Mr. Lincoln's Wife

ANNE COLVER

Mr. Lincoln's Wife

HOLT, RINEHART AND WINSTON

NEW YORK   CHICAGO

SAN FRANCISCO

Designer: Ernst Reichl

81522-0715

Printed in the United States of America

This book is for
Stewart Graff
with love

A Note from the Author

As a playmate of Willie Lincoln in Springfield, young Isaac Diller appears briefly in these pages. He and his family were near neighbors of the Lincolns. In his eighty-ninth year Isaac Diller still remembered Mary Lincoln's special kindness in sending the neighborhood children formal *written* invitations to a party for Willie. He remembered his family's opinion of Mrs. Lincoln as an affectionate wife and mother. With other friends of the Lincolns' Springfield years, he deeply resented the "misrepresentations and reproaches of which [Mary Lincoln] has had to bear more than her share . . . living and dead."

After reading the original draft of this book Mr. Diller wrote me that reading about Mary and her sisters "made them seem like old friends." It was exactly my intention. Mary Lincoln is not a character to be idealized. Her temper was too quick, her mind— and her wit—too sharp, her emotions unstable. Her judgments were often harsh. Yet she had a sense, partly as an inborn politician, partly as a woman who deeply loved her husband, of Mr. Lincoln's greatness. She followed his fate and found herself eventually lost in its vast and lonely shadow.

Documentary evidence on Mary Lincoln is sharply conflicting, ranging from the affectionate neighborhood view of Mr. Diller through the malicious gossip and criticism which a Lincoln-baiting press heaped on the President's wife during the war years, to

A Note from the Author

William Herndon's image of Mary as an unrelenting nag and shrew in his lectures after Mr. Lincoln's death.

I have tried for a portrait rather than a photographic likeness. Perhaps the best keynotes in the extreme views of Mary Lincoln may be found in her husband's own words. In the midstream of his marriage he wrote to Mary from Washington: "When you were here I thought you hindered me in attending to business, but now, having nothing but business . . . it has grown exceedingly tasteless to me . . . I hate to stay in this old room by myself . . ."

And in Mary's reply, "How much I wish, instead of writing, we were together this evening . . ."

The letters on pages 91 and 134 are in my own words. All other letters, recorded speeches, and published references are authentic.

A. C.

PART ONE

Elizabeth's House

One

ELIZABETH EDWARDS was having a family dinner. But not for the Edwards family. The only Edwards at the long oval table in the candelit dining room was Elizabeth's husband Ninian, who sat at the head and carved the roast, and saw that the wine was poured properly. All the others at the table were Todds. Elizabeth had been a Todd.

"When you marry a Todd," Ninian said once, "you renounce all other wordly claims and become simply a Todd."

Not that Ninian resented it. There were few things that Ninian went so far as to resent, least of all anything connected with Elizabeth, whom he regarded with admiration, and a certain amount of awe, as an example of all that a wife should be. But when Elizabeth spoke of The Family she was referring to her own. All other relatives she designated as "Mr. Edwards' connections."

Which was natural enough. By sheer force of numbers, the Todds made other families seem trifling. Robert Todd of Kentucky, Elizabeth's father, had fourteen children. Six by his first wife, and the second round by Elizabeth's stepmother. Adding three sets of grandparents, aunts, cousins, grandchildren, and a battery of uncles who ran to senators and judges, the Todds summed up to a quite magnificent display.

"Being a Todd in Lexington is like being an angel in heaven," a visitor to Kentucky said. "All the best people are."

Along with many other Kentuckians, a number of the Todds had migrated to Illinois. Nowadays there were enough of them in Springfield to represent the family adequately at Elizabeth's table.

"Virtually a quorum," Ninian said.

To the scraggly, growing prairie town of Springfield, the Todds had brought an atmosphere of their own, thick with culture and bluegrass.

Elizabeth had been the first of the Todds to move from Lexington, and shortly after her marriage she was writing back enthusiastic invitations for others in the family to follow. The expanding prairie communities offered opportunities in business and politics that were not dreamed of in Kentucky. Judge Hardin, one of the uncles, had come, bringing his law practice and his nephew, John Todd Stuart, to Springfield with him.

Elizabeth had been careful to point out that there were probably more eligible bachelors to be found in Springfield than in the whole state of Kentucky. It was a fact that Elizabeth's seven sisters, all unmarried, bore well in mind.

Frances, the oldest sister, had responded by coming to live with Elizabeth and in due course she was married from Elizabeth's parlor to Dr. Wallace of Springfield.

Now the second sister, Mary, was taking her turn to visit Elizabeth. Next would come Ann. Then, Ninian observed with a sigh, he supposed they could start getting the halfsisters married. "Though I can't see why so much planning should be altogether necessary," he added mildly. "After all, Elizabeth, you married without assistance, I hope—"

Her case had been different, Elizabeth said. It had happened that shortly before her eighteenth birthday Ninian had come to

Lexington to study at Transylvania University. His father, who was at that time governor of Illinois, had given Ninian a letter of introduction to his friend Robert Todd. The governor would be grateful if Mr. Todd would be kind enough to see that Ninian's sojourn at the university was not too lonely.

Such a happy combination of circumstances, Elizabeth explained, could not be expected to recur seven more times for seven more Todd daughters.

"Besides," Elizabeth added thoughtfully, "none of the younger girls seem to have much initiative—unless perhaps Mary—but *she's* apt to be difficult for other reasons."

The family dinner at the Edwards' was a double celebration. It was Ninian's birthday as well as the occasion of welcoming Mary Todd.

Elizabeth glanced down the table speculatively at her newly arrived sister. Not precisely pretty, but there was a quality of freshness and sparkle in the round, pert face that Elizabeth approved. It was plain, too, that at eighteen Mary had learned the trick of looking her best. Her light-brown hair was parted in the center and dressed in becoming curls behind her ears, and her summer frock of starched, embroidered muslin had short puffed sleeves and a blue sash in just the proper shade to show off her eyes. Her glance was a trifle too sharp to please Elizabeth, but she had a lively, animated way of talking, and could express herself with wit. She might do very well, Elizabeth reflected, if only she didn't develop too many notions of being modern and strong-minded that were so unpopular with young gentlemen.

A few weeks before, Mary had graduated from Madame Mentelle's classes in Lexington. In the autumn she planned to enter Ward's Academy for two years of study. Her visit to Springfield was not, therefore, in the nature of an official one. Still Elizabeth felt it could do no harm to consider the ultimate possibilities.

At the moment, unconscious of Elizabeth's speculations, Mary was listening to an account by John Stuart of his new law partner—a man by the name of Lincoln. John had, it seemed, first met Lincoln when they were volunteers in the Black Hawk Indian War. Later they shared a boarding-house room in Vandalia during a session of the state legislature of which they were both members. John had persuaded his lanky, easygoing roommate to take up law, and had lent him the books and kept after him so diligently that six months later Lincoln had been admitted to the bar.

"Don't see how you did it, John," Judge Logan, one of the uncles, finished a glass of Ninian's excellent port wine and patted his stomach. "I knew Abe Lincoln when he used to pilot a flatboat on the river, and I'd have staked my life he'd never stick to one place long enough to amount to anything. Abe's smart—and he has a knack for politics. I've seen him get up to speak in the Assembly, looking like a scarecrow in those clothes of his, and before he finished he'd have the whole house on his side. Then, likely as not, he wouldn't show up when the question was put to vote. He'd be out fishing, or swapping yarns down at the post office. Abe's trouble is that he doesn't care enough about getting ahead to stay with anything."

"Well, he's staying with the law—so far," John said, "and people are beginning to notice him. He was trying a case last week in Decatur, and a man in the back of the courtroom kept interrupting. All of a sudden Abe stopped speaking and took off his coat. He picked the man up like a sack of meal, carried him to the door, and threw him out. Calm as you please, put on his coat, and said, 'Excuse me, your Honor.' It was that, as much as anything, that won the case for us."

Mary laughed with the others.

"I'd like to meet your Mr. Lincoln sometime, John," she said. "He sounds interesting."

Ninian rose to pass the gentlemen cigars. "I'm afraid you'd

be disappointed, Mary. Abe's hardly what you'd call a ladies' man—"

"Oh, I don't know, Ninian—" Judge Logan leaned back in his chair. "Maybe that's just what Abe needs—a little feminine influence to make up his mind for him, and polish off the rough corners—"

Elizabeth stood up rather abruptly. There was a rustle of skirts as the other women rose to follow.

Mary was the last to push back her chair. She would have liked to stay, instead of going into the sitting room and listening to the latest exchange of gossip about clothes and servants. But Elizabeth's eye was on her. As she crossed the hall, the sound of the men's voices trailed after her. They were still talking about Mr. Lincoln.

During the two months she stayed in Springfield, it seemed to Mary that wherever she went the conversation was certain, sooner or later, to get around to Mr. Lincoln. No two people appeared to agree about him. If one said he was the homeliest man on earth, another was sure to protest.

"I don't see how you can call Abe homely. He's plain, I suppose—but there's something about his eyes that makes you forget the rest of his face."

There were stories about his strength. He could throw any man in the county in a wrestling match. Stories about his uncouth, back-country manners. Yet they said he could match wits with the smartest lawyers on the circuit. There were jokes about the schoolbooks he carried around in his pockets, and was forever studying.

"I asked Abe what he was reading one day," Judge Hardin said, "and he showed me an old first-year grammar. Said he'd never really learned the difference between an adverb and an adjective."

Yet he'd read all of Shakespeare and could argue theories of philosophy with any man in town. He was sad, they said. To look at him sometimes, you'd think he'd lost his last friend. John Stuart said there were hours on end when Abe would look as if all the gloom in the world were settled on him. The next day you'd likely see him down at Diller's drug store with the boys —telling one of his stories that was comical enough to make a cat laugh.

"Whatever comes up, Abe can twist into a joke somehow."

With all the talk, no one seemed to know very much about Abe Lincoln. He had been born in Kentucky somewhere but he said his people were Virginians. "Not one of the first families, though. More like third or fourth."

In the two months Mary never actually got to meet Mr. Lincoln. When she asked why he wasn't invited to the house, Elizabeth was vague.

"He's been up at Vandalia most of the summer. Besides— Mr. Lincoln doesn't take any interest in young ladies."

Mary looked curious. "Don't they take any interest in him?"

"Heavens no!" This was more of John's doing, Elizabeth thought impatiently. What did John Stuart mean, filling the child's head full of nonsense? "Tell me," she switched the subject briskly, "did you enjoy talking to Stephen Douglas last evening? Cousin Lizzie tells me he danced with you half a dozen times. I can assure you Mr. Douglas is considered the most promising young man in Springfield, as well as being quite handsome..."

When the time came for Mary to go home to Lexington she was still disappointed not to have met Abe Lincoln.

Two

FOR THE next two years Mary applied herself at Ward's Academy to the study of classics in French and English, history, poetry, and a smattering of the sciences, and stood near the head of her class. In her spare time she danced, went to parties and picnics, rode horseback, and quarreled with her stepmother. There were afternoon promenades in the Botanical Gardens, musical evenings when the young ladies rendered sentimental ballads or played dashing airs on the pianoforte in candlelit drawing rooms, lectures at the weekly meetings of the Lyceum, and a new model planetarium at the university to be visited and marveled at.

Mary fitted pleasantly into the pattern of social life, but she was not sorry when the time came for her promised return to Springfield. The girls she had grown up with had begun to seem quite tiresome, forever going into raptures over some new love. A visiting lecturer from the East, or somebody's older brother home from college—or, if all else failed, one of the younger university professors, or a new minister.

"I can't see what earthly use there is in fluttering over someone who probably doesn't even know you're alive," Mary told her friend Pat Breckinridge. "If I were in love, it would be with a man who was brilliant and ambitious and could make speeches and do things—" She stopped, rather surprised, wondering what had made her say just that.

Peg was unmoved. "I expect that's because you've always been clever," she said calmly. "But maybe you'll just *think* the man you fall in love with can do all those things."

Two years had brought changes to the raw, young town that Mary remembered. Springfield was still growing. New houses had sprung up everywhere; the streets were lengthening out to push the cornfields farther and farther back into the flat brown prairie. There were new shops around the square, and now the State House, massive and somber, cast an impressive solemnity over everything.

The sign that had read *Stuart and Lincoln, Law Offices* was gone. Mary saw a new one, farther up the block, with gold letters: *Logan and Lincoln, Attorneys at Law.*

So, Mary thought, Judge Logan must have been persuaded after all that Mr. Lincoln could stick at his trade.

Elizabeth pointed out the new developments proudly. "You'll find the town quite different nowadays," she said. "Since they moved the State capital here from Vandalia, we have all sorts of interesting young men coming and going. By the way—" she smiled significantly—"Mr. Douglas has been inquiring for you, Mary. I told him you'd be here in time for the Assembly Ball next week. I hope you've brought plenty of new frocks . . ."

She made no mention of Judge Logan's new law partner.

Mary wore a white dress to the ball, with a sash of deep-pink satin that matched her slippers, and a cluster of late roses from Elizabeth's garden fastened in her curls. Midway through the evening she found a moment for a word with Elizabeth.

"Are you having a good time?" Elizabeth's smile was fond, her glance was sharp.

"Everything is lovely, Elizabeth," Mary said. She fanned herself. "I was just wondering—" she paused—"who is the gentleman over by the door? The tall one, in the black coat—talking to Uncle. He doesn't seem to be dancing—though he looks quite young enough—"

Elizabeth looked. Then she shrugged.

"Oh—that's Abe Lincoln," she said. "I really can't remember whether you met him when you were here before."

"No," Mary said, "I haven't met Mr. Lincoln yet."

Three

ON A blustery evening in February, Elizabeth and Ninian drove Cousin Lizzie Grimsley home from a church supper. It had snowed and sleeted for two days. The roads were rutted with icy drifts and the carriage swayed like a ship tossed on a stormy sea.

Ninian was tired. He disliked church suppers in general, and those under Cousin Lizzie's fluttering supervision most particularly. He was chilled, his shoes were wet from the snow; he wished nothing more than that he were at home, before his own fire.

Elizabeth seemed quite unmindful of the disagreeable elements. With that total disregard of discomfort which Ninian had learned to recognize in women whose minds were on something else, she sat beside him, oblivious to the howling wind and the angry clatter of sleet that whipped against the windows.

"The thing that troubles me about Mary," Elizabeth said, as though they had been discussing the matter, "is that she's got

20

her head full of notions. Where she got them, I'm sure I don't know. I never had any such difficulty with Frances."

Mr. Edwards nodded, suppressing a shiver as a draft whipped through the carriage. Having lived through two courtships, he was familiar with the peculiar difficulties that seemed to be the natural prelude to matrimony.

"The strange part is," Elizabeth went on thoughtfully, "that Mary started out so well. Much better than Frances. There was Mr. Douglas. If Mary had given him an ounce of encouragement, he'd have proposed long ago. Then there was Mr. Tyre— and that nice young clergyman from Decatur—he could quite easily have come to something—" Elizabeth paused. "Really, I can't understand Mary."

It might be, Ninian suggested, trying to keep his teeth from chattering, that Mary didn't want to get married at all.

To this absurdity, Elizabeth paid no attention. "Of course, Mary has always had a mind of her own. That's so difficult where men are concerned. It's a pity though . . ."

When they drew up at the front door, Ninian saw the parlor lights still burning.

"Who's the victim tonight?" he asked.

Elizabeth stepped out of the carriage. "Really, Mr. Edwards —you do speak vulgarly sometimes. It's only Mr. Lincoln again. Why Mary persists in letting him come to call, I can't think. If she has any notion of making Mr. Douglas jealous, she's over- doing it. I've told her so plainly but she doesn't listen. She says—" Elizabeth shook the snow from her mantle energetically —"that she enjoys Mr. Lincoln's mind."

They came into the parlor to find Mary alone. Looking at her sister, Elizabeth could scarcely fail to feel a certain satis- faction. A bright fire—a pleasant room. A girl in a blue dress, with her small, pretty feet resting on the brass fender. A storm outside—and a whole evening of solitude. From experience, Elizabeth had learned that one might sell all other commodities short, in favor of solitude. Such a pity, really, to think it had been wasted on Abe Lincoln.

"Well—did you enjoy your evening?"

Mary looked up, smiling.

"Mr. Lincoln has just gone. He was sorry not to have seen you, but he's leaving for Decatur in the morning, and he has a brief to finish."

Elizabeth walked over to the mantel and straightened an ornament. Running a finger along the underside, she inspected it for dust.

"Tell me," Elizabeth's tone was crisp, "what do you and Mr. Lincoln talk about when you're alone?"

"Not very much." Mary's smile deepened. "A good deal of the time he just sits and looks at the fire."

One morning Elizabeth came to Mary's room with a letter in her hand. It was from a niece of Mr. Edwards who lived in Maryland. Of all things, the girl had suddenly taken it into her head to visit them.

"I never supposed Mr. Edwards was especially fond of Matilda," Elizabeth frowned. "But he quite insists on having her. You and Matilda will have to share a room."

Mary looked up quickly. "What's she like?"

"Oh—quite plain, I think." Elizabeth's tone was reassuring. "As I remember, she was a gawky child. She used to have notions about being a writer. At any rate, she's probably interested in books, and won't expect to go about much. I only hope she won't be troublesome . . ."

When Matilda arrived two weeks later, it was apparent from the number of party frocks that emerged from her trunk that she expected to spend her time at something besides reading.

"I hope I haven't brought too many things," Matilda's smile was engagingly frank. "Mamma and I decided it was better to bring too much than not enough. Especially as Uncle Ninian wrote Mamma that there were so many parties in Springfield nowadays."

Mary rather enjoyed having Matilda share her room. She was pleasant and friendly, and for all her prettiness, she hadn't a scrap of self-consciousness. She seemed to travel on the amiable assumption that everyone liked her as much as she liked them.

Elizabeth observed the two girls with mingled feelings. It was a relief that they were getting on well. On the other hand, Matilda was altogether too pretty for Elizabeth's peace of mind. One thing, at least, she was thankful for. Matilda wasn't the flirting kind—her brown eyes were too level and direct.

It wasn't long before Elizabeth discovered that there were things far worse than being a flirt. Matilda made not the slightest effort to attract attention. Her manner toward the young gentlemen she met was the same candid, pleasant friendliness she showed everyone. Most unexpectedly, the gentlemen responded to this good-natured treatment with an alarming degree of interest. Matilda became the center of every party. Matilda was the most popular girl on picnics. When the doorbell rang in the evening it meant another caller for Matilda.

"You might think," Elizabeth said to Frances, "that Matilda Edwards was the first girl who had ever visited Springfield."

At the end of ten days, Ninian asked his niece whether she was enjoying her stay. They were at the dinner table. Matilda looked up with her quick, friendly smile.

"Why, of course, Uncle. How could I help it, when Aunt Elizabeth is being so lovely to me?"

The next week Matilda met Mr. Lincoln.

He had been in Vandalia attending to some business. On the first day after his return he came to call on Mary and her guest.

"I never saw Abe in better spirits than he was tonight," Ninian said later.

Elizabeth, busy before the mirror, gave one of her curlpapers an extra pull. She said nothing.

It wasn't long before others besides Ninian observed a change in Mr. Lincoln. "Abe's as cheerful as a cricket these days," Judge Logan said. "Whistling around the office—and he's had his boots shined twice this week."

"It looks as though Elizabeth has made another match," Mrs. Stuart said. "Mr. Lincoln has no eyes for anyone since Matilda Edwards came to town."

Elizabeth kept her silence until one evening when Mary had excused herself from a party, saying she had a headache, and Mr. Lincoln had brought Matilda home later. Then Elizabeth faced her husband squarely.

"It's a shame," she said. "Matilda ought to be spoken to, Mr. Edwards. But if I say anything, of course it will only look as though I were taking Mary's part—"

"I can't see what Matilda has done . . ." Ninian glanced up.

"She hasn't done anything. She *never* does anything—that's just the trouble. But she knows quite well that Mr. Lincoln was interested in Mary before she came. I've as good as told her so. Yet she goes on, accepting his attentions as though it were the most natural thing in the world . . ."

Ninian spread his hands. "It's all beyond me, Elizabeth," he said. "A few weeks ago, you were complaining that Mary was wasting her time on Abe. Now, simply because he seems to find Matilda agreeable company—"

"There's a great deal more in it than that, Mr. Edwards," Elizabeth said darkly.

"I can't see that Matilda treats Abe one bit differently than she does any of the others who seem to be taken with her."

"That's precisely my point, Mr. Edwards. It simply isn't natural for a girl to like *every* man who comes her way. It—" she groped helplessly for a moment—"it isn't decent."

24

Spring turned to summer, and Matilda showed no signs of going home. Not all Elizabeth's hints, to the effect that Matilda's family must by now be anxious for a glimpse of her, had any effect.

"Mamma was worried at first for fear I might be homesick," Matilda said. "But when I wrote her how wonderful you were being to me, she said she and Papa were perfectly willing for me to stay just as long as you and Uncle Ninian wanted me."

One July evening the girls came home from a picnic supper, and Mary found Elizabeth downstairs sewing by the lamplight. Matilda had gone straight upstairs.

"Elizabeth," Mary said suddenly, "I'm going home. I can't stand it any longer."

Elizabeth put down her sewing. She looked alarmed. "Sh-sh—dear, Matilda will hear you."

"I don't care who hears me. I'm going back to Lexington. I never liked it here. The men are hateful. They have no manners—and I—"

"Mary—" Elizabeth's voice was sharp. Then it softened soothingly. "If Mr. Lincoln has done something . . . If Matilda—"

Mary took off her wide-brimmed hat and flung it on a chair.

"Mr. Lincoln has nothing to do with it," she said, "nor Matilda either. It's just—" her words broke—"it's just—everything."

Elizabeth rose. "Now, Mary," she said, "stop and think. What would you be going home to? A stepmother who cares for nothing but her own babies. You know how unhappy you were in Lexington—"

Mary cut her short. "I couldn't be any more unhappy than I am here. I couldn't possibly—"

The next morning, at breakfast, Matilda observed quite matter-of-factly that she must go home.

"I hate to think of it." Matilda's smile, warm and affectionate,

25

embraced them all. "I'm going to miss you just awfully—especially Mary."

In the silence, tense and strained, that followed her announcement, Matilda went on placidly. She was going home to be married. There was a Mr. Ramsey—he was older than she was, but very kind. The wedding was planned for October, and Mamma thought she really ought to be planning her trousseau.

For a moment no one said anything. Then Elizabeth spoke.

"Well—" her tone was strangely flat. "I'm sure we're all very happy for you, Matilda. But I should have thought, if you had anything like this in mind, you might have taken us into your confidence a trifle sooner."

Matilda buttered a hot biscuit. She hadn't dreamed, she said, of keeping anything from them. *She* hadn't supposed it made any particular difference.

"Not make any *difference*—well, really—" Elizabeth set her cup down with a smart click. Mary was staring at her plate and Ninian appeared to be wholly preoccupied with the business of lighting his cigar.

"I must say, Matilda," Elizabeth went on, "whether or not you chose to confide in us, there are certain standards of proper conduct for an engagement. One hardly expects a girl who is about to be married to go about as though she were entirely free to accept the attentions of other young men."

Seeing his niece's puzzled frown, Ninian cleared his throat. "Your aunt is intending to say—" he brushed the ash from the tip of his cigar, "that we had ventured to hope, in these weeks, your fancy might settle on one of our local gentlemen."

"Oh!" Matilda's brow cleared. Quite startlingly, she threw back her head and laughed. "Oh, goodness no, Uncle. I never thought of such a thing—though your friends have been ever so kind to me." She helped herself to another biscuit and buttered it thoughtfully. "I suppose," she said, "they were nice to me mostly because they liked meeting someone who wasn't expecting to marry one of them."

Ninian, quite suddenly, was taken with a fit of coughing. It must have been, he explained, that some smoke had got down his throat.

That night Mary lay awake listening to the wind in the trees, and the dry count of the crickets' chirping. Her hands were clenched tightly at her sides. All day, since Matilda's astonishing revelation at the breakfast table, one question had been circling in her mind. In the darkness, she drew her breath.

"Matilda?"

"Yes?"

Mary shut her eyes. "Matilda—have you ever thought—did Mr. Lincoln ever say that he was in love with you?"

There was a silence. Then Matilda's voice. "Why, no."

Mary waited while the pounding, surging tide subsided. She heard the wind again, and the vague familiar sounds of the summer night.

"I thought perhaps since he seemed to like you so much, and you liked him . . ."

"Yes," Matilda said, "I like him very much. If it weren't for—other things . . ." Her voice trailed away. "He talked to me a great deal—mostly about the things he wants to do. I think perhaps he liked to talk to me, because I've always wanted to do something too—only I never knew quite what it was. He seemed to understand that."

"Yes."

"But as for love," Matilda said, "I don't suppose he knows the meaning of the word."

Four

IT WAS amazing, Mary's sisters agreed, the way Mary had taken Mr. Lincoln back without a murmur. Matilda's tracks had scarcely cooled, so to speak, before he was calling on Mary again—with never so much as a word of explanation or apology.

"I can't understand it," Frances said. "Mary, of all people— who's always had so much spirit . . ."

"It's beyond me," Elizabeth said to Ninian, "why Mary should fasten on Abe Lincoln. But since she has, I suppose there's nothing to do but to see that she gets him."

There was no question, in Elizabeth's mind, but that marrying the wrong man was infinitely preferable to not marrying at all. With this in view, she brought her best technique to bear.

Mr. Lincoln remained peculiarly impervious to technique. He called on Mary; he was pleasant. He squired her to local parties with reasonable faithfulness. He ate Elizabeth's food, and smoked Ninian's excellent cigars. But on the subject of matrimony he was as mute as if the holy estate were nonexistent.

It was a good year for Whig politics. William Harrison was running for President and, from the look of things, he had a good chance of being elected. The Whigs in Springfield rallied their forces.

"Reckon this is where Abe gets a chance," they said. "He's one of old Tippecanoe's best rooters in these parts. If Harrison gets in, Abe's sure to get some plum out of it."

One evening there was an item in the paper saying that Mr. Lincoln had been invited to make a speech at a campaign rally near Columbia, Missouri, early in October.

The next morning Mary found Elizabeth sorting linens.

"I've been thinking, Elizabeth," she said. "The Judge Todds down in Columbia have asked me to visit them. I think perhaps I ought to go."

Elizabeth glanced up. "All the way to Missouri?"

"Well, it really isn't so far. And I haven't seen any of them since Cousin Ann was a little girl. I didn't care about going in the summer but now that it's cooler . . ."

Elizabeth contemplated. "Just when were you thinking of going?"

"I hadn't decided really." Mary picked up an embroidered napkin. She folded it neatly, smoothing the edges. "Perhaps toward the end of the month—if that's convenient for you. There's going to be a big rally about then."

Elizabeth gathered up the sheets to be mended and started toward the door. "If you want to go traipsing off to Missouri I'm sure I have no objection," she said.

When Ninian heard the news of Mary's trip he studied the tip of his boot thoughtfully.

"I expect we ought to remember that all's fair in love or war," he said. "In this case, I sometimes wonder which it is."

If the Judge Todds were startled by the abruptness with which their niece announced that she was about to favor them with a visit, they managed to conceal their surprise. Once Mary arrived, she exerted herself so diligently at being charming and agreeable that the judge had to admit she'd turned out the best of any of Robert's children so far.

Mrs. Todd agreed, but she was puzzled. "I never saw a girl so taken up with politics as Mary. She's been at me since the first moment she got here about going up to that Whig rally in Rocheport. She's even got Ann all excited—though before she listened to Mary's talk Ann couldn't have told the difference between a Whig and a Democrat."

On the morning of the rally, Mary was up and dressing before seven. She brushed her hair smoothly and laid out her best hat and a fresh pair of gloves. It was going to be a fair day, thank goodness, which meant there would surely be no last-minute indecision about going. The judge had said he was willing enough to take the girls if the weather was good, but, by heaven, he wasn't going to risk an attack of rheumatism by sitting five hours in the rain just to hear a lot of political windbags spout.

No danger of rheumatism today, Mary thought, as she slipped on three starched petticoats and fetched her new blue frock from the wardrobe. The October sky was serene and cloudless, and the early mist would burn off long before they got to the river. The excursion boats were due to leave at ten.

Promptly at seven-thirty, Mary knocked at her aunt's door. Was there anything she could do to help get ready? She'd already wakened Ann and got her started dressing.

Mrs. Tood blinked. "Heavens and earth, child—whatever have you put on your best dress for? No one will be gotten up much for this sort of outing."

While they were dressing, Mrs. Todd turned to her husband. "You know, Mr. Todd, I wonder if Mary isn't in love," she said. "When a girl gets up before seven and put on her best dress—there's something more than politics on her mind. And it's not like a Todd to be as sugary as all that without a good reason behind it. You keep a sharp eye on Ann today. I don't want her led into any mischief."

The judge pulled on his boots and straightened up, puffing. "Sophie, for the love of mercy, stop fretting. It won't do Ann a bit of harm to get waked up a little—and Mary's all right."

There was a crowd at the docks when they arrived. The sun was already hot. When her uncle went to see about tickets, Mary asked which boat the speakers were taking.

What difference did that make? the judge inquired testily. He took off his hat and mopped his forehead. It was all very well, taking the girls on an outing, but blame it all, what did Mary think she was doing—running the election?

The news came that the speakers' boat was being held till later. They went aboard another steamer. The whistle gave a long, ear-splitting shriek, and everyone leaned over the rail shouting and waving handkerchiefs.

"*Tippecanoe and Tyler too!*"

"*Hurray for Harrison!*"

Mary turned to Ann.

"Isn't it exciting?"

The whistle shrieked again. The side-wheel paddles sucked into the muddy river.

The low shores, green and rolling, moved slowly past, while the boat's engine throbbed like a laboring heart against the swift, downstream current. Sitting between Ann and the judge, Mary kept up a lively conversation. She was charming, gay, prettily attentive to the judge's comfort. She glanced down the river at intervals, where the speakers' boat might be following. And her blue eyes, beneath the brim of her new hat, were bright with expectancy.

By midafternoon, Ann felt her new-found enthusiasm for politics beginning to wane. It had been thrilling at first to be part of the crowd, cheering and applauding as one speaker after another was introduced. But as hour after hour passed, the long-winded speeches, the sweeping gestures, began to take on a wearisome monotony. The sun, hotter now, beat down on their heads, and the benches were uncommonly hard.

Ann glanced at her father. He was dozing, arms folded, his head sunk onto his chest. A long career in politics had indoctrinated him to hours of oratory.

She whispered to Mary. "Do you think we might get some lemonade? They're selling it—right over there—"

"Sh-sh, not now." Mary frowned. Her glance was on the platform, where a group of new speakers, in black coats and tall hats, were just arriving.

A short, stout gentleman came forward. "Ladies and gentlemen—your attention please. The next speech this afternoon was to have come from our distinguished and eloquent supporter from Illinois—the well-known Mr. Abraham Lincoln—"

The stout gentleman paused. Mary leaned forward.

"Due to an unforeseen concatenation of events, the forces of nature, over which not even the Whig party has complete control—*as yet*—" scattered laughter and applause—"our good friend Mr. Lincoln has been delayed . . ."

Mary's hands tightened. She heard the stout gentleman bellowing on. One of the later boats had been grounded in the shallows. Mr. Lincoln's appearance was unavoidably prevented. Meanwhile, craving the indulgence of his listeners, the stout gentleman begged the honor of presenting that incomparable patriot, that prince among statesmen, the Senator from . . .

Mary stood up.

"All right," she said, with a suddenness that made Ann blink, "let's go and get some lemonade."

Long after the speeches were over Mary saw him. At first she could scarcely believe her eyes. But no one else, surely, could be as tall, nor look quite like that, his face so tanned and weather-beaten, his dark hair rumpled and uncombed. He was standing near the empty platform, his coat hanging over one arm, talking to some men gathered around him.

"Look," someone in the crowd said, "ain't that Abe Lincoln?"

Remembering later, Ann couldn't help thinking it was strange the way Mary had changed all of a sudden. One minute she'd been cross and queer, not a bit like herself, acting as if she wished she hadn't come. The very next moment, she was all cheerful, smiling. Then the way she'd taken Papa's arm and said, oh, by the way, she'd almost forgotten, but there was a friend of Mr. Edwards' from Springfield she had promised to look up. Someone Mr. Edwards was particularly anxious to have her uncle meet . . .

Before Ann really knew what was happening, she found herself being towed along toward the platform, Mary talking all the while, explaining how fond Mr. Edwards was of his friend Mr. Lincoln. If Mr. Lincoln was staying in Columbia, mightn't it be nice if they could ask him to dinner. "If Auntie wouldn't mind, that is?"

Sounding surprised and a trifle winded, the judge gruffled an answer. If Ninian set such store by this fellow, he guessed it'd be all right.

Waiting to greet Mr. Lincoln, Mary felt suddenly shy. She had never seen him like this, surrounded by people who stepped up to shake his hand, and greet him respectfully, asking how things looked for the Whigs up Illinois way. He seemed like a stranger—pleasant and self-assured. There was no awkwardness about him now.

He hadn't seen her yet. A broad-shouldered man had crowded in front of Mary and she hung back, wondering whether she ought to speak.

There was no time to decide. The large gentleman stepped aside, and Mary found herself looking into Mr. Lincolns' eyes. He stared as though he couldn't credit what he saw. Then wonderfully, unbelievably, his face lighted up.

"Miss Mary—" He put out his hands to take both of hers. "I didn't know you were here."

He smiled down so warmly, with such a hungry welcome in his eyes, that Mary felt the shyness go out of her in a wave of exultant tenderness.

Her hat, she realized, was all askew. The blue frock, so fresh and pretty that morning, was bedraggled and stained with lemonade. She knew her face must be flushed and shiny from the heat. Yet for the first time she could remember, Mary was conscious of feeling really pretty. She drew her hands away gently.

"Yes—" she said. "Yes, Mr. Lincoln, I'm here . . ."

On the boat going home that evening, Mary stood alone by the rail. A sharp breeze blew her hair and whipped the muddy surface of the river below. Out here alone the voices and band music were lost in the darkness. There was only the rush of wind and the steady churning of the paddle wheels.

Watching the wake sweep out in a shining path through the black water, Mary saw a stray log drawn suddenly from its aimless, drifting course into the white swirl. She saw the log bob and twist against the relentless strength that swept it up, until, at length, it was left behind, and vanished in the dimness of the river.

For that little while, the log had been like something caught up by a fate—strange and exciting—that drew it without warning or destination, and would not let it go.

Five

"I RECKON you were wrong about Mary being in love," the judge told his wife when he was undressing that night. "She wasn't out of my sight all day—and I'll vow she never so much as spoke to a single person, outside of that lawyer friend of Ninian's from Springfield. She says that Ninian wants us to have him for dinner. So I asked him for tomorrow."

The next evening it was plain that Mr. Lincoln was making a most favorable impression on the Todds. For the most part, Mary was silent. She heard the easy, agreeable way Mr. Lincoln talked to the judge, and the pleasant courtesy with which he addressed Mrs. Todd. Mary wondered why he so seldom seemed like this in Springfield. Only when Matilda had been there had she seen him so charming. She put the thought hastily aside. Matilda was far away. And Mr. Lincoln was smiling at her across the table.

Mary looked down at her plate.

"If Mary were my child, I'd give her a good talking to for being so unmannerly," Mrs. Todd said later to her husband.

"Anyone would suppose she might have put herself out a little to entertain that nice Mr. Lincoln, especially since Ninian asked us to invite him here. But he might as well have been a fly on the wall for all the notice she took of him."

"I guess it didn't make much difference to Mr. Lincoln," the judge said comfortably. "He seemed to enjoy himself well enough. I don't wonder Ninian's taken with him. He's got a likable way and plenty of horse sense. I reckon a man as smart as that has too much to think about to worry over whether the girls notice him or not."

When he had bade them good night, Mr. Lincoln said he expected to stay in Columbia until Friday morning.

By noon on Thursday, Mrs. Todd was beginning to be alarmed about Mary. From having been so bright and friendly, the child had suddenly taken the queerest streak. She wandered around the house as though she didn't know what to do with herself. She'd take up a book, frown at it for a minute or two, and then throw it aside to go and stand at the window—staring out at the street and hardly answering when she was spoken to. Once, when she was holding a skein of wool for Mrs. Todd to wind, someone knocked at the front door and Mary had jumped as though she'd been shot—and barely apologized for dropping the wool and getting it all tangled.

At the table, Mary made the merest pretense of toying with her food. When Ann ventured to speak to her, she answered with such rude impatience that poor Ann's eyes filled with tears.

Mrs. Todd wondered if she could have been mistaken about Mary. Perhaps she wasn't in love at all, but only coming down with something. Mrs. Todd frowned. It would be so awkward to have the child ill, particularly if she were going to be difficult like this. And sickness in the house always put the judge into such a wretched humor.

36

Mary pushed back her plate suddenly. "I just don't feel like eating," she said, "I think I'll go lie down."

Alone in her room, Mary found she couldn't rest. She felt half smothered by the compress Mrs. Todd had insisted on putting on her forehead. Perhaps if she got up and wrote a letter to Peg Breckinridge . . .

Halfway through the first page, she tore it in two. It was no use. No use. She came back to the bed and sat down, pressing her hands against her eyes. He wasn't coming. He wasn't going to write—or send any message. She had been stupid to think he would. It was stupid to keep on hoping. Stupid . . .

She dug her hands tighter, until sharp darts and wheels spun against her eyelids. Suddenly, out of the forlorn misery, she saw herself standing at the rail of the excursion steamer. She remembered the night wind, and the river current, swift-flowing and relentless . . . and the moment when Mr. Lincoln had smiled as he took her two hands in his.

After supper that evening, Mrs. Todd settled herself by the sitting-room lamp with her mending. It was a mercy that Mary's headache hadn't developed into anything after all. Mary had insisted on putting on one of her prettiest frocks for supper and chattered and laughed through the meal. It was plain that at least she wasn't going to be ill. All the same, there was something about the child that made Mrs. Todd uneasy. The way she'd stop right in the middle of saying something, for no reason at all, and look toward the door.

Well, young girls were apt to be trying. Particularly nowadays, when they had such notions about being independent, and heaven only knew what else. She ought to be thankful that Ann showed so few signs of having any ideas at all.

Ann was at the piano now, aimlessly picking out tunes with one finger from a book of new songs. As she hit the fourth wrong note in succession, Mary jumped up.

"What about a game of checkers, Uncle?" she asked abruptly.

At nine-thirty Mrs. Todd put away her mending.

"Time for bed, girls."

In spite of her aunt's objections, Mary managed to coax the judge into one more game. The evening mustn't end yet, she thought desperately. Please—not yet. Even though there wasn't any hope . . . She bit her lip, trying not to let herself notice the curious, whistling sound of the judge's breathing as he bent over the board, pondering his next move with nerve-racking deliberation.

"Remember to lock up," Mrs. Todd stifled a yawn. "And don't let Mary sit up too late, Mr. Todd. She ought to have a good night's sleep. . . . Come along, Ann."

Ten minutes later there was a knock at the front door. Mary didn't raise her eyes from the board. *It couldn't be.* Of course it couldn't. It was absurd to think anyone would be calling at this hour.

She could hear old Peter's step, shuffling and slow, going down the hall toward the door. A pause, endless, unbearable. Then quite unmistakably, a gentleman's voice was asking for Miss Todd.

"I'm afraid I've won this time, Uncle." She began to clear away the checkers, careful to keep her fingers steady. "But I'm sure you won't mind too much. Here's Mr. Lincoln come to see you."

The judge had scarcely settled down to a comfortable talk about some of the nonsense that went on in the law courts and the lollygagging young fools in the legislature nowadays, when he was startled to have Mr. Lincoln ask if Miss Mary would care to come for a walk. The judge got to his feet, thankful that his wife was upstairs and out of earshot. He was not certain she would approve the invitation. Still, any friend of Ninian's was bound to be all right. And Mary didn't seem to object too much.

The night air was cool and sweet after the stuffy, lighted parlor.

"I hope you didn't mind my asking you to come out," Mr. Lincoln said. "It seemed kind of a shame to miss a pretty night."

Mary lifted her face. "As a matter of fact, before you came I was wishing I could get a breath of air."

"Which way shall we go?"

"I don't know . . ." Mary pointed. "That road over toward the hill looks pretty."

They walked rapidly in the darkness until, Mary stumbled over a loose stone. Mr. Lincoln stopped and took her arm.

"You're not tired? You don't want to go back, do you?"

"Not a bit," she said quickly. "Only—" she laughed a little, "you forget what long legs you have, Mr. Lincoln."

He started again, more slowly, still holding her arm. "That's right, I do. If I start to gallop again you just call *whoa.*"

At the end of the road they turned onto a side path and went in silence until they reached the top. They stood looking back over the trees and rooftops. Overhead, the sky arched clear and starry. The spice of autumn was in the still air.

"When I get up on a hill like this," Mr. Lincoln said, "it makes me feel as if I could do a lot of things. Makes it easier to think."

Mary said nothing. She had never felt really alone with him before—never like this. Always before there had been that sense of a wall high and guarded that cut him off. Now there was no wall. She stood quietly, her hand resting on his arm.

"How old are you, Mary?"

She turned, surprised by the question. It was the first time he had called her Mary.

"Twenty-one," she said.

"I'm thirty-one."

He was silent, seeming to ponder something. Looking up, Mary could see the outline of his head in the dimness.

"There's a big difference between us," he said slowly. "I used to think, a long time ago, that by the time I was thirty I'd know what I really wanted to do. I guess I don't know any better now than I ever did. There was a time, a while back, when I used to think I'd like to try preaching. I gave that up because I couldn't decide what I wanted to preach. Then I thought about studying to be a doctor, but that didn't seem just right either. Finally I started on law. I reckon that was about the only thing left."

Mary glanced up. "You're not sorry, are you?"

He shrugged. "Not most of the time, anyway. There are still a lot of questions I haven't answered. Some, I guess I never will." He stopped. After a little he turned and looked down. "I don't make much sense," he said. "Right now, anybody else would be talking about you instead of me. They'd be saying how pretty you looked, wouldn't they?"

"I—don't know."

"I mean," he said slowly, "if they felt like I do. They'd want to ask you whether someday you might be willing to think about—getting married."

Mary stood perfectly still. The moment had come so suddenly she was afraid to speak. Afraid that the least whisper, a single breath drawn too deep, might break the spell. The silence was like a spun thread, fragile and shining, between them, all but breaking.

"Maybe I oughtn't to mention it when I've got so little to offer. But would you think about it, Mary? Sometime?"

"If . . . you wanted it . . ." Her words were scarcely a murmur in the dark.

She felt his shoulder. The solid strength of it. Somewhere, above her head, she heard him sigh. Then, a little awkwardly, he took her in his arms. For a minute they were close, not speaking.

When they said good night, Mr. Lincoln took her hand. In the light from the window she could see the strange sadness in his eyes.

"If you ever feel you've made a mistake, Mary, you must tell me. Will you promise that?"

"Yes . . ."

It was the only promise he had asked her to make.

The thread, shining and tenuous, trembled between them.

"Good night, Mary."

"Good night."

He let her hand go gently.

She watched from the doorway until he turned the corner. He had not looked back.

Six

BACK IN Springfield everybody was talking about the elections. It was beginning to look as though the Whigs had it for sure. The whole West was behind Harrison and the National Road. Van Buren was out just as sure as the sun rose Thursdays. They'd heard Abe Lincoln hadn't got to make his speech in Missouri after all, but he'd said he guessed it didn't matter much. Everybody at the rally was going to vote Whig anyway.

Elizabeth looked Mary over with an experienced eye.

"I must say the change seems to have done you good," she said. "I've never seen you look so well."

Privately to Ninian, however, Elizabeth reported that the trip had apparently not accomplished much. "I'd hoped it might bring things to a head with Mr. L. You'd think, in all conscience, that having her chase him all the way to Missouri would wake any man up to speak his mind. But I can't get a word out of Mary—though it's plain from the way she acts that *something* happened."

For a week—two weeks—nothing was said. Mr. Lincoln was out of town making a last round of campaign speeches. Whenever his name was mentioned, Mary was vague and evasive.

At length Elizabeth came straight to the point.

"I know perfectly well, Mary, that there is something between you and Mr. Lincoln. And since you are living in my home—"

"For the purpose of finding a husband—"

"Please don't be difficult, Mary. I am responsible for you while you are here, and I have a right to know what your intentions are."

Mary was silent. Caught thus, in the full cold light of Elizabeth's good sense, the thread seemed perilously threatened. If she refused to speak, Elizabeth might question Mr. Lincoln. He'd be back in a few days now. If Elizabeth or Ninian said anything, the frail, sweet thread would surely break.

Mary drew a breath. Briefly, hating with her whole soul the necessity of putting wordless things into words, she told what had happened the night on the hill.

"Well," Elizabeth laid aside her sewing, "I must say I'm surprised that he actually got to the point." She paused thoughtfully. "You say he *did* ask you to marry him?"

"We—spoke of it. But nothing was decided . . ."

Elizabeth nodded.

"Naturally not. After all, Mr. Lincoln has had no chance to speak to Mr. Edwards. But as soon as he returns—"

"Oh, *no*—" Mary stopped quickly, aware of the look in Elizabeth's eyes. "I mean, there mustn't be anything said. Until we're both quite sure, that is. Just for now, we must keep everything secret."

"Secret?" Elizabeth raised her brows. "There's nothing disgraceful, I hope, about being engaged."

"I can't explain, Elizabeth, but you *must* let me do this my way. Don't you see? There are reasons—"

Elizabeth did not see. "I've tried to be patient with you, Mary. I've tried to help you. But if you won't confide in me I don't know what more I can possibly do."

"You can let me alone," Mary said, choking back the sob

that rose suddenly in her throat. "Just . . . let me *alone*. That's all . . ."

It was more difficult when Mr. Lincoln came back to Springfield.

Elizabeth said nothing further on the subject of the engagement, but there was a reserve in her manner, an air of silent, martyred patience, that made the atmosphere electric with her waiting.

Mary waited too. In the days and the nights she waited for a return of that moment when they had stood on the hill together. But everything seemed so different here in Springfield. Mr. Lincoln was very busy, for one thing. Mary reminded herself of that when he was late for appointments, or forgot them altogether. No doubt it was only because he was tired that he seemed distraught and far away when they were together. After the elections were over, surely it would be better . . .

Elections came and went. The Whigs swept triumphantly into office. Still Mr. Lincoln's abstraction did not lift. He was kind. He continued to be reasonably attentive. But when he came to call he was more and more often silent, his eyes lost in some unreachable sadness that left Mary helpless and frightened.

She began to make new excuses. He was overtired—perhaps he was ill. Perhaps he was worried for fear she had regretted her promise. Lying awake, she could think of a thousand reasons to explain his strange, unfathomable silence. In the darkness, she could still call back the moment when his arms had held her close. She could believe in it then. She could believe it would come back.

In the morning there was only another day to face—and the cool, unspoken question in Elizabeth's eyes.

Near Christmastime, around the stove at Diller's store, they said Abe was looking kind of seedy lately.

44

"Don't know what ails him. You'd think he might perk up a little, since the elections. But he looks as washed-out as a cat in a cistern. You don't reckon he's sick, do you?"

"Abe's not sick," Mr. Diller said. "Josh Speed was in a couple of days ago, and he says it's nothing to worry about. He says back in New Salem, when Abe got like this, they used to call it the Lincoln Blues."

"Well, Abe's got a bad case this time. What's eating him, do you suppose?"

Mr. Diller rubbed his chin.

"I wouldn't want to say for sure," he said. "But judging from a few remarks I've heard dropped lately, I'd say Abe's got Todd trouble."

On Christmas Eve, John Stuart dropped by the Edwards house with a bundle of packages for the children. It was a raw night out, with rain that soaked the ground and turned the streets into muddy rivers.

"It doesn't look much like a white Christmas," John said, taking off his wet coat. "Unless the winds pull around north before morning, we'll have nothing but more mud."

He started toward the fire, rubbing his hands briskly, then, as he caught sight of Mary, he stopped short.

"Hello—what's Mary doing here? I thought all the young people had gone to the dance over at Mrs. Browning's."

There was an awkward silence. Ninian coughed. As a matter of fact, Mary had been expecting to go, he explained. It seems Mr. Lincoln had been detained.

"I daresay Abe's had trouble finding a carriage." Ninian was careful to avoid Elizabeth's eye. "What about a spot of brandy, John, to celebrate the holiday?"

John stood with his back to the fire, looking at Mary thoughtfully.

"It seems a shame to deprive all the other gentlemen of your company, Mary. My carriage is outside. Why not let me drive you to the Brownings'? Then if Abe shows up later—"

Mary stood up suddenly. There were bright spots of color in her cheeks. The folds of her crimson skirt rustled stiffly.

"Thank you," she said. "It's not necessary, John. I didn't want to go to the dance anyway. I wish you'd all stop pretending to be sorry Mr. Lincoln forgot to come for me—when I know quite well you're actually delighted."

"Oh, now come, Mary," John's smile was easy. "You mustn't take it so hard. You know how thoughtless these Yankees are—and Abe's worse than most. I daresay he would have forgotten his head long ago if the Lord hadn't thought to fasten it on his shoulders. I still think it's a pity, to let that handsome dress go to waste—"

Mary turned away. "I hate the dress," she said. "I wish I'd never seen it. I wish I'd never seen any of you. Or Springfield—or anyone."

"Mary," Elizabeth's tone warned her sharply. "You're upset."

"What if I am upset?" Mary said. "A precious lot you care so long as you can run everyone your way and manage everything, just as you did with Frances—"

"Now, Mary," John's smile grew a shade less bland. "There's no reason to turn on Elizabeth like that. She's not responsible if Abe takes exception to some of the things people are saying."

Mary whirled on him. "And just what *are* people saying?"

"Well, nothing much." John shrugged. "Only there seems to be a general opinion that your family doesn't look very kindly on Abe as a match for you. I don't know just how the talk got started, but—"

"There—you see?" Mary flung the words at Elizabeth. "You see what you've done with your meddling? You've ruined everything just because you couldn't hold your tongue. And after you promised not to tell—"

"I'm sure I don't know what John is talking about," Elizabeth said. "I've told no one anything."

"Except Frances, I suppose. And Uncle Judge and Cousin Lizzie—"

"Don't be a fool, Mary. I hope I still have the right to speak to my own family confidentially."

A choked sound came from Mary's throat.

"You might as well have told the whole town and been done with it. Don't you suppose I know why you're all scheming and plotting to keep me from marrying Mr. Lincoln? You pretend it's because he's not good enough for me. Because he's poor and you think his manners aren't elegant enough to suit your fine Kentucky taste. You're jealous because you know I love him and he loves me. And that's something that never happened in this family before. It never happened to Frances and it never happened to you—"

"*Mary!*" Elizabeth's voice cut like a knife. She took her sister by the shoulders. "Stop this hysterical nonsense *at once!*"

Mary twisted her shoulders.

"I won't stop. You can't make me be quiet. You know Mr. Lincoln will be a great man someday. Everyone says so—everyone believes it. And that makes you jealous. You and Ninian and John and Frances—"

"I warn you, Mary, if you go on like this I shall send Ninian for a doctor. I'll tell him you are out of your mind."

Mary wrenched herself free. She pushed back the curls that had tumbled across her face.

"Very well . . ." her voice dropped, "I'll stop." She went slowly toward the door, stumbling a little over the hem of her frock. "It doesn't matter. It's all spoiled anyway . . ."

Later, when Elizabeth went upstairs to see to the children, she returned to tell Ninian and John that Mary was in bed, apparently asleep.

"I'm sure I don't know what to do with her." Elizabeth set her lips. "Mary always had a temper, but I must say I never expected such an exhibition as she made of herself tonight."

John sighed.

"It's all most unfortunate, certainly." He helped himself to the brandy, frowning. "Still, it may not do any harm to have Mary realize the way people are talking. If she has any pride, after all—"

"Well, she hasn't," Elizabeth said. "I should think that was plain enough. Mary's made up her mind she's going to marry Abe Lincoln and nothing in heaven or earth can stop her."

"Except Abe Lincoln," John said slowly. "Abe can be stubborn himself. Especially when he gets an idea that people are trying to make up his mind for him. I've no doubt he's fond of Mary. All the same, you can't blame him for being skittish. A man doesn't exactly relish hearing the opinion of his future in-laws before he's got around to asking for it."

Ninian, twirling the stem of his brandy glass, said nothing.

It was New Year's afternoon when Mr. Lincoln came to the Edwards house again.

Elizabeth and Ninian had gone to make a round of calls, and Mary was alone in the sitting room. At half past four the winter dusk was deepening. Through the long windows, Mary watched the fading twilight, cold and blue. In a minute now, Joseph would be coming in to draw the curtains and light the lamp on the center table. Hearing his step in the hall, she straightened.

"You expecting company this evening, Miss Mary?"

"I—don't think so, Joseph."

He lingered a moment, stopping to put fresh coal on the fire. In the flickering light, Mary's dress of scarlet wool glowed softly.

"Mis' Edwards didn't say anything about tea," Joseph said. "Would you like a nice hot cup?"

Mary shook her head. "No, thank you, Joseph. I'll just wait."

When Mr. Lincoln came in, shortly after five, he said he couldn't stay for tea.

"As a matter of fact, Mary," he blurted out as though he were afraid to hesitate, "I've got to talk to you."

"Yes, Mr. Lincoln?" Mary felt her smile go suddenly stiff. Looking up, she saw such a depth of misery in his eyes that she stretched out her hand in quick alarm. "Mr. Lincoln—what is it?"

He stared at her, not speaking, his face marked with shadows. Then he drew a long breath.

"I don't know how to say this, Mary. I wish I could make it easy, but I can't." He was silent a moment, seeming lost in some far-off thought. "I can't get married," he said finally.

There was a silence.

"Well?" Mary heard her own voice, sharp and brittle. Feeling everything go out from under her, the room, the bright fire, the soft light from the table lamp, she clung to the word, steadying herself against it. "*Well?*" When he didn't answer she asked finally, "Why should you tell me that, Mr. Lincoln?"

He lifted his hands, and let them drop.

"I didn't know . . ." He paused. "I couldn't help but think maybe you were—expecting me to marry you."

Mary sat motionless. Not all the thinking, all the despair, the doubts and questions in the long nights, had prepared her for this. She must say something. Tell him he was mistaken. Anything to show she didn't care. To hide this awful, unbelievable moment. She groped for the words. But nothing came.

Mr. Lincoln went on. He was sorry, more deeply sorry than she could know, if he had said or done things that would lead her to think he intended, or could possibly intend, to marry anyone . . .

"*Anyone*, Mr. Lincoln?"

He seemed not to notice the irony. It wasn't a question of his feeling for her, he said earnestly. He had always held her in the very highest esteem, but she must surely see for herself the reasons why marriage was impossible. He had no money, no confidence of ever having any. He had debts . . .

Mary listened in stony silence while he struggled on. It was as though, having once made the plunge, some dogged, painful honesty forced him deeper and deeper. "I want to do what's right, Mary. If you think we ought to get married, if you honestly feel it would make you happy . . ."

"*Happy?*" The word was bitter and strange on Mary's lips.

Still his voice went on. "Your happiness would be worth anything in the world to me, Mary. You must believe that." There was no doubting his distress, his utter humility. "But I've got to tell you the truth. If we were ever to get married, and you weren't happy, I'd never forgive myself. These last weeks, I haven't been able to think about anything else. Josh Speed would tell you—"

"Thank you," Mary said. "I hardly think we need to call in any witnesses."

Mr. Lincoln sighed.

"Maybe it was wrong to tell you," he said, "but I've been nearly crazy, worrying. I tried to write you a letter, but I couldn't seem to get it right. Josh said that wasn't the way to do it. He said I ought to talk to you face to face. He said the only fair thing was to find out how you felt about it—" He broke off as Mary stood up.

"That was gallant of Mr. Speed, I'm sure." A wave of pure fury swept over Mary as she pictured what the scene must have been. The two men sitting together in the room they shared over Josh Speed's store, both in stocking feet, no doubt, with their coats off and their galluses comfortably let down, discussing the state of her heart.

"Another time, Mr. Lincoln, I might suggest that when you are in any doubt about a lady's feelings, you would do better to consult her directly, however delicate Mr. Speed's perceptions may be."

Still frozen in anger and unbelief, she turned toward the door. When he made no move to follow she looked back, and saw him watching her with eyes so full of misery and sorrow that her heart gave way.

"Oh, Mary—" he said. "Mary—"

She went to him swiftly, and he put out his arms. She pressed her face against his shoulder, feeling her own tears, hot and blinding. For the first time since the night on the hill they were close again. Drawing back a little, she looked up and saw the tears in his eyes too. For one last moment the shining thread held.

Then with a sound like a low, choked moan Mr. Lincoln took his arms away. He turned.

"Good-bye, Mary . . ."

She made no answer. When she heard the sound of the outer door closing, she stood where he had left her.

The next Sunday Elizabeth came home from church with the news that Mr. Lincoln had left town. Josh Speed had put his store up for sale, and the two of them had started out not saying where they intended to go nor for how long.

"No one seems to know what took Mr. Lincoln," Elizabeth said. "It's my opinion he's out of his mind."

Ninian pointed out that there might be other explanations. "Just because a man does something you didn't expect, Elizabeth, it doesn't necessarily indicate insanity."

Elizabeth was firm. She wasn't the only one who had noticed how queerly Mr. Lincoln had acted. Judge Logan said he hadn't done a scrap of work for the past month. Just mooned around the office and talked about going out west somewhere to start farming. "Cousin Lizzie told me she saw him going down the street New Year's evening about suppertime, splashing along through puddles like something demented, and *carrying* his hat and coat, if you please, as though it weren't the dead of winter. When Lizzie spoke to him, he just went rushing on."

It was all most regrettable, to be sure. At the same time Elizabeth could hardly fail to be relieved at having the impasse between Mr. Lincoln and Mary so unexpectedly resolved—and in a manner that could not possibly be construed as any reflection on Mary. When Frances reported that she had heard a rumor that Mr. Lincoln had proposed to Mary, and been driven to despair by her refusal, Elizabeth was so struck by the appropriateness of the story that she admitted that she had suspected as much.

"Did Mary tell you that?" Frances inquired sharply.

"Well, not in so many words," Elizabeth shrugged. "But Mary would scarcely be likely to speak of a matter so delicate and painful."

"We have to remember, Frances, that Mary has always been *sensitive*. A thing like this is bound to be a shock. But she'll get over it in time." Elizabeth sounded brisk, almost cheerful. The more she thought of Frances' explanation, the more suitable it seemed, and therefore quite undoubtedly true. It was even rather romantic. And Elizabeth was not one to deny that a hint of a broken heart in the background never harmed a young girl's chances with other young gentlemen.

As the days passed Elizabeth began to think quite kindly of Mr. Lincoln.

For Mary the days passed like some endless, monotonous dream which she could never quite believe but never waken from. Gradually she realized that there would be no wakening. What had seemed unbelievable had really happened. Mr. Lincoln had meant the things he said and now he was gone. She could never know what he was thinking, never know anything about him. Unless, of course, he should write. It was a forlorn hope, but after a time he did write, from Kentucky, saying that he was well, that he and Josh Speed were just traveling for the present, that the weather had been bad. He hoped Mary was well. Above all, he hoped she would be happy.

It was a strange letter, full of bad conscience and unhappiness, but giving no return address. Tearing it to bits, dropping the pieces into the fire, Mary felt the last slim shining strand slip from her fingers.

Seven

THE DAY Mary heard that Mr. Lincoln was back in Spring-field, she and Elizabeth were in Smith's dry goods store. They were at the woolens counter. Long afterward Mary could re-member the exact pattern of the printed challis she had been looking at when she heard someone in the next aisle speak casually.

"I ran into Abe Lincoln this morning—looking very well too. He says he's back in Judge Logan's office. We all thought he might go to Washington on some government appointment, but I guess that fell through when President Harrison died."

Mary's throat had gone dry in a faint, sick wave, half of ex-citement, half of dread. She remembered putting down the cloth and closing her eyes. *Dear God, suppose she should open them and see him standing there* . . . Instead, she had met Elizabeth's sharp glance.

"I think we've shopped long enough for one afternoon, Mary. We'll choose a pattern for Ninian's dressing robe an-other time."

The next days Mary lived in a misery of anticipation, searching the mail each morning for a letter, feeling her heart pound every time there was a strange step at the front door—alternately resorting to panicky excuses to stay home lest she encounter him somewhere and inventing needless errands downtown that would take her by his office.

The weeks passed, and there was no word from him, no unexpected meeting. Life subsided gradually to normal. When at length she did see him, one frosty December morning, Mr. Lincoln was coming out of the post office. He had his collar turned up, against the cold, and his eyes were deep and gray in his bronzed, lean face. He seemed glad to see Mary. They talked pleasantly for a few minutes; Mr. Lincoln told her she was looking well.

After that, there was no more waiting for the postman. Mary no longer started whenever someone knocked at the door. They met now and again, always by accident, but as Mr. Lincoln's work took more and more of his time, the occasions grew less frequent, and though there was plenty of company at the Edwards house, Mr. Lincoln never seemed to be included. In the family, it was thankfully observed that Mary had got over her nonsense at last, and when Judge Logan came to dinner, he seldom took occasion, any more, to tell amusing anecdotes about his partner.

Mary went home to Lexington for a summer visit. When she came back she struck up a sudden friendship with Mrs. Simeon Francis, whose husband owned the Springfield newspaper. Elizabeth was relieved when Mary took to spending an occasional afternoon at the Francis house. It gave her an interest outside herself, and seemed to cheer her up. Elizabeth concluded that a youngish and sympathetic friend was precisely what Mary had needed.

One morning in early October Mrs. Francis sent a note asking if Mary would come to tea that afternoon. She had a friend coming whom she was specially anxious for Mary to meet.

"I daresay it's some friend of Mr. Francis," Elizabeth said. "He meets a great many interesting gentlemen in his work. You can wear your new blue merino. If you like, I'll lend you my beaver jacket . . ."

Polly Francis was waiting near the door when Mary came in. Mary could hear the sound of voices in the parlor, but Polly opened the door to a small sitting room.

Mary saw a tall man standing before the fire. His back was toward her.

"You two be friends again," Polly said, and closed the door.

Afterward Mary was never sure whether the meeting had been by accident or by design. There had been hints from Polly Francis. Remarks, dropped casually, to the effect that all was not well with Mr. Lincoln. He was lonely, unhappy. He had been heard to say he wished the clock could be turned back, that he could have another chance to right certain mistakes he had made. Looking back, Mary found it difficult to account for the way her heart had pounded while she walked toward the Francis house that afternoon—for the sudden confusion, half expected, that gripped her when Polly closed the door and left her face to face with Mr. Lincoln. She could remember how they looked at each other, solemn and questioning—the way he had started to say something polite, and had stopped, and simply held out his arms. Walking toward him, Mary knew the truth for the first time. She had thought once that Mr. Lincoln needed her. She had dreamed of his future, thinking he needed someone to spur him on, to be tactful, to guide him toward the destiny that everyone seemed, rather strangely, to expect of him.

In that instant, held next to his heart, Mary knew it was she who needed him. She would go on needing him, as long as she lived, with an intensity that left her shivering and helpless.

One thing more she knew that afternoon. This time no one should interfere. Not heaven or earth or Elizabeth would break the shining thread again.

On a November morning, gray and lowering, Ninian met Mr. Lincoln on the square in front of the State House. Mr. Lincoln was hurrying along, his head bent against the wind, as though anxious to get somewhere faster than his long legs would take him. At first he started to pass, but suddenly he drew himself up. Speaking rapidly, with no trace of his usual roundabout drawl, Mr. Lincoln said, without preamble, that he and Mary were planning to be married.

Ninian took off his hat.

Mr. Lincoln, after a moment's hesitation, removed his also, and the two men stood facing each other soberly.

Eight o'clock in the morning, beneath a slate-gray sky, with their fellow townsmen jostling past them on their way to business seemed a curious place for such an announcement, but Ninian did his best. He put out his hand.

"This is a surprise, Abe . . ."

Mr. Lincoln nodded. Having blurted out his tidings, he seemed incapable of further comment, and merely stood, gloomily inspecting the lining of his hat.

"Have you—" Ninian cleared his throat, "settled on a date yet?"

Mr. Lincoln nodded again. "We're counting on doing it this evening, Ninian. If it's convenient for you and Mrs. Edwards. Mary thought," he added, "it might be a good idea not to say too much about it ahead of time."

Ninian cleared his throat again. "This will be a surprise for Elizabeth, but I'll tell her." There was a pause. Ninian put out his hand once more. "I'm sure I wish you every happiness, Abe. You and Mary both. Now and in the future."

Mr. Lincoln shook hands.

"Thank you, Ninian," he said solemnly. "I'm sure you mean it."

That evening turned out to be impossible, since Elizabeth had already arranged to entertain the Dorcas sewing circle at her home. But the following night Mary and Mr. Lincoln were married in the Edwards parlor.

"I never heard of such a thing," Elizabeth said helplessly. "There's no time to arrange anything. Mary hasn't even a wedding dress. And if I'd known, for one minute, why Mary was sneaking off to visit Polly Francis—"

"You'd better take the chance," Ninian said, "before Abe changes his mind again."

Toward candlelighting time on the day of the wedding, the wind pulled round to the east. The dusk brought a gray rain that blew across the prairie, rustling on the dry corn shucks, whining against the shutters, wanting in.

"It's a poor kind of time for a wedding," Frances said.

All day she and Elizabeth and Cousin Lizzie Grimsley had worked helping in the kitchen, tacking up greens around the improvised altar in the parlor.

Stepping down from the ladder, after adjusting a branch of laurel, Cousin Lizzie sighed so that her stout waist seemed about to burst its dove-colored satin bounds. "Is Mary dressing now?"

"I expect so, Lizzie." Elizabeth was worrying about the punch. "Why?"

"I don't know—" Lizzie clasped her hands uncertainly, "it seems as though someone ought to be with her."

The sisters exchanged a glance.

"Mary's all right." Frances bent to straighten a chair. "No one can say, certainly, that she's going into this with her eyes closed. We've told her plainly enough she was making the mistake of her life. Abe Lincoln doesn't amount to a row of pins, and never will. But Mary won't listen. She's got some notion in her head she's going to make him over." A thin smile curved Frances' lips. "Once she's married, I daresay Mary will discover it's not as easy as it looks to change a husband."

"Oh, Frances." Cousin Lizzie's pale eyes filled with distress. "Mr. Lincoln adores Mary. I can see he does."

"If that's the case," Frances put down the hammer, "I can only say he conceals it remarkably well. I passed him in the street this afternoon, and if ever I saw a sorry looking sight, he was it. He looked more as if he were headed for an execution than a wedding."

Lizzie clasped her hands nervously. "I only hope Mary is going to be happy."

Ninian came in as she spoke.

"Precious few people," he said, "are cut out to be happy, Lizzie. Unless I miss my guess, Mary's not one of them. If you're bound to be sorry for someone, it's Mr. Lincoln you'd better worry about."

During the ceremony, Lizzie couldn't help feeling Ninian must be mistaken. Mr. Lincoln didn't look a bit sadder than usual, only dignified and solemn, the way a man ought to look while he was getting married. In his long black coat, with his hair combed down so neatly, he was almost handsome. Ninian was very clever, of course. But then, Lizzie reflected, so was Mary.

One thing Lizzie was thankful for. Elizabeth had got Mr. Dresser, the new Episcopal rector, to read the service. The sight of him, in his impressive vestments, made Lizzie feel easier. The Lord, at least, must have lent his backing to the proceedings. She listened to the words of the ceremony.

"For better for worse . . ." Mr. Dresser's words rose above the beat of rain against the shuttered windows. "For richer for poorer . . ."

(It must be richer certainly, Lizzie nodded. Mr. Lincoln couldn't very well be much poorer.)

58

"In sickness and in health . . ."

(They needn't worry about that part, both of them were healthy enough.)

"Till death us do part."

(Those words always made Lizzie sigh.)

When the moment came for Mr. Lincoln to slip the ring on Mary's finger, his friend Judge Brown, who was standing up with him, took the gold band from his pocket.

"With this Ring I thee wed . . ."

Mr. Lincoln's voice, repeating the words, did have a mournful sound. Perhaps it was only the effect of the silent room, Lizzie thought. The wind howled and shuddered until the candles on the mantel flickered and melted wax dripped down their sides.

Mr. Lincoln's voice continued.

". . . I thee endow with all my worldly goods and chattels, all my lands and tenements . . ." Judge Brown stirred uneasily at his side. A look of alarm came over his face.

"Great Scott, Abe," the judge's nervous whisper carried through the hush, "the statute fixes all of that."

It was the only time during the afternoon that anyone saw Mr. Lincoln smile.

The bride and groom left for the Globe Tavern where they were planning to board, temporarily, Elizabeth was careful to explain, until they had time to find a house. The other guests lingered over the supper table. They agreed it had been a pretty wedding. Mary had looked sweet.

Mr. Lincoln was apologetic about the accommodations he had engaged. The tavern, a square structure of weather-beaten clapboard, was not prepossessing from the outside. The rooms, on the second floor front, Mr. Lincoln said he guessed were nothing extra when it came to style. But Ed Boliver, who owned the Globe, was a friend of his, and a good fellow, and had promised to do what he could to make things comfortable. They were to have lodging and meals for four dollars a week; it had seemed about the best he could do on such short notice.

Mary smiled reassuringly. She was quite certain it would do nicely. Climbing the dark and rickety stairs, her hand on Mr. Lincoln's arm, she stepped across the landing and into a new world of tenderness and hope.

The low-ceilinged rooms, the dingy furnishings and the doleful, liver-colored paper that hung in blistered and peeling strips on the walls, could not mar the enchantment—not even the thought of what Elizabeth would say when she saw the worn carpeting and the grimy curtains at the windows.

Over the iron bedstead hung a steel engraving of Washington crossing the Delaware. When Mr. Lincoln, inspecting it, observed that it looked as though the General was determined to sink or swim, but probably expected the former, Mary seemed not to hear.

She had crossed to the window and stood looking out. She was thinking of a moment, two years before, when she had stood at the rail of an excursion steamer and watched a log bobbing and twisting, drawn by the swift, relentless pull of the ship's wake. She remembered the stars arched high above. Stars and the night wind and the churning wake in a dark river. They were part of a pattern that made the shabby, close room behind her fade into insignificance.

"You know, Mr. Lincoln, I was just thinking . . ." She turned, her eyes full of a shining eagerness.

"Yes?" His voice seemed to come from far away.

Mary shook her head, feeling the words escape her. She looked at him, so tall that the top of his dark head was barely below the ceiling. She remembered when Polly Francis had said, "I think Abe Lincoln must be the loneliest man in the world."

It would be different now, Mary thought. He wouldn't be lonely ever again.

"I was going to say—" Mary smiled, "I think the rooms are very nice."

He smiled too, lighting up his whole face, so that the strangeness in his eyes was gone.

Mary went to him quickly. The last shadow of doubt went out of her heart. In the silence she heard him draw a long breath.

"I hope you won't be sorry," Mr. Lincoln said.

PART TWO

Mary's House

Eight

On a late June morning, when mackerel clouds were scudding across a blue sky, Mary sat by her window in the Globe Tavern. She was sewing the last of a dozen linen shirts for Mr. Lincoln. She came to the end of a seam and stopped to rest her eyes from the fine stitches. Elizabeth said it was absurd to spend hours putting tucks in shirt bosoms that were only meant for every day. There were so many things Elizabeth found absurd.

"I mean to have Mr. Lincoln the best-dressed lawyer on the circuit," Mary said. She was careful not to add that when she laid out his things for a trip, the fresh pile of linens were often left behind on the bed. His suitcase had been stuffed, instead, with the odd collection of books and newspapers that Mr. Lincoln insisted on taking with him.

As Frances pointed out to Mary, marriage had wrought no miracles in Mr. Lincoln thus far. After eight months of Mary's most diligent efforts, he seemed surprisingly much as he had always been. Not that he put up any active resistance to improvements. Indeed, he was invariably agreeable. When Mary suggested that it was not always necessary to go about at home in stocking feet, Mr. Lincoln nodded. When she pointed out the custom of using the butter knife to serve his plate, he said he hadn't a doubt it was a good idea. He simply continued, without argument, to do precisely as he had always done before.

In the first weeks after they were married, Mary had set about to reorganize a number of things. First there were the rooms to be fixed up. Fresh white curtains to be made and hung. A new spread for the old iron bedstead, a desk to be arranged for Mr. Lincoln. And shelves for the books.

Dear heaven, the books. Mary remembered the days when she had struggled with the problem of disentangling Mr. Lincoln's belongings from the confusion of books. A pair of muddy boots wrapped up in his second-best broadcloth coat. An umbrella, ancient and rusty, crammed with his shirts. His stovepipe hat stuffed with an assortment of socks—no two of them mates, and all in shocking condition. And scattered through everything, spilling out of the most unlikely corners, came books and more books. Geometry texts, spellers, grammars, arithmetics. Plato's dialogues, a dog-eared volume of Shakespeare. A copy of some Hindu religious writings, and a worn black Bible, bulging with newspaper clippings of a humorous and illiterate journalist. Books of philosophy, physics, poetry, and jokes.

Books were all very well, Mary said, but books belonged on shelves, not mixed in with what properly went into bureau drawers. She had sorted them carefully, but in spite of all her system the books had a way of getting unsorted and appearing in weird places. One night Mr. Lincoln would be reading *Othello*. The next evening Mary was careful to lay the volume of Shakespeare, with a marker, beside Mr. Lincoln's chair. When they came up after supper, his gaze would wander vaguely around the room. What had become of those papers he'd been reading? The ones with the pieces by J. Flannigan?

"I threw those out a week ago, Mr. Lincoln. I supposed you

were finished with them. They were only cluttering up the room, gathering dust . . ."

Mr. Lincoln would give no sign of being annoyed. He would simply descend to the woodshed and prowl around until he found the missing papers in the rubbish, and likely bring up a few discarded magazines for good measure.

The next night, when Mary had conscientiously stacked the papers on his table, Mr. Lincoln would scatter them all over the floor and ask where the Shakespeare had disappeared to.

"I put it away on the closet shelf," Mary said shortly. "There's no more room in the bookcase."

There were other, less tangible changes. In those early weeks Mary had attacked them energetically. There was the matter of Mr. Lincoln's policy about money. He talked a great deal about being poor and saddled with debts, but it didn't take Mary long to discover that the reason they had no money was simply because Mr. Lincoln had a curious reticence in regard to charging his clients for services rendered. Half the time he was so easygoing about collecting fees they were never paid at all.

Mary was sensible. "There's no earthly sense in not being paid for the work you do, Mr. Lincoln. Charity is well enough where it's deserved, but nine times out of ten your clients who say they can't afford to pay have more money than you have. You must simply be firm."

"Yes," Mr. Lincoln sighed. "I suppose I must."

"I'll say one thing for Mary," Elizabeth admitted. "She's certainly building fires under Mr. Lincoln."

"The question is," Ninian said, "whether Abe will turn out to be noninflammable."

In the spring, when it was time for Mr. Lincoln to travel the circuit, Elizabeth had asked Mary to come back to her old room at the Edwards house.

"Mr. Lincoln certainly can't expect you to stay cooped up in those miserable rooms for two whole months, Mary. Besides, with the baby coming, you oughtn't to be alone."

Mary had replied that she was very well where she was. Now that the rooms were fixed up with what Mr. Lincoln called her trimmings, she had grown quite fond of them. And she was hardly alone, with Ed Boliver and his wife right there in the house.

As a matter of fact, Mary had found the weeks while Mr. Lincoln was on the circuit as pleasant as any she could remember. Even when the June heat had begun, and the dust blew thick from the prairies, she didn't mind staying indoors most of the time. Elizabeth made it a point to bring her sewing over several afternoons a week, although Mary troubled less and less about returning the visits.

"Why don't you come out for a drive, Mary? It would do you good. I don't know how you stand being stuffed under this hot roof."

"I daresay I shall have plenty of time to go driving," Mary said, "when I have a carriage of my own."

"Very well, if you want to be stubborn . . ."

It was easier when Cousin Lizzie or Polly Francis came to call.

"I don't care what anyone says," Lizzie confided one afternoon, "I think you're being perfectly wonderful, Mary. I said to Elizabeth just the other day . . ." She paused, squinting while she threaded a needle. "I said there's no sense in worrying about Mary. Mary knew when she married Abe Lincoln that things weren't going to be a bed of roses—just at first, anyway. But you'll never hear a word of complaint out of Mary, I said, no matter how it may turn out."

The best days were when no one came at all. Then she didn't have to be explaining, guarding, forever on the watch for unspoken criticism of Mr. Lincoln. It was nice to do as she pleased. To read, or sew, or write letters.

Writing to Mr. Lincoln, she could forget all the uneasy moments when they discovered how extraordinarily different two people could be. The moments when Mary had found her quick decisiveness blunted and sidetracked by the peculiar, maddening slowness of Mr. Lincoln. His odd silences, that left her puzzled and hurt. The curious, roundabout unpredictability of his nature. They had both been startled by those moments, and troubled.

But in her letters, long and gossipy and affectionate, Mary could picture everything just as she wanted it to be. The future stretched out then, lovely and exciting. There were no remarks from Elizabeth to spoil it, no patient sympathy from Frances. Not even the presence of Mr. Lincoln, often so disturbingly solid and uncompromising.

In Mary's letters Mr. Lincoln could be all that she had dreamed.

There were times, in those early summer weeks, when Mary remembered the old days in Lexington. The way the family used to pack up for the annual pilgrimage to Orchard Springs. The pleasant, orderly commotion of departure. Piles of starched petticoats and fresh muslin dresses heaped on the beds, and the servants hurrying around under Miss Betsy's watchful eye, packing hampers of picnic food for the journey. Carriages piled full of luggage, nurses for the babies, the jingle of harness as the horses pranced smartly in the driveway. Then the big, rambling, frame hotel up in the Kentucky hills. Candlelight in the dining room, and the large round table that was always reserved for the Todd family. New arrivals bowing. The fiddlers playing during dinner and later, in the ballroom, for dancing. Picnics and horseback rides, beaux and young ladies, flirtations and tears. The mammas sitting in the rows of rocking chairs on the verandas, exchanging gossip and symptoms in mysterious whispers.

Lying awake sometimes, in the hot bedroom over the tavern,

Mary would twist about, trying to find some comfort for the nagging ache in her back. She remembered how it had been at home when her stepmother was expecting a new baby. The busy preparations in the nursery—and Mammy Jane, who had nursed all the Todd babies, waiting on Miss Betsy hand and foot. Rubbing her back, gentling her forehead with cologne-scented handkerchiefs, Mammy Jane ordering Mr. Todd to keep his cigars away from Miss Betsy's room. All of them fussing over Betsy, treating her like something delicate and precious.

The important thing was, Mary reflected, the thing that Elizabeth could never understand, was that she wouldn't have traded places with Betsy for the whole world. Not for anything under shining heaven.

The evening Mr. Lincoln arrived home he and Mary walked over to Elizabeth's for supper. Afterward, on the porch, the air was like a bake oven, motionless and stifling.

Elizabeth fanned herself.

"You haven't told us any stories yet, Abe," Ninian said. "I've never known you to come home without a supply of new ones." He rose to offer his guest a cigar, but Elizabeth pointed out sharply that the smoke might bother Mary. About time, she thought, that Mr. Lincoln was reminded of Mary's condition.

They left early. On the way home, walking beside Mr. Lincoln, Mary was aware of an odd, perverse disappointment. Now that he was here, all the wonderful anticipation of seeing him had been lost somehow. At a crossing she stopped suddenly. Mr. Lincoln turned.

"What's the matter, Mary? You don't feel sick, do you?"

Mary bit her lip. "It wouldn't be strange if I did. The way you rush me along—"

"I'm sorry, Mary; you should have told me I was going too fast."

The next minute she pulled her arm away. "Heavens and earth, Mr. Lincoln. You don't have to creep."

He speeded up again, without comment.

The rooms were unbearably hot that night. Sitting on the edge of the bed, Mary saw that Mr. Lincoln kept glancing at her as if he were wondering what to say. Let him wonder. Mary set her chin stubbornly, but in spite of anything she could do her lips began to tremble.

"Mary, won't you tell me what the trouble is?"

She blinked back the tears furiously. "There isn't anything to tell. I just—don't feel well, that's all."

He stood looking down at her, his expression so helpless and puzzled that she turned away and buried her face in the pillow.

"Do you want me to get the doctor, Mary?"

She shook her head, pressing her face tighter. A wave of something curiously like homesickness swept over her. Couldn't he see for himself what the trouble was? Couldn't he have said just one word, after all those weeks, about having missed her? Couldn't he have acted a little bit pleased about being home again, instead of sitting like a wooden Indian all evening? Mary could imagine what Elizabeth and Ninian had said after they left.

"I don't see why you had to be so rude and hateful tonight—" her words were muffled against the pillow. "When you've been gone all this time, and Ninian and Elizabeth were trying to be nice—"

There was a silence, then she heard him sigh.

"Well, I'm sorry." He sat down beside her on the bed. "I didn't mean anything. To tell you the truth, I wasn't thinking much about Ninian and Elizabeth. I guess I'd been looking forward to getting home and seeing you again—" He broke off, startled by the suddenness with which Mary sat up and faced him.

She flung her arms around his neck.

"Why on earth couldn't you have told me that before? I've

been so miserable and lonesome, thinking you weren't glad to see me—"

"Well, I don't know, Mary," he patted her shoulder, "I reckon I thought you knew that."

The long summer heat broke at last. Rains poured over the prairie, freshening the dark earth and bringing the shriveled corn to life.

Coming home in the midst of one storm, Mr. Lincoln found Mary in the parlor downstairs, her face white, her hands over her ears. Always terrified of thunder, she had come to look for Mrs. Boliver and found herself alone. Now she clung to Mr. Lincoln, shaking. After that he was careful to leave his office and hurry home at the first rumble of a storm—when he remembered.

A few weeks later Ed Boliver was carving the supper roast in the tavern kitchen when the scullery maid clattered down the back stairs. She had been up to fetch some linen and heard Mrs. Lincoln calling.

"You'd best go quick," the girl said. "Mrs. Lincoln is going on something awful, and in her condition, I'm scared—"

Ed took the steps two at a time, his long white apron tripping him.

Mary was waiting at her door, her face streaked with tears. Talking rapidly, in a feverish voice, Mary told Ed he must go to Mr. Lincoln's office at once. Something had happened to him. She was certain of it. He'd never been late coming home without sending her word. It was two hours past his usual time.

She clutched at Ed's arm. "Please find him for me. Hurry. Please hurry!"

Ed promised hastily. He untied the apron.

The moment Ed was out of the house, Mary rushed to the front window. She watched him down the street, saw him turn the corner into the square. Counting the minutes, she waited. Her eyes strained down the empty street. A thousand images of disaster tore at her heart. If something had happened, if Mr. Lincoln didn't come home, she couldn't bear it. She couldn't...

Two men came around the corner—and for a moment everything in Mary's mind seemed to stop. The men came nearer. She saw Mr. Lincoln's stride. He was saying something to Ed. Then, just before they turned in at the tavern gate, she saw Mr. Lincoln stop and throw his head back. He was *laughing* ...

Something blind and dark rushed at Mary. She turned from the window and ran through the hall, down the stairs, half stumbling, clutching at the banister. As Mr. Lincoln came up the step she flung herself at him; sobbing and trembling, unaware of his dismayed astonishment, she clung to him.

"Why, now, Mary, there's nothing to get so riled up about."

Nothing! He called it nothing that he'd kept her waiting more than two hours without one word, when he knew quite well she'd be beside herself with worry. She threw the words at him bitterly, heedless of Ed's embarrassed stare and the curious glances of the tavern guests who laid down their knives and forks to listen.

"How could you make me suffer so, Mr. Lincoln? And then *laugh* about it. How could you?"

He touched her arm. "I'm sorry, Mary. I hadn't any idea you'd be upset. I just stopped at Diller's on the way home, and got into a game of checkers. That was all."

That night, long after Mr. Lincoln was asleep, Mary lay stiff and wretched, staring into the darkness. It was true, she thought. Everything Elizabeth had said, all of Frances' mean little hints, were true. Mr. Lincoln didn't care about her really. He didn't care any more than to forget her for a game of checkers. He didn't care, and he didn't understand, and he never would. In a million years, he never would.

She was alone. She'd given up everything in the world for him—believing in him. Now she was alone. He might as well be a thousand miles away as lying there beside her, never even hearing when at last she got up and went into the other room. Huddled in the old pine chair, the night shadows bleak around her, she rocked slowly back and forth.

There were faint streaks of dawn in the windows when Mary leaned stiffly over the bed and touched Mr. Lincoln's shoulder.

"Mr. Lincoln—"

His eyes opened.

"*Mr. Lincoln—*"

"What is it Mary?" He sat up, seeing her face, in the half light. She was shivering.

"You'll have to go for the doctor, Mr. Lincoln. As quickly as you can . . ."

For a long time everything was a blur. A blur of sleep that dropped between the stretches of pain. Through it all, through the sleep, and the sound of her own moaning, through the doctor's voice, calmly reassuring, and Elizabeth's directions, brisk and experienced—through everything there was the knowledge, cold and bitter, that she was alone.

It was evening when Mary opened her eyes. For a time everything seemed unreal, out of focus, as though she had wakened to a strange world. Gradually, the familiar outlines came back. The bed, the walnut dresser, the windows beyond, squares of dull blue in the twilight.

Slowly, she began to remember. The doctor's voice had said, "You have a boy, Mrs. Lincoln. A good, healthy boy."

Strange that the room should be so still. She turned her head a little, surprised at the effort it required, and saw Mr. Lincoln sitting by the bed, his hands resting on his knees, his head bent. In silence, Mary lay watching the look in his deep-set eyes, locked beyond her reach. Like an echo, weak and faint, the memory of the long night returned. And the loneliness . . .

"Mr. Lincoln . . ."

He turned.

"Mr. Lincoln, what were you thinking about just then?"

He didn't answer for a minute. Looking down at his hands, he drew a long breath.

"I was thinking about something I heard yesterday, down at Diller's, that Reverend Dresser wants to sell his house. The white frame one, over on Jackson Street. I don't know whether it's anything you'd want, Mary, but it's got a nice yard. I was thinking we might buy it . . ."

"You mean," Mary could scarcely trust her voice, "right away, Mr. Lincoln?"

"Well, yes. If you like the place." He looked at her doubtfully, as if she might not approve. "We ought to have a real home now—for the little fellow. He's a fine boy, Mary."

Mary smiled. She put out her hand, and with his touch she felt the last doubt vanish. Her eyes closed, she lay content in the utter sweetness of the moment.

After a while Mr. Lincoln said, "We've got one thing to be thankful for. Elizabeth says the baby doesn't look like me a bit."

Nine

IT WAS the twelfth of February, and Mary was planning a special dinner for Mr. Lincoln. Elizabeth and Ninian had been invited. It was the first real party Mary had given in the new house, and everything must be just right. Since early morning she'd been busy, dusting and polishing. She set the table with the best silver and embroidered linen, and spent a good hour showing Aggie, the Irish girl who came three days a week now, exactly how the dinner must be served.

By five o'clock everything was ready. Not even Elizabeth, Mary thought, could find a speck to mar the perfection. Fires burned in the grates. In the warm light the horsehair and mahogany furniture gleamed. Starched curtains framed potted geraniums on the window sills. A smell of roasting turkey, rich and plummy, drifted from the kitchen.

Mary went upstairs to feed the baby before she changed her dress. It had been worth all the trouble to have the house so pretty. Worth all Aggie's crossness and impertinence, and her bitter groans that Mrs. Lincoln made her work so hard her poor bones cried out to the holy saints for mercy.

Drawing the bedroom blinds against the winter dusk, Mary fixed the baby's gruel, and bent over the walnut-spindled cradle to take him up. Thank heavens, he seemed to be in one of his amiable moods. It would be too awful if he should decide to take a howling fit while Elizabeth was in the house. Elizabeth was very firm on the subject of howling babies. There was no excuse for it, she said, since babies, like husbands, only needed proper handling to keep them contented or at the very least quiet.

It would have been nice, Mary thought, to have had the birthday dinner a surprise for Mr. Lincoln. But experience had taught her that Mr. Lincoln wasn't the surprising kind. As surely as she planned an unexpected party, he'd choose that night to be an hour late for supper, or worse still he'd bring some crony home from the office. Why not come along for a bite? he'd say cordially. He guessed Mary'd be able to scare up enough for an extra, and she'd be tickled to have the company.

It wasn't that Mary objected to providing extra food. She was always ready to welcome a guest, particularly if he happened to be someone she thought Mr. Lincoln ought to know. It was the *sort* of people Mr. Lincoln chose to bring with him.

"Where on earth do you *find* them, Mr. Lincoln?" she asked despairingly. "Don't any decent people ever come into your office?"

"Well, I don't know, Mary," Mr. Lincoln would rub his chin, "I thought he seemed like a nice sort of fellow . . ."

"He had a five days' growth of beard, and the most abominable table manners I've yet to see. Stuffing himself like a pig."

"That shows he enjoyed the food anyway. He said it was the first real Kentucky meal he'd had in months. I should think that would please you."

"Kentucky meal, my foot. From the amount he ate, it was more likely the first food of any sort he's sat down to in a week. And if he ever clapped eyes on Kentucky, which I doubt, you can be sure he never set foot inside any decent house. You're the most gullible man I ever saw. Anyone could flatter you out of house and home."

"I guess that's so, Mary. Maybe the trouble is I don't get enough exercise resisting flattery. If you'd care to give me a little practice at home . . ."

At least, Mary sighed, there was no danger of his turning up with any strays tonight. She had told him about the party, and reminded him again the last thing before he left for the office, and he had promised solemnly to be on time.

She wiped a rim of milk from Robert's mouth and laid him in the cradle, winding his flannel band tightly to strengthen his spine, before she slipped on his nightgown. As an extra precaution, she left him a sugar-tit to suck until he went to sleep. Tiptoeing out, she paused a moment to listen. If he were going to roar, he'd start the instant the door was shut. There was no sound. Mary drew a breath of relief.

Looking in the hall mirror, she was thankful to see that her lilac moire looked as becoming as new. She fastened the waistband and settled the full, rustling skirt. It was a mercy, certainly, that she hadn't got fat after the baby. Not even Elizabeth could find fault with her figure. She parted her hair and brushed it smoothly, fluffing the curled ends behind her ears. There . . .

She was starting down the stairs when the sound of voices made her draw back. Ninian and Elizabeth weren't due for half an hour, and these were strange voices. She peeked cautiously over the banister. Two bonneted heads were visible in the hall light, and the top of a bald head, gleaming pinkly.

What on earth?

It couldn't be, it simply *couldn't* be that Mr. Lincoln had forgotten. But there was his voice now—explaining that Mary would be along in a minute.

"She's just upstairs, getting her trotting harness on," she heard him say cheerfully.

Mary felt a sharp prick of anger as she heard them laugh. How *could* Mr. Lincoln speak like that? And bringing strangers home after she'd reminded him so carefully. Well, she wouldn't go down. She would simply wait until he came up to find her, and then tell him that he had to get rid of them, somehow, before the Edwardses came. . . .

But the next moment, having caught sight of her skirt through the banisters, Mr. Lincoln called her.

"Come along down, Mary. I have a surprise for you."

Surprise, indeed. There was no escaping now. The strangers had turned to follow Mr. Lincoln's glance and stood gawping while Mary gathered her skirts in one hand and started down, her lips set in a tight, straight line. Name of heaven, wouldn't one suppose the man might at least have enough sense to show them into the parlor, instead of lining them up in the hall and shouting at her, as though he were announcing a train?

Mr. Lincoln put his arm around Mary's shoulders. These were old friends, he said, looking for all the world as though he had something to be pleased about. Mattie and Tom Renfrew, from New Salem, and their daughter Ella.

"I've been bragging to Mattie and Tom about what a fine wife I had," Mr. Lincoln said, "but I figured they'd never believe me until they'd seen for themselves." He turned to the visitors. "Now, isn't she just as good as I said?"

Mary could have wept. Being paraded like this before his bumpkin friends, as though she were something Mr. Lincoln had acquired at an auction. And of all the moments he could have chosen to put on such an absurd display . . . She nodded, as slightly as possible. "How do you do?"

The two women's smiles wavered uncertainly before the chill in Mary's voice.

"Very pleased, I'm sure." Mrs. Renfrew drew her shawl closer, obviously abashed by the spectacle of Mary's elegance.

The girl Ella said nothing. Her stare, beneath a country bonnet gaudily festooned with a row of nodding purple pansies, was hostilely appraising, and there was a look of touch-me-if-you-dare in her prominent black eyes.

Tom Renfrew, plainly not a party to the social qualms of his womenfolks, stepped up to grasp Mary's hand and wring it heartily. "A treat to meet you, ma'am. I'll own I thought Abe was stuffing us with all his talk about getting himself such a grand wife, but he didn't overshoot the mark a mite. No, sir, not a mite."

Mary allowed herself the faintest shadow of a smile as she extricated her fingers from the calloused grip. "It's always a pleasure to meet Mr. Lincoln's old friends," she said coolly. "I'm only sorry you couldn't have come earlier, in time for tea."

There was an awkward silence, while the Renfrews digested this. Mr. Lincoln, bland and cordial, came to the rescue. With never so much as a by-your-leave, or a glance in Mary's direction, he said supper was better than tea anyway, and of course they would stay.

Mrs. Renfrew pulled at her shawl again. Her glance hovered unhappily between Mary's frigid countenance and the dining room beyond, where the table, set for guests, was plainly visible. "Well now, Abe, that's kind of you, but I don't know as we ought. If Mrs. Lincoln's expecting company, she don't want a lot of strangers horning in . . ."

For an instant, Mary took hope. It was on the tip of her tongue to suggest another evening, but Mr. Lincoln gave her no chance.

Nonsense, he declared, they were staying to supper and no more argument about it. He clapped Mr. Renfrew soundly on the shoulder. "Come right along and make yourselves comfortable while I fetch out the elderberry wine." Paying no more attention to Mary than as if she had been a wax dummy standing by in helpless dismay, Mr. Lincoln led his friends past her into the parlor.

The dinner exceeded Mary's worst expectations. With the arrival of Ninian and Elizabeth, the Renfrews lapsed into a frozen and dreadful silence, from which Elizabeth's air of astonished disapproval did nothing to retrieve them. Sitting on the edges of their chairs, they seemed immobilized by the sight of Elizabeth in her jet-embroidered silk, and Ninian, slim and elegant, with his satin waistcoat and patent-leather boots. It was the boots that appeared to impress the Renfrews most deeply. They eyed them with a kind of mournful fascination until Mr. Lincoln appeared with glasses and wine.

Mrs. Renfrew, noticing that Mary and Elizabeth refused the wine, shook her head nervously. But Mr. Lincoln laughed.

"Now, Mattie, don't you be put off by these womenfolks." He filled her glass. "You'll never get me to believe you've signed the pledge behind my back."

Mrs. Renfrew tittered slightly, glancing apologetically at Mary. "You be careful now, Abe. You know I never could stand much."

Miss Ella accepted her glass without argument. After a few warming sips, she seemed suddenly restored to the power of speech and looked coquettishly at Mr. Lincoln.

"Abe, do you remember that story you used to tell in New Salem about the farmer that had to pull the pig out of the quicksand?" She turned to Mary. "It was the funniest thing I ever saw, the way he used to act the whole thing out. No matter how often we heard Abe tell that one we'd laugh to busting every time."

For one excruciating moment, Mary caught the look on Elizabeth's face. From the dining room across the hall came sounds of rattling silver and the ominous clank of glassware. Gritting her teeth in despairing rage, Mary could picture Aggie's struggles with the problem of adding three extra places to the table.

Mr. Renfrew, wrenching his gaze with difficulty from

Ninian's boots, set down his empty glass with a thud. I'll tell you, Abe, this is a real toney place you've got here." He stood up, thrusting his hands deep into the pockets of his homespun trousers. "Of course, we'd heard you were doing well, but I reckon folks in New Salem are going to be mighty proud when we tell them how you're set up here. Isn't that right, Mattie?"

Mrs. Renfrew nodded. "We always were proud of Abe. We used to say he'd get on someday, when he got his mind to it."

"Yes, *sir*," Mr. Renfrew teetered on his heels. "We knew we could count on Abe to do big things. Many's the time I've said that, Abe, back in the days when you used to bring your extra pair of pants around, to see if Mother could squeeze on one more patch." He chuckled. "I reckon your wife don't have to worry about patching your britches nowadays, do you, ma'am?"

The last remnants of Mary's smile congealed.

"I guess not and that's a fact," Mr. Renfrew went on, undismayed. "I hear you're making quite a name in politics, Abe." He turned to Ninian, genial and expansive. "I suppose you're in politics too, Mr. Edwards?"

Ninian crossed his knees, letting one foot swing lightly. "Yes and no, Mr. Renfrew. I've lived with politics all my life, so to speak. But I can't say any fires of statesmanship burn in my breast, as they do in Abe's. Personally, I've always felt I'd rather just sit back and watch the show."

Mr. Lincoln smiled. "You've got the right idea, Ninian."

"Maybe so. Maybe so," Mr. Renfrew pondered, frowning. "All the same," he bent his eye sternly on Ninian, "it's a good thing for this country we've got young fellows like Abe here, that are willing to get right in the show and aren't afraid to get their elbows skinned."

At a signal from Aggie, Mary rose abruptly.

"Dinner is waiting, Mr. Lincoln," she said. "We'll go in."

It was close on midnight when Mr. Lincoln came upstairs. Ninian and Elizabeth had mercifully departed as soon after dinner as was possible. Feeling that she could bear no more, Mary had excused herself, saying she had a headache. Her departure had failed to cast the slightest blight on the Renfrews' evening.

Undressed and in bed, Mary lay listening to the laughter and voices from below. It was absurd, of course, to let that sound make her feel lonely. She ought to be feeling merely angry. And she was angry. But, oddly, it wasn't so much Mr. Lincoln she resented now, as Ninian and Elizabeth. Remembering the way they had exchanged glances over Mr. Renfrew's pompous remarks and Mrs. Renfrew's cackling, country laugh, Mary felt a sudden surge of indignation.

The Renfrews had been quite impossible, of course, and it *was* infuriating of Mr. Lincoln to have dragged them in and spoiled her party. All the same, there was no need for Elizabeth and Ninian to assume that she was ashamed of Mr. Lincoln's friends. She remembered the gleam of amusement in Ninian's eye as he watched the Renfrews go off into fits of laughter over Mr. Lincoln's stories, and the way Elizabeth had raised her brows, ever so slightly, at Ella Renfrew's frequent giggling references to the old days when she had been on very intimate terms indeed with Mr. Lincoln.

Closing her eyes, Mary realized that her head really did ache. She had meant to punish Mr. Lincoln and snub the Renfrews by coming upstairs early. Now, most perversely, she seemed to be the only one who was punished.

When, at last, she heard Mr. Lincoln's step on the stairs, Mary turned her back and lay still. She could hear him moving about the room, getting ready for bed, winding his watch, fastening the blinds. She had expected him to try, somehow, to make amends, but the silence only grew longer. What on earth was he doing now, not making a sound?

Mary turned and sat up.

He was over by the window, standing with his hand on the back of a chair, staring down at the floor, with a queer, half-closed expression in his eyes.

"Mr. Lincoln . . ."

"Well, what have I done wrong now, Mary?"

She was startled by the words. She hadn't meant to scold. She only wanted to call him back. But at the sound of his voice, cold and patient, all her anger rushed out. He knew well enough what he had done, she said. She had worked all day, trying to have things nice for the dinner—and he had ruined everything by dragging home those ridiculous people. As if that weren't enough, he'd spent the whole evening flattering them, encouraging their stupid jokes, giving them too much wine. He had ignored her, been rude to her family. He was stupid, boorish, utterly inconsiderate of her feelings.

"For weeks I've slaved over this house, trying to make it nice for you and your friends. I get no thanks from you. You don't even notice what I've done. When I have Elizabeth and Ninian here, instead of always going to their house, as though we were poor relations, you insult them and make a fool of me. I don't see how you expect me to go on trying . . ." her voice broke, miserably.

For a long moment Mr. Lincoln did not speak. Then he came over to the bed.

"Well—" he said, "I'm sorry, Mary."

He leaned over to blow out the lamp. In the blackness the dying wick left a tiny glow that shone for a minute and then winked out, leaving an odor of oil smoke, faint and acrid.

After a while, Mr. Lincoln spoke again.

"There were times," he said, "when I'd have gone hungry if Tom and Mattie Renfrew hadn't been willing to give me supper. I reckon it wasn't always convenient for them to have me, but they'd never let on they weren't pleased to see me."

84

There was not the slightest trace of reproach in his tone. After a pause he said, "Well, good night."

In the darkness Mary could hear him turn over, feel him settling down to sleep. She was tired now, too utterly weary to think any more. She only knew that everything had got confused and wrong, and that somehow she had been the one to blame. Only, it wasn't fair. It wasn't fair . . .

Long after Mr. Lincoln was asleep it occurred to Mary that no one had wished him a happy birthday. Unless, perhaps, the Renfrews had remembered.

Ten

THE YEAR Robert was three there was a new baby, Edward, in the walnut-spindled cradle. That summer Mr. Lincoln ran for Congress.

Down at Diller's they had a flock of new stories to tell about Abe and the campaign. One they never got tired of repeating was about the time he went to hear his opponent, old Peter Cartwright, make a speech in a big revival tent. Cartwright had been an old-fashioned hellfire and brimstone preacher. The trouble was, people said, he couldn't keep his politics and his religion straight. He'd start out telling why he ought to be elected to Congress, but before he finished he'd be pounding on the table and asking how many wanted to come to Jesus and be saved.

The day Abe went to hear him, sure enough, old Cartwright puffed along on the tariff and states' rights for a while, and then he peeled off his coat and asked everybody in the audience who wanted to repent their sins and go to heaven to stand up. There was a scuffle in the tent. One by one people got to their feet till they were all standing except Abe, down there in the front row.

Reverend Cartwright leaned down from the platform and pointed a finger. "Brother Lincoln, if you don't want to go to heaven, speak up and tell us *where do you expect to go?*"

Abe had stood up, cool as you please, and picked up his umbrella.

"Why, I expect to go to Congress, Brother Cartwright," he'd said. Then he'd put on his hat and walked out.

Two weeks later, when the votes were counted, Abe had beat the old preacher two to one. He was elected to Congress.

You'd have to get up early in the morning to get ahead of Abe, they said at Diller's. Good thing he was going to Washington too. Reckon Abe'd show the government money wasters a thing or two.

Mary heard the news proudly. This would show Elizabeth and Frances and Ann, the newest sister to live in Springfield, that Mr. Lincoln was a success.

Getting packed and ready to leave kept Mary busy the next weeks. It seemed a pity to be breaking up when she'd hardly more than settled the house. But Mr. Lincoln had been elected. He was going to Washington. The path Mary had dreamed of was opening now.

One might think to hear Mary talk, her sisters agreed, that Mr. Lincoln was going to be an ambassador at least. "Ninian says it will be a shock," Elizabeth said, "when Mary discovers that a congressman's wife is no more noticed in Washington society than a new lamppost. But never fear. If Mary doesn't meet a soul, she'll give us to understand that Mr. Lincoln is the shining hope of the Whig party and they have dinner at the White House every second Tuesday."

By the end of November they were ready to leave. Mr. Lincoln was turning over the law office to his junior partner,

Billy Herndon. He and Mary and the children would take the steamboat down the river to Kentucky. They planned to visit in Lexington with the Todds for a month.

"I notice," Ann said dryly, "that Mary took good care not to have Mr. Lincoln visit Lexington until now, though they've been married five years, and I know for a fact Papa has written every summer to invite them. I daresay Mary thinks now Mr. L. is going to Congress, she can show him off better."

The visit was a success.

After some of the things they had heard, the Todds were apprehensive about meeting Mr. Lincoln. They expected a cross between a homespun backwoodsman with an ax over his shoulder, and a spellbinding orator who might overwhelm them with flights of political rhetoric. It was a surprise to find him so normal.

The night the Lincolns arrived, the Todds were lined up in the front hall, Southern style, to welcome the visitors. Mr. Todd and his wife stood nearest the door. An assortment of uncles, aunts, and cousins came next, then the Todd children, starched and pinafored, in descending stair-steps down to the red-haired baby Alex, who was the same age as little Robert Lincoln. In another group the household servants stood together, waiting curiously to catch a glimpse of Miss Mary's husband.

Mammy Jane told Mary she'd been surprised by Mr. Lincoln's size.

"The way Miss Elizabeth wrote, we pictured him kind of weazened like," she said.

All the Todds agreed that Mr. Lincoln was considerably more prepossessing than they expected. Not handsome certainly, but there was something about his eyes that kept him from being homely. And you couldn't help seeing he had a friendly knack. Later they discovered he knew a good horse when he saw one, and could argue politics in true Kentucky style.

As for Mary, she seemed prettier than any of the family remembered. Her face was round and pert, her eyes bright, her curls as soft. And her tongue was just as sharp.

"I can't see that Mary's temper has improved noticeably," her stepmother said. "But at least she's kept her figure after two babies, and that's something."

For all the talk about the Lincolns being poor, Mary was as well-dressed as any of the Todd ladies. She talked a great deal about their house in Springfield and Mr. Lincoln's increasing law practice. His new partner, Mr. Herndon, she said proudly, was one of the most brilliant young lawyers in the state of Illinois.

Mr. Lincoln seemed mildly puzzled by hearing their affairs described so glowingly.

"I don't see why you want to make us so fancy, Mary," he commented privately. "The way you tell it makes me sound like such an important fellow that being just a congressman is a measly comedown."

Mary smiled. "There's no harm in putting your best foot forward, Mr. Lincoln."

"I know," he said. "I wish I could remember which the best one is."

With the Todd children, Mr. Lincoln scored a complete success. It took them a few days to get used to the idea that young Robert and Eddie were not in the least bit awed by their parent. After that the young Todds made full use of the lovely uncle in their midst. It was novel, and slightly confusing, to see a papa whom nobody seemed to be afraid of. A papa who never scolded, or bothered about his dignity.

Following Robert's example, timidly at first, the Todd children were soon tagging devotedly after Mr. Lincoln. When he settled himself to read in Mr. Todd's library, they swarmed over him, begging for a story. He carried the smaller ones piggyback, got down on all fours to play bear, and didn't mind having his hair mussed even when there were visitors.

"I don't see how you can be a real papa," Alex Todd observed. "You don't wear whiskers or get mad."

Mammy Jane confided to Mary that she never had seen a gentleman take to children like Mr. Lincoln. "Mr. Lincoln isn't a bit like white folks," Mammy said.

Nevertheless Mary was pleased to notice an improvement in Robert's manners under Mammy Jane's training. Even the baby Edward settled into the schedule of the Todd nursery in a most orderly way. There were no more tantrums, no evenings when supper was a nerve-racking ordeal of trying to ignore ear-splitting howls from overhead.

It was lovely, as Mammy Jane said, that Mr. Lincoln was so devoted to the children. But Mary found a little more discipline far easier on the nerves.

Young Robert, however, took full credit for his popular parent. "Alex says he likes my papa much better than his papa," he announced at breakfast to the assembled family. "And so do I."

Grandmother Parker made the comment that pleased Mary most.

"I like your Mr. Lincoln," she said. "He has good eyes and good hands, and he made me laugh more than I have for twenty years." She folded her blue-veined hands. "I don't wonder you're proud of him. Your Mr. Lincoln is a gentleman, Mary."

Eleven

From Washington, Mary wrote home to Elizabeth that they were comfortably settled in a boarding house on Capitol Hill.

... Our rooms are *small*, but adequate, and afford a pleasant outlook toward the Capitol building. Mrs. Spriggs, who owns the house caters to a most *select clientèle*, mostly the families of Congressmen, officials, *etc.*, which makes the atmosphere at meals lively and stimulating.

Social life in the city is extremely active. The ladies, take a prominent part in all affairs, political and otherwise, and there is much of what Mr. Lincoln calls "flourishing about in carriages." Theaters, balls, receptions and formal visiting take a *great deal* of time, and everywhere we see the very latest in fashionable gowns.

The city, on the whole, is disappointing. There are a few fine homes, mostly around Lafayette Square and the President's House —but we must frequently pass through the meanest, unpaved streets and everywhere is *mud!*

The town is seething with talk of emancipation, *pro* and *con*. But for all the abolitionist talk that emanates from the Capitol, I have never seen slavery more in evidence or more abused than in Washington. Almost every day we see slaves, often chained together and in a miserable condition, led up Pennsylvania Avenue . . . to the Slave Pen—a disgraceful shambles which occupies a block adjoining the Smithsonian Gardens.

Mr. Lincoln's speech, criticizing the President's action in prosecuting the Mexican War has, as you have no doubt read, attracted much attention. . . .

I thank fortune we keep well, and the Washington climate appears to agree with us so far. The precious boys are lively as ever, and we all enjoy ourselves. . . .

"It sounds well enough, I must say," Elizabeth observed to Ninian. "But if I know Mary, there's plenty she hasn't written."

What could one write about evenings spent alone in a boardinghouse parlor, sewing or reading—except to say that they were very dull?

And why trouble Elizabeth with the information that the problem of fitting two active and hitherto totally unrestrained children into the pattern of city boardinghouse life had led, on a number of occasions, to criticism from Mrs. Spriggs and some of the other guests?

It was true that Mr. Lincoln was making his mark in Washington. More and more frequently now he was invited out. Mary couldn't help but be pleased when he was pointed out and recognized.

"See that man over there—the tall one in the plug hat? That's Abe Lincoln. Comes from out West somewheres. Kind of solemn-looking duck, but he can tell a comical story when he gets started. They say even Daniel Webster comes down to the Capitol post office at lunchtime to hear Lincoln's yarns."

One evening, Mr. Lincoln came home with the news that he'd been asked to Sunday breakfast at Mr. Webster's house.

Mary looked up from her sewing.

"Why, Mr. Lincoln, that's wonderful. The most important people in Washington go there." She pursed her lips thoughtfully. "Let me see, I should think my green velours ought to be just about right. Or perhaps the ladies dress more formally. Perhaps my black silk—" she stopped, aware that Mr. Lincoln was looking at her with a peculiar expression.

"To tell you the truth, Mary," he shifted uneasily, "I didn't hear anything about ladies being invited."

Sometimes, having her supper upstairs with the children when Mr. Lincoln was working late or had been invited to join a group of men at an evening bowling party, Mary would be in tears when Mr. Lincoln came home.

"I'm sorry you don't like it better here, Mary," he said. "Maybe if you got out a little more—"

Mary shrugged impatiently.

"How am I to 'get out,' when there's no one to leave the children with? And where, pray, would I go? Without a carriage I'd be a fine sight parading the streets and hopping over mud puddles."

"Well, I don't know," Mr. Lincoln sighed. "I should think you might make friends here in the house. Mrs. Spriggs seems nice."

Mary gave her shoulder a sharp twitch. "Thank you, Mr. Lincoln. I think I prefer to wait until the time comes when you see fit to introduce me to some of your friends you talk so much about."

Mr. Lincoln shook his head.

"I don't meet anyone but men, Mary. They never seem to ask me whether I'm married."

When June brought the first wave of hot weather, Mary took the boys back to Springfield. It was only sensible to get them out of Washington during the months when epidemics of malaria and typhoid swept over the city.

They agreed that she would return in the fall. But when October came, the trip was delayed for one reason and another. First Mr. Lincoln was away, speaking in New York, and attending to various political matters in New England. Then he wrote that Mrs. Spriggs was extremely sorry she had no rooms available for Mary and the boys at present. With Washington so crowded, it wasn't easy to find another place that would suit them. Perhaps later, after Christmas . . .

Mary went back to Lexington. It was a relief to have the children under Mammy Jane's competent hand again, and she and Mr. Lincoln exchanged affectionate letters.

Mr. Lincoln wrote:

Dear Mary:

In this troublesome world we are never quite satisfied. When you were here I thought you hindered me some in attending to business but now—having nothing but business—it has grown exceedingly tasteless to me . . . I hate to stay in this old room all by myself . . .

I went yesterday to hunt the plaid stockings as you wished, but found . . . not a single pair I thought would fit "Eddy's dear little feet." I have a notion to make another trial tomorrow morning . . .

And are you entirely free from headache? . . . I am afraid you will get so well and fat and young as to be wanting to marry again. Tell Louisa I want her to watch you a little for me. Get weighed and write me how much you weigh.

I did not get rid of the impression of that foolish dream about dear Bobby till I got your letter written the same day. What did he and Eddy think of the little letters father sent them? Don't let the blessed fellows forget father . . .

Most affectionately . . .

From her comfortable bedroom in the Lexington house, with the windows open to the warm May evening, Mary answered:

My dear Husband:

. . . I feel wearied and tired enough to know that this is Saturday night—our babies are asleep . . . little Eddy recovered from his spell of sickness. Do not fear the children forget you. I was only jesting.

Even E's eyes brighten at the mention of your name . . .

It is growing late, these summer eves are short. I expect my long scrawls, for truly such they are, weary you. . . . How I wish, instead of writing, we were together this evening. I feel very sad away from you.

My love . . .

PART THREE

The President's House

Twelve

Looking back, Mary was often startled to find that she could remember things without really feeling them. Days vanished into weeks, and weeks into years, and the long, soldierly line marched over the horiozn, taking all reality with it—except for a few landmarks that rose like peaks, snow-capped, still visible.

That was the spring Mr. Lincoln won the big case for the Illinois Central. It was when we added the second story to the house . . . It must have been the summer they paved the sidewalks around the square . . . Remember the winter Robert took the croup and was awfully sick . . .

There was the birth of Willie, and the year before that when they watched little Eddie die of fever. Mary could still feel the agony of sobs that wracked her, the fury with which she had refused to let her child die. She had hated Mr. Lincoln then for being calm. But later she had seen his face across the small, open grave and read there such a bitter, unspoken grief that her heart broke for him.

There was a morning when Mr. Lincoln had leaned over the spindled cradle and looked at another baby boy. This one was

Thomas, named for Mr. Lincoln's father, but Mr. Lincoln said he looked like a tadpole, with such a big head on a long, thin body, and they called him Taddie.

Taddie was his father's favorite, Mary said.

"Funny thing," they often said down at Diller's. "It looked for a while there as if Abe was set to do big things. Going off to Congress, and sassing the President, hobnobbing with Daniel Webster and all. But nothing much seemed to come of it. Guess he decided Springfield was good enough for him, after all."

One winter morning Mary was in the kitchen, delivering a lecture to Katie, the current Irish girl. It had rained all day, with no sign of clearing. The barn roof had developed a leak. The boys had been noisy and troublesome, and Mr. Lincoln was late for supper. Now Katie was in one of her unreasonable moods.

Mary glanced at the hall clock. It was past eight. The younger boys ought to have been in bed and asleep, but they had wound up the long day by a furious quarrel. The repercussions still drummed in Mary's ears.

It had begun when Willie had gone out to the woodshed to find that Tad, for want of better amusement, had hung his turtle. It was a pet turtle, and Willie was attached to it with the passionate devotion he lavished on all small creatures. He was still in the shed, loudly refusing to abandon the limp remains, his usually mild and placid nature roused to a storm of indignant tears.

Taddie, banished to bed in disgrace for his barbarous deed, was by no means penitent. Mary could hear him banging his head against the wall, while he shrieked with rage against the indignity of his punishment.

In the parlor, Robert was reading. Like his father, Robert had a maddening talent for burying his nose in a book and remaining completely oblivious to other people's difficulties. He was expected, during Mr. Lincoln's absence, to take care of the fires, but he had forgotten, as usual, and the house was damp and drafty.

How, demanded Katie shouting above Tad's roars, was she to do her work, when no one else did theirs? The fire in the range was half out, and not a stick of wood had Robert fetched.

"You should have got it yourself then, or else reminded Robert," Mary tried not to shout back.

That, said Katie, tossing her head, was not her work. As if she hadn't enough to do, cooking and scrubbing all day and picking up after the boys, who ought to be taught to do for themselves, they were certainly old enough, and somebody at her heels every minute telling her to do this, do that, she tried hard to please, goodness knows, though there were some people the saints in heaven couldn't satisfy, but there was one thing she wouldn't do and that was break her back carrying wood, not for the blessed saints themselves, she wouldn't . . .

Mary put her hands over her ears suddenly.

"For heaven's sake, Katie, stop talking. I'll get the wood myself."

After one thunderstruck moment Katie began untying her apron. Never, she muttered, never in her life had she expected to see the day when she would be shouted at. And by a lady, too. Supper or no supper, Mr. Lincoln or no Mr. Lincoln, Katie McGonnigle would stay no longer under this roof. She was leaving.

Mary struggled in from the drafty shed with an armload of wood, just in time to witness Katie's flouncing departure. She dumped the logs into the woodbox and came back to the shed where Willie, shivering and tearful, still hovered over his turtle. She had snagged her new lace cuff on a frayed end of bark, and driven a splinter into her finger.

"Willie, you *must* come to bed. I won't stand for another moment of this nonsense. The turtle is dead and nothing's going to bring it back to life."

Willie only clung to the bench tighter, his round face white and tragic.

"I'm going to wait for Papa," he said, between chattering teeth. "Papa can fix my turtle, I know he can."

Mary pushed back her hair, her lips trembling.

Dear heaven, why must they all, forever, wait for Papa? Even Katie had announced, darkly, that she wouldn't set foot out of the house until Mr. Lincoln came. Whose fault was it that the house was not properly managed? It was Mr. Lincoln who was late to meals and turned up with unannounced guests expecting to be fed. It was Mr. Lincoln who went blandly on his way, forgetting his chores, and leaving Mary to cope with unchopped wood and sidewalks piled with snow.

Katie would never think, of course, of blaming *him*. In Mr. Lincoln's presence they were all as mealy-mouthed as sucking doves. Mr. Lincoln was such a kind-spoken gentleman, God love him. And though they complained, loudly, that Mrs. Lincoln drove them past endurance and they were plagued beyond bearing by the boys' naughtiness, it never seemed to occur to them that Mr. Lincoln might occasionally lend a hand in managing his children.

You'd better do what Mrs. Lincoln says . . .

I reckon your mother knows what's best . . .

It was the most he could be counted on to offer in dealing with domestic problems.

"I should like to have the angel Gabriel change places with me for a week and see whether he could make this house run properly," Mary had exclaimed once.

Mr. Lincoln had looked over the edge of his book.

"That might be a good scheme, Mother. While you were in heaven, you'd probably be able to suggest a few improvements."

It was going on nine when Mr. Lincoln came into the house. He paused at the stairs, whence Tad's shrieks still issued, then he walked straight to the kitchen, to be confronted by Katie, bag packed, arms folded, and murder in her eye. Briefly, in highly explicit terms, Katie informed him of her reasons for leaving.

Mr. Lincoln put down his hat.

"Katie," he said, "I don't blame you."

He stood a minute, looking at his supper on the cooling range with an eye so sad and hungry and altogether weary that Katie's heart misgave her. But she squared her shoulders.

Mr. Lincoln sighed. He reached in his pocket and drew out a silver dollar. "Katie," he said, and the voice of him she had to admit would pull tears from a stone, "if you were to have an extra dollar every week, just between you and me, and not a word to another soul, do you think you could see your way clear to stay?"

Katie stared at the dollar, her blue eyes suffused with a sudden tenderness.

It wasn't, she said, that she wanted to leave *him*. And to part with the boys, especially little Taddie, God love the innocence of him, would surely break her heart. Still and all, Katie shook her head, she couldn't live under the roof with any woman that treated her so. Just because a teacup had got broke—and cracked already it was, and just slipped out of her fingers—Mrs. Lincoln had said she'd take twenty-five cents out of her wages to pay for it. And it wasn't the money she grudged, but the shame of it. On top of that, scolding and shouting at her when she couldn't carry in the wood fast enough, on account of her back . . .

Mr. Lincoln reached in his pocket again.

"If you had twenty-five cents to pay for the cup, Katie, and another twenty-five not to mention this to Mrs. Lincoln, and an extra fifty cents—do you think you could tell her you were sorry?"

"Well, sir," Katie set down her bag, "it wouldn't be for the money, if I did." She pocketed the silver firmly. "But I'd never hope to see the day when Katie McGonnigle would disoblige a Christian gentleman like yourself. I'll stay."

Mr. Lincoln went up, two steps at a time, to Taddie's room.

"Now then, Tadpole, what seems to be the trouble?"

Sobbing and twisting against his father's shoulder, Taddie poured out a wildly grieved account of his injuries.

Mamma had hitted him because he had just touched Willie's stinky old turtle. And she had hurt him bad, and the turtle had been deaded anyway . . .

Mr. Lincoln listened, saying nothing. Hoisting the boy higher on his shoulder, he crossed the hall to his bedroom and opened the bureau drawer.

"Taddie," he said, pulling out a small brown sack, "do you think a peppermint drop would make you feel like going to sleep?"

Taddie made a grab for the bag. Then he choked back a last sob, doubtfully.

"Can I have them all, Papa?"

"Well, I expect so."

Taddie rubbed his nose.

"Can I eat them now?"

"Well—"

"If I don't tell Mamma?" Taddie's glance was sidelong. "Can I?"

"I guess so, Taddie; only mind, you mustn't cry any more or tease Willie about his pets."

On his way past the parlor door downstairs, Mr. Lincoln paused to remind Robert about the fires. Then he went out to the shed. Mary was still trying to coax Willie back to the house.

He put his hand on Willie's shoulder and turned to Mary.

"Is something wrong here, Mother?"

The last remnant of Mary's control snapped.

"Something wrong *here*, Mr. Lincoln?" she demanded. "Where isn't there something wrong in this house, I should like to know? Katie is leaving because Robert refused to mind the fires. Taddie had to be spanked and put to bed because he hung Willie's turtle. Now Taddie is crying himself sick and Willie insists on staying out here where we shall both catch our death—and you come in, three hours late for supper, and ask if something is *wrong*."

"Well, Mother, it seemed the quickest way of finding out."

"Now you've found out, perhaps you can do something with this wretched boy. He won't budge from his stupid turtle that was dead hours ago."

Willie's furious wail cut in.

"He's *not* dead, Papa. He's *not*. I saw him move. See, Papa, look at him. You *see*—"

Mr. Lincoln bent down. Then he lifted the turtle's box and took Willie's hand. "I'll tell you what we'll do, Willie. We'll take the turtle up to your room. Then he won't take cold, and neither will we."

"Mamma won't let me," Willie gulped, his eyes turned on Mary accusingly. "She doesn't like my turtle. She says he's *dead*—"

"Oh, I think Mamma will. Please, ma'am," Mr. Lincoln asked politely, "may we have safe-conduct into Willie's room for one turtle, guaranteed to be harmless, free from vicious habits?"

Seeing the small, wan smile that dawned on Willie's forlorn countenance, Mary turned on her heel. "You can do anything you like," she said icily, and marched into the house.

In the kitchen, Katie looked up from the stove where she was warming the kettle of stew over a fresh fire. Very red of face, not meeting Mary's eye, she mumbled something about having changed her mind and being sorry the old cracked tea-cup had broke itself.

Mary said nothing. Passing through the hall, she heard the sounds of briskly crackling flames. Robert was on his knees before the hearth.

She went upstairs.

Taddie lay curled up to sleep, the covers smoothed neatly, and as she bent over him he gave her an angelic smile, all the more touching because his subdued moments were so rare, and because of the way his puckered lip made the smile twist to one side.

Poor baby, he was all worn out, his cheeks were stained with tears, streaked and grimy. Taddie's tempers always vanished in sweetness and Mary never failed to be disarmed by the way he could forgive his punishments. There was none of Robert's silent, passive stubbornness. None of Willie's shy, secretive ways that made his occasional outbursts so frighteningly intense. With Taddie everything was on the surface, good and bad alike.

Of all her babies, Mary thought, Taddie was the most truly her own.

It wasn't until she bent down, tenderly, to wipe his cheeks that she detected the unmistakable odor of peppermint drops that lingered on the rosy curve of Taddie's smile.

Standing in front of the mirror, smoothing her hair, Mary looked at her reflection. She could see the lines, no longer to be denied, around her eyes and the corners of her mouth. Lines that came from too often pressing her lips into the tight downward curve of exasperated weariness.

Her head ached and she had no appetite left for the belated meal, yet suddenly she found herself wishing she could tell Mr. Lincoln she was sorry she had been angry. Perhaps she could make him understand. Perhaps he might even console her—as he could cajole Katie, and give Taddie peppermints, and bring Willie's turtle back to life.

It was no use. He would have forgotten already that there was anything for her to be sorry about, just as Katie had forgotten, and Taddie, and Willie.

It would be easier, certainly, to forget as quickly as they had, Mary thought. Yet a shadow looked over her shoulder into the mirror—the shadow of a future that would not let her forget. It was a shadow of hope and faith—of a President's house —of the greatness which, through all the everyday rub, she had never stopped seeing in Mr. Lincoln.

She turned away from the mirror, not sure whether she had seen something real or only a dream, and went downstairs to a cold supper.

Thirteen

IT WAS beginning to look as though the slavery issue would have to be decided, after all. The Whig party had held out as long as it could, trying to straddle the ticklish question, and had finally died, still straddling. The Democrats managed to keep themselves on the fence, but sooner or later they'd have to make the jump.

"The North won't let slavery alone," Mr. Lincoln said, "and the South can't afford to give it up. One way or another they're bound to meet head on."

He was back in politics now, helping to form the new Republican party that was made up of leftover Whigs and a few Democrats who were tired of their own party's quibbling. Still, in spite of the Republicans' firm stand against the extension of slavery, Mr. Lincoln hadn't altogether made up his mind.

More and more, people spoke of the possibility of war, of secession, and a split country. But mostly they talked without really meaning it. In the prairie summer, while the sun rose and set just as it always had, and the corn grew tall in the fields, war seemed a far-off and impossible thing.

"If there should be fighting," Elizabeth asked one afternoon, "which side would Mr. Lincoln take?"

Mary, wary of the sudden move, was still cautious. Mr. Lincoln hadn't decided. There were many factors to be considered. Moral rights were one thing, but property rights were quite another, and so long as the Constitution guaranteed both, who could be certain which was right?

Elizabeth bit off her thread. It wasn't so much a question of being right, she observed crisply, as being anywhere at all. If Mr. Lincoln didn't hurry up and decide, he might very well find himself nowhere.

When Mary said the same thing to Mr. Lincoln, he shook his head.

"It's like the old Scotch elder who used to make the same prayer every Sunday: 'O Lord, point me right, for Thou knowest if I get pointed wrong, Thou, Thyself, can't change me.'"

After a minute, he said, "I wish someone would point me right."

Mary went on with her mending. As she bent over Willie's sock, her heart pounded with new hope.

That summer Stephen Douglas came back to Springfield. He was running for the Senate, on the Democratic ticket. It was up to the Republicans to put up a man strong enough to give him a run for his money, and money was something the Democrats had plenty of.

"Don't know as they'll get anybody fool enough to try to beat Douglas," they said down at Diller's. "Douglas is the best vote-getter in Illinois—and always was."

Mr. Douglas was married now. There were those who hinted that his wife, who was young and very handsome, already had her eye on something more important than the Senate. Adele Douglas was smart, and she knew that if Mr. Douglas could win this election, the Democrats were likely to put him up for President. And if money and good looks and influence could turn the trick, she meant to see to it that he had them.

When the Republicans first began to talk of running Abe Lincoln against Douglas, Mary was annoyed by Mr. Lincoln's indifference to the suggestion. This was the first chance he had had since his one term in Congress had come to nothing. She had begun to lose hope that there would ever be another. Now here it was, and Mr. Lincoln only looked gloomier than ever.

"The only chance I can see," he said, "is the chance to take a skinning. With the Democrats pouring money into Illinois, Douglas can't possibly lose. Anyway, he's the most popular man in the state."

Mary set her chin.

"And how did he get to be so popular, I should like to know? Not by magic, Mr. Lincoln. He went out and worked for it and you can do the same thing, if you've a mind to."

Mr. Lincoln shrugged. There was only one stick big enough for Douglas to stub his toe on, he said, and that was slavery. Douglas was too smart to risk committing himself there. He'd walk the fence, same as he always had, and get the vote on both sides.

"Unless," Mary said, "someone is smart enough to push him off that fence. Unless somebody asks him point-blank to state his mind."

Some weeks after Mr. Lincoln was nominated, he surprised everybody, most particularly his opponent, by challenging Mr. Douglas to a series of public debates that would put the slavery question fairly and squarely up to the voters.

"I'd like to know how Abe Lincoln expects to argue anybody down on something he hasn't made up his own mind about," Elizabeth said.

It seemed that Mr. Lincoln had been doing more thinking than Elizabeth or anyone else except Mary, and perhaps Billy Herndon, realized. For weeks Mary had collected newspapers and magazines and poured over them. Those she could not find at home, she asked Mr. Herndon to send from the office. She wrote to her family to send papers from the South. Every article she found on the slavery question she clipped and pasted into notebooks.

The notebooks were for Mr. Lincoln. Mary left them, without comment, on the breakfast table in the mornings and beside his reading chair each evening. While Mr. Lincoln read them she searched the latest columns for more articles to clip and paste.

Mr. Lincoln studied the arguments from the South. They not only supported slavery for Negroes—but for the lower class of white workers as well. In the so-called free society of the North, the Southern papers said, there were thousands of servile laborers who were incapable of self-government and yet were given the power to vote. The time was coming when the North must rid itself of this burden of ignorance and incompetence. It was natural for some men to be masters and some slaves, as natural as for parents to take responsibility for their children. Late or soon, all thinking people must come to see this. There were groups of powerful interests in the North that were beginning to listen to these arguments—and believe them.

That was the way the wind was blowing. And having felt its cold breath, Mr. Lincoln was ready at last to answer.

On the morning after he had challenged Mr. Douglas to debate the slavery question, Mr. Lincoln came down to find a new notebook by his breakfast plate. He looked up, "Still more, Mother?"

Mary was helping his plate from the stove. She did not turn. "Still more, Mr. Lincoln," she said. "You've declared war on Mr. Douglas. You'll need plenty of ammunition to win it."

One summer day the two candidates spoke to a crowd under the broiling sun. Men were bareheaded and in shirt sleeves. The few women fanned themselves and dabbed their faces with handkerchiefs. Mr. Douglas had spoken longer than usual and in spite of his eloquence the audience was weary. By the time Mr. Lincoln rose to reply they were shifting restlessly.

Mary, standing in the crowd, looked around uneasily as Mr. Lincoln began. His words came slowly at first. Then, as he caught the attention of group after group, his voice rose with quiet strength.

"When . . . you have succeeded in dehumanizing the Negro; when you have put him down . . . and extinguished his soul . . . are you quite sure that the demon you have roused will not turn and rend you? . . . Our reliance is in the love of liberty which God has planted in us. Our defense is in the preservation of the spirit which prized liberty as the heritage of all men, in all lands everywhere. Destroy this spirit and you have planted the seeds of despotism at your own doors. Familiarize yourselves with the chains of bondage and you prepare your own limbs to wear them. . . ."

Listening, Mary found herself caught up with the others. Even from a distance, every line of Mr. Lincoln's face was familiar. She knew each inflection of his voice. The shirt he wore was one she had made. Yet his words were new. The words—and something more. A kind of spirit that came from him and from his listeners, like something that had slept a long time and was wakening. The crowd sensed it; she could feel their response in the silence around her, in the upturned faces.

The current, dammed over the slow years, was flowing now.

Mr. Lincoln finished speaking and pulled out a red cotton handkerchief to wipe his forehead. There was applause. The audience stirred, beginning to break up. A few went to the platform. Mary could see Mr. Lincoln reaching down to shake hands. She stood quite still. Presently she was surprised to find tears in her eyes.

That was one of the few times Mary heard Mr. Lincoln speak that summer. Most of the time while he was away campaigning, she stayed in Springfield. The current hired girl was as unreliable as her predecessors, and couldn't be left to take care of the boys. For another thing, there wasn't enough money in the Republican chest to pay her traveling expenses.

While Mr. Douglas and his wife and party swept into one town after another in a private railroad car, Mr. Lincoln usually arrived carrying his own suitcase after a long, dusty ride in a day coach.

"We have to make up in elbow grease for what the Democrats put on in show," Mr. Lincoln said. He worked hard, coming home between speeches so tired that Mary watched him anxiously.

For all the fanfare of the Douglas tour, Mr. Lincoln was holding his own.

"The way Douglas lands in a town with a brass band and a cannon firing salutes makes it look as if he'd fought the country and just succeeded in conquering it," Mr. Lincoln told Mary. "I have a hunch some folks might rather see a candidate look like an ordinary sort of fellow."

There were others who were more skeptical.

"I don't see why you can't work up a little more show," Elizabeth said to Mr. Lincoln one evening when he and Mary came for supper. "People like to be entertained. There are bound to be plenty who vote for the party that makes the most noise. It makes them feel safer."

"Like whistling in the dark," Mr. Lincoln agreed. "We have plenty of dark, but we can't seem to work up the whistle."

From Chicago Mr. Lincoln wrote Billy Herndon that the newspapers were divided. Some called Douglas bombastic and hollow. They said his best qualification for senator seemed to be a handsome wife. Others said Lincoln was a Republican backwoodsman who could split infinitives as well as rails.

"You can gather they don't care much for either of us," Mr.

Lincoln added, "but don't tell Mother what they said about Addie Douglas."

The most serious charge against Mr. Lincoln was that his outspoken statements on slavery were setting one half the country against the other. When he warned about the possibility of war he was preaching war, the Democrats charged.

Answering, Mr. Lincoln said that there was a difference between a horse chestnut and a chestnut horse.

After the last debate one woman said, "All the time Mr. Douglas was speaking I felt *so* sorry for Mr. Lincoln. Then when Mr. Lincoln spoke I felt *so* sorry for poor Mr. Douglas."

It was a long summer for Mary. With Mr. Lincoln away she had the house to take care of and only the boys for company.

"You might go down to Lexington," Elizabeth suggested.

The thought of the big house, with cool shaded rooms and long evenings on the veranda while Mammy Jane bathed the children and put them to bed was tempting. But Mary shook her head. "When Mr. Lincoln comes home, he needs a family here and as much food and rest as I can coax him to take," she said.

From the start of the campaign, no one seemed to have much doubt about the outcome. Lincoln had put up a good fight. Starting from way behind, he'd made Douglas sweat for every vote. Still no one was surprised, in November, when Douglas carried the state.

"Nobody expected me to win," Mr. Lincoln said, "except Mary."

He was wrong. Mary hadn't thought he would be elected any more than anyone else had. But when it was over, and Mr. Lincoln was back home, she knew one thing for sure. She had been right when she kept him from taking an appointment from President Taylor as governor of the Oregon Territory.

He had thought perhaps they ought to go—seeing no possibilities for anything very promising where they were.

Mary had been firm. He should not go. Now she saw that she hadn't been mistaken.

Mr. Douglas was going back for another term in the Senate, but after the debates there had been a sudden end to the talk of putting him up for President the following year.

Mr. Lincoln had been defeated. All the same, he had said some things that wouldn't be forgotten.

Money was scarce in the Lincoln house all winter. Mary gave up the hired girl altogether. But while she cooked and scrubbed and mended the boys' clothes, she was happier than she had been in a long while. If she had moments of doubt, she only needed to remember the afternoon she had heard Mr. Lincoln speak and the look on the faces of the people around her—listening.

Fourteen
VVVVV

WITH MR. LINCOLN back at the law office, money began to come in again, and the bills were paid. Mary still had no help in the house, but Robert was going to Exeter Academy in the fall.

"I can't see any mortal sense in sending Robert halfway across the country when there are schools right here in Illinois," Elizabeth said.

Mary was firm. "I mean to have the best of everything for the boys. I've always intended Robert to go to Harvard, and he needs a year at a good eastern school to prepare him."

Elizabeth looked at her curiously. "What does Mr. Lincoln say to all this?"

"Mr. Lincoln leaves such things to me," Mary said. "He's devoted to the boys, but he has no more ideas about planning for their future than a kitten. So long as they learn to read and write, I don't suppose he'd ever notice. He doesn't realize that the boys must have their chance—but I do. And I mean to see they have it."

A few weeks after Robert left for Exeter, Mary's younger sister Emilie came to visit. Mary was fond of Emilie, and she hoped Emilie might marry and settle down in Springfield. But shortly after her return to Lexington, Emilie wrote that she was engaged to Ben Helm. They would be going to live in Georgia as soon as they were married.

Reading Emilie's letter, full of happy plans for the future, Mary felt uneasy. Three of her sisters were already married to Southerners. All her brothers were living in the South. And the dark prophecies of secession and war grew no less.

She wondered sometimes how much Mr. Lincoln regretted having lost the election to Mr. Douglas. He seemed completely taken up with his law work again, and though there were occasional visits from gentlemen who came to smoke their cigars in the parlor and confer with Mr. Lincoln, he spoke little about politics.

"I'm glad for your sake, Mary," Elizabeth said, "that Mr. Lincoln has gotten over this nonsense of running for office and settled down to business. I daresay it was a disappointment to you when he lost the campaign, but I suppose we all have to learn sooner or later that our husbands aren't cut out to be great men. Taking things by and large, Mary, I don't mind saying Mr. Lincoln has turned out a good deal better than I expected."

One winter evening, after supper, Mr. Lincoln came into the sitting room where Mary was darning socks. Instead of picking up a book, he sat down on the sofa, his elbows on his knees. Tad and Willie were asleep. The house was very still.

Out of the silence, Mr. Lincoln said, "I was talking to Jesse Fell this afternoon."

Mary nodded. She didn't know Jesse Fell. She was wondering at the moment whether she had remembered to tell Robert in her last letter about the new shirts she was sending him. When Mr. Lincoln didn't go on, she looked up.

"Yes?"

Mr. Lincoln pushed his rocking chair back. "Fell's got some notions about the elections next fall. He seems to think that if the Republicans put up the right man, they might stand a chance to get in."

Mary rolled up a sock and rubbed her eyes. She made an effort to listen.

"He said," Mr. Lincoln looked at the ceiling, "they were thinking of putting me up to run. But I don't know . . ."

For a moment Mary continued to inspect a hole in one of Willie's socks. Suddenly, as though an explosion had rocked the familiar, firelit room, the meaning of Mr. Lincoln's words dawned on her. She leaned forward, gripping the sock so tightly that she stretched the hole bigger.

"What did you tell him, Mr. Lincoln?"

"Why," he seemed surprised, "I told him I didn't think much of the idea. I said if they were looking for someone who stands of being elected they were barking up the wrong tree. Seward, back in New York, or Chase, or Simon Cameron—any of those men are better known than I am."

"Mr. Lincoln—" Mary stood up, not noticing the lapful of socks that spilled at her feet. "Mr. Lincoln, you don't mean to sit there and tell me you refused."

"Not exactly, Mother. I told Fell they'd better think it over. After all, nobody outside of Illinois has ever heard of me."

"No," Mary said, "but they will, Mr. Lincoln. They *will* hear of you."

Hearing the fierce intensity in her voice, Mr. Lincoln glanced up again. There wasn't any use, he said, taking this too seriously. It was only a conversation between friends. He just thought he'd mention it.

Mary shook her head. From deep inside her a strength seemed to rise. All the hopes, all the efforts she had squandered for so many years on a thousand things that never really mattered were suddenly concentrated. She stooped and gathered up the scattered socks from the floor and put the basket on the table.

"Mr. Lincoln, you must listen to me." Mary sat down facing him. This was the moment she had always known was coming. The tide was running swift and full. "You must decide what you are going to do, Mr. Lincoln. Now—before it's too late. Before the chance is gone—"

"Now, Mother, there's no call to get excited. You can't force a thing like this. Besides, there's no such luck for me."

Mary watched him steadily. "There's no luck about being President, Mr. Lincoln," she said. "These things can be forced. They must be."

For a minute, in the still room, he seemed to catch the light that burned in her eyes.

"Promise me you won't answer that way again, Mr. Lincoln. Promise me . . ."

For a moment more her glance held his. Then Mr. Lincoln smiled.

"Well," he said, "it seems kind of early to be making campaign promises—" His voice dropped back into the easy drawl. "If it makes you feel any better, Mother, I'll promise that the day they come and knock at the front door and ask me to be President—I won't say no."

The snowball gathered slowly.

For more than a month the days came and went much as usual. Mr. Lincoln was busy at the office. Willie fell off the porch and sprained his knee. Mary's grandmother died in Lexington and left her a legacy of a thousand dollars and her amethyst brooch.

During those weeks Mary was careful not to let Mr. Lincoln see that she was waiting. For the first time in years she showed no irritation when Mr. Lincoln was late for meals or the boys tried her patience. It was as though a calm, deep and certain, had dropped over the house.

The snowball still gathered.

By the time spring came, people in Springfield were beginning to say they'd heard talk of Mr. Lincoln being put up for the nomination. It seemed an unlikely kind of idea. Still, they mentioned it.

When Elizabeth heard it from Ninian, she spoke to Mary. Mary only shrugged, and said it was far too early to listen to rumors.

Mr. Lincoln had to go to New York, to make a speech at Cooper Union. Before he got back to Springfield the news of his speech had spread all over the country. Newspapers everywhere had reprinted his words—along with editorials praising or condemning his stand.

In the late spring there was a week of unseaonably raw weather, and both Tad and Willie came down with colds. When Taddie's cold settled in his chest, Mary insisted on sitting with him at night until, worn out with nursing and anxiety, she came down with a chill herself.

Cousin Lizzie Grimsley was sent for, and for several days she took care of the house while Mary rested. When Cousin Lizzie went home, she was puzzled.

"I can't make Mary out," she said. "You know how particular she is about her house—and yet the whole time I was there she hardly seemed to notice what was going on. Half the time I don't believe she even heard what anyone said until Mr. Lincoln came home. Then she'd want to sit up and fix her hair—and start to fuss if his supper wasn't ready the minute he wanted it. You might think they'd been married a week, instead of nearly eighteen years."

One morning after Mary and the boys were well again, another letter came from Emilie. She was married now, and very happy. But she couldn't help being troubled by all the talk of secession. Did Mary suppose there was really going to be a war? More letters came from Lexington. Was it true, as they kept hearing, that Mr. Lincoln might run for President and, if he were elected, he would abolish slavery?

Mary replied at length. There was some talk of Mr. Lincoln

being nominated, she said. As for slavery, he was opposed to it as an institution and bitterly opposed to extending it in any form. But he was not an abolitionist and never had been. And no President, she added firmly, would have the power to amend the Constitution and abolish slavery.

The weather grew milder. It was time to fetch down the summer clothes from the boxes in the attic and let down the boys' trousers.

As the days lengthened, and the sun shone warmly on the apple tree in blossom outside Mary's window, there was no lessening of the tension that hung over the country. Storm signals were raised now. North and South were being drawn inexorably apart. Violent words were hurled back and forth. The founding fathers and Holy Writ were quoted liberally on both sides.

The most plentiful commodity on the market, Mr. Lincoln said, seemed to be hot air.

Not many in either North or South took much stock, for all the shouting, in the idea of an actual war. It was only a little group of radicals, mostly in New England, that went so far as to say they wanted to fight. New England was very far away. But the little group had lighted the fires, and the fires kept on burning.

They were trying to pin Mr. Lincoln down now. He had spoken against slavery. If it came to slavery or war, which would he choose?

"You'll have to tell them something, Mr. Lincoln," Mary said. "If you don't, you'll wind up with neither side trusting you."

"I don't know why they should," Mr. Lincoln said, "when I don't trust either side."

"It doesn't settle anything just to keep on saying there's wrong on both sides, Mr. Lincoln. There must be right on both sides too."

"Yes," he said. "That's just the trouble."

The snowball was rolling too fast to be stopped. No one seemed to know how it had happened, but people everywhere were getting the idea that maybe this man Lincoln could do something to straighten out the mess. He wasn't one of those name-callers anyway. If Lincoln thought there was a chance of bringing both sides around and stopping this thing short of ruining the whole country—well, maybe he was the man to do it.

One rainy morning in May, the Republican National Convention met in Chicago.

Mary was up early, helping Miranda with breakfast, and the boys were already at the table when Mr. Lincoln came into the dining room. Mary turned, a pot of coffee in one hand and a plate of hot biscuits in the other. For a moment she and Mr. Lincoln looked at each other, then Mary smiled.

"Sit down, Mr. Lincoln. You look as though you need a good breakfast."

She poured his coffee, and put out a helping of strawberry preserve. He sat staring at the food, seeming lost in thought.

"I was just thinking, Mother," he said finally, "I'd better bring in some wood before I go down to the office. It's kind of chilly—maybe you'd like a fire."

Mary looked up quickly. It was the first time she could ever remember his offering to do anything around the house without being reminded.

"That's all right, Mr. Lincoln," she said. "Miranda or I can fetch the wood just as well as not. It's no trouble."

By midmorning the rain had stopped. Willie had gone to school and Taddie was playing in the yard. The house was tidy for the day, and Miranda had started dinner. Mary went to the front window and stood looking out on the familiar street. There wasn't any use, of course, expecting news. It would be several days before the convention got around to actually deciding. In the meantime she might as well find something to keep her busy.

She was upstairs sorting sheets to be mended when the front door banged, and Taddie came pounding up the stairs shouting breathlessly that Papa was coming down the street.

"Is he the Prestendent yet, Mama?"

"No, no; of course not, Taddie." Mary hurried past him, not pausing to notice the mud he had tracked onto the clean stairs. She met Mr. Lincoln at the front door.

"Mr. Lincoln, what is it? Has something happened?"

He turned to hang up his hat.

Nothing had happened, only there was no hope of getting anything done at the office. The place was full of people, all with nothing in particular to say and wanting to say it fast.

"If it's all right with you, Mother, I guess I'll just stay home today."

That was Wednesday. All day Thursday and half of Friday they waited. Mr. Lincoln walked downtown every few hours to bring a fresh batch of telegrams. Between times there were streams of visitors, arriving at the most unlikely hours, and letters, messages, and more telegrams.

The house was in a turmoil. Meals were interrupted a dozen times, there were cigar ashes all over the furniture, the polished floors were tracked with footprints, and the boys were in such a stew of excitement that Mary gave up hope of keeping them in any sort of order.

Reports and rumors came from the convention. Billy Herndon had gone up to Chicago, and he telegraphed long bulletins. Mr. Lincoln's name had been given an ovation, but Seward got an even bigger demonstration. Most people seemed to think Lincoln's chances looked good, but it was still anybody's guess how the convention would vote.

By Friday morning, there were dark shadows around Mr. Lincoln's eyes.

"I'll be glad when it's over," he said gloomily. "There never was much of a chance."

"Nonsense, Mr. Lincoln. Nothing's over yet—and you'll feel

differently when you've tasted Miranda's pancakes. She's the first girl I've ever had that knew how to make them properly." Mary handed him his plate and passed the syrup jug.

It was barely eight o'clock, but Mary had already straightened the house, planned the meals, and given Miranda directions for the day. It was the only time she had the house to herself.

"I should think you'd be fagged out," Mr. Lincoln said. "But you look more as if you were fixed up for a party."

Mary smiled. She had gone up before breakfast to change into her blue sprigged muslin, and her hair was brushed and shining. It was unusual of Mr. Lincoln to notice.

"Heavens and earth," she said, "one of us has got to keep cheerful."

While Mary got Willie off to school and helped Miranda clear away the breakfast things, Mr. Lincoln followed her about, his hands in his pockets. She was surprised and touched by the way he seemed to turn to her, as though he needed her reassurance. After all the years, after the bitter, rebellious times when she had felt shut out of his life, it was strange that he should come so close now just when there was so much to pull him away.

By nine o'clock another telegram had come from Billy Herndon. Balloting would begin this morning, it said; everyone was sure of a quick decision. By afternoon, at the latest, there should be news.

Mr. Lincoln read the message and handed it to Mary.

"I wish it weren't Friday," he said. "It always was an unlucky day."

"I daresay it's just as likely to be unlucky for Mr. Seward," Mary put down the telegram and handed him a list. "If you're planning to go downtown before noon, Mr. Lincoln, I'd be obliged if you'd stop at the grocery. We're out of vanilla and eggs—and Miranda wants to bake a cake."

It was a little past twelve when Mr. Lincoln came home. He walked straight through to the kitchen.

"Here are your things, Mother."

There was a note in his voice that made Mary turn quickly.

"While I was getting the vanilla," he said, "Ed Boliver came across from the office to tell me they'd got the news that I'd been nominated." He looked at Mary with a queer mixture of surprise and sheepishness. "I guess they really meant it, after all, Mother."

Miranda was outside, hanging up wash. Taddie had gone across the street to play. In that moment, they were alone in the house, facing each other across the packages. Mary came around the table.

It was true, she thought. This was the moment she had believed in and waited for. Now it had come; surely all the impatience and misunderstanding and failure would be washed away.

She put out her hand.

"I knew this would come, Mr. Lincoln," she said. "I've always known it."

Mr. Lincoln took her hand, looking down at her.

"Well—I'm glad you weren't disappointed, Mother," he said.

The rest of the day was a confused dream. People appeared from nowhere and popped up in every corner of the house, shaking hands, shouting the same congratulations over and over. A band, hastily assembled, marched down Jackson Street and blared out a noisy serenade, half off key, and a dozen times during the afternoon Mr. Lincoln went out on the front porch to shake more hands.

Telegrams came every few minutes. Tad or Willie came rushing in with the latest ones. There was no restraining the boys now; it seemed to Mary they were everywhere, stumbling over visitors' feet, hanging on Mr. Lincoln's coattails, their cheeks and pockets stuffed with candy they received from the strangers with shrieks of delight.

Elizabeth and Ninian were there, and Ann and Frances and the John Stuarts. Cousin Lizzie, bursting with pride, told anyone who would listen about the strange feeling she had the very day Mary married Mr. Lincoln—that he would turn out to be a great man.

On all sides Mary heard them talking about Mr. Lincoln. How they'd always said Abe had something about him that was different.

"Seemed like he was almighty slow getting started, though—"

Even her sisters seemed awed by the news. When they offered to stay and help Mary serve refreshments she accepted gratefully. Her cup was too full to leave room for bitterness.

At eleven that night, the house still milled with people, and there were outraged howls from Tad and Willie when Mary finally marched them upstairs. Worn out herself, she managed somehow to get them undressed and into bed. But at that very moment a fresh burst of music blared from the street below, and both boys were up again. Taddie danced on the bed, loudly demanding to *see the noise*.

With a sigh of resignation, Mary carried him to the window.

"Look, Mamma, at all the sticks on fire—" Taddie strained against her shoulder.

It was a torchlight parade. In the flaring lights the street and yard looked strange and unfamiliar. People crowded about the front step, shouting ragged scraps of campaign songs above the raucous band.

"Hurray for Lincoln!"

"Three cheers for Honest Abe!"

Taddie drooped against Mary's arm, overcome with sleep at last, but Mary still stood, holding him. She looked up from the noise and lights below to the arch of sky and the fixed unreadable pattern of the stars.

Fifteen

THE QUIET summer weeks were a relief to Mary. Mr. Lincoln worked in the office, preferring to stay in Springfield and leave the early campaign speaking to Sumner, Chase, and the others.

Except for the great bundles of mail each day it might almost have been any other summer. The strawberry season, followed by the raspberry season, were each accompanied by the usual church suppers and rounds of private ice-cream parties. Robert was home from Exeter, and in August word came that he was accepted for the freshman class at Harvard. The boys picked cherries and peaches from the trees in the yard and Mary put up preserves as usual.

Stephen Douglas had been nominated by the Democratic party. The old rivals faced each other once more. "If Douglas wins this time," Frances said, "even Mary will have to admit she chose the wrong beau."

The July days passed. The campaign grew more intense. Still Mary remained serene.

"I must say," Elizabeth admitted, "Mary is taking this a great deal better than I expected. She scarcely mentions the election and I haven't heard her speak a cross word to Mr. Lincoln in weeks."

Even when Fido, the brown dog shared between Willie and Tad and their best friends, the Roll Boys, persisted in climbing onto Mary's clean spread, she put him off the bed gently. It occurred to her that neither she nor Fido might be in this house another summer.

Autumn came and the tensions grew tighter again. Mr. Lincoln was speaking almost constantly. Whenever he was at home the parlor was filled with visitors and cigar smoke. Mary was torn between welcoming the callers properly and trying to keep some order in the household. One afternoon she cuffed Fido for bringing a bone into the kitchen. Willie and the Roll boys and young Isaac Diller were in the kitchen. She turned to see their shocked faces.

"I'm sorry," she said, not knowing whether she spoke to the boys, or Fido, or herself. "I'm sorry. In a few days this will all be over."

On election morning Mary woke before daylight. She saw Mr. Lincoln, already dressed, standing by the window.

"I couldn't seem to sleep," he said. He came over and sat down on the bed.

Mary watched him, thinking how tired he looked. She wondered how he really felt about being President. It occurred to her that not once, in all the months, had he ever said what he wanted.

While she dressed, Mary glanced out at the gray morning. The trees looked bare and cold, and a sharp wind rattled the windows. It was like the morning of her wedding day. From across the hall, she could hear the boys arguing about something, Willie's voice low and persistent, Taddie's growing shrill as it always did when he was on the verge of tears. Dear heaven, did they have to start quarreling so early on this of all days.

When she went in, Willie was sitting cross-legged on the floor.

"Taddie won't put on his clothes, Mamma. He won't even start, and I'm all dressed. He won't be ready in time to see Papa be President, will he, Mamma?"

Taddie, still in his nightgown, glowered from the bed.

"I want to put on my Sunday suit," he said, his lip quivering. "And Willie won't let me. He says I can't put it on, but I want to help Papa."

"He's silly," Willie said flatly. Wearing a Sunday suit won't help Papa. He's a crybaby."

"I'm *not—*" Taddie's face darkened furiously as the tears started down his round cheeks. "I'm not crying—are I, Mamma?"

"He is too. Look at him."

Mary bit her lip. If only everything needn't put her so on edge. She pulled Willie to his feet and ordered him downstairs; then she took Tad into her lap and began to dress him, pulling on his clothes with angry jerks.

Abashed by her set face, Taddie stopped crying and watched her warily.

"Are you cross because Papa is going to be Prestendent, Mamma?"

Mary stopped, a stocking half on, and drew him quickly toward her. "Oh, Taddie—it's only that I—I'm tired this morning."

He smiled, instantly forgiving. "That's all right." He glanced up again, artfully.

"I *can* put on my Sunday suit, can't I, Mamma?"

"Of course, dear, if you want to."

As she got up to fetch it, Taddie beamed. "Willie will be mad," he said complacently.

At breakfast there was more trouble. Taddie, swollen with triumph, refused to touch his porridge, and when Mary ordered him to eat it or go back to bed, he shook his head.

"I don't have to," he announced. "I don't have to do anything I don't want to, because my Papa is going to be Prestendent." With a defiant gesture, Taddie pushed the plate away, upsetting his milk on the tablecloth. A dribble splashed down on his Sunday trousers.

Willie was ecstatic. "Taddie's spoiled his Sunday suit. Look, Mamma—"

Mary put down her napkin, but before she could move or speak, Mr. Lincoln, without a word, rose and carried Taddie upstairs. When he came down, his face was grave.

"I've put him to bed, Mother. It's where he belongs, poor little chap, he's all worn out." He sat down. "Please God, this will be over today and we can settle down to being a family again."

Down at the State House they had reserved a room for Mr. Lincoln, where the returns would be posted as they were telegraphed in. When he was ready to go, Mary went to the door with him. Mr. Lincoln took his hat from the peg.

"Well . . ." he hesitated. "I'll be back as soon as I can, Mother."

Mary nodded. "I'll send Willie down at noon with something hot for you to eat."

He waited a moment longer, looking at his hat.

"Good-bye, Mary," he said.

She watched him down the street. It was still early—no one much was out yet—and he walked alone, rapidly, his tall figure leaning into the sharp November wind.

At noon Mary sat down to dinner with the boys. Taddie, unchastened by a morning in bed, was full of conversation.

"Isn't Papa Prestendent yet, Mamma?"

"Of course not *yet*," Willie said. "It takes a long time, doesn't it, Mamma?"

Taddie shook his head, unconvinced. "We have to go on

the train tonight," he insisted. "Miranda said so. And Willie has to leave his turtle here—and his new kitten. And we have to leave Fido. This is how the train goes—*whooooo . . .*"

Willie's face puckered. "I *don't*. I don't have to leave them. If I have to leave them, I won't *go* to Washington. I'll stay here . . ."

Mary tried not to listen. Her eyes burned—dear God, how long was it since she'd slept a night through?

When she had packed a basket for Willie to take to Mr. Lincoln, and sent Taddie out to play, Mary went upstairs. Three o'clock . . . four. She lay down on the bed but when she closed her eyes, the house seemed filled with a strange whispering. . . . *When would he come home? When would he come? When . . .*

It was dusk when Mary went downstairs. She told Miranda to light the lamps, and went to call Taddie just as Elizabeth and Frances came up the front walk. They asked if there was any news.

At eight o'clock Mary sent Miranda to put the boys to bed and gave them each a nickel to be good. A boy knocked on the front door with a message from Mr. Lincoln. The first returns were showing him ahead, but it was still too early to tell. They ought to know for sure by midnight. The boy said, grinning, he guessed Mr. Lincoln was the calmest man in town. Everybody else had gone clean crazy.

Mary went into the sitting room and took out her basket of mending. It lay in her lap, unopened, while she stared into the fire, waiting . . .

It was one o'clock when she heard footsteps outside, and rose to go to the door. It must be another messenger. There was a sound of voices, and singing. Then she heard Mr. Lincoln.

"All right, boys, go home and get some rest now."

He stepped inside and closed the door.

"Well, Mother," he said, "I've been elected."

Mary looked at him. At his face, his hat, at his eyes, deep-set, remote. Suddenly, without will, she burst into tears, pressing her face against his coat.

His voice was patient, full of mild surprise, as he patted her shoulder.

"Why, Mother," he said, "I thought you wanted me to be President."

Sixteen

THE NEXT morning Mary woke with a start, to find Mr. Lincoln gone, and no sound from the boys' room across the hall. Her first thought was of something wrong, then she heard voices from the dining room below. Sinking back, she lay still, smelling coffee and bacon, thinking of plans for the day.

There was so much to be done. Food to be ordered, clothes to be decided on, a letter to Robert . . .

Downstairs she found Mr. Lincoln opening a stack of messages. He showed her a telegram offering congratulations and pledging personal support to the new President. Mary smiled when she saw the signature: STEPHEN A. DOUGLAS.

"I can't think of anyone I'd rather have back me," Mr. Lincoln said.

It was raining again. After breakfast Taddie settled down with an illustrated paper on the parlor floor. There was a strange quiet over the house, a sense of letdown that hung heavily. Instead of going to the office, Mr. Lincoln went into the sitting room and stretched out on the couch.

Coming in a few minutes later, Mary found him asleep. She

tucked an afghan over him and tiptoed out, pausing at the parlor door to warn Tad to be quiet. Taddie glanced up at her thoughtfully, one hand resting on his stomach.

"I think, Mamma, I ate too much porridge."

Mary felt his forehead.

"I think," he said more urgently, "I'm going to be sick . . ."

She led him hastily upstairs. When he was safely in bed, she came down to the kitchen. Miranda was sitting by the table, her head in her hands. She was full of rheumatism, Miranda said, and down with a cold besides. Mary sent her to her room, then she carried wood to make a fire in Taddie's room, and went back to the kitchen to see what she could find for lunch.

When a kettle of soup was on the stove, and the downstairs was swept and dusted, Mary sat down at the desk, remembering the letter to Robert. He would have heard the election news of course, but he'd be anxious for more details, and there was so much to tell.

She drew a sheet of paper toward her. The only sound in the still house was the slash of rain against the windows. Taddie was quiet upstairs. Across the hall, Mr. Lincoln still slept. Presently, dipping her pen, Mary began to write.

My dearest Robert,

I fancy you can imagine, without my telling you, what excitement and rejoicing there is this morning over the glorious news. If only you could be with us today. I believe your dear father's happiness would be complete. But we shall be together again soon, *in Washington*, where so much that is new and wonderful awaits us all. Your father is too busy to write to you himself just now, but he sends you dearest love. The little boys are well, and quite bursting with pride and joy—as, indeed, are we all . . .

Toward the end of November, Mr. Lincoln was to go to Chicago, where he would meet Mr. Hamlin, the vice-president-elect. There was to be a reception in honor of Mr. Lincoln at the Tremont House. Mary was going too. At the last moment, in spite of Elizabeth's protest that it was quite impossible, Mary decided to take the boys.

Next day on the train Willie and Tad looked very smart in their new worsted suits, with peaked caps and square-toed, buttoned black boots. They were enchanted with everything, most of all by the brass band that met them in the Chicago station, and the delegation of welcoming gentlemen who were decked out in badges and cockades.

When Mary heard Mr. Lincoln introduce his family to the committee and say, "These are my boys," she smiled.

Elizabeth seemed a thousand miles away.

The days in Chicago were a complete success. At the hotel, Mary engaged a woman to stay with the children and it was obvious that Mrs. Porter, plump and friendly, was pleased to be employed by the new President's family. She treated Mr. Lincoln and Mary with beaming awe. As for Tad and Willie, Mrs. Porter told Mary again and again that they were the best-behaved little gentlemen she had ever seen.

Accustomed to the lean and frugal diet of Springfield, Mary relaxed gratefully under the steady stream of Mrs. Porter's flattery. Indeed, everywhere in Chicago they met with such kindness and approval that even Mr. Lincoln was impressed.

"I guess they like us, Mother," he said.

On the night of the reception, Mrs. Porter helped Mary dress. Her new rose satin gown looked very well, and not the least bit homemade, which was a credit to the efforts of Mary and Cousin Lizzie. When Mr. Lincoln came in, dressed in his evening clothes, and Mary took his arm, Mrs. Porter stepped back and clasped her hands. They were to enjoy themselves she said, and never give a thought to the boys, who would be quite safe and sound, the lambs.

Elizabeth seemed two thousand miles away.

At the reception, surrounded by admiring and friendly guests, Mary realized that now for the first time in her life she was free of the thousand invisible strings that kept her tied to the past. All the old failures and mistakes were forgotten. Here there was no past, no one to remember anything. It was wonderful how comforting strangers could be. It would always be like this, Mary thought, once they were in Washington. . . .

Seventeen

Two WEEKS before Christmas Mary made a trip to New York. There were a great many things to buy before she would be ready for Washington; clothes for herself and the boys, and new decorations to be ordered for the White House. She would go up to Cambridge and visit Robert. He'd need cheering up before his first Christmas away from home, Mary told Mr. Lincoln. Cousin Lizzie, hastily consulted, agreed to come and stay with the boys while Mary was away.

Mary found New York even more exciting than Chicago. The newspapers printed columns of gushing comment about the new first lady. Shops and hotels vied with each other for the privilege of her patronage. Mary found herself blossoming in the warming glow of limelight.

It was lovely to find herself recognized and catered to. People were curious about her, and she took their curiosity for kindness.

She read about herself in the society reports and saw herself described as handsome and stylish, witty and poised. Though she smiled over an occasional florid paragraph, she took the praise to her heart.

She spent a good deal more money than she had intended. By the time she boarded the train to Boston to visit Robert, she had quite lost track of her accounts. But surely it couldn't have been an unreasonable amount since the people in the shops had seemed to expect it. And they had been so tactful and pleasant about the matter of credit. There was no need to worry. Nothing, they had assured her, need be paid for until it was *quite* convenient. Indeed, they had often seemed so reluctant to discuss prices at all that it seemed almost as though they were making her gifts of the things she selected.

Sitting back in the train, Mary drew on her black glacé gloves. It was a good hour before they were due in Boston, but she was ready to step off the train, comfortably assured in her new traveling suit of gray velours from Stewart's, and the stylish bonnet the clerk had exclaimed over so admiringly. Robert would be pleased, she thought, to see her looking smart.

She smoothed the fingers of her gloves, thinking with pleasure of the many more pairs, just like them, in her trunk. She had felt a little guilty, buying so many gloves, especially the white ones for evening. But the nice young clerk had assured her that six dozen pairs were not a whit more than she would need.

Miss Harriet Lane, who had been the White House hostess for her uncle, President Buchanan, thought nothing of ordering *her* gloves by the dozen, the girl had told Mary. A single evening of handshaking at a reception would wear out two or three pairs, and the girl had said such flattering things about Mary's small hands.

Mary smiled, remembering the others who had been so kind. The Metropolitan House had given her the finest suite of rooms and the choice table in the dining room. At Stewart and Company, Mr. Stewart himself had sent orders that the entire store was at Mrs. Lincoln's disposal.

Mr. Stewart says this lace is not to be shown to anyone until Mrs. Lincoln decides whether she will choose it for her inaugural gown . . .

Mr. Stewart wanted most particularly for you to see this sable cape, Mrs. Lincoln . . .

Miss Nelson, do come and see how this bonnet suits Mrs. Lincoln. . . .

Mary sighed, still smiling at the memory.

Then there had been Mr. Montrose, the delightful young gentleman in the decorator's shop who had had such excellent ideas about the new furnishings that would be necessary for the White House. Mr. Montrose talked a great deal, very rapidly, with a good many gestures. He assured Mary that he knew the White House *intimately*, and that it was, confidentially, in a most shocking state of disrepair. Too many administrations had come and gone, leaving remnants of barbaric taste behind them. Mrs. Lincoln would truly be doing a service to the nation in renovating the public rooms.

Put that way, Mary could hardly fail to listen. It was remarkable the way Mr. Montrose's selections seemed to coincide with her own. Together they fingered brocades and tapestries, and studied the effects of carpets and draperies. Whenever the subject of price was mentioned, Mr. Montrose waved it aside. Economy, said Mr. Montrose, was scarcely the object when it came to decorating the President's house.

Best of all the new things she and Mr. Montrose had decided on, Mary loved the crimson draperies they had chosen for the East Room. She remembered how Mr. Montrose had described the room to her: white and gold and crimson, with crystal chandeliers. Even now, on the train, she could close her eyes and see the picture.

The train jerked, drawing into the station. A kerosene lamp was lit in the coach. By its light Mary saw her reflection in the dark window. She set her bonnet straight and drew the new sable cape about her shoulders. The cape had been an extravagance, but surely she was entitled to one special treat after the years of homemade dresses. She had worn it to surprise Robert. Besides, he might have brought some of his friends to meet her . . .

Mary saw Robert at once, standing alone a little back from the crowd. She saw him catch sight of her, saw his glance, sober and reserved, taking in her new costume as he came forward, hat in hand.

"Well, Mother." He stooped to kiss her cheek.

It was always a surprise to find how serious Robert looked. Mary let him guide her through the station, collecting her luggage. She saw the slight lift of his dark brows when he counted the pile of bags and cases.

"All these, Mother?"

"Why, yes, dear." She added rather hurriedly that the trunks had been sent directly on to Springfield—so at least they hadn't those to bother with.

Robert said nothing.

On the way to the carriage, he explained that he had engaged a hotel room for her. His hand was on her arm, urging her along through the station at such a pace that Mary drew back laughing. "Do wait a moment, dear—I've hardly had time to look at you. Must you rush me so?"

He paused dutifully. But there was a strained, embarrassed look about his mouth.

"Yes, of course, Mother, but don't you think we'd better . . ."

She saw then what the trouble was. Someone had recognized her and pointed her out. People in the station were turning to stare. Mary smiled back at them unperturbed, but Robert frowned.

Mary lowered her voice kindly.

"You mustn't mind, dear, if people seem to be curious. They're bound to be—but it's only because they're friendly and interested. Oh, Robert, there's so much to tell you. Father sent his love of course, and he's very well. The boys are well too, though Willie had a cold when I left. But Cousin Lizzie writes that he's quite over it now." She stopped suddenly, aware that Robert was hardly listening. His face was flushed and he kept his head down. It was only natural. The dear boy wasn't accustomed yet to being stared at. Once they were alone, it would be easier.

But in the carriage, Robert sat stiff and straight at her side. Mary answered his perfunctory questions about the journey, the weather in New York. She heard herself replying quite formally. There was a moment's silence, awkward and self-conscious. She cleared her throat.

"How are your studies, dear?"

"Well enough, thanks."

Another silence. Mary turned to look out of the window at the glimmer of twilight in the winter streets. Boston looked so cramped and crooked after New York. But so pretty. Turning to mention this, she caught Robert's glance resting on her cape. He looked quickly away, but she touched the fur apologetically.

"I expect you think I'm rather grandly gotten up for traveling, Robert, but I didn't know—I thought perhaps we might be dining with some of your friends—"

No, Robert said quickly, he hadn't planned anything special. He thought she might be tired. "I thought just a quiet dinner at the hotel, in your room—"

Of course, Mary said quickly, that would be nice. It was considerate of Robert, though she didn't feel at all tired.

At the hotel desk there was some confusion. The management had, it seemed, thought best to put Mrs. Lincoln in a somewhat larger suite than the young gentleman had engaged. They had not quite understood the circumstances. The manager hurried forward. He hoped Mrs. Lincoln would be entirely comfortable. It was the sort of attention Mary had found delightful in New York. Here, with Robert beside her, she hurried through the formalities as rapidly as possible. When the door of the suite closed behind the last lingering attendant, Mary put off her sable cape and sighed with relief.

"Now we can have some peace," she said, "and really talk."

But somehow, in the dark and formal sitting room with its massive furniture and hangings of bilious green, the things she had planned to tell Robert seemed to evaporate. It was a relief when Robert rang for the porter to ask for a fire, and occupied himself with the business of ordering dinner.

The next afternoon, when Robert came to take her driving after his classes, Mary felt the odd discomfort in him again. As they stepped into the carriage, several people gathered to watch them. A woman in a bedraggled cloak and outlandish hat suddenly seized Mary's hand. She wished God's blessing on Mr. Lincoln, a noble man if ever one lived. Mary smiled kindly, as she bobbed a curtsy and hobbled away down the street, but Robert glowered, climbing into the carriage.

"How on earth do you stand things like that, Mother?"

"Like what, dear?" Mary was tucking the robe over her knees. "Oh . . . you mean the woman just now? She meant no harm, poor soul. There was nothing I could do but be polite—"

"But it makes such an absurd show of you." Robert frowned. "Curtsying to you—as though you were a queen or something. I can't see how you endure such fussing—but you seem to, well —almost enjoy it."

Mary was silent for a moment.

"The fussing, as you call it, Robert, isn't for me," she said. "It's for your father. I think you must realize that."

When Robert made no reply, Mary tried again. It had never done to be sharp with Robert. He was so unlike the younger boys. With Robert, she knew, the least hint of criticism was enough to send him into one of his queer stubborn silences.

"I'm sure you are as proud of your father as I am," she began gently.

"Well, naturally—" Robert shifted uneasily. "But that's hardly the point. Just because Father is going to be President needn't change everything. Even you don't seem the same. Your clothes—and the way you fix your hair. And you always seem to be watching people, as though you were waiting for them to recognize you."

For an instant Mary struggled with the angry hurt that rose in her. It was suddenly impossible to feel her child grown completely apart, judging her. It didn't matter that Robert wasn't pleased with her appearance, that he disapproved of the clothes she had thought he would admire. It didn't matter that he should seem embarrassed and unhappy. It only mattered that he shouldn't escape her so entirely. She must reach him some way—bring him back.

"Robert—" Mary put her hand out, touching his sleeve, "you mustn't feel so. I haven't changed. I . . ." The next moment Robert was looking down at her hand, and the little-boy expression had come back into his face.

"Well, I'm sorry," his voice was reluctant. "I didn't mean anything, I guess."

"Of course not, dear." Mary drew her hand away quickly. Robert had always hated to be touched.

After that, things were quite easy. But when Mary asked whether he would care to ask one or two of his classmates to dinner with them, Robert was evasive. It was a bad time, he said. With midterms coming on they were up to their ears studying.

"And besides, Mother—there's no use parading."

Mary drew back, bewildered.

"I should hardly call it that, Robert—asking your friends to meet your mother."

"But you don't understand." Robert shook his head patiently. "They'd all think they had to be polite. About Father, I mean."

"And why shouldn't they be?"

"Well, it's just that I can't help knowing how they really feel—most of them, anyway. You think just because people stare at you they're friendly—but Boston isn't like New York —or the West. People here think Father is nothing but a back-woodsman. One of the Boston papers called us a family of clod-hoppers."

"Yes," Mary said, "I saw that article. That was the one that said we'd track mud into the White House and keep pigs on the front lawn, wasn't it?"

When Robert made no reply she smiled forgivingly. "I know it hurts you, dear, seeing such things written about your own family. But we haven't long to wait now. Once your father is in office, all this criticism will be forgotten."

On the train going home Mary fell into conversation with a woman who was on her way to visit her married son in Chicago. They passed a number of pleasant hours discussing their children. Before long Mary found herself confiding other things as well. About her stay in New York; the new clothes she had ordered and the little chambermaid in the hotel who had wept with pleasure over the box of handkerchiefs Mary had given her when she left. She even described the crimson drapes she and Mr. Montrose planned for the White House.

The woman listened sympathetically to everything. "I can imagine how delighted your son must have been to have you visit," she said.

Mary agreed, smiling. She told how considerate Robert had been, how he had taken care of everything for her at the hotel, even to ordering their dinner.

While they talked the miles between Boston and Chicago stretched out behind them. Mary found the edges of her disappointment fading. The strained moments, the awkward silences, and the hurt at Robert's seeming disapproval were lost in a warm sense of her own good fortune in the eyes of this friendly stranger.

"Truly, Mrs. Lincoln—" the woman sighed, "from all you've told me, I think you must be the happiest woman in the world."

Eighteen

THE NEW year that dawned in Springfield on a clear frosty night brought little sign of hope for the country. After the brief calm that had followed the election, the storm was rolling around again. The Southern states were seceding, one by one. Violence was open now—in both North and South. Between them, like a gaunt shadow of hope, stood the man in Springfield.

From everywhere came fresh demands. Mr. Lincoln must act. He must do something, say something. Promise the South security, promise to compromise. Promise anything that would save the country.

The weeks passed, and he did nothing.

Mary had long letters from her family. From Lexington, from her brothers in New Orleans, from her sister in Alabama, from Emilie Helm. From her uncles, cousins, friends. And in all the letters there was a new determination, a note of bitterness. The South had made up its mind. The South did not mean to give an inch. It was time the North, and Mr. Lincoln, learned that. They were seizing arsenals, arming themselves, organizing to fight for their life as an independent nation.

Mary showed the letters to Mr. Lincoln.

In Washington, old Buchanan counted the weeks until he could finish being President. Someone said he was like a poultice sitting on the festering head of rebellion. He was tired and confused, waiting only to go home.

Just as Mr. Lincoln waited in Springfield through the cold days of January, and the North and the South waited.

Mary waited too, and while she was waiting she read. She sent Willie and Tad to buy every newspaper they could find, and borrow others. Democratic, Republican, abolitionist, independent—Mary devoured every word.

Coming home one evening, Mr. Lincoln found Mary beside a cold fire in the sitting room. The boys were in bed. She looked up from the heap of papers scattered about her chair. Headache pounded behind her eyes.

"Well, Mother," he asked, "what news have you found for me today?"

Mary pushed the papers away and stood up.

"The same as always, Mr. Lincoln. Hatred and blame and bitterness. All of them say you must decide—you must speak—" She stopped, her hands stretched toward him, then she pressed them to her head. "If only this would end," she said. "If the fourth of March would come."

She was startled by her own words. For how many years she would have given anything for her husband to be President. Now the moment had come and she had spoken as if it were not a beginning but an end.

Each morning there were new stacks of letters for Mr. Lincoln, for Mary, even for the boys. Letters with advice, questions, ugly threats. Letters demanding favors, asking for appointments, for offices, for money. Letters offering prayers and blessings, sending good luck charms. Letters from old friends, from enemies, and from foolish, rambling crackpots.

Every morning Mary sorted them, slitting the envelopes,

turning the pages, searching each word. Sometimes the letters seemed to engulf the room where she sat, the desk, the pen she held. Words and words. Who could ever answer them, with good words or bad?

When she lay awake at night the bad words wove a spell of fear. And gradually fear moved in, familiarly, like an old friend come to stay. It made itself at home, dined with her, and went to market, sat with her while she mended, watched in the evenings while she read stories aloud to the boys. It followed her to bed, whispering troubled dreams, until it wakened her to the stillness of the house, and the sound of a train whistle over the prairie, and Mr. Lincoln's breathing, deep and slow.

A cry from Taddie's room at night and Mary would jump out of bed, shivering with dread. Long after she had found the boys sleeping safely, she would lie awake, staring into the dark. Listening . . .

The weeks of waiting dragged into February. They were to leave Springfield on the tenth, and Mary plunged with relief into packing and arranging, thankful for anything that kept her days busy and sent her to bed at night too tired to think or feel.

One afternoon Willie came home from school to find his turtle dead. It lay in its box, a small, lifeless shell, and no amount of gentle prodding or coaxing would move it. Willie carried the box to the attic where Mary was sorting the contents of an old trunk. His blue eyes were full of tears.

"He's dead, Mamma," Willie said. "I can't make him alive this time."

Mary had just taken Robert's first pair of boots from the trunk. She still held them as she turned to look into the turtle's box. Then she gathered Willie in her arms and wept.

That evening Willie showed his father the turtle. When Mr. Lincoln said he was sorry, Willie looked reproachful. "Mamma cried hard," he said.

But it was Mr. Lincoln who took Willie upstairs to bed and sat beside him in the dark until he fell asleep.

When he came down Mary sat by the reading lamp. Her hands lay in her lap. She spoke quietly.

"Mr. Lincoln . . ."

He did not turn, but Mary could see his reflection in the mirror above the mantel.

"Mr. Lincoln, what are you going to do?"

His face looked strange and guarded.

Mary stood up. "War is in the air," she said. "The whole country is breathing it. Everyone is waiting for you to decide—to speak—" She clenched her fists. What made him act this way? As though he were paralyzed, unable to speak. He had spoken often enough in the past for what he believed. Against slavery. For the Union. What held him now, when everything depended on his words? Why must he only talk of being patient, of seeing the justice on both sides, of letting events take their course? She looked in the mirror again. There was no clue in his reflected image. She turned to a fresh batch of newspapers on the table.

"If you won't listen to me, Mr. Lincoln, at least you must hear these." She turned the pages, hunting for places she had marked, but when she thrust them at him, Mr. Lincoln put his arm up, covering his eyes.

"Mary, for God's sake—let me rest."

She drew back as though his voice had been a blow. The papers fell from her hands and she stooped to gather them up and throw them in the fire.

After a moment she took the box with Willie's turtle and started for the kitchen. Waiting for the coffee to boil for Mr. Lincoln's supper, she glanced again at the empty turtle shell. Such a small thing, she thought, to have made her weep so bitterly.

While Mr. Lincoln had his supper, Mary took out her sewing. She tried to think of things to talk about that would sound cheerful. A farewell party she was giving for Willie and Tad. She'd invite the Remann children and the young Dillers, and their other neighborhood friends. She spoke of Robert's last letter, and the news that Emilie and Ben Helm were expecting a baby.

Mr. Lincoln listened, answering now and then. He told a new story he had heard at Dillers. When he went to lock up for the night, he stopped by Mary's chair and touched her shoulder.

"I suppose it will be easier when this part is over," he said.

She took his hand, resting it against her cheek. He seemed so lonely standing there.

"I'm sure it will," she said.

For three days they had a bonfire in the side yard, and burned the accumulation of old papers, lettters, broken furniture, and worn-out toys the attic had brought forth. Mary watched the strange collection disappear in the flames. The yellow sled they had pulled little Eddie on. A tuft of faded strawflowers that had stood on the mantel in the parlor when the house was new. A velvet bonnet, dusty and streaked, that Mary had meant, each winter, to wear again because Mr. Lincoln had liked her in it. The dog-eared grammar text that Mr. Lincoln had carried in his suitcase when he rode the circuit, and his old surveyor's gear. A rusty black umbrella from goodness knew where and a gray wool shawl the moths had got into . . .

Tad and Willie stood by, alternately fascinated at watching the odd fragments smolder and wither in the crackling blaze and dismayed to see the last remnants of their once treasured playthings go onto the heap.

The morning his red express wagon was brought out to be burned, Taddie wept so loudly that Mr. Lincoln promised it could go to Washington.

It was an endless process, Mary declared. As fast as the old things were sorted and cleared out, there were new ones arriving. Every mail brought its quota of gifts. Peculiar parcels of ungainly shapes and sizes were stacked in the front hall. Unpacked, they disgorged a weird assortment of articles. There were hats of every size and pattern to fit the presidential head. An Indian chief's war bonnet, and a ceremonial squaw robe for Mary. Western boots, elaborately tooled and studded with silver. A Pennsylvania spinster sent a china cake plate she had decorated for the White House pantry. There was a gaudy assortment of sofa cushions, some with embroidered mottoes: "God Bless Our Noble President," "Hurrah for Old Abe." Handkerchiefs, jewelry, pipes, cigars and a hundred copies of an antitobacco pamphlet. There were neckties, shaving mugs, fancy waistcoats of every known material, Bibles, and always more hats.

Mary was in despair, but the boys pounced on each new bundle in fits of delight.

"If nothing else comes of all this," Mr. Lincoln said, "we have enough hats to last us a lifetime."

One morning a crate was brought to the door with a pair of gray doves huddled sadly in one corner. These were rescued by Willie, who revived them tenderly, and immediately inquired of his father whether he might take them to Washington.

Mr. Lincoln glanced over the top of his book. There was no reason, he supposed absently, why not.

Emboldened by success, Willie seized the moment to bring up the subject of Fido. If Papa didn't mind the doves, could they please take Fido with them?

Mr. Lincoln was doubtful. "Your mother's planning on having things kind of fancy when we get to Washington," he said. "I don't know that she'll want a lot of animals mussing the place up."

Oh, said Willie quickly, Fido wouldn't muss anything. He could live in Willie's and Tad's room. And just go out the kitchen door to play.

"*Please* say I can, Papa." Willie hung on his father's chair. "Please say so."

Mr. Lincoln sighed.

"Well, as far as I'm concerned, Willie, I don't see any great objection. But you'll have to ask Mamma. She's the boss."

A few minutes later, Mr. Lincoln looked up from his book again. Mary, her sleeves rolled up to the elbow, her hands floury from the pastry board, stood in the doorway.

"Mr. Lincoln," she demanded, "what's this about your giving Willie permission to take that wretched dog to Washington? *And* a cageful of birds from dear knows where? He says you promised him."

"Now, Mother, I did no such thing. I told Willie he must ask you."

"And why, pray, should he ask me?"

"Well, I didn't know how you might feel about it."

Mary set her lips. "You know perfectly well how I feel about it. Of all absurd notions, to traipse into the White House like some band of Gypsies with a traveling menagerie. Besides, Fido belongs half to the Roll boys."

"That's true," Mr. Lincoln said. "How could we know which half was ours to take?"

"But you said I *could*, Papa. You promised—" Willie hopped on one foot in an agony of uncertainty.

Mary saw his tears gathering and the last of her patience vanished.

"Truly, Mr. Lincoln, I can't understand how you could deliberately raise the child's hopes, and then make a joke of it. It's positively heartless to disappoint him now."

At these ominous words, Willie's tears spilled over and he set up a howl that drowned out the sound of someone knocking at the front door.

A moment later Miranda appeared, ushering in three frock-coated gentlemen who had arrived to pay their respects to the future President just in time to see Mary march past them, her eyes blazing, as she dragged Willie, kicking and protesting behind her.

Upstairs, while she tried vainly to silence Willie, Mary kept one ear cocked for the sound of voices below. Dear heaven, they'd surely think she was murdering the child to hear him scream so. And nothing she could say, no promises of a new pet in Washington, or the good home Fido would have with Bud and Johnny Roll, would quiet Willie.

Willie didn't *want* a new pet. He wanted Fido. Papa had said—he had *promised*—until Mamma said he couldn't.

Mary saw the resentment in his eyes. She was the one Willie would blame for losing Fido, and it wasn't fair. It wasn't fair that she should forever take the blame, simply because Mr. Lincoln could never bear to say no. Willie looked up, still unconsoled, his lower lip pushed out accusingly.

"Papa *said* it," he repeated sadly, "and Papa is going to be the President. I thought presidents could do anything they wanted to."

Mary was silent, feeling curiously helpless.

"I used to think that too, Willie," she said, in a different voice. "I think we were both wrong."

Nineteen

THE LAST week in Springfield moved too swiftly, with too many things to be done, to leave room for doubts.

Each morning Mary made new lists and memorandums to be checked off. She arranged with Elizabeth and Frances who would come to Washington for the inauguration. Robert came home from Cambridge to travel with them, and finding the confusion at the Lincoln house not to his taste, he went to stay with the Edwardses.

At the last moment Cousin Lizzie Grimsley was invited to join the traveling party and she was in a quiver of gratitude and delight.

"You might think Lizzie had been appointed to the cabinet," Ann said. "Personally, I'm willing to go to Washington for Mary's sake, but I'll be thankful when all the fuss is over and we can settle down again."

The night before they closed the house the Lincolns held a farewell reception. The whole town was invited.

From seven o'clock until after midnight people gathered on the steps and in the front yard, waiting to join the line inside and shake hands. They came alone or in groups, mostly in families. Some drove in from the country and hitched their horses around the Courthouse Square. A number of old friends had traveled from New Salem to wish Abe good luck.

Every window in the house was lighted. Willie and Tad, gloriously reprieved from the sentence of bed time, sat on the gateposts like happy gargoyles. Each time the crowd took up a chorus of the campaign song, *"Old Abe Lincoln Came Out of the Wilderness,"* they added a chant of their own. "Do you want to see Old Abe? Give us a five cents and we'll show you Old Abe." Long before midnight their pants pockets were bulging with nickels.

Mary stood beside Mr. Lincoln in the parlor to receive their guests. She smiled and shook hands. Catching a brief glimpse of herself in the mirror opposite, she thanked fortune she had persuaded Cousin Lizzie not to add any trimming to her white moire gown. The low neckline showed off her pearl necklace and the white flowers in her hair. The candlelight was kind to the weary lines in her face.

When the Renfrews came past, with others from New Salem, Mary gave them a specially warm smile.

"I'll own," Elizabeth said to Frances, "there are times when I have to admire Mary. She's been up since before six this morning, and working like an Indian ever since. To look at her, you might think she had nothing to do all day but dress for the party."

Frances nodded. For her own part she was exhausted. It was barely nine o'clock and half of Springfield had yet to arrive, all parched with thirst and famished, to judge from their onslaught at the refreshment tables.

"Beg pardon, ma'am—"

Frances turned to make way for a stout gentleman who was attempting to squeeze his way past her. A trickle of punch splashed onto Frances' sleeve. The stranger whipped out a grimy handkerchief and mopped energetically at the stain.

"I didn't aim to do that, ma'am—" The man's face, throttled by his collar, flushed several shades deeper. "I was just going to say howdy to Abe in there, when the feller pushed me—"

Still muttering apologies, the stout gentleman lumbered off. Frances looked ruefully at her sleeve.

"Impossible creature," Elizabeth said indignantly. "Where in the name of mercy do you suppose Mr. Lincoln picked *him* up? Sometimes, I'm just as thankful Ninian wasn't a success at politics when I see the sort of thing Mary has to put up with. On my word, though, I believe Mary actually enjoys it."

"After all, she could hardly complain," Frances smiled thinly. "Mary was the one who nagged Mr. Lincoln into this whole thing. Though I shouldn't want to see my husband in Mr. Lincoln's position. Mr. Smith says he's heard there are people all over the country who are so opposed to Mr. Lincoln that they've signed papers taking an oath to keep him from reaching Washington alive. You'd think Mary might be worried, but when I tried to tell her, she only flared at me. She says the rumors come from people who are jealous of Mr. Lincoln."

Elizabeth shook her head. "Poor Mary, I don't suppose she'll ever get over thinking we're consumed with envy of Mr. Lincoln. All the same, we oughtn't be too hard on her. I daresay she'll find out soon enough her bed isn't all roses."

The next morning they closed the house and took their luggage to the Chenery House, where they would sleep the last night, before taking the train. Mary and Mr. Lincoln went to the Simeon Francis' for supper. Walking back to the hotel afterward, they passed the corner of Eighth and Jackson.

Mary looked across at the house. She couldn't remember ever having seen it completely dark before. The windows, curtainless and blank, stared forlornly into the night, and under the big elm in the side yard she could see the last remnants of their bonfire. She stood a minute.

"I've thought sometimes I'd be glad when this moment came," she said. "Now I feel as though I couldn't go at all."

"I know, Mary," Mr. Lincoln touched her arm. A night wind blew across his words. "We've seen good times and bad ones. But it seemed as though even the troubles got to be old friends."

A telegram from Washington was waiting at the Chenery House. There had been threats against Mr. Lincoln's life. Security measures must be maintained. It would be safer if Mr. Lincoln took the train for Washington alone. Mrs. Lincoln and her party could follow separately.

Mary read the telegram when Mr. Lincoln handed it to her. She read the words unbelievingly at first, then indignantly.

"Mr. Lincoln, they can't order us this way. If you are in danger we will go with you—" Her voice broke. Her hand reached toward him. "Don't leave me alone. Please, Mr. Lincoln..."

No one heard her.

People crowded around Mr. Lincoln in the hotel room. Reporters, politicians, men who wanted favors, a woman who had read his horoscope. Mr. Nicolay, his new secretary, was trying to keep them in order. Mr. Lincoln tried to listen, tried to answer.

Mary went to look at the boys and found them sleeping. Then she undressed and lay down to look into the darkness.

The plans had been made. Mr. Lincoln would travel to Washington without her. No one had heard her voice. She wondered if anyone would hear it again.

The next morning Mary and the boys stood with the crowd at the depot and heard Mr. Lincoln make his farewell speech to his friends in Springfield. They watched the train pull out. Then they went back to the Chenery House.

That evening Mary ordered supper at five o'clock.

"We'll go to bed early," she told the boys. "We all need sleep."

When there was a knock at the door, Mary thought it was the waiter. She sent Willie to answer. He came back with a telegram.

Mary's hands shook as she opened it. The next moment she crumpled the paper and held it to her cheek.

Willie watched anxiously. "Is anything the matter, Mamma?"

"Nothing . . . nothing." Mary hugged him. There were tears of relief and joy in her eyes. "They want us to join your papa. We have to find a train that will take us to Indianapolis . . ."

They were in time to wish Mr. Lincoln a happy birthday as the new party came aboard the inaugural train. Mary saw everything through steam that hissed from the engine and a mist of tears. She heard the boys shout as they saw their father. A little girl brought her an armful of roses and she bent down to take them.

Her hand was on Mr. Lincoln's arm, as if, this time, she did not mean to let him go.

Back on the train the ladies laid off their wraps in the special parlor car. They gathered around the stove to warm their hands. Cousin Lizzie took the roses Mary handed her. She asked Mr. Lamon, who had come as Mr. Lincoln's bodyguard to find a vase for them.

Mr. Lincoln said it was nonsense to have a guard, but Washington insisted. "At least Ward Lamon is the only man taller than I am," he said.

Mary felt safer when she saw Mr. Lamon. But later an alarm went through the car. A black bag had been found.

"*A bomb—*"

Mary heard the word first. Then there was a babble of voices and a scream from one of the ladies.

No, no—it wasn't a bomb at all. A grenade. Someone had come into the car and left it. The fuse was lighted. If it had gone off . . .

Oddly, it was Mary who seemed the most composed.

When the danger was past she ordered hot coffee for them all.

"Truly, you're wonderful, Mary," Cousin Lizzie said. Her knees were still limp. "Even Ann says so."

Mary said nothing. It would have been difficult to explain that after months of imagined dangers, a real one was far less frightening.

There were stopovers, welcoming committees, speeches and dinners and receptions. At Pittsburgh Mr. Lincoln addressed a huge crowd in the Municipal Hall. More bunting, more flags and cheers. More flowers for Mary.

After the one incident of the grenade, there were no further alarms.

The evening before they reached New York, Mary went into the sleeping car where the boys had been put to bed. They had made the long trip remarkably well. But at supper she noticed that Willie was pale.

She glanced at Taddie, sprawled in the berth spread-eagle fashion, already sleeping soundly. Across the aisle, Willie lay very still, his head hidden against the pillow. Mary bent down, touching his shoulder. She sat beside him.

"Willie—"

There was no answer.

"Willie, tell me what's the matter dear. Are you sick?"

There was a silence, then Willie's muffled voice.

"I'm not sick . . . I'm feeling sad about Fido."

While Mary explained that Fido was surely quite happy at home with the Roll boys, Willie lay motionless, still turned away.

Fido wouldn't have liked the train at all, Mary said. He would have had to be in a box, nailed up all these days. She had been thinking, Mary went on, that when they got to Washington, they would have a big stable of their own. They might be able to have a pony . . .

"Of course, Taddie is still young to have such a responsibility. But if you could help look after the pony, I think we might manage . . ."

The shoulder under Mary's hand relaxed a little.

"Mamma—" Willie's voice was small against the clack of the train wheels.

"Yes?"

"Do you think Papa could find a black pony? An all-black one?"

"I think so, Willie."

There was a sigh. "Good night, Mamma."

Walking back through the swaying car, Mary heard the train whistle, as it wailed and died away. She had heard the whistle a thousand times in the night, back in Springfield, while a train shrieked into the darkness. Now it was different. They were moving forward, boldly, surely—past sleeping towns, where the whistle would be heard for a moment, lingering and mournful, then dying in the stillness.

The last stopover was in Albany, where they were entertained by the mayor at a large breakfast.

"It's a mercy they didn't build any more cities along the line," Mr. Lincoln said. "Mother would have run out of dresses."

They parted that evening, in New York. Mr. Lincoln and Ward Lamon and the other gentlemen were to go directly to Washington, while Mary stayed at the Metropolitan House with Robert and the little boys until the day before the inauguration.

Tired from the long trip, Mary went to bed early, but she could not sleep. She remembered the things Ann had told her, rumors that assassins had sworn Mr. Lincoln would never reach Washington alive. She remembered the grenade in the black bag.

Once, near dawn, Willie cried out in his sleep.

It was noon that day when the telegram came. All morning Mary had been in an agony of fear, and when the porter handed her the envelope, her fingers were trembling so that Robert had to open it.

Mr. Lincoln was safe in the capital.

Mr. Seward was at the station to meet Mary and Robert and the boys in Washington. It was pouring rain. Mary saw drops of moisture on Mr. Seward's coat.

Mr. Lincoln couldn't come himself, Mr. Seward explained. Some important callers had come in at the last minute. He would be waiting at the hotel, where everything was ready for them.

The red plush lobby at Willard's Hotel was thronged with people. Walking quickly through, her hand on Robert's arm, Mary was aware of a buzz of comment as they passed. People turned, one or two smiled, and she smiled back, trying not to show the mounting agitation that pounded in her heart. But when they reached the second-floor suite and Mr. Seward opened the door, Mary saw Mr. Lincoln alive and safe, and such a flood of relief rushed over her that she could scarcely breathe. He stood with his back to the door, holding a sheaf of papers in one hand. Mr. Lincoln was speaking to one of the strangers in the room, not noticing that the door had opened. Then Mary saw him turn. A smile of welcome came over his face.

"Oh, Mr. Lincoln—Mr. Lincoln—" Mary forgot the strangers and put her arms around him.

Mr. Lincoln seemed surprised. "Now, Mother, I wouldn't cry. You see they haven't shot me yet."

Twenty

SPECIAL GUARDS were stationed in the hall outside Mr. Lincoln's room that night. A detachment of soldiers was on duty in the lobby downstairs. The city teemed with people, coming and going all night long, roaming the streets as though it were broad daylight. And there was ugly talk of violence. Some said there were five hundred men in the city, all armed, who had sworn a pact that the new President would never sleep in the White House.

Somewhere in the crowds that milled and shouted in the streets, five hundred men waited for morning.

Mary sat with Robert and the boys and the others of their party to watch the inaugural ceremony. Everything was going smoothly. Old Chief Justice Taney, looking small and shriveled in his black robes, had administered the oath while Mr. Lincoln towered above him. Now Mr. Lincoln was speaking.

". . . We are not enemies, but friends. . . ."

She watched Mr. Lincoln's face, and the faces of the men who sat near him, listening, and wondered what they were thinking. She wondered if they could hear, beneath the sure, even flow of his voice, the deeps of melancholy and doubt she knew were in him. The present, with its triumph, was real—but the price of the triumph was real also. The endless weeks of waiting, the bitterness, the discouragements and loneliness—the dark horizon of the future—were all part of the moment.

Stephen Douglas sat directly behind Mr. Lincoln. Mary could see the outline of his stocky shoulders. His face was impassive, as he listened. He held Mr. Lincoln's top hat on his knee. What was he thinking now? That he might have been standing where Mr. Lincoln stood? Was he sorry, disappointed, bitter? Or was he half thankful that he only waited, holding Mr. Lincoln's hat?

Taddie, in the seat beside her, squirmed restlessly, and started to whisper. Mary put her finger on her lips. She could see Robert next to Taddie, then Willie, and Elizabeth.

Mr. Lincoln finished speaking and stepped back. There was a general stir, applause. Cheers rang from the audience. Mary saw Mr. Lincoln turn and glance at her.

Cousin Lizzie clapped her hands vigorously, pausing to wipe her eyes. Robert was applauding. Mr. Douglas rose, and handed Mr. Lincoln his hat. They were shaking hands now—Mr. Seward, Mr. Chase, Mr. Cameron . . .

Mary drew a long breath. She saw Elizabeth leaning toward her.

"I must say, Mary, I think Mr. Lincoln did very well."

They drove up Pennsylvania Avenue in the new carriage that had been sent for Mr. Lincoln from New York. A dress coach, of dark maroon, with scarlet brocatel upholstery. Beside them, in the thin March sunlight, rode a special guard of honor wearing bright scarfs and rosettes of orange and blue. In the seat next to Mr. Lincoln, General Winfield Scott, commander of the army, looked out at the cheering crowds that lined the broad street. The old general's eyes, beneath his cockaded hat, were pale and wary, watching.

At the White House, Mr. Lincoln took Mary's arm and they went in together.

An elderly attendant sat on a high stool by the door, a ring of large brass keys dangling from a chain on his belt. He climbed down stiffly to shake hands with the new President and his wife and introduced himself as Edwards.

Looking into Edwards' sharp old eyes, Mary realized with a qualm that he must have seen many presidents come and go.

Close behind Mary, pushing ahead with shouts of excitement, came Willie and Tad. Their copper-toed boots clattered noisily as they slid across the parquet floor, and made a dive for the wide staircase that curved upward from the reception hall.

"I'll race you down the banisters, Willie!"

Mary caught Taddie just in time, pulling him back as she saw old Edwards' dour glance. She kept the boys hands firmly in hers while they walked through the downstairs rooms. But when they looked in the East Room, at the end of the corridor, Taddie broke away again. He and Willie rushed about the long room, poking and prying and chattering like squirrels.

"Look, Mamma, the piano's made of gold. Only the gold is all coming off in peelings."

Taddie stopped suddenly, his face puckered.

"Mamma—is *this* the White House?"

Mary said nothing. She stood in the doorway, looking with dismay at the room she had pictured so many times. The room she and Mr. Montrose had discussed. White and gold and crystal, Mr. Montrose had said. But the white walls were streaked and grimy. The gilt on the frescoes was chipped, and the crystal chandeliers were gray with dust. The long windows, where the crimson draperies would hang, were bare and cracked, and the cold March sunlight shone on dingy, ill-assorted furniture and faded carpeting.

Mary turned to Mr. Lincoln. He was standing beside her, his eyes narrowed, lost in some thought of his own.

"We'd better get back to the others," Mary said.

They were gathering in the broad reception hall. Mary saw Elizabeth's expression as she and Ninian came in—the quick, appraising look, the slightly lifted brows. There was to be a luncheon for the new Cabinet members in half an hour, and the ladies, Mary realized, would expect to be shown upstairs to their rooms.

Taddie pulled at Mary's sleeve.

"Mamma, can I go see my room now? Can I unpack my red wagon?"

"Mamma—" Willie was on her other side, hopping excitedly. "Can I go out and look at the barn? I want to see where my pony will stay."

She sent them along, and then turned to her guests, but before the last carriage had drawn up at the front door the boys were back again. Willie's lip was trembling indignantly. There was a man out in the barn, Willie said. A very cross man, who had told them to go away and not bother him, and nobody was to come fooling around the stables.

"Isn't this our house now, Mamma?" Willie's round face was troubled. "Don't we *live* here?"

There was an abrupt wail from Taddie. Overcome by this new and hostile world, he buried his face against Mary's skirt and burst into tears.

"I don't want to live here, Mamma. I don't like this place."

Mary looked about distractedly. What on earth could she do with the boys while they got ready for the luncheon? No servants were in sight. She glanced at Edwards, but one look at his glum, wizened countenance discouraged her. Suddenly her eye lit on a pleasant-looking young officer, assigned for the day as an aide to the President, and Mary smiled hopefully. Would he, she asked the young man, be kind enough to walk out with the little boys for half an hour or so, and show them the grounds?

Instantly, sensing the looks the others exchanged, and the

slight, frozen pause before the young officer answered, Mary realized her mistake. Mr. Lincoln stepped forward.

"Never mind," he said to his aide. "The boys can come with me." He offered them each a hand. "Come along, we'll see if the cross man can be persuaded to let me into the barn."

Mary bit her lip, feeling embarrassment sweep hotly over her. To think the new President must spend his first half hour in office minding the children, before he had a chance to lay aside his hat. She had a sudden conviction that Addie Douglas would have managed very differently.

"Let's go upstairs," Mary said, and turned quickly to avoid Elizabeth's eye.

In the room that was to be hers, Mary stood looking about. It was pleasant enough, large and square, with long windows that faced across the sloping grounds down toward the river and beyond to the hills of Virginia. But the furnishings were even drearier than those downstairs. She looked at the limp blue curtains, and thought of the crisp, starched ruffles at the bedroom windows in Springfield. The bedstead was carved walnut, large and gloomy, covered with a counterpane of faded rose print. Mary laid her bonnet on the bare dresser. She had an uneasy sense of being an unbidden guest in someone else's house.

From across the hall, Mary could hear Elizabeth speaking.

"I should think the country could do better than this for the President's house. The furniture might have come out of the ark. And half the carpets are worn clear through . . .

Then Ann, chiming in sharply. "If I were in Mary's place, I'd hire some decent servants. The only ones that have taken the trouble to show themselves are an incompetent-looking lot. And the way they treated us—as though we were sightseers. I call it disgraceful."

"I'm sure Mary will have everything running smoothly in no time." That was Cousin Lizzie, sounding nervous and apologetic and proud all at the same time. "With all the lovely things she ordered from New York . . . And Mary's always so clever about managing—"

Mary closed her door sharply and crossed to the window. She ought to be fixing her hair, getting ready for the luncheon. She looked down on the lawn, such as it was. She hoped the ground wasn't as damp as it looked. If Tad got his feet wet and came down with one of his colds . . .

This was the moment she had waited and planned for, Mary thought. And when she woke up tomorrow morning it would still be real. Tomorrow and tomorrow . . . Those were words Mr. Lincoln used to read aloud by the fire in Springfield. It was a long time, she realized, since Mr. Lincoln had read Shakespeare to her.

She went over and sat down on the bed. Now she knew what made her feel like this. She was homesick. Homesick, like Taddie. Homesick for a house she knew and a familiar room, and one cross Irish hired girl instead of a staff of strange servants. She put her hands over her eyes. . . .

There was a knock at the door, and Mary braced herself. That would be Elizabeth telling her she must get ready for lunch.

Instead, a tall Negro woman stepped into the room. Her name was Lizzie Keckley, she said. She had come recommended by Mrs. Breckinridge, who thought perhaps there might be work for her at the White House. She was a seamstress. She had made dresses for Mrs. Jeff Davis and other Washington ladies. Or she could help with the unpacking.

Mary considered a moment. There was some last-minute fitting to be done on her gown for the ball that evening. How soon could Mrs. Keckley start to work?

"I can stay now if you wish."

"Then do, by all means."

Mary stood up. There would be so much to do these first days, she said. A good deal of entertaining, no doubt, and callers to be received. If Mrs. Keckley were experienced with children, she might help with the boys. They needed someone to keep an eye on them.

Mrs. Keckley nodded. She was very fond of children. "I have a son of my own, ma'am, going on eighteen."

"My oldest boy is just the same age." Mary's tone warmed. The younger boys needed someone to keep an eye on them this afternoon. They were quite keyed up with today's excitement.

"And tired from the long trip." Mrs. Keckley nodded. "We'll have a walk in the park and an early supper and they'll be ready for bed. Don't worry about them, Mrs. Lincoln."

Mary felt a surge of relief. She turned to smooth her hair and met Mrs. Keckley's glance in the mirror.

"May I make one touch?" Mrs. Keckley brushed back one curl over Mary's shoulder and straightened the collar on her blue dress. "Now you look just right," she stood back, smiling.

Walking out to meet the others for the luncheon, Mary held her head high. Some of the strangeness had worn off. This was her home.

Twenty-one

By evening, when it was time to dress for the ball, Mrs. Keckley had read aloud until the boys fell asleep. She had adjusted Mary's new gown expertly; Mary's hair was dressed; her gloves and flowers waited on the bed. When Mary was ready, Mrs. Keckley went to help the other ladies dress. Later Ann drew Mary aside.

"Mark my word, Mary, you have a real treasure in Mrs. K. Mind you don't let her slip through your fingers though. If Mr. Lincoln talks and jokes with her, as he always does with servants, it will certainly spoil her, and that would be a pity. If I were you, I should speak to him about it. And quite firmly."

"If you were me, Ann, everything would be managed perfectly. I haven't a doubt." Mary's voice was sharp, but she smiled. She was determined not to let Ann nor anyone else spoil things for her tonight. She complimented Cousin Lizzie on her coffee-colored gown so kindly that Lizzie's eyes filled with tears of pleasure.

The ball was held at the Union Building, a few blocks from the White House. Stepping out of the carriage, Mary held her head high.

The servant problem—and war—could wait until tomorrow.

All of Washington, the newspapers said, was at the ball that night. All of Washington, however, seemed to include some unexpected elements. The fashionable Southern set—the cave dwellers—were there in full force, having come apparently for the purpose of commenting on the appearance of the new President and his wife. For weeks their dinner tables had seethed with stories of the Republican interlopers. Now, having seen for themselves, the inner circle found their worst fears confirmed. It was plain to be seen that the Lincolns were rustics. Westerners, to begin with, and definitely antislavery, which was shocking.

"Quite, quite impossible . . ." they murmered. "They say poor Mr. Lincoln never owned a pair of boots until he was elected. No doubt it's having to wear them now that makes him look so sad . . ."

"One can't help rather pitying *him*. What can one expect of a backwoodsman who's been shoved into the limelight by an ambitious wife?"

"I've heard that he lives in mortal terror of her temper . . ."

Miss Kate Chase and her father, the new Secretary of the Treasury, were late arriving. When they came in, there was already a crowd. Mary was aware, nevertheless, of a stir of interest. From all over the hall, people turned to look, to watch Mr. Chase shake hands with the President, to see what Miss Kate, slim, elegant and red-haired, was wearing, and how she greeted the President's wife.

Miss Kate was pleasant. If her manner was somewhat languid, Mary had already gathered that this was the badge of social distinction in Washington. Mary felt Miss Kate's fingers, slim and boneless in hers. They rested a shade longer, Mary observed, in Mr. Lincoln's.

"How too awful—such a crush—" Miss Kate's glance swept over the room. "Doesn't it make you feel quite dreadful having all of us come just to stare at you, Mrs. Lincoln? Though

I must say," a smile of unexpected sweetness lighted her delicate oval face, "you look as though you were quite enjoying it. Doesn't she, Mr. President?"

"Being stared at is something one gets used to, I expect," Mary said.

Miss Kate lifted one slim shoulder. "I daresay you're right, Mrs. Lincoln. Personally, I find it very trying, but then, of course—" again the smile, candid and disarming, "you've had so many more years of experience than I."

As Miss Kate drifted away in the crowd, her white-gloved finger tips resting lightly on her father's arm, Mary stared after her. She saw the elegant poise of Miss Kate's small head. She looked barely more than twenty, yet Mary noticed that she greeted the older guests, particularly the gentlemen, with an air of easy familiarity. Miss Kate was wearing white too, but her gown was cut simply, without trimming, and she wore no jewels. Her shining red hair was parted in the center and drawn smoothly into a low knot at the back of her neck.

Mary looked down. Suddenly she felt short and tightly laced and middle-aged. But the next moment she remembered something she had heard a woman say about Miss Kate in New York. "Kate Chase is bound and determined her father will be President," the woman had said. "She's twice as ambitious for him as he is for himself, and that's saying a great deal. If she doesn't get her wish, it will be a bitter disappointment—and Kate's not used to being disappointed."

A smile, not unlike Miss Kate's own, curved Mary's lips. Beauty or no, middle-aged or no, she reflected that between herself and Kate Chase she held the trump card.

As the evening wore on Mary became increasingly aware that there were a great many people at the ball who had nothing whatever to do with society. Mingled with the more fashionable element, rubbing elbows with the cave dwellers and diplomats, was a large and motley assortment of guests who appeared to have wandered in simply for the show, and were bent on improving the occasion by seeing how much they could eat and drink. They roamed about, gawking and commenting, pocketing souvenirs, making such forays on the refreshments that the supper tables were turned into a shambles.

Alarmed to discover that the food had vanished along with virtually all the silverware and napkins before the evening was half over, Mary appealed to Mr. Lincoln.

"What are we to do, Mr. Lincoln? The tables are quite bare. They've even carried off most of the centerpieces—and there are still dozens of guests who haven't been served."

"I don't know," Mr. Lincoln shook his head. "Unless we send out for some loaves and fishes."

It was also apparent, however, that no one except Mary was seriously perturbed by the situation. Washington partygoers seemed to accept the presence of the barbarous horde as a matter of course.

"You mustn't let it worry you," Mrs. Breckinridge said cheerfully to Mary. "These sightseers turn up everywhere nowadays. We're quite accustomed to them."

Elizabeth remained scandalized. "Pigs are pigs," she said firmly, "whether Washington is accustomed to them or not."

Only Cousin Lizzie seemed to approve of the party. Shortly after midnight she came up to Mary, her face flushed and shining.

"Isn't it wonderful?" Lizzie fumbled with a drooping curl over her ear. "I never *saw* so many people, Mary. And just to think they all came just to meet you and Abe. I should think you'd be flattered to death. Everyone seems to be having *such* a good time. You know that Miss Chase, Mary—the one with a plain dress. I never dreamed she'd recognize *me*, but she was ever so friendly. And when she smiles she's really quite nice looking, in spite of being a redhead. I could see she's tremendously taken with you, Mary. She asked me all sorts of questions. About your house in Springfield and the boys—" Lizzie paused for breath.

"I've no doubt you answered them—fully." Mary's words were edged.

"Oh, yes. She was *so* interested. And I know she admires you. I heard her telling Mr. Lincoln that you looked like a fashion plate. She said she never expected to see one come to life—right out of *Godey's*. So, you see—"

Mary's patience snapped. "For mercy's sake don't be such an eternal fool. Can't you see Kate Chase was only making fun of me—of us all?"

"Why, Mary . . . I didn't . . . I'm sure she . . ." Lizzie's eyes were round and hurt.

Mary turned away. She couldn't bear anything more. Not tonight. She bit her lip, pushing back her own tears of exhaustion, and looked up to see Mr. Lincoln coming toward them.

"Well, Lizzie, you've been quite a belle this evening," he said. "Every time I caught sight you had a new gentleman in tow—" He paused, looking from Lizzie to Mary, while the smile died slowly out of his eyes.

He put his hand on Mary's arm. "I guess it's time we were getting home, Mother," he said. "The party seems to be about over. And it's been a long day."

PART FOUR

House of Cards

Twenty-two

EARLY the next morning Mary woke to discover Tad and Willie hanging on either side of her bed, arguing noisily.

Seeing her eyes open, the boys left off their discussion and began telling her, both at once, that there were people in the hall outside. Lots and lots of them. Tad was bouncing excitedly. All sorts of people, he went on, right outside the door there. Queer-looking men, mostly, and some ladies too, and they were all talking about getting in to see the President. One of them, Willie said, had given him a silver dollar just to tell which was the door of Old Abe's office. And another had offered Tad a pinch of snuff.

"See the dollar, Mamma? It's a real one."

"Watch me take snuff. See?" Tad sneezed.

"The people are all over the stairs, Mamma. They're all *over*."

Mary sat up. She couldn't think what the boys were prattling about. But when she opened her door and looked out, there, sure enough, were a number of odd-looking individuals, lined up, leaning against the wall, smoking cigars, and generally making themselves at home. Several of them turned to gape at her through the partly open door.

"Hello—who's she?" one man inquired. He hadn't troubled to remove his hat.

Mary slammed the door. She dressed hastily, sent the boys off to Mrs. Keckley, and marched down the corridor to Mr. Lincoln's office. A few of the bystanders, seeming to recognize her, fell back grudgingly to let her pass. She went in without knocking.

"Mr. Lincoln—"

He was alone at his desk, writing something.

"Mr. Lincoln, have you seen those people out there?"

"Not yet, but I expect I will." He looked up mildly. "That's what they came here for."

"Who on earth are they, Mr. Lincoln? Coming in like this before we've even had breakfast—"

"Office seekers, Mother." Mr. Lincoln put down his pen. "That's one commodity I understand this house never runs short of."

"How did they get in?"

"By the front door, I suppose."

Mary folded her arms.

"They'll have to wait downstairs then," she said shortly. "I won't have the creatures cluttering up the halls, staring at us as though we were waxworks. One of them actually gave Taddie snuff. You'll have to speak to someone, Mr. Lincoln—at once."

"All right, Mother, I'll see what I can do." Mr. Lincoln took up his pen again and stared at it thoughtfully. "The trouble is, I suppose, I'm the one to speak to."

That day and the next passed, and nothing had been done. The house swarmed with the favor seekers, crowding the staircase, pushing their way to the front of the line, clutching their credentials and arguing over the relative merits of their claims.

Now and then one of the visitors would wander out of line and appear in one of the private rooms, where he would generally stand, gawking and unabashed, until requested to leave.

By the end of the week Mary was unnerved. Quite as she might have expected, Mr. Lincoln had done nothing whatever.

"After all, Mother," he said, "I can't very well turn them out. These are the people who voted for me."

"And since when, I should like to know, does voting for a man include the privilege of walking into his family's bedrooms at all hours of the day and night?"

Plainly, if anything was to be done, Mary saw that she would have to do it. She spoke to Mr. Nicolay, Mr. Lincoln's secretary, and Mr. Nicolay, looking harried but patient, said he would speak to Mr. Hay, the other secretary, who would consult Mr. Stoddard, the third secretary. But without definite orders they were not sure ...

The orders, Mary said, were quite definite. In the future uninvited callers would wait downstairs. She would be obliged if Mr. Nicolay would act on the order promptly, since Mr. Montrose was expected from New York that afternoon to confer with her in the matter of redecorating the rooms.

Unfortunately, an hour before Mr. Montrose's arrival, a large group of young gentlemen presented themselves at the White House with the patriotic intention of mobilizing a volunteer company to protect the President and defend Washington in the event that Rebels should invade the city. For want of other space, old Edwards ushered them into the East Room, and there Mary discovered them when she came in with Mr. Montrose. The zealots, unable to restrain their feelings while waiting for an audience, were milling about the room, leaping onto chairs and vowing heroically that if they were given guns, they would bivouac where they were.

Mr. Montrose, already tired by his journey, seemed totally undone by the spectacle of so much virility.

Eventually the volunteers, including their several unmilitarylooking leaders who declared their desire to be commissioned as brigadiers, were sent to the War Department. And Mr. Montrose was able to rally himself, with some difficulty, to the questions of upholstery, carpeting, and color schemes.

As weeks went by, the influx of office seekers dwindled to a steady but manageable trickle, and Mary was discovering that, in Washington, problems were often best settled by allowing them to settle themselves.

In household matters, however, Mary declined to be passive. But when she attempted to change the more archaic customs of management the White House staff proved to be immune to suggestion. In the memory of the oldest usher, who dated back to the Van Buren administration, things in the White House had always been done a certain way. No new President's wife was expected to give orders. She was tolerated only so long as she was willing to live and learn.

"It's absurd," Mary told Mr. Lincoln. "When I try to give an order in the kitchens, I'm told it can't be done that way because Mrs. Madison said fifty years ago it was to be done some other way. Who's running this house, I should like to know? Dolly Madison or me?"

Mr. Lincoln looked at her thoughtfully.

"Neither one, so far as I can see, Mother," he said.

Cousin Lizzie was more sympathetic. "If you ask me," she said, "half these servants ought to be discharged. They're positively insolent to you, Mary. And the things they say behind your back are disgraceful. They grumble over the least thing that makes extra work, and they call you stingy and unreasonable just because you object to their wasteful ways. One of the kitchen maids told me she'd been here through four administrations, and you were the first mistress that ever came down to the kitchens every day. Spying, she called it—" Lizzie's nose grew pink with indignation. "She said it was plain to see that you weren't used to having servants, since you weren't willing to trust them. I took pains to tell her, you may be sure, that you'd been brought up to expect good service, and they needn't think they could hoodwink you with their slovenly ways."

It was a relief all around when Mary discovered that a trip to New York would be necessary before she and Mr. Montrose could decide on the final details of the new furnishings.

For his part, Mr. Lincoln said, if Mary was set on adding a few frills to the house, he had no objection.

"You and Lizzie run along," he said. "Enjoy yourselves. Stay as long as you like."

Once in New York, Mary found herself soothed by the long discussions with Mr. Montrose about designs and fabrics, during which each deferred to the other's opinion. They were always charmed, in the end, to discover how perfectly their tastes agreed. In the matter of lace curtains they were particularly harmonious, with the result that Mary found she had ordered a double set for every window in the house. It was disconcerting to contemplate the probable cost, but Mr. Montrose slid so delicately over the matters of price and credit that Mary hesitated to mention actual figures.

While she was in New York it seemed a pity not to look at a few of the new styles in spring clothes. And the clerks at Stewart's and Lord & Taylor's were as eager as ever to be of service. Encouraged by their friendliness and Lizzie's raptures over the gowns and bonnets, Mary ended by ordering a good many more than she had intended. But there was bound to be a great deal of entertaining in Washington, and, as Mr. Stewart himself said, it would never do for the first lady to be outshone. Miss Kate Chase, he added thoughtfully, had been up only last week to buy her spring wardrobe.

Mr. Lincoln brought the boys to the station the evening they arrived in Washington. He looked tired, but he seemed pleased to have Mary home again. He listened amiably while she told about the new plans for the house, and he neglected considerably to inquire about the cost of anything.

When Lizzie commented later on this singular omission, Mary smiled.

"Mr. Lincoln has no notion of such things," she said indulgently. "He likes to have the house in proper style, and he's always pleased to see me in what he calls 'fine feathers,' but he has no more idea than a kitten what it will mean to live up to our position here. I daresay he fancies a few yards of bonnet trimming and a new pair of shoes are all any woman needs to be dressed for a whole season."

By the end of the week Mr. Montrose had sent down drapers and upholsterers, and there was frantic activity in the house. Mary supervised and directed, but even in the midst of the hammering and confusion, Mr. Lincoln remained oblivious to the upheavals going on around him. When, one morning, he tripped over a man with a mouthful of tacks who was laying the new stair carpet, Mr. Lincoln only murmured a vague apology and went on his way.

"You'll see, though," Mary said confidently, "how delighted Mr. Lincoln will be when everything is done."

Lizzie sighed. "I do think you're wonderful, Mary. Mr. Lincoln is a lucky man to have a wife who does so much for him."

On a Friday morning in April the last curtain and the final strip of carpeting were in place. The old house had come to life again. Falling plaster had been repaired. Rooms that had been bare and dreary glowed with new paint. Fresh damasks covered the furniture. The new red carpets glowed richly. Windows were hung with lace curtains and drapes.

When Mr. Montrose had gone, Mary went back for one more look at the East Room. The gold-and-white walls were perfection. Small rainbows spangled the ceiling in the light reflected from the crystal chandeliers. The crimson draperies gave the crowning touch.

Mary walked down the long room, touching a chair here, a sofa there, standing a moment by the keyboard of the newly gilded pianoforte. Let Washington come and see the house now. They were so fond of talking. This would give them something to talk about.

It was noontime. Mr. Lincoln would be coming down from the office, and she would show him everything. He'd worked so hard these weeks, been so preoccupied and worried by all the new demands they were pressing on him. She thought, smiling, how astonished he would be to discover all she had done.

Out in the hall, Mary was surprised to see Mr. Seward coming in the front door. It seemed an odd time for the Secretary of State to call. She started to speak, but he brushed past with barely a nod, and hurried toward the stairs, just as Mr. Lincoln appeared at the landing. Both men looked grave. Mary saw that Mr. Lincoln held a telegraph blank in his hand.

"You've seen this news?" Mr. Lincoln handed the message to Mr. Seward.

"That's why I came," Mr. Seward said. "If it's true that they've fired on Sumter—it means war."

The two men came down the stairs together.

"We'd better find Cameron," Mr. Lincoln said, "and see what he knows."

They went out the front door, Edwards watching from his perch on his high stool, his old face gnarled and impassive.

Neither of them had noticed Mary, where she stood waiting.

In a single hour Washington was in a turmoil. No one had expected *war*. They had talked of it without really believing in it. Now that it had come, everyone was angry. Congress, having stewed and frittered for months, boiled over in a fury of oratory. Everybody wanted to blame somebody, and the President was the likeliest target.

"The North doesn't stand a show. We're caught unprepared—and Lincoln's responsible. With all this prattle of peace, to get himself elected, he's left us a fair target. Now we're done for."

Other factions, equally bitter, shouted that it was the President who had deliberately shoved them into war.

"If he'd been man enough to own the South was right, we'd never have had to fight. But he's harped on slavery, like a blithering preacher, until he's pushed us into the chowder."

The volunteer companies, in their sashes and sabers, took on a new meaning. All over the North, men were mobilizing, moving toward Washington. *Sign up now. March on Richmond, and we'll be home before the summer's out*, the recruiting posters read. Companies of three-month volunteers joined up, promising their families they would be back in time to help with the harvest.

On a bright spring morning the Pennsylvania Fifth, the New York Twelfth, and the Massachusetts Eighth paraded up the avenue in Washington. Their flags whipped smartly in the fresh breeze, their drums rolled, bayonets flashed in the morning sun. At the White House gate they wheeled to pass in review before the President.

Mary stood beside Mr. Lincoln, watching them march by. She saw the faces, young and eager. They wore bright sashes; most of them smiled broadly as they passed. Mr. Lincoln did not smile back. His eyes, fixed on them, seemed to be looking at something far away.

All along the avenue, windows stood open in the soft spring air. From inside, now and then, came sounds of music. Rebel tunes, clear and tinkling, signaling a thin defiance from the Southern ladies at their pianofortes. The strains of "Dixie" mingled with the blare of fife and drum, and the steady clump of marching feet.

Here came an odd-looking company, dressed in gaudy uniforms with red fez caps and pantaloons of vivid blue. The New York Fire Zouaves—a volunteer brigade led by a dashing young colonel who rode before them, his saber drawn. He heard the pianos tinkling, turned and gave an order, and the next moment his corps band struck up smartly.

> "Then I wish I was in Dixie!
> Hooray! Hooray!
> In Dixie's land we'll take our stand,
> To live and die in Dixie . . ."

The crowd lined along the sidewalk caught the joke and a roar of laughter went up. The bystanders took up the words.

> "Away, away, away down South in Dixie!
> Away, away, away down South in Dixie!"

The defiant pianos were silenced. Windows banged shut.

"The North has stolen everything," the Southern ladies cried. "Even our tunes."

When the Zouaves marched past the White House portico, Mr. Lincoln's face relaxed for the first time as they struck up "Maryland, My Maryland." General Ben Butler had occupied Baltimore that morning, and Maryland could be fairly claimed.

Mary, looking at the Zouave colonel, recognized young Ellsworth, a lad who had read law for a few months in Mr. Lincoln's office in Springfield. She remembered him pleasantly, as a blond, round-faced boy. Riding past now, he grinned at Mr. Lincoln, and winked broadly. Mary saw Mr. Lincoln's hand raised in salute.

That afternoon there was an informal reception for the soldiers at the White House. Mary stood with Mr. Lincoln, shaking hands, greeting them all. She was pleased to find them friendly, eager to talk. When one of the Pennsylvania boys, in a burst of confidence, told her she looked like his mother, Mary was touched. She promised to write to his mother and tell her how well he was.

The boy blushed under his freckles. "Ma'd be all perked to hear from you, ma'am," he said. "She didn't think much of my signing up, but Pa said if Old Abe wanted me to fight, I'd best fight. Pa thinks a whole heap of Mr. Lincoln."

Mary looked at the thin young face. "How old are you?" she asked gently.

"Going on eighteen, ma'am."

Mary was silent. A fear, swift and cold, touched her heart, but she pushed it away. She said, "I have a son, about your age. I can imagine how your mother felt to see you go."

"Yes, ma'am." The boy looked troubled, then he brightened. "Pa says three months'll be over before we know it though. And I can go home again."

"I hope so," Mary said.

When the boys had gone, Mary spoke to Mr. Lincoln. Did anyone really suppose the fighting would be over before the summer was out?

Mr. Lincoln hesitated. He was sitting forward in his chair, his shoulders slumped. The talk in Congress, he said, was all of making the war a short one. "They say the South will give in quick enough, once they see we mean business."

Mary pursed her lips. "I wonder if the Confederate boys are signing up for just three months," she said.

Twenty-three

THE NEXT day was Sunday. Ellsworth, the young Zouave colonel, came to dinner. He was full of talk of getting his boys in the "mix-up," and Tad and Willie were entranced.

"What would you do if you saw a Reb coming at you?"

"Shove a bayonet through him—like this—" Ellsworth skewered Tad on the end of a fork, and Willie squealed with delight.

"What will you do with old Jeff Davis if you catch him?"

"Hang him on a sour apple tree."

"What is a Zouave anyway?"

Ellsworth laughed. "Ask anyone in New York. They'll tell you a Zouave is an Irishman, plus three yards of red flannel sash."

After dinner Ellsworth borrowed a carbine from Mr. Stoddard and showed the boys the manual of arms. They watched the clockwork motions in high glee, until one "shoulder arms." Ellsworth was standing too near the south window, and the muzzle of the gun crashed through the pane of glass. Ellsworth was dismayed for a moment, then he grinned.

"You see, boys," he said, "what we'll do to Johnny Reb."

Having young Ellsworth with them made the big house seem almost like home. Mary suggested that he stay at the White House while he was stationed in Washington, but Ellsworth was firm.

"I've got to stick to my boys," he said. "They're a troublesome lot of Irishmen. If I weren't on hand to look after them, half the company would be tarred and feathered before the week was out."

On an afternoon when Mary was out paying calls, Mr. Lincoln found a slip of paper on his desk. It was a bill from a firm of merchants in New York, to the sum of several thousand dollars owed for carpeting furnished as per order, installed in the East Room, main corridor, state dining room and staircase in the White House. Mr. Lincoln looked at it for a moment.

"Mr. Hay, do you know anything about this?"

Mr. Hay studied the bill carefully. He cleared his throat. Since Mrs. Lincoln had taken charge of all the decorations and repairs, perhaps she might know, he said. Or possibly Mr. Stoddard.

Mr. Stoddard was sent for. As junior secretary he kept the household accounts. Mr. Lincoln showed him the bill. So far as he could see, Mr. Stoddard said guardedly, the statement seemed correct.

Mr. Lincoln asked whether Mr. Stoddard knew if any more such bills might be expected.

Well, yes, Mr. Stoddard nodded. With the painters and the upholsterers and the carpenters, there might be quite a few more. He paused, glancing at Mr. Hay.

There was a silence.

"I wish you had consulted me about this sooner," Mr. Lincoln said.

Mr. Stoddard's uneasiness grew more marked. Mrs. Lincoln had taken charge of everything, he said. She had understood that it was customary for Congress to appropriate a certain sum at the beginning of each new administration for necessary repairs to the White House. In this case, since Mrs. Lincoln has found so much that needed doing, it might be necessary to ask for a larger amount.

Mr. Lincoln's smile was thin. "At a time like this," he said, "with an army to raise and the country howling about taxes, I hardly think Congress could be persuaded that flossing up the President's house is a necessary expense."

He took the bill from Mr. Stoddard, folded it, and put it in his pocket.

"When the other bills come in, bring them to me. I'll make up the extra myself."

"Yes, sir."

"And, Mr. Stoddard, I would appreciate it if nothing were said of this. It would be too bad," Mr. Lincoln rubbed his chin, "to have Mrs. Lincoln upset."

It was useless to hope that any morsel of information that might contribute to the fashionable pastime of criticizing the new administration would remain unnoticed. The Washington grapevine was well developed. Within a few days the tea tables and drawing rooms rocked with delight over the story of Mrs. Lincoln's new furniture.

Someone had heard, straight from an usher who had been in the White House for years, that Mrs. Lincoln had bought three trunkfuls of lace curtains to hang nowhere at all. They'd heard the President had gone into a towering rage. One of the maids said she wouldn't be surprised if he'd actually beaten her.

It was too shocking, really. Fancy anyone spending such sums at a time like this with the country at war. The secesh ladies, who sympathised romantically with the South, shook their heads virtuously.

Furthermore, they added, it must never be forgotten that Mrs. L. was a Southerner herself. For all she talked so freely about sympathizing with her husband's politics, she had three brothers under the Confederate flag. And mind you, they said, blood is thicker than politics.

Going over her mail with Mr. Stoddard one morning, Mary put down a letter suddenly. "Mr. Stoddard," she pushed the remaining stack toward him, "will you read the rest of these? I . . . can't stand any more . . ."

Mr. Stoddard glanced up to see tears in Mary's eyes.

"Take them away." She gave the letters another push. "Burn them, do anything you like, only don't let me see any more, please."

He glanced through a few of the letters, frowning. They were the sort that came every day now. Ugly, anonymous scrawls, most of them—though now and then there was a carefully written one, no less bitter because it was written in a neat hand on elegant stationery. He picked several at random . . . The President's wife was a spy—she sympathized with the South. . . . The President's wife was a traitor to the South. . . . She went to New York to buy expensive clothes . . . She entertained at fine dinner parties while soldiers were starving and dying in the field . . .

He pushed the others aside. The abuse and bitterness were familiar to him. Each morning the President's mail was filled with just such ravings.

Mary spread her hands.

"Mr. Stoddard, why must they hate us so?"

Twenty-four

A WHITE HOUSE reception was planned for the last week in April. Mary worked for days over the arrangements, ordering the refreshments from Maillard's in New York. It was her first chance to entertain the Washington ladies, and she meant to show them she knew how to do things properly. The house was done to the perfection of Mr. Montrose's taste. Mrs. Keckley had Mary's new gown ready.

Watching the preparations, Mr. Stoddard was doubtful. He hoped the party would go well—after Mrs. L. had gone to such trouble. But with the talk that was going around in Washington, especially in the secesh ladies' circles, it seemed there wasn't anything they'd stop at to make things hot for the President. It would be a shame, Mr. Stoddard thought, if the ladies decided to take out their feelings on Mrs. L.

On the night of the reception, Mr. Lincoln was late. He had been at his desk until the last moment, while Mary fumed impatiently outside the study door. She had sent the barber in to shave him and trim his hair while he worked. Finally Mr. Stoddard was directed to warn him that he must dress at once. His clothes were laid out and ready, and Mr. S. was to remind him once again not to fail to put on white gloves.

Mary and Cousin Lizzie were in the East Room when Mr. Lincoln appeared. He stood a minute, looking around the big room. There were flowers in tall vases, and the crystal chandeliers sparkled in the candlelight. The carpet, at which Mr. Lincoln glanced with a new respect, was soft beneath his feet. The crimson draperies filled the room with color. Mr. Lincoln raised his eyebrows.

"Kind of dolled up tonight, aren't we, Mother?"

Mary came to straighten his tie, smiling up at him. She wore a new gown of watered silk, cut low over her round, smooth shoulders, and with a full skirt sweeping into a train.

"Our cat has a long tail tonight," Mr. Lincoln said, looking at the new dress. "Seems to me some of the tail might have come in handy at the top."

"Don't be old-fashioned, Mr. Lincoln. It's the style to have necks cut low this season. I daresay you'd find nothing out of the way if Miss Chase wore a low neck—or any of the other young ladies." She gave his tie a final pat. "There, you look very fine. Now do, for pity's sake, remember to stand straight and not slouch. And don't put your hands behind your back while you talk to the ladies. It offends them."

"Well, Mother, you don't leave me much margin for error. But I'll do my best. Before the evening is over I'm sure I can think up a few new mistakes."

Mary glanced up sharply. His face was solemn and his voice sounded meek. But she detected a twinkle in his eye. "Mr. Lincoln," she rapped his wrist sharply with her fan, "being President hasn't improved you one bit. First you aggravate me and then you make a joke."

She tried to keep her own expression serious, but as she took his arm they were both laughing.

They stood together by the East Room door while the Marine band struck up a lively tune from the hall outside. Mary heard the usher's voice, announcing the first guests.

Three gentlemen from the Senate shook hands with the President and bowed stiffly to Mary. One of them mumbled something about regretting that his wife had been unable, at the last moment, to come. Mary failed to quite catch the words. She only nodded brightly, and the gentleman, a trifle red of face, moved on. A delegation of congressmen came next, then Judge Stevenson, who murmured over Mary's hand that Mrs. Stevenson was indisposed and sent regrets.

More congressmen—then a group from the French embassy, among them one woman who was presented to Mary as the wife of one of the attachés. She was a sallow little creature, all in black, who gazed at Mary out of sad dark eyes and remarked mournfully, in broken English, that it was a charming occasion, and she was enchanted to be present.

Carriages arrived steadily. The outside corridor was jammed, and the sound of voices rose above the music. Guests were announced, made their bows, and passed quickly into the crowd.

"The Secretary of the Treasury, Mr. Chase."

Mary lifted her shoulders. Her smile grew a shade brighter. Mr. Lincoln was shaking hands.

Mary was surprised to find Mr. Chase alone.

"Where's Miss Kate?" she asked. "Isn't she with you?"

Miss Kate was desolated, Mr. Chase explained. A headache, at the very last minute had kept her at home. She begged that Mrs. Lincoln would understand.

Mary was on the point of replying quite conventionally when something in Mr. Chase's bland face made her pause. The next instant, in a stinging, bitter flash, Mary realized what was happening. In the whole roomful of people, not one woman of any real social position in Washington was present. The cave dwellers were having their revenge on the "antislavery Westerners." It was a colossal, unbelievable snub.

Mary's smile stiffened. She lifted her chin.

"Indeed, Mr. Chase, please tell Miss Kate that I do understand—quite." She drew her fingers away.

The minutes passed. Minutes of humiliation, sick and cold, while Mary kept her smile fixed and unfaltering, and the ruins of the evening crumbled slowly. Gentleman after gentleman appeared, shook hands, and moved on. Then suddenly, the usher's voice rang clearly:

"The Honorable Stephen Douglas and Mrs. Douglas."

Mary turned swiftly toward the door. Adele Douglas, her blonde curls smooth and shining, her figure elegant in rose brocade, was coming in.

There was a stir—an almost tangible wave of surprise and disbelief—among the guests who stood near the door. They turned to stare like boys caught in the midst of a prank that hadn't quite come off.

"Dear Mrs. Lincoln—" Mrs. Douglas took Mary's hand. Her voice carried clearly in the hush. "How charming everything looks."

It was then, for the first time, that Mary found herself weakening. Her knees trembled; she felt her smile waver uncertainly. The next moment she felt Mr. Douglas' hand on hers.

"I'm glad we're not too late," he said. "I was hoping to ask you for the honor of the first dance."

The band had just struck up a waltz. Mr. Douglas held out his arm.

"May I?"

Mary nodded. They walked past the guests to the reception hall where the floor had been cleared. She looped up her train and Mr. Douglas smiled.

"This is like old times, isn't it?" he said.

Twenty-five

COLONEL ELLSWORTH had one more Sunday dinner at the White House before the news came that the Confederates were threatening Alexandria. He and his Zouaves were ordered to move south. They sailed down the Potomac that same evening. Ellsworth was apologetic for the condition of his company. Rounded up from the bar at Willard's, and other favorite haunts, some were noticeably the worse for wear.

"They'll be all right, though," Ellsworth assured Mr. Lincoln. "It's action they've been spoiling for, and once they get a taste of it, you'll hear well of them, sir." His face, beneath the peaked red cap, looked young and eager.

Mr. Lincoln smiled. "They'll be all right," he said. "I'm sure of it."

Two mornings later, a telegram was delivered to the White House.

Mr. Lincoln found Mary and the boys at breakfast. Before he sat down he told them that Colonel Ellsworth was dead. He had been shot in the back and killed instantly by a rebel innkeeper in Alexandria, while he was climbing the stairs to fly the Union flag from the inn roof. He was still holding the flag, Mr. Lincoln said, when he fell.

The news came as a blank shock. Willie and Tad burst into a storm of weeping and rushed at their father, burying their heads against him.

Mary looked at Mr. Lincoln, dazed and unbelieving.

"It can't be true," she said. "It can't be . . ." Her eyes were on his, pleading. As if he might somehow make the truth untrue.

He shook his head.

"It's just the beginning of the truth," he said slowly. "I suppose we must learn to get used to it."

Mary insisted that the funeral must be at the White House. She made the arrangements for the service.

Late in the evening Mary saw the light burning under Mr. Lincoln's study door. It was seldom, in these days, that she ventured to disturb him but after a moment's hesitation, she knocked softly and went in. He was sitting at his desk, a letter before him, and he looked up as she came to stand beside him.

"I've been trying to write to Ellsworth's parents," he said. His face, in the circle of lamplight, was worn and heavy.

Mary saw the last lines he had written. ". . . to the memory of my young friend and your brave and early fallen child. . . . May God give you that consolation which is beyond all earthly power . . ." While she watched, he signed the letter and laid down his pen.

Mary took his hand and laid her cheek against it. "Do you know, Mr. Lincoln," she said, "when I was in Lexington there was a doctor in town named Jackson. He used to come to our house often. I remember how he told us that my little brother Alex made him think of his little brother Jimmy. Jimmy was very like Alex, he said, gay and naughty and always into mischief. I heard this afternoon that Jimmy Jackson was the man who killed Ellsworth." Mary paused. "And then I heard that one of Ellsworth's men had killed Jackson. I suppose in the

South tonight they're wanting revenge against the man who shot Jimmy Jackson—and here we're crying murder because Jimmy killed Ellsworth."

"Yes," he said. "And one cry is like another . . ."

The morning they brought Ellsworth back to Washington was mild and sweet. Sitting next to Mr. Lincoln in the East Room while the funeral service was read, Mary felt the warm breeze through the black draperies she had hung to cover the crimson curtains. She looked at the flag-covered coffin, and thought of Ellsworth, going through the manual of arms to amuse Tad and Willie, and breaking a window in the south parlor. The glazier's marks were still fresh on the new pane. She saw this room, thinking how she had worked over it, wanting so to have it handsome to impress Kate Chase and the other ladies. She remembered the deep lines of tenderness and grief about Mr. Lincoln's mouth as he had sealed the letter to Ellsworth's parents, whom he had never seen. Hearing the words of death, measured and final in the shadowed room, Mary felt a numbing helplessness. The spring sunshine shattered around her in shining, jagged fragments.

✳❀✳❀✳❀
Twenty-six
ᴡᴡᴡᴡᴡᴡᴡ

Tʜᴇʏ sᴀɪᴅ that in Washington nowadays a man had to be a Westerner to get anywhere.

"Unless a fellow's been a rail splitter—or at least a hog caller —he don't stand a show with Abe's gang. What's Lincoln up to anyway? Playing politics and finding jobs for his Republican friends while the South steals a march on us."

Mr. Lincoln said: "These Democrats hold tight to their seats. If the news got out there was a post office being given away at the South Pole the road there would be paved with frozen Virginians."

For three months Washington had watched the Northern troops arrive, march through the city, and disappear across the Long Bridge to join the Army of the Potomac. The first enthusiasm for the shining brigades in their brave uniforms had begun to wear thin. All this hoopla was well enough, people said, but what became of the soldiers after they marched south?

"Why don't they fight? We've sent the troops and the money. What's Lincoln waiting for?"

"If we don't get a move on, the war will be lost before we've begun it. The boys signed up for three months, and the time's 'most out already. Why don't they take Richmond and finish the thing?"

The generals were after Mr. Chase for more money, but the treasury was empty. The Secretary appealed to Congress. Congress said they couldn't raise any more money till they had something to show for what they'd spent already. People had no heart for this war anyhow. Unless they saw some signs of action soon, they'd lose patience altogether. Chase went back to the Cabinet, and the Cabinet appealed to Mr. Lincoln.

"There's such a thing as striking while public opinion is hot," they said nervously. "Every newspaper and minister and ten-cent orator in the North is howling for a victory."

"Yes," Mr. Lincoln said, "and so is the South."

"But the longer we wait, the better chance the South has to prepare. If you could persuade General Scott to make some sort of move—just to keep people quiet—"

"Well," Mr. Lincoln said, "I'll talk to Scott again. "But I don't promise results."

When the President called on General Scott in his parlor, the old man sat with his gouty leg propped on a stool. Mr. Lincoln faced him, his tall hat on the floor beneath his chair, his hands resting on his knees. The blinds, drawn against the hot June sun, made shadowed stripes across the flowered carpet.

"Hang public opinion," old Scott said. "What do your fool congressmen and preachers know about a war? Just let us attack once—and get beaten. Then where would your public opinion leave you?"

"Nowhere," Mr. Lincoln said. "But that's where we seem to be right now."

The general shifted his leg.

"McDowell's down there on the Potomac trying to get an army together," he said. "He's not a bad general—the best we could get for the Union side. But the troops they send him are schoolboys signed up for three months. They think war is some kind of a holiday they can go home from in a few weeks. It takes some doing to lick boys as green as that into an army, Mr. Lincoln. And it takes money. You can tell your blasted politicians that."

Mr. Lincoln sighed. "What about the regular army, General? The country's been supporting one all these years."

The old man snorted. "The regular army is lined up against the Union, fighting for the South—the best of them, anyway." He reached out to pour himself a drink. "Better have one with me before you go," he said, as Mr. Lincoln stood up. "Good whisky's the only thing to keep a man alive in weather like this. . . . No? Well, I hope you'll excuse my not seeing you to the door. Can't move around much, with this confounded leg."

"That's all right, I can let myself out," Mr. Lincoln stooped and picked up his hat. "I'll tell the Cabinet what you've said. I believe you and General McDowell know best, but it's a hard job keeping these fellows from blowing the roof off."

Hearing the outer door shut, the general drained his glass and leaned back, easing his collar. Queer chap, Lincoln. Not half bad, as politicians went. None of the usual poppycock—and he had the decency to give a man credit for knowing what he was about. He'd never have the stuff to amount to much of a soldier. Too apt to shilly-shally around and see two sides to a question. But he wasn't a fool like Seward and Cameron and Chase. Thinking they could run an army from their danged department desks.

The air in the shuttered room was close and heavy. The general grunted at the sharp twinge of pain in his leg. His grizzled chin dropped forward, and his eyes closed . . . He couldn't see that this war they'd cooked up made much sense on either side. You spent your life building up a decent army. Then it split in two and began to fight itself. Sense or not, though, it was war. And war was still a soldier's business, even when you had your own men against you. It was hard to think of them—Jeb Stuart, Jackson, Longstreet, Beauregard, Joe Johnston . . . the best officers that ever came out of West Point. All gone to fight for the South. And you were left in the soup, with a mess of brigadiers who'd never fired a gun and troops so green they wouldn't burn with a fire under them.

And the danged politicians.

"The generals say we can't fight without more money, and Congress won't raise any more money without a fight," Mr. Lincoln told Mary. "I can't tell where the head ends and the tail begins."

"You'd better listen to the generals," Mary said. "I don't trust Chase, or Seward either. They're both jealous of you, Mr. Lincoln. Like as not they're trying to scheme things so that the war goes badly, and you'll be discredited."

"Now, Mother, they're not as bad as all that."

"I have eyes, Mr. Lincoln. What I say is true. Everyone knows Chase wanted to be President. If only you weren't so blind, you'd see that he'd stop at nothing now to take the honor away from you."

"Well, he's welcome to the honor," Mr. Lincoln said, "if he'll find some way to get us out of this hash."

The last of June melted into July, and the heat grew worse. It hung over the city while Congress stewed and sweated. The Cabinet met in shirt sleeves. Secretary Welles lifted his beard to fan his neck with a large palm leaf. They consumed gallons of the iced ginger beer Mary sent up.

And still the war hung stalemate.

For Mary, the days were endless. It was impossible to keep the boys quiet. They raced and played and rode Willie's pony until they were exhausted. When night came they were too restless to sleep, and complained fretfully of headaches. Mary held long conversations with Mrs. Keckley over the dangers of malaria and typhoid, and the menace of the old sewage canal that wound past the foot of the White House grounds and spread its foul smells and disease.

Now that Cousin Lizzie had gone home to Springfield, Mary had no one but Mrs. Keckley to talk to. Mr. Lincoln was busy all day and half the night. When he came to meals he sat staring at his plate, eating little and hardly seeming to hear when Mary spoke. It was too hot for Mary to go driving, and there was nothing left to do. After the long years of work, with the constant pressure of time at her heels, leisure was like a friend long lost and grown unfamiliar.

As for callers, there were none. The Red Room, which Mary and Mr. Montrose had decorated so charmingly as a place where she would receive visitors, stood empty and unused. Kate Chase and the Southern ladies had seen to that. Miss Kate's pointed tongue grew no duller with the passing months, and she had the ear of every important person in Washington. When the news came of Stephen Douglas' sudden illness and death, Mary felt she had lost her only friend in Washington.

Mary, alone in the White House, had the ear of no one save the President, and he could not be counted on to listen.

In the confused hate that boiled up everywhere, criticism that had begun as dinner-table gossip was taken up and given the dignity of serious charges. Anything that would make the President look bad was welcomed by nine-tenths of the press. Stories about the President's wife were relished as spicy side dishes. The President's wife was extravagant. She was vain and ill-tempered. She was a meddler, interfering with her husband's decisions, and playing politics to satisfy her personal grudges. She was accused of being a spy. Rumors of her Confederate sympathies, enlarged and glorified, were trotted out and paraded before the country.

It might be a good idea, Mr. Lincoln suggested one morning, if Mary were to take the boys and go away for a while. To the mountains or the seashore. Just until the hot spell blew over.

Mary flared up instantly.

"Do you want to get rid of us, Mr. Lincoln?"

Of course not. He was patient. He'd only thought she might enjoy a little change. Washington was no kind of place in summer, and the boys seemed to be all tuckered out.

So long as Mr. Lincoln must stay, Mary said, there was nothing, *nothing* that would induce her to leave him. She would be miserable every moment she was gone, knowing he needed her with him.

Mr. Lincoln said no more.

It was a relief when Ben Helm, Emilie's husband, came for a few days' visit. He brought messages from Emilie and the others at home, and Mary welcomed him eagerly, hungry for news. While Ben was at the White House, Mr. Lincoln offered him a commission in the Union army.

"We need young men like you," Mr. Lincoln said. "And it would be a fine thing for Mother if she could have Emilie here. To tell you the truth, Ben, it's been kind of lonesome since we came to Washington."

Urged by Mary, Ben wavered. He'd like to say yes—but there were some men in New York he'd have to talk to first. Men who had been at West Point with him. Southerners, like himself.

The day Ben left, Mary put her arms around him.

"Try to come back, Ben," she said. "We need you."

A week later Ben's letter came, addressed to Mary. He'd thought it all over. She was to tell Mr. Lincoln that he was deeply honored by the President's offer, but now that he had talked with his friends, he couldn't see his way clear to accepting. There was one man in particular, Colonel Robert Lee, who had just resigned his post at West Point to go home to Virginia. "He didn't try to influence me to join the Confederacy," Ben wrote. "Lee told me he is not in favor of secession. He is so opposed to this war that he hopes never to draw his sword in it—but he cannot fight against his own people. Nor can I."

Ben hoped Mary and Mr. Lincoln would understand.

Mary encountered General Scott at the White House a few days later. His leg was still troubling him and he leaned heavily on his cane. She told him about Ben's letter.

"I remember Ben when he was a boy at West Point," the general said. "And Robert Lee was on my staff in the Mexican Wars. He was the best soldier I ever saw."

The old man was silent a moment, sucking in his cheeks. "Pity we had to lose them." He looked at Mary out of pale, expressionless eyes. "I can understand how Lee felt. I'm a Virginian myself."

Twenty-seven

On a summer morning Mary found a letter in her mail signed by one Rebecca Orville, requesting an interview with Mrs. Lincoln.

Mary showed the letter to Mr. Stoddard.

"You'd better let me find out who this woman is before you answer," Mr. Stoddard said. "People are trying all sorts of queer tricks nowadays."

"Nonsense," Mary brushed aside his caution impatiently. "Anyone can see this person isn't planning any mischief." She took the letter. "I shall write today, and ask Miss Orville to come and see me. It can't do any harm, certainly."

The afternoon when Miss Orville was expected, Mary ordered tea served in the Red Room. She was ready promptly at four, pleased at the prospect of a visitor who had nothing to do with politics or official society. For the first time, with some surprise, Mary realized how lonely she had been in Washington.

Five minutes later one of the pantry maids knocked at the

door and hurried in. Please, there was a woman waiting with a note from Mrs. Lincoln, and what should they do?

What should they do? Mary echoed sharply. Why, show her in, of course. She had left word that a caller was expected. Why on earth hadn't Edwards had her properly introduced.

"But, Mrs. Lincoln," the maid looked flustered. "This woman is *colored*. Edwards told her there must've been a mistake, ma'am. He sent her around to the kitchen to wait."

Mary spoke firmly. "There has been no mistake. Please bring Miss Orville to me at once."

"In here, Mrs. Lincoln?"

"Certainly."

"But what shall we do about tea, ma'am? You ordered it served—"

"Serve it, of course." Mary ignored the girl's look of outraged dignity. "Now fetch Miss Orville, and mind you're civil about it."

A few minutes later a young woman, quiet and well mannered, was shown in. Mary greeted her kindly, apologizing for the delay and misunderstanding at the door. She talked pleasantly, anxious to put Miss Orville at her ease, but it was impossible to overlook the glaring insolence of the pantrymaid who appeared with tea. Without waiting to serve the guest, the maid disappeared, slamming the door behind her.

Mary saw the embarrassment on her guest's face. She saw also that the tea was half cold, and the only refreshments were a few stale-looking cakes carelessly arranged on an ordinary kitchen plate.

Mary rose and handed Miss Orville her cup.

"I'm very glad you could come today." She offered the cakes. "I hope I'll be able to give you the advice you wanted."

Miss Orville explained that she was a teacher. She was also a member of the colored Presbyterian church on Fifteenth Street, and through the church an effort was being made to supply some sort of school for the Negro children in Washington.

"There are a great many free colored people in the city, Mrs. Lincoln," Miss Orville said. "We're respectable people. Quite a lot of us own our own homes, and pay taxes. But we haven't any way of educating our children."

The District had laws, she said, forbidding Negroes to enter any public building, and this included the schools.

"We do as much as we can for ourselves. We have our own teachers, and we've been holding classes for the children in the church. But we're crowded there. We need a regular school building."

They had raised the necessary money, Miss Orville said, but their plan had been blocked by a number of Washington citizens who were objecting to the idea of educating Negro children. Unless they could get some support from influential people, the whole plan would be lost.

The woman talked quietly and well, and Mary listened sympathetically. She would speak to Mr. Lincoln at once, she promised, and see what could be done.

"We're very grateful for your kindness, Mrs. Lincoln," Miss Orville said.

They talked for a few minutes about the difficulty of keeping children amused in hot weather, and the danger of malaria. Then Miss Orville rose to leave.

Remembering the difficulty with Edwards, Mary was careful to escort her guest to the door. As they walked through the hall, Mary saw Edwards' glower of disapproval. He climbed down from his stool, and at the very moment when he swung open the front door and Mary turned to shake hands with Miss Orville, a carriage swept up beneath the portico outside and a driver in mulberry livery stepped smartly from the box.

Mary froze. There was only one carriage in Washington with that livery. Secretary Chase was arriving for a Cabinet meeting. Mary's eyes caught sight of Miss Kate, slim and elegant, a parasol tipped over her sharp, pretty face.

The carriage whisked away. But from Miss Kate's amused, astonished glance, Mary knew that the little scene of the President's wife shaking hands with a Negro woman on the White House steps had not gone unobserved.

There was no chance for Mary to speak to Mr. Lincoln about Miss Orville's plan that evening.

The Cabinet meeting dragged on until ten o'clock. Then General Scott arrived, to stump up the stairs and remain closeted with the President for another two hours.

It was late when Mr. Lincoln came to bed, but Mary was still awake. He told her that a plan of attack had been drawn up. General McDowell would move his army against Beauregard at Manassas, while General Patterson held the other half of the Southern forces in the Shenandoah Valley.

"Some of our officers say we still aren't ready," Mr. Lincoln said. "But Scott finally gave his consent tonight. I only hope it's the right thing."

He lay down on the bed, one arm across his face.

Mary turned down the lamp. "Try to sleep, Mr. Lincoln," she said gently.

Even as she spoke, she knew they would both lie awake.

News of the plan for attack spread through Washington the next day and was hailed with delight. The long, dreary delay was over, and the city came out of its summer doldrums to celebrate. Around the bar at Willard's they toasted the end of the war.

"We can't lose," they agreed with a keen sense of military strategy. "Now the fool politicians have quit their wrangling, we can beat the South and be done with it. It stands to reason —we've got more men, more generals, more equipment. The measly Rebs will run like rabbits once they see we really mean to fight."

The young officers, riding up from the Potomac camps the evening before the attack, raised their glasses in a fine spirit of defiance. They had never seen a battle, most of them, but the light of victory shone brightly in their eyes.

"We'll show the measly Graybacks a thing or two," they vowed. "Just let us throw one good scare into them and they'll kite for home fast enough."

Returning to their camps, late in the hot night, the officers sounded off false alarms to see what their troops would do. When the men came scrambling pell-mell out of the tents, the officers were doubled up, convulsed by the killing spectacle of the men, half dazed with sleep, brandishing their guns and rushing about with shouts that the Rebs were on them.

It was a great success.

Even old General Scott caught a trace of the prevailing cheer, and admitted things didn't look quite as bad as he had expected. A smile lighted Mr. Lincoln's tired eyes when he heard that, but Mary shook her head.

"They forget one thing, Mr. Lincoln. The South will be fighting for its life in this war. Our men, most of them, will only fight because they've been told to."

Mr. Lincoln stood at the window of his study, looking through a glass toward the Virginia hills. From a steepletop in Alexandria the stars and bars of the Confederacy floated defiantly in the breeze.

Mary stood beside him.

"At least there's one consolation," she said drily. "With all the talk of attack and victory being shouted about in Washington, the South can never complain of being taken by surprise."

Between the generals and the cabinet members, Mr. Lincoln was in conference the next day and night. Mary still found no chance to tell him about Miss Orville's school. But she spoke to Mrs. Keckley.

Mrs. Keckley was mending a pile of the boys' clothes. When Mary had finished, she laid aside one of Taddie's plaid socks.

"I know Miss Orville. She is right, Mrs. Lincoln. We need schools for our children. We need them desperately. But we must be careful. We must move slowly—"

"Slowly?" Mary echoed. "But children don't move slowly. They grow—they don't know how to wait—"

Mrs. Keckley took up another sock and threaded her needle.

"A good many of us have to learn to wait," she said.

The next morning Mary spoke to Mr. Stoddard.

"I like this plan of Miss Orville's," she said. "She's sensible and honest. I've promised to come and see the building where they plan to have the school. As soon as Mr. Lincoln has more time, I'll consult him about it. He's quite certain to approve—"

She broke off as Mr. Stoddard glanced up, embarrassed. Tactfully he suggested that Mrs. Lincoln's taking up such a plan might be awkward. Washington people might misunderstand. There would be talk.

"Talk?" Mary's brows rose sharply. "There's talk enough already, I should think. They can't say worse things of me than they have, Mr. Stoddard. This, at least, would have the novelty of being true."

Mr. Stoddard shook his head. With feeling running so high, Washington was full of people waiting for a chance to jump on anything to discredit the President. And for the President's wife to sponsor a school for Negroes . . .

He paused. It was the devil and all trying to explain what he meant, with Mrs. L. sitting there watching him, touchy as a firecracker and refusing to see what was as plain as a nose on a face. Of all things for her to have gone and got herself keyed up about . . .

"They've accused me of being a Southerner and a spy," Mary said. "Wouldn't this prove that I'm not pro-slavery?"

Mr. Stoddard hesitated again. "I'm afraid people who circulate such stories aren't likely to be convinced by any sort of proof, Mrs. Lincoln."

"Then what am I to do, pray? Just sit by and do nothing at all?"

"Well, for the present, it might be best. In these times, one can't be too cautious—"

Whack! Mary's fist came down on the table between them.

"Mr. Stoddard, I will not hear that word *cautious* again—" Mary's eyes blazed. "Every fool in this city talks of nothing but being cautious. You sound like Mr. Lincoln, forever saying we must go slowly."

"Mrs. Lincoln, *please*," Mr. Stoddard glanced uneasily at the door. "You may be overheard."

"I haven't the slightest doubt I'm being overheard, Mr. Stoddard. Every word I utter in this wretched house is overheard, with servants peeping and spying at the keyholes for some new gossip to spread all over town. And you talk to me of caution. I've tried your precious caution, Mr. Stoddard, and what has it got me? Nothing but hatred and lies. Spiteful, vicious lies about me—about Mr. Lincoln—even about my children."

"Yes, yes—I know." Mr. Stoddard mopped his forehead. "I realize it's been most trying. We can only be patient, Mrs. Lincoln, and try to understand . . ."

"Mr. Stoddard—do for mercy's sake stop trying to soothe me." Mary's voice trembled with fury. "You talk to me as though I were ill—or out of my mind. I shall thank you to remember that I'm neither. I know quite well what I'm saying. I'm sick of caution. Sick to death. Ever since I came into this house, I've heard nothing but that hateful word. I must be cautious. I must be careful. I mustn't do this or that for fear of being misunderstood. I can't go into a shop to buy a new dress without being accused of extravagance. I must hold my tongue and smile no matter what lies they spread about me.

I daren't read the letters from my own family because they happen to live in the South and I'll be called a spy. *I'm* spied on and talked about in my own house but I can't discharge a servant who is insolent for fear of having more vile stories spread about me. Then you tell me I must be patient and try to understand—"

Her voice broke bitterly. "You are the one who doesn't understand, Mr. Stoddard. How can I be patient when I'm humiliated every day of my life? When I'm a prisoner in this house, afraid to think or speak—"

"I know, Mrs. Lincoln. Believe me, I see how difficult its been. Still, you must think of your position—"

"My *position*!" Mary flung the word back at him furiously. "My position is a laughingstock, Mr. Stoddard. Washington has seen to that. They've hounded me and made a fool of me, until you and the others pity me. Don't you think I read the letters my son Robert writes to me? Asking me to be more careful, more discreet, because there has been so much talk. What do you think I care for my position when my own son is ashamed of the lies he hears about me? And you dare to sit there telling me I must think of my position. You're a fool, Mr. Stoddard. A blundering, self-important fool!"

Mary sank back in her chair. The anger died out of her in a shuddering wave, leaving only misery. She covered her eyes, feeling the tears against her fingers, helpless and shaming. Through the spinning emptiness she could hear Mr. Stoddard's words. His distressed apologies. He hadn't meant to upset her. She must try to calm herself, not to allow herself to get so overwrought. No matter how unreasonable he thought her, Mary realized, he must try to make amends now. He must cater to her, humor her, give in to her. Not because he had an ounce of respect for her—merely because she was *Mr. Lincoln's wife*, and so she mustn't be offended.

She dropped her hands.

"It's quite all right, Mr. Stoddard," she said. Somehow, she must get out of this ridiculous and shameful scene. She stood up, shakily, and smiled at him, a smile that bit deep in the corners of her mouth. "You see—there's no reason to be alarmed. I'm quite myself. I shall send Miss Orville a check and explain that I can only offer my personal support for the school at this time. And I promise—" her voice was still level, "that I shan't embarrass the President, nor you, Mr. Stoddard, by mentioning the subject again."

The Union attack was set for Sunday morning, July twenty-first, at dawn.

It was convenient, having the date and hour posted in advance. Half of Washington, it appeared, was making plans to drive down the night before to be on hand and watch the show. It was worth going twenty miles, after all, to see the Union victorious. "Southern chivalry will bite the dust," they said. "Watching the Graycoats run will be a treat for sore eyes."

By sundown on Saturday all the preparations had been made. Senators, judges, congressmen, and lesser dignitaries had marshaled their carriages for the drive. Newspaper correspondents, sightseers, and assorted visitors in the city had besieged the local stables for hired hacks. After one last round for luck at Willard's bar, they were off to battle.

All that night the Long Bridge over the Potomac rumbled beneath the carriage wheels. By morning Washington was practically a desert. Everyone who *was* anyone had gone.

It would never have done to leave the ladies behind. They were as anxious as any to see the fray, and nearly every party had its quota of crinoline skirts and gaily ribboned bonnets. The ladies obligingly squeezed themselves into corners to make room for the loaded picnic hampers at their feet, and they set the sultry night air ringing with their gallant cries.

"On to Richmond!"

Tad and Willie, kept awake by the brave shouts of the departing cavalcade, grumbled bitterly at being left out of the fun.

"But *why* can't we go, Mamma? We want to see the Johnny Rebs run too."

That night McDowell and Sherman sat late, talking with their lieutenants. The tent flaps were pinned back to let in the faint breeze, and the candles flickered, throwing shadows on the grave faces bent over the maps.

On the far side of Bull Run Creek, beyond its yellow, muddy banks, were Beauregard and Jackson, Longstreet and Joe Johnston.

The moon, rising late, shone clear. High and impartial, it floated through the night, making the tents bright where the soldiers turned restlessly in a half-sleep, waiting . . .

Twenty-eight

THE SABBATH morning broke hot and red.

All day, in Washington, the telegraph wires clicked, bringing news. McDowell had attacked. Things appeared to be going well. The plan was working like a charm. By three o'clock that afternoon, Mr. Lincoln rose from his desk. He went to find Mary.

"Well, Mother, it looks as though they've pulled it off." He stuffed the latest batch of telegrams into the pocket of his gray coat. He might walk down to Scott's house, Mr. Lincoln said, and see what the old general thought of the news.

Mary was waiting at the front window when Mr. Lincoln came back.

"Well?" she looked at him closely. "What did Scott say?"

"He said it was danged hot." Mr. Lincoln sat down and pulled out a red cotton handkerchief to wipe his face. "But he admitted things looked pretty favorable."

There was a lull in the telegraph messages.

"I guess the worst is over, Mother," Mr. Lincoln said. "Why

don't we order up the carriage? A breath of air might do us both good."

They drove for an hour. Everywhere in the streets the people seemed in high good humor. Some waved as the President's carriage passed. Now and then a voice was raised in cheerful greeting.

"Good luck, Abe!"

"Hurray for Lincoln and our side!"

Mr. Lincoln smiled and waved back.

"Our stock seems to have gone up, Mother," he said.

When they came back to the White House, Mr. Nicolay was on the front step with word that Mr. Seward was waiting at the War Office for the President. "I'll just walk over and see what's on his mind," Mr. Lincoln said.

Mary felt a sudden alarm. "It's bad news, Mr. Lincoln," she put her hand on his arm. "Don't try to hide it from me—"

"Now, Mother," he patted her hand consolingly, "there's no use getting fired up. Seward didn't say anything was wrong. He's probably got some bee in his bonnet he wants to tell me about. You and the boys go ahead with supper. I'll be as quick as I can."

All through supper, while the boys gabbled noisily about the news of the battle, Mary waited for the sound of Mr. Lincoln's step.

By eight o'clock he still hadn't come. Willie was teasing for a story. Mary looked at his flushed face. He and Taddie had been up since dawn. She had been too preoccupied to notice how long they had stayed outdoors, racing in the hot sun.

"Please, Willie, you and Tad go to bed like good boys." Her glance was on the door, wondering if she heard a step. "Mrs. Keckley will read to you."

"As long as we want her to, Mamma?" Taddie's eye, never slow to catch a bargain, brightened. "Until we go to sleep?"

As the boys rushed upstairs, Mary followed slowly. She ought to be more firm with them really. They were getting so out of hand. But it was difficult, with the house always filled with people, and hours so irregular.

Where *was* Mr. Lincoln? Why didn't he come?

She turned abruptly and went to the wardrobe, to fetch out a bonnet and gloves. There wasn't any reason to stay here. She could send for the carriage and drive awhile. It was barely dusk. Out of the house at least she could breathe.

As the carriage turned down the avenue, Mary leaned back. It was better now. The heaviness, the vague uneasy feeling was gone.

At the corner in front of Willard's Hotel the carriage was stopped. A crowd was gathered to block the street. They seemed to be listening to a man who was waving a paper. Mary tried to catch his words, but they were lost in the noise and confusion.

Everyone seemed to be shouting something. But it couldn't be good news, Mary thought. The faces she saw looked angry and frightened. Suddenly a woman screamed, close by the carriage.

"They're coming—the rebels are coming!" The woman waved her arms. "They're marching on the city. We'll all be killed—murdered . . ."

Still screaming, the woman ran closer to the carriage. The startled horses plunged. There were more voices now.

"We're lost—they've beaten us . . ."

"Our troops are routed . . ."

"They're marching on us—we'll be killed . . ."

The coachman struggled to quiet the horses and steer them clear of the crowd. But it was already too late. Someone had recognized Mary. They closed in around her, screaming and shaking their fists. Jeers and hoots rose in a frightening chorus.

"There she is—look!"

"There's Mrs. Lincoln!"

A rough-looking man, bolder than the rest, pushed his way through the crowd and leaped onto the carriage step.

"Lincoln's to blame for this!" The man pushed his face close to Mary. "*He'll pay for it*. We'll make him pay for it. Just see if we don't."

Mary felt the man's breath, fuming with whisky. She saw the coachman turn and raise his whip but she managed to speak in time. At her sharp command the whip was lowered.

The man still clung to the step, pouring out a stream of abuse.

Suddenly a girl at the edge of the crowd brandished her fringed parasol. "Hurray for Jeff Davis!" The girl's voice rose defiantly. "The South has won! Three cheers for Beauregard."

A tall gentleman flung his hat into the air. "Old Beau has knocked the damned Yankees into a cocked hat."

Another man seized the tall Southerner's topper and drove his fist through it. "There's your cocked hat for you."

In the brawling confusion, the coachman wheeled the horses, and whipped them up. The carriage swayed perilously. Mary clung to the side. The next minute they were clattering up the cobbled street while the howling melee died in the distance. One woman followed a little way, still shouting.

"She's a spy! Lincoln's wife's a spy . . ."

Old Edwards had been dozing on his perch by the door when Mary came in.

"Has—Mr. Lincoln come yet?" she caught her breath.

Yes, a little while ago. He'd gone upstairs with Mr. Seward and Mr. Cameron. There was a Cabinet meeting, Edwards said. He was looking at Mary's white face.

"Are you all right, ma'am?"

Mary nodded. Her hands shook as she tried to straighten her bonnet, but she managed to turn toward the stairs. Once her hand was on the banister, she felt safer. She paused, gathering her strength.

It was nearly one o'clock when Mary heard the door of the Cabinet room open, and the sound of departing steps. She went out into the corridor and waited. Mr. Lincoln didn't seem surprised to see her still dressed.

"What is it, Mother?"

Mary hurried to him. "Mr. Lincoln, is it true what people are saying? That we've been beaten?"

"Yes, it's true. We lost today."

"But the things they said, Mr. Lincoln. I was out on the street and I heard them. They said our army was routed and the men were deserting—"

"We don't know yet," Mr. Lincoln said. "We don't know how bad it is."

"Mr. Lincoln, how could it have happened? How could everything have gone wrong so suddenly? You said yourself— General Scott said, this afternoon—"

He shook his head slowly. "Our men did their best," he said. "McDowell did the best he could."

"How do you know that, Mr. Lincoln?" She must make him listen. "They could have tricked you into this failure, because they hate you—because they want the people to blame you. They *are* blaming you, Mr. Lincoln. The people I saw tonight were saying terrible things."

"Yes, I know." He paused. "Well, when the news is bad, I suppose they have to blame someone."

It was no use. He hadn't even heard her. He would listen to the others, trust the others, believe every word they said. But when she spoke, he didn't hear.

Twenty-nine

ᐯᐯᐯᐯᐯᐯᐯᐯᐯ

IN THE morning Mary woke to see rain. Gray and listless, it fell like a chilling curtain after the days of heat. She dressed quickly, smoothing her hair, and crossed to Mr. Lincoln's room. The door stood half open. She saw the bed untouched.

Down the hall, in front of the study, Mr. Hay was standing guard. He touched his lips warningly as Mary came near.

"Mr. Hay, where is Mr. Lincoln?"

"In the study sleeping. People kept coming in to see him all night. They'd come back from the fight, and he wanted to hear what they could tell him."

"You should have called me, Mr. Hay. Mr. Lincoln should have had something to eat."

Mr. Hay had seen to that, he said smoothly. He had ordered up coffee and eggs and more coffee later.

"But surely he can't be warm enough, sleeping on that couch. It's turned so cool. He'll need a blanket, Mr. Hay."

Mr. Hay had attended to that also. He had fetched a quilt from his own room and put it over Mr. Lincoln.

Mary bit her lip. She looked over Mr. Hay's shoulder. The door was still closed.

By nine o'clock the cavalcade of visitors had begun again. All day they came, steady and monotonous as the rain. Congressmen and senators—the sightseers who had started out so confidently to see the battle won were back now. Their eyes were wide, their voices hoarse, as they described the horrors they had seen. The utter rout of McDowell's army. The stampede on the field. The disordered panic-stricken retreat of the Union troops.

They were full of indignant stories. Of officers lashing their men back into line. Of deserters throwing down their guns and running wildly off the field into the woods.

In awestruck tones the sightseers told how narrowly they had escaped with their own lives. Their carriages had been all but wrecked by the deserting soldiers who had cut loose from their regiments and were crowding the roads north.

Sitting at his desk, Mr. Lincoln heard the accounts. "I congratulate you, gentlemen," he said dryly, "on winning the race."

By late afternoon the returning stream of carriages had stopped. The soldiers, on foot, began to straggle in. Their boots, still caked with Virginia mud, left tracks on the new stair carpet as they filed up to Mr. Lincoln's office. The stories they had to tell were briefer. After walking twenty miles, they hadn't much breath left to shout.

The fight had been going all for the North, they said, until midafternoon. Then something had happened. No one could quite tell what. The enemy had taken a new hold and begun rushing them. Before they could counterattack, Jackson's troops had been on them. They came like a gray wave—with a yelling that was like no sound they'd ever heard. The Union officers had done the best they could—some of them, anyway

—but the men were running wild. Companies had broken up. Everybody was too scared to pay much attention to orders. And those confounded carriages that had come down from Washington were cluttering up the field. The ladies were screaming blue murder. It had been a rout.

Mr. Lincoln sat listening. Listening to anyone who would come in and talk. Listening to excuses, explanations, stories of the long trek back to the city. Of roads jammed with men who were lost or who had deserted, retreating helter-skelter through the night—of the carriages, forcing their way through, refusing to stop and pick up those who had fallen by the way. Stories of wounded men who had walked all night long, supported by their comrades . . . Listening . . .

Coming downstairs into the front hall that afternoon, Mary found a group of soldiers who had just left the President's office. They were standing by the door, looking out at the rain. Seeing their wet coats and muddy boots, and the exhaustion in their faces, she paused and asked where they were expecting to go. They turned, staring at her.

They didn't rightly know. Nobody seemed to know what they were supposed to do.

"I guess we can find some place, ma'am."

Mary turned toward the corridor.

"Come with me," she said, and led the way to the East Room. "You can make yourselves comfortable here. I'll have a fire built, so you can dry your clothes, and we'll see about some food right away."

Within an hour kettles of soup and coffee were boiling on the big ranges in the kitchen, and Mary was supervising trays to be sent up to the East Room.

When one of the soldiers told her there were more men outside, lying on the benches in Lafayette Square, Mary sent Mrs. Keckley to bring as many as she could. They came in, rain soaked and dazed with fatigue, and were sent to the East Room.

When she came up from the kitchen, Mary found the men silent, grouped about the fire. A few were perched gingerly on the edges of the brocaded chairs and sofas, but most were sitting on the floor. One or two stood up as she came in. But none spoke.

Most of the men had taken off their wet coats, and Mary saw that a few had wounds they had bound up clumsily themselves. She hurried upstairs to find Mrs. Keckley, and together they ransacked the linen closets for old sheets to tear into bandages.

Working with Mrs. Keckley to bind up wounded arms and ankles, trying to help a boy whose leg was broken, Mary felt a new strength.

After the long weeks of being no one, she was needed.

Another night passed and there was no sign of a Rebel invasion of the Capital. Not a single citizen was murdered in his sleep. Washington began to relax.

People came out of the first hysterical shock of defeat and took time to look around and get mad. What, they demanded indignantly of each other, had gone wrong with the glorious Army of the Potomac that had boasted so loudly of victory the night before the battle? The army that was scattered and disgraced now. Somewhere there must be a scapegoat in all this. They meant to smoke him out.

Congress and the Cabinet said it was the generals' fault.

The generals, soothing their smarting pride, said the meddling politicians were to blame.

And where was Lincoln in all this, people asked. Lincoln wouldn't say yes and he wouldn't say no. While the air was thick with hurtling brickbats, Lincoln sat tight, refusing to come out and say who had been to blame.

"For mercy's sake, Mr. Lincoln, why don't you stop all this argument?" Mary said impatiently. "Admit the Rebels fought too well for us, and be done with it."

Old General Scott thought otherwise.

"It wasn't Beauregard and Jackson who beat us," he said to Mary. "It was our own blockheadedness. Too many cheers ahead of time." He rubbed the silver head of his cane. "People think they can win a war just by yelling loud enough that they're going to. Now they've found they're wrong, and they want to chop off a few heads to make themselves feel better. McDowell's head will be the first to go, though he doesn't deserve it. Patterson's too. If anyone's to blame, it's me—for being fool enough to let them talk me into a fight I knew we weren't ready for. But they'll never think to take my head off. It's too old and tough to give them any satisfaction."

"Do you think Mr. Lincoln was wrong?" Mary asked.

"Of course he was wrong. The politicians are always wrong." The general thumped his stick. "Lincoln might learn, though." He looked at Mary. "He might turn out to be a pretty good President. Only try to keep him from taking these things too hard. He's got a long way to go yet."

Thirty

IN THE weeks that followed, Mary found herself remembering the old general's words. It all happened just as he had said it would—McDowell and Patterson were in disgrace. Still the grumbling, the endless criticism went on.

"Why don't they do something? They got us into this war— and now they sit and talk—and get us nowhere."

The more they railed, it seemed, the less Mr. Lincoln was willing to commit himself to any policy. Hour after hour, he sat in his study listening.

"In the name of heaven, Mr. Lincoln, what more is there for you to hear?" Mary said. "You listen to every Tom, Dick, and Harry who wants to air a crackpot scheme. You take every word your Cabinet utters as gospel."

"Well, Mother, I have to trust someone."

Mary leaned toward him. "You're the President, Mr. Lincoln. Trust yourself."

He shook his head.

"I wish I could, Mother. But there are places too big for one man. Maybe war is one of them."

Robert came home in August, after a month's visit in Springfield. He told his father he'd been thinking seriously of enlisting. Half his class at Harvard were in the army already. It looked queer for him not to sign up.

Mr. Lincoln looked at him. "You haven't mentioned this to your mother, have you, Bob?"

Not exactly, Robert said. He'd tried leading up to the subject once or twice, but she hadn't been encouraging.

"I expect not." Mr. Lincoln sighed. "Your mother's been upset lately. Things have been pretty hard on her since we came to Washington." He hesitated, weighing a paperknife. "I know it's asking a good deal, Bob, but I'd appreciate it if you could kind of let this thing slide for a while. Maybe later your mother might get more used to the idea."

Robert shrugged. Later might be too late, he said. The war might be over.

Mr. Lincoln gave him an odd glance. "I guess there's no call to worry about that. From the looks of things, I'm afraid you'll have plenty of time. Only—don't tell Mother I said that."

Robert didn't mention the matter again, but Mary was uneasy. The last day before he left for Cambridge she asked him to promise her not to enlist.

"It's your father I'm thinking of, Robert. He has so much to trouble him these days. It wouldn't be fair to add another worry."

Robert was silent.

"When you've finished your education there will be plenty of time to talk of enlisting. And besides, you're not strong enough—"

"Oh, Mother, for heaven's sake."

"Well, it's true, Robert. You've always had a delicate chest—" She put her hand on his arm. "Please, dear, promise me you won't think about it any more."

"I should think you might realize how it makes me look," Robert said. "With my own father calling for volunteers, I can't join up because my mother says I have a weak chest. It makes me feel like a fool."

"Oh, Robert," Mary's eyes filled with tears, "How can you speak to me so? When I'm asking it for your father's sake—"

"All right, all *right*, Mother. I've promised. Isn't that enough?"

Mary pulled away her hand. Her world, rocked for a moment, came back to its precarious balance.

"Yes, dear," she said.

The nights were the hardest times now. With the late summer heat hanging over the city, Mary lay staring into the stifling darkness. Often she got up and crossed to the boys' room, only to find them sleeping. Down the corridor she could see the crack of light under the study door.

She would tiptoe down and stand listening. There was no sound, but often she could see the shadow of Mr. Lincoln's steps pacing back and forth.

One night she opened the door without knocking and went in. Mr. Lincoln was standing by the map rack. He was in his shirt sleeves. His dark hair was rumpled.

"Is something wrong, Mother? Is one of the boys sick?"

Mary shook her head. She pushed one of her thick braids across the shoulder of her robe. "I only thought we might talk a little . . ." She paused, wondering now what it was she had meant to say. She crossed to where he stood and put her head against his shoulder.

"Oh, husband, husband . . ." she whispered.

He put his arm around her, not speaking. She felt him draw a long breath.

"I wish things were easier here for you, Mother," he said. "Maybe if you took the boys and stayed a few days in New York . . ."

Before she closed the door, Mary looked back.

He was studying the map again.

Thirty-one

TALKING TO Mr. Lincoln one morning, Mary suggested that they give a dinner for Cabinet members and their wives. They had had no company for a long time.

"I believe a party would do us all good," she said.

After the long dull drag of summer, it was nice to have something to plan for. Mrs. Keckley was to make a new gown for Mary.

On the morning before the party, Mary tried on the dress for a last fitting. While Mrs. Keckley knelt beside her, pinning and snipping, Mary talked more cheerfully than she had in weeks. A thunderstorm the night before had cooled the air. The trees looked fresh and green again. The earth smelled sweet.

Tad and Willie, quiet for once, were playing checkers on the sewing-room floor.

Mary had decided to make the dinner a larger affair. She had ordered the caterers from New York again, and it seemed a pity to go to all the trouble for only the Cabinet.

"Mr. Lincoln needs cheering up," Mary said. "And he always enjoys a party, though he does fuss about having to dress for it."

She lifted her arm, so that Mrs. Keckley could adjust the waistline.

"What do you hear from your son these days, Mrs. Keckley? You told me he was in Tennessee, didn't you?"

Mrs. Keckley drew a basting shorter, stroking the gathers with a pin.

"Could you turn just a shade, Mrs. Lincoln? There—that's right. No, my son has left Tennessee. He's in the army now."

"Really?" Mary looked down in surprise.

Mrs. Keckley nodded. "He enlisted two months ago—in Ohio." She hesitated. "They put him in a white company. He says the men are very friendly."

"I should think you must be anxious about him."

Mrs. Keckley nodded again, quietly. Just at first, she said, she had been disappointed to have him interrupt his schooling. Now she was more used to the idea.

"When I told Mr. Lincoln, he said I ought to feel very proud. He said—" Mrs. Keckley paused to gather up the pins and cushion, "that we must all learn to be anxious in these times. And then, of course, I'd expect my son to do whatever he thought was right, no matter how I felt about it."

"Yes," Mary said. "Yes, I suppose so." She turned to look into the long mirror. The dress looked lovely. Yet somehow the pleasure had gone out of the moment. Mr. Lincoln had praised Mrs. Keckley for letting her son go into the army. Did that mean he thought Robert should enlist, as so many college boys were doing? She brushed the thought away quickly.

"The dress is beautiful, Mrs. Keckley," she paused. "I hope you'll let me know when you have news of your son."

"Indeed I will, Mrs. Lincoln. It's kind of you to be interested."

Mary watched Mrs. Keckley brush the silk ravelings from her neat black skirt. Her only son two whole months in the army, Mary thought, and she had never mentioned it.

Except to Mr. Lincoln.

From the look of things, Mary reflected, the dinner was starting out well. She smiled graciously at Mr. Seward on her right. He was looking quite agreeable. His sharp eyes and long nose seemed less noticeable than usual.

Mr. Chase, on her left, was bland and impassive. She saw him eying the centerpiece, a concoction of white sugar doves and icing roses, topped by a gilded eagle with spread wings.

Conversation generally was going well. Looking down the candlelit table, Mary saw that Mr. Lincoln was telling a story. At the laugh that went up when he finished, Mary smiled. She'd been right to think a party would do him good.

"Miss Kate seems to have positively thrived on our wretched summer weather," Mary said to Mr. Chase. "She looks charming tonight."

It was after the entree that the general spirits showed signs of sagging. The evening had turned miserably warm. Beads of perspiration glistened on Mr. Chase's forehead. Mr. Seward stared at his plate as though his tussle with stuffed breast of guinea hen had left him quite exhausted.

Mary searched desperately for a fresh topic of conversation.

Suddenly the voice of a senator, midway down the table, boomed out. Had anyone ever heard of anything more outrageous, the senator demanded, than the uppityness of the free Negroes in the city lately? You wouldn't believe it, but there had even been some sort of scalawag notion of Negroes setting up a school for themselves.

The general lethargy, stirred by the senator's vehemence, gave way to a flurry of murmurs.

"Absurd," said someone.

"Too, too preposterous."

There was a pause, then the delicate voice of Miss Kate, came clearly down the table.

"Do tell us more, Senator." Miss Kate bent toward him. "I'm sure Mrs. Lincoln will be particularly interested." Her smile, flicking Mary's glance for an instant, was barbed. "I believe Negroes have their rights, quite as other people have. But one is hardly expected to invite Negroes to take tea with one. Don't you agree Mrs. Lincoln?"

For an instant, while everyone turned to look at her, Mary could feel her cheeks flaming. She saw the long row of faces, waiting expectantly, and the centerpiece with its sugar roses that had begun, ever so slightly, to melt.

"Judging from some of the people who *are* asked to tea in the best Washington circles," Mary said, "I think one might do a great deal worse."

Miss Kate's smile remained serene. "That's very witty, Mrs. Lincoln. I'm afraid, all too true. But quite seriously, I wonder if we aren't making a mistake to let the Negroes feel that this war is being fought for them. In all fairness to *them*, I mean. One wouldn't want them to get an exaggerated sense of their importance." She turned to the other end of the table. "Do you think I'm right, Mr. Lincoln?"

Mary held her breath, waiting for his answer.

Mr. Lincoln folded his hands. All the way down the table Mary heard his knuckles crack.

"It seems to me, Miss Kate," his tone was mild, "it's like worrying in a tug of war for fear the rope might get to feeling too important. It's important, all right—but whichever side wins, I don't know that the rope expects to get much fun out of it."

A little past eleven Mary went upstairs. After the incident at the dinner table, conversation had been strained and difficult, and Mary, watching the party slowly crumble into boredom, had felt helpless to revive it.

She climbed the stairs slowly, too tired to care that the dinner had been a failure. A headache, that had begun dully early in the evening, had grown into a drumming throb of weariness.

She was halfway down the hall when a sound from the boys' room made her pause. They must surely have been asleep long ago. Mary opened the door just in time to see Taddie hurl himself from the foot of his bed with an ear-splitting scream.

The room was in wild disorder. Sheets were dragged off the beds, a chair was upset, and Taddie, in his nightshirt, danced up and down over the prostrate form of Willie.

"*Boys!*" Mary's voice cut through the noise.

Taddie turned, his eyes blazing with excitement. "We're playing war, Mamma. Look—Willie is dead now. He's a Johnny Reb, and I've shooted him dead. Be dead, Willie. You're *dead*."

Willie, on the floor, writhed convulsively. "O-oo-oh, I'm dead. Help, help, I'm dead—"

"Look—Willie is dead!" Tad's scream was ecstatic. "Now I'm going to shoot his head off with a big cannon." He leaped onto the bed and took aim. "BANG, BANG, BANG! Look, Ma—"

Willie's foot caught the leg of a table that held a vase and sent it crashing to the floor. Mary made a quick move. She yanked Willie to his feet. Just as his outraged howls were added to the din, Mr. Lincoln appeared in the door.

"*Papa!*" Both the boys hurled themselves on Mr. Lincoln. "Papa—Papa, Mamma *hurt* Willie." In a burst of sympathetic wails, Taddie buried his head against his father's knees. "Mamma *hit* Willie—and she hurt him, Papa—"

"Hush, Willie." Mr. Lincoln's voice was mild. Over the boys' heads, he surveyed the room. The stripped beds, the upset chair and table, the broken vase and scattered flowers.

"Well, Mother," he said, "it looks as if the war has reached us at last."

When Mr. Lincoln came into her room, Mary didn't look up. She lay across the bed, the new dress crushed beneath her.

"The boys are all right now, Mother," Mr. Lincoln said. "I got them to bed."

Mary didn't answer.

"Willie was sorry about the vase. I don't suppose he meant to break it." Mr. Lincoln paused. "I guess all the fuss over the party was too much for you . . ." His voice was kind, a little puzzled.

Mary didn't move. In the silence she could feel him standing beside her. There had been a hundred times when she had lain awake, and wished she might look up to find him beside her. Times when she tried desperately to reach him through the frightening loneliness.

Now he was here and she could find no words. There was no use trying to speak of the long nights, and the dreads that came like shapeless mists. No use to ask for comfort. No use to speak of the party that had gone so flat and wretched. She might have liked to thank him for standing up for her, answering Miss Kate. But he'd say she was imagining things.

She lay still. Let him think it was only the heat, and being tired, that made her like this.

He waited a minute longer. "Well, you'll feel better tomorrow, Mother, when you've had a good sleep."

He touched her shoulder before he went out, closing the door carefully behind him.

The next morning at breakfast Mary said, "I think you're right, Mr. Lincoln. The boys and I need a vacation."

They might spend a few weeks at Saratoga Springs. The early autumn was the pleasantest time of year to travel. Saratoga wouldn't be too crowded, and she might try the waters. On the way home, they could stop in New York. Perhaps Robert could join them for a visit.

But when the moment came, a few days later, to say good-bye, Mary clung to Mr. Lincoln, weeping.

"I can't go, Mr. Lincoln. Please don't make me. Let me stay with you, please. I'll be better, I promise."

She heard his voice, mild and surprised.

"Now, Mother, there's nothing to feel so bad about. You and the boys will have a fine time and you'll be home again before you know it."

On the train, Mary leaned back. As they pulled out of the station, through the flat, bedraggled outskirts of the city, she sat motionless, lulled by the steady clack of the wheels. They gained speed, rolling north, and the low green hills began to appear. Mary straightened.

At the Springs, where the nights were cool, she would surely sleep. And when they came back, everything would be different. She could try again. Things would be better. They needn't stay away long. Only until she was rested. Then she could begin again . . .

Thirty-two

IT WAS late October when Mary came back to Washington. The weeks had passed quickly at the Springs, with the waters in the morning and a drive every afternoon on the smart promenade past the United States Hotel with its millionaires' piazza where Commodore Vanderbilt sat, and young Jim Fisk with kiss-curls on his forehead.

It was pleasant to dress every night for dinner, and to hear voices and music and laughter, and no talk of war. To sit on the verandah, while the boys went pony riding, and listen to the latest gossip. Gossip about Jim Fisk and Mr. Astor and Madame Jumel with her wigs and parasols and laces and airs. Gossip that had nothing to do with Washington.

At first Mary had worried about Mr. Lincoln. But he wrote often and assured her that he was delighted to hear that she and the boys were enjoying themselves. He was getting on all right. The only sad news he sent was the information that Mrs. Keckley's son had been shot in a skirmish with rebel troops on the Tennessee border, and had died a few days later of a fever that had developed from the wound. Mrs. Keckley had borne the loss with courage and fortitude, though it was an over-whelming blow—and she had begged him not to tell Mary, for fear it would mar the pleasure of her holiday. But he had thought she would want to know.

Mr. Lincoln was at the station to meet them when they ar-rived in Washington. Seeing him come down the long plat-form, Mary was struck, even before they were close enough to speak, by the change in his appearance. Surely his shoulders hadn't been so stooped, nor the lines set as deeply around his mouth.

He was glad to have them home again, and pleased to see Mary looking rested and well.

"You look very grand in your new feathers, Mother," he said, admiring the bonnet she had bought in New York. He swung the boys up to his shoulder, pretending to groan over their weight, and for once Mary was grateful for his ability to act as though the past simply didn't exist. But driving up the avenue, Mary kept turning to look at Mr. Lincoln, conscious again of a subtle difference.

It wasn't long before Mary discovered that Mr. Lincoln wasn't the only person who had changed while she was gone. There was a new spirit in the city, a settling down to the grim business of war that showed itself in a hundred ways. Social feuds and scandals had been abandoned in favor of the far more diverting pastime of armchair strategy. Everyone, it ap-peared, had become a military expert overnight. Conversation nowadays was all of encampments, platoons, maneuvers, biv-ouacs.

"Washington," Mr. Lincoln said, "has decided to accept the war, after all. Even in the best families."

In its new phase of patriotism, the city was inclined to view the President with a more tolerant eye.

The first evening she and Mr. Lincoln went to the theater

together, Mary was astonished to see the audience rise and cheer when Mr. Lincoln stepped into the box.

General McClellan had taken General McDowell's place as commander of the Army of the Potomac.

McClellan was handsome and young, with a fiery eye and a great reputation for fearlessness. A rash of McClellan badges and pennants appeared everywhere. On lapels and hatbands, adorning ladies' muffs and tippets.

When Tad and Willie played soldier now, they wrangled bitterly over which one should have the honor of being "Little Mac."

"We have a novelty in office seekers today, Mother," Mr. Lincoln said one morning. He handed Mary a letter dated from Springfield. Ninian Edwards had written to say that he had suffered severe business losses during the past months. He was close to bankruptcy. Was there any possibility of an opening in a government appointment for which Mr. Lincoln would think his qualification suitable? He hesitated to ask for favors, but at Elizabeth's suggestion he ventured to write.

Mary looked up from the letter. "What do you intend to do for him?"

"Whatever I can," Mr. Lincoln said.

A few days later Mr. Lincoln told Mary that Ninian had been offered a captain's commission, in charge of commissary distribution for the Springfield area.

❋✿❋✿❋
Thirty-three
⋁⋁⋁⋁⋁⋁

It was a regular thing nowadays for visiting regiments to be entertained at the White House. One afternoon, talking with a group of Massachusetts volunteers, Mary discovered that a number of them were former Harvard students. Young Oliver Wendell Holmes was among them, a soft-spoken lad with a good wit and admirable manners. Another handsome boy was a grandson of Paul Revere. Some of them, Mary learned, had recently left their classes to join up.

Afterward, Mary spoke to Mr. Lincoln. "These boys are enlisting," she said. "But Robert mustn't be allowed to. He has his education to finish. Besides, it wouldn't be fair—Robert would be in far greater danger than the others, being the President's son . . . You must forbid Robert to go, Mr. Lincoln," she said.

He turned from the window. "Robert is a grown man, Mary. He will decide for himself, just as these others did."

"Robert isn't the only one to be considered. There are other reasons—"

"There are always other reasons, Mother. If we considered all the other reasons, we'd have no soldiers in the army."

"Yes—yes, I know, Mr. Lincoln. But this is different—"

Mr. Lincoln shook his head. "It's not different," he said.

General Scott was being retired. There was a dinner for him at the White House. McClellan was there, with gold braid and polished boots.

Mary was troubled and sorry to see old Scott go. He sat next to her at dinner, his grizzled countenance sleepy and impassive while McClellan spoke with a great display of energy and courage about his future plans for the army.

When Mary told General Scott he would be sadly missed in the Capital, the old man roused himself and turned to look at her.

"I can't say I'm sorry to go," he said. "They've given me everything I could require for my last days—even a successor."

Mary saw him glance down the table at McClellan.

"I only hope," Mary said, "your successor will be worthy of you."

The old man sighed. A sigh that was half a yawn.

"I'm too old for anything," he said, "even opinions."

At four o'clock one rainy morning in November, General Scott left Washington. He had received the thanks and tribute of Congress and the President. General McClellan came to see him off, muffled in a heavy cape, dramatic as always, as he clattered down the avenue in the pitch dark and the beating rain.

Surrounded by his cavalry officers, sneezing and shivering in their dripping uniforms, McClellan stood in the drafty station, trying not to show his impatience to see old "Fuss and Feathers" on his way. General Scott shook hands with them all. He puttered about, seeing to his luggage, sending courteous wishes to Mrs. McClellan and the baby.

With General Scott gone, McClellan was in full swing. Mr. Lincoln spoke to him one day.

"We have put a terrible lot on you now."

McClellan smiled quietly. "I can do it all."

Once, when the President was kept waiting for an appointment with McClellan, Mr. Hay protested the general's cavalier behavior.

"Never mind," Mr. Lincoln said. "I'll hold McClellan's horse if he'll bring us a victory."

Christmas came, and Tad and Willie hung their stockings over the mantel in the south parlor.

The first snow fell over the camps where McClellan's army waited. There had been another victory for the South at Ball's Bluff. Surely soon McClellan would be ready to begin. But McClellan still called for more time, and troops and money and supplies poured down from the North to disappear across the Potomac into silence.

All quiet along the Potomac, people said. All *too* quiet. But for the most part they were still content to pin their faith to McClellan's star.

The weeks went on, and winter settled in. The country waited.

Mary held, from day to day, her truce with fate.

Thirty-four

MARY WORKED regularly at the hospital now. One raw February afternoon she came home to find that Willie was feverish and had been put to bed by Mrs. Keckley. She hurried to his room. Willie was sitting up, a red wool sock wrapped around his throat. He was entertaining Taddie with a long, excited story about a little lame robin who couldn't fly south when the other robins did, and would have starved and frozen except for the sparrows, who brought him food and gave their feathers to make him a warm cover.

Taddie caught Willie's cold, and for several days Mary was hardly out of their room. She read to them, rubbed their chests with camphor, dosed them with herb tea, and scolded Tad for hopping out of bed in bare feet.

"I'm afraid poor Taddie has taken it the worse of the two," Mary told Mr. Lincoln. "He's like Robert—these things always go to his lungs."

Taddie was a troublesome invalid, complaining loudly when he felt badly and bursting into irrepressible spirits the moment he showed signs of improving.

Keep them quiet, the doctor had told Mary, and they would be all right in a few days. But there was no keeping Tad quiet. He squirmed and fussed and bounced until by evening he had brought on the fever and was coughing worse than ever.

One night Taddie was crying and restless. Mary sat by the bed stroking his hot forehead and telling him stories until he fell sleep. When she rose, stiff and chilled, to go back to bed, she paused to bend over Willie and was surprised to find him awake, looking up at her.

"Do you feel badly, Willie?"

He shook his head.

"I was just listening to the story you told Tad," he said.

Unless Taddie was better by morning, Mary told Mrs. Keckley, she meant to have the doctor again. But when he woke, the fever was broken. Mary sighed with relief. By afternoon both boys were so much improved that she went for an hour's drive, breathing the misty winter air gratefully after a week indoors.

That evening at dinner Mary spoke cheerfully to Mr. Lincoln about the White House reception planned for the following week. It was to be the largest affair of the season. All the diplomatic corps was invited. The Marine Band would play for dancing.

Two days before the reception Taddie was up and out, quite well again. But Willie was still in bed. His cold was better, but he remained white and listless. Mary questioned him anxiously. Was he in any pain? No. Was there anything he wanted? Willie hesitated. Nothing special, he said, only it would be nice to see his pony.

"So you shall, dear." Mary was touched by the politeness of the small voice. So unlike Taddie's stormy demands. "Tomorrow morning, if you're better, Papa will carry you to the window, and Taddie can ride the pony right onto the lawn where you can see him."

That night Mary was wakened by Taddie calling. She hurried across the hall to find Tad sitting up, huddled in his nightshirt.

"Something's wrong with Willie, Mamma. He keeps saying funny things and when I talk to him he doesn't answer."

Willie was awake, but when Mary bent over the bed he pulled away from her touch. His skin was dry as scorched paper.

"Is Willie very sick, Mamma?" Tad leaned over from his bed. "Will he have to take medicine again?"

Mary went to call Mrs. Keckley. They stood together looking down at Willie in the shaded lamp light.

"It may be only the fever working out of him," Mrs. Keckley said. "I've seen it this way—and in the morning it may be quite gone."

In the morning Willie's fever had not broken. The doctor came, and looked grave. The cold had gone into the chest, he said. There was nothing they could do but watch and wait.

At the doctor's words fear plunged into Mary's heart. She looked at Willie. He twisted fretfully, trying to say something, but his voice was choked and unfamiliar. Through a rush of tears Mary bent and gathered him in her arms, begging him to tell her what he wanted.

Over Mary's head the doctor looked at Mrs. Keckley. It might be best, he said, to have a nurse for Willie. Then Mrs. Lincoln would have a chance to rest. In a case like this, it was often better for the mother to stay away as much as possible. The slightest emotion, however natural, could be upsetting.

Mary looked up. "I won't have a stranger," she said quickly. "No one understands Willie as I do. No one else will take the same care of him . . ."

The doctor looked at Mary curiously for a moment. Then he stood up and closed his bag. He would come in again toward evening, he said. Then they'd see.

When the doctor was gone, Mary still knelt by the bed.

Willie was quieter now. She smoothed the tangled hair back from his forehead. They wanted to push her away, she thought. But she wouldn't let them. Not when Willie needed her.

Late in the afternoon Mr. Lincoln came in and sat by Willie's bed, watching.

A little past midnight Mary hurried into Willie's room. She had wakened from a heavy sleep, fancying she heard him call. But he lay quietly. The night light threw vague shadows on the wall. There was no sound but a hoarse breathing.

Suddenly the anxious waiting was more than she could bear. She went to find Mr. Lincoln. He was still dressed and reading.

"Mr. Lincoln, I'm so frightened about Willie—" she drew her blue robe closer and shivered. "There must be something we can do, Mr. Lincoln. Isn't there something?"

She spoke almost as if she were one of the strangers who came to him for help. She had seen them waiting outside his office, standing patiently, their faces heavy with trouble or grief, trusting him to somehow make things right.

Mr. Lincoln stood up and took off his spectacles.

"Come here, Mary," he said.

They faced each other in the circle of lamp light.

The night silence made everything strange and unfamiliar, yet they were closer than they had been in a long time. Mr. Lincoln talked. His words were simple. There was nothing momentous, no magic wisdom in what he said. But Mary was quieted. In the stillness of the room, in the sound of his voice and in his plain, worn face, she felt for a few minutes the strength and comfort he had given to so many.

At the doctor's insistence, next morning, a nurse was sent for. Mary made no protest. When the woman arrived, she watched Willie lie back, quiet under the sure, impersonal touch. She saw how docilely he took the spoonfuls of barley water he had refused from Mary.

All day Mary hovered in and out of the sickroom. Downstairs, the caterers were getting ready for the reception, spreading the long tables, clearing away furniture, taking charge in the kitchens. The florist's men arrived, bringing garlands of laurel and tubs of potted palms for the East Room.

Mary moved through the preparations in a dream, giving orders, making decisions mechanically. "Mr. Lincoln says it's too late to recall the invitations," she told Mrs. Keckley. "We must get through this somehow."

By evening, when it was time for Mary to dress, the doctor had come again. For the first time he said Willie was better. Mary went in one last time before going downstairs, to find Willie sleeping. His breathing was easier, and his cheeks felt cooler to her touch.

The nurse stood by the bed. The shaded light fell softly on the white satin of Mary's gown and caught the gleam of pearls at her throat and wrists.

"You look very handsome, ma'am."

Mary fancied she caught a trace of resentment in the woman's voice. No doubt she, like so many others, thought it out of place for the President's wife to be entertaining in satin and pearls while just beyond the river an army lay camped in the snow, without enough blankets to protect them from the damp and freezing night.

"This is the only reception we have had all winter," Mary said quickly. "I wish we needn't have had it at all but even in wartime the President is expected to entertain for the foreign diplomats."

"Naturally." The nurse smiled. She leaned down with a possessive gesture to smooth the sheet over Willie's shoulder where Mary's touch had disturbed it. "I only hope the noise of the dancing won't be too loud. It would be a pity, when I've coaxed the poor lamb into such a nice sleep."

Mary bit back a sharp answer. She turned to the nurse. "I promise you he won't be awakened," she said. "I gave orders this morning that there is to be no music."

The evening was a success. The embassy guests were elegant and gay. Light voices mingled with the rustle of fashionable silks and brocades in the palm-filled East Room. As one gentleman after another bent over her hand, Mary greeted them graciously. Her smile was fixed and bright. Through the sound of voices, her ear strained for a call from upstairs.

The Washington ladies were there in force, Mary observed. Even the cave dwellers. After a year of war the old sport of snubbing the President's wife had grown stale. The more exciting topics of battlefield strategy and the shortcomings of the generals had taken precedence at fashionable tea tables.

Kate Chase, charming in pale yellow brocade that set off the flame of her red hair, greeted Mary cordially. She asked kindly for news of the sick boy.

Mary was touched and grateful.

She made several more visits to Willie's room. Once she found Mr. Lincoln just leaving.

The nurse was encouraging. Willie was quiet. He had taken a bit more broth.

It was late when the last guests were gone. Mary and Mr. Lincoln went upstairs together. Mr. Lincoln took her arm.

"Well, Mother, it was a nice party. I was proud of you tonight."

The compliment, so rare from his lips, made Mary look up quickly.

Still together, they stopped one more time in Willie's room. He slept with his head turned to one side, the long lashes shadowing his cheeks. The nurse, wrapped in a comforter, drowsed by the night lamp.

Mary bent to touch Willie's forehead and straightened, meeting Mr. Lincoln's glance. Their eyes held, and in that moment something from all their years together hung between them. A hot summer night in Missouri, on a hill with the stars overhead, a bleak hopeless New Year's afternoon, the shabby rooms in the Globe Tavern, the morning when Robert was born, and the black night when little Eddie lay dead between them. The torchlight parade, the crowds, the handshaking, the roses for Mary. Willie's dead turtle.

For better for worse ...

❋❋❋❋

Thirty-five

∨∨∨∨∨∨

THE DAY after the party was gray and stormy. Mary stayed at
her desk in the morning, writing letters, while downstairs the
men carried away the extra chairs and dismantled the long
tables.

Willie wakened late, rested from the long sleep. When Mary
went in he asked if he could have his kitten please, to sleep on
the bed.

"Of course you may, dear. I'll send Taddie to fetch her
from the stables."

When Tad brought the kitten in, the nurse frowned. She
didn't like animals in a sickroom. They poisoned the air and
carried all manner of disease. The doctor would surely dis-
approve. Besides, the child was not to be excited. It might bring
on the fever again.

Mary hesitated. But seeing the light in Willie's eyes as he
reached out for his pet, she hadn't the heart to disappoint him.

"Just for a little while," she said, holding the kitten down for
Willie to stroke the gray fur. "Surely it can't do any harm,
when it pleases him so much."

By afternoon the sun had warmed the air with the false mild-
ness of early spring. Willie was sleeping again, his arm wrapped
contentedly around the curled-up kitten, and when Mr. Lincoln found an hour free from appointments and suggested a
drive, Mary felt safe in going.

It was dusk when they came home. The sun had vanished,
leaving a chill in the sharp wind. Edwards, opening the door,
stepped back quickly to avoid the draft. Mrs. Keckley had
brought a message from the nurse. Mrs. Lincoln was to go upstairs as soon as she came in.

Mary knew at once that Willie was worse. He had wakened
with a chill, the nurse said. Now the fever had taken a queer
turn.

"I don't like the looks, ma'm. I shouldn't be surprised if it's
going into the typhoid."

Mary knelt by the bed, still in her coat and bonnet. She
pulled off her gloves, rubbing her hands to warm them before
she touched Willie's blazing cheeks. This mustn't happen. It
couldn't. She spoke to Willie, coaxing him, but there was no
light in the dull eyes that stared back at her.

It was another hour before the doctor came—an hour while
Mary felt the strength drain out of her with every moan, every
restless spasm of the boy's thin body. She hardly knew when
the doctor had gone again, and Mr. Lincoln came to stand at
the foot of the bed, for a long while, in silence. Much later,
when they came and helped her to her feet to lead her across
the hall to her own room, she followed numbly, only partly
aware of Mrs. Keckley helping her undress, holding a cup of
hot milk to her lips.

Alone in the darkness, when they had left her to sleep, Mary
lay still. She hadn't noticed when they tiptoed out, or felt the
icy stiffness that crept slowly over her. She only knew that
Willie was dying.

Living the hours blindly, hardly knowing day from night,
Mary hovered between her room and Willie's. When they

said she must either control herself or else be forbidden to come into the sickroom, she would promise to be quiet. But the tide would rush over her, and she flung herself with fury against the fate that would take her child.

Mrs. Keckley watched by Willie's bed during the times when the nurse slept, and Taddie was left to roam the house. There was nowhere for him to go—nothing to do that wouldn't make a noise and disturb Willie. He wandered into his father's study and amused himself pulling colored pins out of the war maps and making paper hats out of the piles of letters stacked on the desk. There was a meeting of the cabinet one afternoon, and Taddie crawled under the long table. He was an Indian in the forest, and the circle of black-trousered legs were trees through which he peered at a skulking, stealthy enemy. At length Mr. Lincoln pulled Tad out and took him on his knee.

"It's hard on a little fellow, having to keep so quiet," Mr. Lincoln said to the gentlemen.

Dozing one night, in her chair by Willie's bed, the nurse roused to a faint sound. The door opened softly and Mr. Lincoln stood there.

He came near the bed.

When the nurse came back, he hadn't moved. "I've fixed some hot tea, sir. Why don't you take a little?"

"Thank you." Mr. Lincoln took the cup.

He stood holding it, not drinking. "This is the hardest trial of my life," he said. "I wish I knew why these things must come."

"Perhaps to make us better, sir."

He looked at her. "Do you really think that?"

"I know it, sir. I lost my own two children, and then my husband. But I can't feel bitter. It was God's hand that took them, and I've learned to love Him all the more."

He still looked at her. "Did you always feel like this?"

"No, not for a long while. But blow after blow came. And then I began to learn."

For a long while he didn't speak.

"I'm glad you told me," he said finally. He handed back the cup.

"But you haven't taken the tea, sir. Would you like some fresh?"

"No. But I'm grateful all the same."

The next evening, after the doctor left, Mary lay awake. She heard the sound of Mr. Lincoln's step. Back and forth. She had heard him walk like that in the nights after the news of battles. He had grieved then for other men's sons—now it was for his own. Back and forth. At the sound, Mary felt a swift, unreasoning resentment. In her own sorrow, sharp and immediate as a knife plunge, it hurt her to know that he had grieved as much for the others as he did now for his own. That he would mourn so for all who must die.

When she could hear his step no longer she went to the door and called.

"Mr. Lincoln, please come."

She went to him, sobbing. "Mr. Lincoln, Willie is dying. I know it. But they won't let me go to him. The doctor says I disturb him."

He answered patiently at first. She was worn out and overwrought. There was nothing she could do for Willie. If the nurse could keep him quiet . . .

When she made a move toward the door, Mr. Lincoln held her back.

"Mary," he said, "Mary—wait—"

His voice went straight to her heart. It was the only time she remembered his holding her, asking for her help. She reached toward him.

The next moment Mr. Lincoln spoke steadily.

"Go back to bed, Mother," he said. "I'll stay with Willie myself. You try to rest."

When Mary wakened later there was no sound in the darkness. She crossed to Willie's door, and stood listening a moment. Then she knocked, and heard Mr. Lincoln's answer.

"Mr. Lincoln, may I come in now?"

He opened the door and took her arm, not saying a word. He was still dressed, and Mary saw Mrs. Keckley sitting beside Willie. The nurse, busy at the bureau where the medicines were kept, did not turn. Mary went toward the bed. She sat down next to Mrs. Keckley. Willie's hand lay outside the covers, but she made no move to touch it. Holding herself very still, trying desperately to do right, Mary watched Willie's face—listening for his shallow breath.

She was there, motionless and dry eyed, when Willie died.

The thin gray light of dawn was at the windows when Mr. Lincoln came into Mary's room. There was a dry sound in her throat. Beyond her will, she heard the sound of her weeping. Through her tears she could see Mr. Lincoln facing her as he had that other night. But there was no strangeness in him, no strength or magic. She saw only her husband watching her helplessly.

"Go away," Mary flung herself against the pillow. "You don't understand. Go away and leave me."

"Mary—Mary, why do you torture yourself this way?"

"You can't know, Mr. Lincoln . . . You can never know . . ."

On the morning of Willie's funeral, Mary was too ill to go to the service. Mrs. Keckley was to stay with her. Before he went downstairs, Mr. Lincoln came in, wearing the black coat that had been new for his inauguration. He sat by the bed a few minutes. The lines were drawn deeply around his mouth. He sat quietly, his hands resting on his knees.

Mary closed her eyes, shutting out the sight of him. In the utter calm of his silence she felt reproached for the tempest of her own grief. If either of them could speak, she thought wretchedly, there might be some help. But there was a remoteness in his face, as if he had some secret understanding that held other mortals away. It was a wall against which her tortured spirit bruised itself.

After a while Mr. Lincoln stood up.

"There were people outside the house this morning, Mother," he said. "Some of them were kneeling—praying for us. They tell me that all over the country, when they heard the news, people prayed for us."

A bitter cry broke from Mary's lips.

"What good can their prayers do us, Mr. Lincoln? They can't help Willie—nor us—"

"I suppose they can't, Mother. All the same, I'm glad they prayed."

Thirty-six

THE AIR was moist with the smell of spring when Mary was able to be out again. She moved absently through the days, dressing herself, going through her mail with Mr. Stoddard, reading to Taddie. On pleasant afternoons, when Mr. Lincoln ordered the carriage, she drove with him. She tried to talk, to smile, to come back to the life of those around her.

"You must think of Mr. Lincoln," people had told her. "You have Taddie and Robert. You must be brave."

She listened to their voices, feeling only emptiness. They couldn't know that a world could die, leaving only bitter shadows. In the emptiness, like a brooding ghost, she saw her own failure. Even in her sorrow for her child she had failed again, somehow, so that they whispered about her, shaking their heads.

There was no escaping. She was bound to the bargain she had made. There was no going back.

The snowball of war rolled on, piling up its burden of defeat and misery, of treachery and jealousy and blood. There was trouble now between the new factions that wrangled and bickered for control. They were opposing McClellan more and more openly. He was slow, overcautious, worse even than old Scott had been. They complained to Mr. Lincoln, and Mary saw him harried and worried until it seemed his shoulders must break beneath the weight of malice and confusion heaped on him.

Only from the West was there any good news. A man named Grant had captured Fort Donelson from the Rebels. Later Mary heard that her brother Sam had been killed in the fighting, on the Confederate side.

Seeing how, in spite of all his anxiety, Mr. Lincoln still had time to be patient with her, Mary tried to respond. In little ways she tried to meet his kindness. But the strange listlessness that held her did not lift. She would look up out of a long silence and find his eyes on her, watchful and troubled. They were together more than they had been in a long while, talking of everyday things, of old times in Springfield—of anything that would not touch on the soreness of grief. They were friendly, considerate of each other—affectionate.

All the time, beneath the surface calm, Mary felt a dark gulf of silence widening between them. In the first days after Willie's death there had been no way to speak. The language of their suffering was too different. Now, as the silence lengthened, it was like a wedge, forcing them apart, driving deeper day by day, making them strangers who could only try to cover the loneliness with cautious phrases.

When summer drew near, Mary spoke of taking Taddie away with her. He ought to be out of the city—to have other children to play with.

"Perhaps we might try the seashore," Mary said. "Some quiet place, where no one knows us . . ."

"Whatever you think best, Mother," Mr. Lincoln said.

One afternoon Mary and Mrs. Keckley were in the sewing room. Mary had finished lengthening the sleeves of Taddie's jacket. She sat twisting the silver thimble on her finger.

"Mrs. Keckley," Mary said, "I wonder sometimes how you bore your trouble so bravely when your son was killed. It must have been very hard for you, and yet you never complained. I'm afraid we must have seemed not half sympathetic."

"I wasn't brave at all, really, Mrs. Lincoln. There were times, in the first weeks, when I felt as if I couldn't go on living. I don't believe I could have gone on if it hadn't been for Mr. Lincoln. But he seemed to understand everything and to comfort me. . . ." She was silent a moment. "I can never forget what he did for me."

Mary said nothing. She was thinking how often she had heard these words, from soldiers she talked to in the hospital, from the wives and mothers of other soldiers. *I can never forget how Mr. Lincoln gave me the courage to go on . . . Mr. Lincoln helped me when no one else could . . .* It was strange and bitter that he could give comfort so freely to these others. The strangers could still come close to him. But when she searched for their path, Mary knew that somehow she had lost the way.

There was a pleasant-faced young woman Mary had engaged early in the year to take charge of the household supplies. The woman worked well, minded her own affairs, and fitted into her position so unobtrusively that beyond an occasional glimpse, Mary was seldom conscious of her presence in the house.

One afternoon the woman brought tea to Mary's sitting room. The chambermaid was ill, and there was no one else to carry up the tray.

Mary thanked her, adding pleasantly that she hoped the woman was finding her work agreeable.

"Very satisfactory, thank you." The reply was prompt and courteous. She touched the tray, straightening a corner of the embroidered cloth. "You have such beautiful linens, Mrs. Lincoln, it's a pleasure to take care of them. I noticed a snagged thread in your lace tablecloth and I took the liberty of mending it."

Mary glanced up in surprise. She noticed that the woman's hands were soft, and the nails carefully trimmed and buffed. She made no comment, but, coming into Mr. Lincoln's study a few mornings later, when he was away, Mary was startled to find the woman standing before the rack where the war maps hung.

She turned as Mary entered, making an excuse about having come in to see whether the curtains needed laundering, and left the study quickly. That afternoon, Mary spoke to Mr. Lincoln.

"I don't like the way that woman acts, Mr. Lincoln. She's always snooping about, making excuses to come into our rooms."

"Now, Mother, there's no use imagining things," he said. "The woman's decent and well behaved, and she's got a nice face—"

"A nice face," Mary shrugged. "I believe that woman came here deliberately to spy on us, and I mean to find out who she is."

The next day Mary was informed by Mrs. Keckley that the woman had gone. She'd packed her things the night before, and walked out without a word to anyone.

Less than a week later Mr. Stoddard showed Mary an item in the newspaper. A woman, calling herself Edith Connell, had attempted to take a position as chambermaid in the home of the Secretary of State. Having become suspicious of the woman's manner and appearance, Mr. Seward ordered her to be investigated, and the woman had been identified as the widow of a Confederate officer who had been killed at Bull Run. Arrested and taken to the Old Capitol prison, she admitted that she had recently been employed by Mrs. Lincoln as a servant. Sufficient evidence in the form of letters and maps had been found in her possession to convict the woman as a spy.

"I haven't mentioned this to the President," Mr. Stoddard said.

"Then don't." Mary handed back the paper.

Years ago she had learned that there was no satisfaction in saying "I told you so" to Mr. Lincoln.

The incident strengthened Mary's determination to be rid of the steward who was in charge of the White House servants and supplies. She dismissed the man personally without consulting either Mr. Stoddard or the President.

Mr. Stoddard was alarmed. The steward had held his position through several administrations. He could make things very disagreeable if he chose to take revenge by spreading gossip about the President's household. And there would be plenty of ears in both social and political circles all too eager to listen.

Mr. Lincoln took no notice of the change except to observe, after a few weeks of meals planned and supervised by Mary, that the cook seemed to be improving.

Mary, for once, was content to say nothing.

Before Mary left for Narragansett, Adelina Patti was in Washington. Mr. Lincoln had heard Patti sing once, at a concert in New York, and had met her afterward at a reception. He asked to invite Patti to the White House.

Mary knew he was making another effort to distract her. She smiled at him, trying to rouse herself from the listlessness that still hung over her empty days. "I'll ask her for tea if it would please you, Mr. Lincoln," she said.

The afternoon Patti came, Mary was late coming downstairs. She found her guest in the East Room talking to Mr. Lincoln. Mary paused a moment on the threshold. She had dressed carefully, taking extra pains to look well.

Patti was charming. Slender and young, she wore wine-colored silk, and a tricorn bonnet of ostrich plumes that curled around her fresh, pretty face.

It was the first time in weeks that Mary had entertained a

stranger, but Patti was so friendly and unaffected that the conversation went easily.

When tea was finished, Patti smiled at them. "I've had a lovely time," she said. "I should like to thank you. I can't tell clever stories, as Mr. Lincoln does—" she spread her hands— "but if it would please you I can sing."

She crossed to the gilt piano.

From her place by the tea table, Mary listened to the lovely voice that rose and swelled until it filled the room as effortlessly as the late afternoon light that streamed in the long windows. The light fell on the crimson curtains, on the graceful curve of the singer's throat, on a bowl of deep-red roses that stood on the piano. It shone on Mr. Lincoln's face and on the stiff folds of Mary's black silk dress.

The song ended, and Patti paused, letting her hands rest on the keys. Then, more softly, she began again. "The Last Rose of Summer" . . . Her young voice was full and tender on the melody. When it was done, the sweet notes died in the silence.

Mary had left her chair and gone to the window. She stood looking across the lawn, her back to the room, and she did not turn when the singer rose from the piano. She heard Mr. Lincoln saying something in a low voice, then Patti's soft exclamation of dismay.

They knew she was weeping, Mary thought, even though she had made no sound. She could hear them going toward the door. Still she did not turn. Mr. Lincoln would make her excuses. . . . They would think she had wept because of the song—and Willie. They would be understanding and considerate, and they would pity her. But they couldn't know that she wept for something more. For a sadness she could not understand—for the bitterness of a world gone hopelessly wrong.

++*+*+*
Thirty-seven
ΛΛΛΛΛΛΛΛ

THAT SUMMER the North was defeated at Gaines Mill.

Later, in August, there was a second disastrous battle at Bull Run. At Gaines Mill the Union troops had been within sight of Richmond. For a few days there was hope in the North, then the furious onslaught of Stonewall Jackson's brigade turned the tide and McClellan's advance into Virginia was ended.

Washington, accustomed now to defeat, took the news with glum calm. But Mary, home from a visit with Taddie to the seashore, was dismayed to find that even in the bitter weeks while the army of the North was being beaten back, the politicians and the generals still played their old jealous game; wrangling for power and blaming each other for each new failure.

"It goes badly with us," Mr. Lincoln admitted. "The lessons of war are hard to learn. But if we can stay on God's side, we may learn them yet."

"It seems to me, Mr. Lincoln," Mary said, "that one good general could help more than God just now."

"I expect so," Mr. Lincoln sighed. "But until we can lay our hands on the right man, we'll have to struggle along with the Almighty."

Less than a week later came the news of Antietam. At last it was a victory for the North—but McClellan had succumbed to one of his fits of caution at the crucial moment and let Lee and Jackson escape with their exhausted troops and retreat to safety unpursued.

Coming down to dinner after a meeting of the Cabinet, Mr. Lincoln sat staring at his plate.

Mary watched him. "They've been at you again, Mr. Lincoln," she said. "I can tell from your expression."

"Well, partly at me, and partly at each other. And between times they were picking on the generals."

Mary put down her fork. "If I were you, I shouldn't put up with their quarreling another day."

"I don't know what else I can do, Mother. I can't very well stay away from the Cabinet meetings, the way Seward does when things don't go to his taste."

"*Seward—*"

Mr. Lincoln smiled, in spite of his weariness. "The way you say that name makes it sound as if there were no worse word in the English language—unless maybe it would be the way you can say *Chase.*"

"Or *Stanton—*" Mary said. She made a face mimicking Stanton's so perfectly that they both laughed.

Months before, when Cameron had resigned and Mr. Lincoln had appointed Stanton as the new Secretary of War, Mary had been indignant.

"For pity's sake, Mr. Lincoln," she had demanded, "must you forever pick men who despise you? Stanton snubs you and talks against you. Mr. Stoddard says Stanton calls you a gorilla."

"But if I were to choose only my admirers for the Cabinet," Mr. Lincoln had said, "I might not have enough to go around."

Now Mary learned that Stanton was urging Mr. Lincoln to

get rid of General McClellan and get some action into the war.

"Stanton is right, Mr. Lincoln," she nodded.

He looked up. "You sing a different tune on Stanton these days, Mother. I thought you didn't trust him."

"I'd sing a hundred different tunes if it would end the war sooner."

Mr. Lincoln was still doubtful. "If I fire McClellan, there's no one to take his place," he said. "Besides, I've heard McClellan is the only one of our generals the Rebels have any respect for. They call old Burnside 'the Tortoise,' but they admit McClellan takes watching."

"That's something in his favor, I suppose," Mary said. "If he can't be respected by his own side, it's nice to think that the enemy approves of him. Still and all, Mr. Lincoln, it's a sorry picture."

"Don't give up yet, Mother," Mr. Lincoln started upstairs. "It's like a preacher I heard once. The first week his first sermon was called 'Hell.' The next Sunday it was 'Hell Continued.'"

Mr. Lincoln went up to Sharpsburg to have a look at McClellan's headquarters.

"Everything was in fine order," he told Mary gloomily when he got home. "McClellan keeps his camp neat as a whistle. All the guards wore nice white gloves. They bowed me in with wonderful style. Little Mac makes them polish their boots every morning and stand as straight as wooden soldiers . . ." He paused. "Sometimes, I'm afraid, they're just about as harmless."

But Mr. Lincoln had enjoyed being with the men. There were some rebel prisoners in the camp. "They were fine-looking boys," he told Mary. "I was afraid they might bear me a grudge, but they seemed willing to have me come in and shake hands."

Several of the captured soldiers had been members of Stonewall Jackson's brigade. Mr. Lincoln had asked them questions about their commander.

"A surprising thing they told me," Mr. Lincoln said, "was that Jackson makes his soldiers kneel down and pray with him, and they don't mind doing it." He rubbed his chin. "I'd swap all the supplies in the Union army for one general who could get his men to follow him like that."

The best the Union could do was to spin the wheel and try a new general at the top. Less than a week after Mr. Lincoln's return from the camp, General McClellan was relieved of his command, and old Burnside was the only successor whose record was so uneventful that everyone could agree on him.

"It seems a pity," Mary said, when she heard the news, "that we must choose our commanders for their harmlessness."

Winter set in early. As the days grew short, and the sun shone pale, the hopes in the North congealed like the mud in the frozen streets. With only old Burnside to look to, people said the chances of beating the Rebs seemed mighty thin.

In December, after a week of cold, mean rain, Burnside finally attacked at Fredericksburg. But Lee and Jackson rallied. Refreshed by the long interval since their retreat from Antietam, they carried the day.

Another victory for the South.

A pall of despair hung over Washington. For three days after the battle, the wounded poured into the city. The hospitals overflowed. Those who could not be cared for were left on stretchers or huddled on park benches.

Mary could no longer bear to look out of the windows that faced Lafayette Square. The wounded lay in endless rows—so many that there was no way to help them.

"Close the blinds," she told Mrs. Keckley.

The blinds could not shut them out. Mary paced her room,

seeing nothing, hearing nothing but the sight and sound of suffering just across the square.

One afternoon there was a knock at her door. A caller was waiting for Mrs. Lincoln, the maid said. The caller was a Miss Orville.

Mary went down, gathering her strength with each step, to the Red Room where she found Miss Orville. The young woman rose quickly.

"I hesitated to call, Mrs. Lincoln," Miss Orville said, "knowing the loss you have suffered. But I must tell you that schools for our colored children in Washington have been started. And how grateful we are to you."

Mary answered slowly. "How can you thank me?" she said. "There was so little I could do. I tried, but everyone told me I must be cautious—*cautious*. I couldn't really help you . . ."

Miss Orville answered quietly: "You gave us encouragement when we needed it, Mrs. Lincoln. You gave us more help than you knew."

Miss Orville's words had a new meaning for Mary. Since Willie's death she had given up her work at the hospital. Now she went back, wanting to help, but she found everything confusing. It was very different from the leisurely mornings when she had rolled bandages and scraped lint. Then there had been time to talk with the patients, to help them write letters. Now every inch of space was jammed with beds. Men lay on the floor or in the corridors. Only the most desperate cases were treated at all.

In the midst of such suffering need, Mary found, ironically, that there was nothing for her to do. People brushed past her, too busy and tired to stop. She managed to find bottles of water, and a cup, but many of the men were too weak to drink. Others moaned in delirium or turned their faces away, with teeth clenched to choke back their moans.

After hours of being jostled about, feeling in everyone's way, Mary left the hospital, feeling drained and ill by the sight and sound of so much pain that she was powerless to help.

Driving home, she leaned back in the carriage, her head and eyes aching, her ears ringing with the men's pitiful cries. When the coachman reined the horses sharply, she looked up. A wagon train of wounded was crossing in front of them to Lafayette Square.

"Dear God, no more," she breathed aloud.

But the procession seemed endless. Ragged, shivering, filthy, the men were unloaded from the springless ambulances that had brought them over the miles of rutted roads from Fredericksburg. Unloaded, like so many head of butchered cattle, to lie in the cold, the stretchers lined in rows across the square.

Suddenly Mary leaned forward. She saw a small woman in a long gray cloak, moving among the men. A wagon of supplies was drawn up in the street, from which the woman carried food and water and a hamper of medicines and bandages. Followed by two rough-looking orderlies, she went from stretcher to stretcher, bending briefly over each. One of the orderlies, following close behind, carried a basin and sponges. Mary saw how the woman washed the mud from the men's faces, caked as hard as turtleshells. She watched the woman's motions, calm and skillful, taking no time to linger over the wounded, speaking only a word, or giving a low request to the orderly. The eyes of the men followed her progress with silent patience.

Watching, drawing her fur mantle closer against the cold, Mary wished she dared offer to help the woman. But her experience in the hospital had made her cautious. She thought, with a twinge, that Mr. Lincoln would never have hesitated. He would have been among the men, talking to them. But it was a language Mary did not know.

She spoke to the coachman, telling him to take another way around the square . . . But in that instant her eye was caught by a young soldier on a stretcher by the edge of the park. Something in the line of his cheek and the way his dark hair fell over it was so startlingly like Robert that Mary felt her heart lurch.

Her hesitancy was forgotten. Giving a quick order, Mary got out of the carriage. Unmindful of the raw wind, or the curious stares of the men, she knelt on the frozen ground beside the wounded boy. There was no blanket over him. She saw that he had one leg shot away. The stump was wrapped in clotted bandages.

As Mary bent down, he turned his head weakly, and opened his dark eyes. In spite of the cold, his face burned with fever, but there was no delirium in his look, only an expression that wrung Mary's heart with its hopelessness. The boy's eyes closed again. He lay still, not even shivering. From under his long lashes, so like Robert's, tears rolled down his cheeks. Suddenly, the boy was not only Robert, but Willie and little Eddie. With the full tenderness of a mother, Mary took her handkerchief and wiped his tears away. The boy didn't move or look at her again.

Mary stood up. She turned, dazed, into a circle of curious faces. She heard a young soldier whisper, *"That's Lincoln's wife—"*

The lad stepped forward, touching his cap. He had one arm in a makeshift sling, and a dirty bandage on his forehead.

"Is there something I can do, ma'am?"

Mary looked at him. "I must get a blanket for this boy," she said. "It's very cold—"

The soldier stared. He said something about the others who lay in the wind, with no blankets either—but Mary didn't listen. She saw the woman in the gray cloak. The woman didn't glance at Mary. She was dipping slices of bread in a bowl of whisky, bending over each man in turn to feed him. When the woman was near enough, Mary spoke.

"Please," she said, "is there anything you can do for this boy? He's very badly hurt—"

The woman's eyes met Mary's, direct and unemotional. She showed no slightest sign of recognizing the President's wife. She turned to look down at the soldier.

"If he could just have a blanket," Mary said.

"There are no blankets." The woman's voice was low and well bred. "There's nothing I can do until they send me help from the hospital."

The woman moved on, calm, unhurried, and Mary was left. She glanced around once more. There must be someone, surely, who would do something . . .

A slight stir behind her made Mary turn. The next moment she was face to face with a tall, dark-haired gentleman who gazed at her with an expression of astonishment.

"My God, Mrs. Lincoln, what are you doing here?"

It was Senator Sumner, elegant in black broadcloth and beaver hat.

"Mr. Sumner, I'm so glad you're here—" Mary felt herself sway toward him. "You'll help me, won't you? Please—"

"Yes, of course." The senator's glance took in Mary's tear-stained face, her muddy skirt, and the circle of onlookers. "You must get back to your carriage, Mrs. Lincoln," he put his hand firmly on her arm.

Led toward the curb, Mary pulled back. She tried to explain about the boy. That she must help him.

There was nothing they could do, Mr. Sumner said, urging her on. The poor fellow was only one among so many . . . They were at the carriage. Perhaps, the senator suggested, if Mrs. Lincoln were alone, he might ride back with her. It was only natural that she should be upset by such harrowing sights . . .

Mary looked back one last time. The boy lay perfectly still, his eyes closed. If only he hadn't looked so like Robert.

"I'm sorry," Mr. Sumner said. "Was the boy," he hesitated, "someone you knew, Mrs. Lincoln?"

"No. Oh, no." Mary was vaguely conscious of something uncomfortable in the senator's glance.

"I thought perhaps," he said, "since the poor fellow was in Confederate uniform—"

Mary turned, her eyes blank. "Was he?" she asked. "I didn't notice. I don't wonder you hurried me away, Mr. Sumner. It must have been quite awkward—"

The senator cleared his throat. Mary saw his look of relief as they drew up before the White House door.

"Mr. Sumner," Mary said, "that woman in the gray cloak—who was she?"

"That was Miss Barton. Didn't you recognize her? I'm sure Mr. Lincoln has met her . . ." he stopped, aware of an odd silence.

Mary shook her head. She had heard of Clara Barton, but she had pictured a large and military figure—nothing like the small woman in gray with her quiet, genteel voice.

"I daresay the President has a great many visitors," the senator went on hastily. "Miss Barton's a remarkable woman, no doubt of that. A good many people think she has no business following an army right into the battlefield. But she's persistent as a horsefly, I've heard. Generally manages to get where she wants to." He paused again. "Most people seem to be pushed into war. A few, like Miss Barton, push themselves in. Either way, it's a miserable business. But I'm afraid there's nothing to be done about it."

"No, nothing," Mary agreed. "Except perhaps to thank God for someone like Miss Barton."

Thirty-eight

ON THE FIRST day of the New Year Mr. Lincoln signed the Emancipation Proclamation declaring all slaves free.

A few Sundays later, driving home from church with Taddie beside Mary, the carriage followed a train of army wagons jogging up the avenue.

"Are they going to a fight, Mamma?" Tad craned his head for a better view. "There's a lady in that wagon. Do ladies go to fight too?"

Mary followed Taddie's glance. Seated in the back of a canvas-covered ambulance, dressed in a gray cloak and bonnet was a woman Mary recognized.

"That's Miss Barton, Tad," she said. "She can go with the soldiers because she's a special person."

Taddie looked interested. "Will she have a gun, and kill Rebs?"

"No, she's a nurse. She'll take care of the soldiers who are hurt and try to make them well again."

"She won't try to make the Rebs well, will she?"

"I expect she will—when rebels fall prisoners on our side."

"Why?"

"Because she's a nurse, and a nurse's work is to take care of sick people, no matter whose side they fight on."

"But I thought we wanted all the Rebs to be dead. Bad people should be dead."

"Rebels aren't bad, Taddie. They're people—just like us."

"Do they have little boys at home?"

Mary nodded.

"Will the little boys be sorry if their papas get killed?"

"Yes. Very sorry."

"Then why do we shoot them?"

"Because we're at war. They are fighting us because they believe in things we think are wrong."

"Do they think they're wrong?"

"No."

"Will they think they're wrong if they get killed?"

"Oh—I don't know, Taddie. Perhaps not. It takes years and years sometimes for people to know whether they were wrong."

Taddie was silent. The wagon train ahead had slowed to a stop. As their carriage turned out to pass, Mary caught a closer glimpse of Miss Barton, her gloved hands folded in her lap as properly as though she were going for a Sunday drive.

That afternoon Mary was in her sitting room. She had ordered the carriage, hoping Mr. Lincoln would go for a drive. When she found he was working, she sent Tad and Mrs. Keckley in the carriage.

Mary picked up a copy of *Leslie's Weekly*. The house was very still. She turned the pages idly until the sight of her name caught her attention. An announcement, devoid of comment or explanation, read:

The reports that Mrs. Lincoln is in an interesting condition are untrue.

Mary smiled wryly. Grandmother Humphreys used to say that a lady's name would be seen in print only twice, once when she married and once when she died. In the event of a breach of taste against any lady in this regard, Grandmother Humphreys always added serenely, the lady's nearest male relative was under moral obligation to shoot the editor.

There were other magazines on the table. Mary knew well enough what the gushing society columns would report of the recent White House entertaining, including descriptions, complete with prices, of her newest purchases of gowns. There would be the inevitable reference to "the First Lady's gallant display of courage in brightening the Washington scene with gaiety despite the gloom and destruction of war that engulfed the nation. . . ."

Once she would have read the columns. She might have clipped a rare favorable paragraph to send Elizabeth. Now she pushed aside the pile and crossed to the window.

Looking down through the dusk, she watched a rising wind that searched the bare trees below. She wondered where Miss Barton was now. The wind must be cold, coming through the canvas flaps of an ambulance that jounced over rutted roads. Still—Mary's fingers toyed with the edge of Mr. Montrose's lace curtain—Miss Barton was somewhere.

Somewhere where she was needed.

EARLY ONE April morning Taddie bounced out of bed to look at the weather. This was the day—the wonderful, exciting day. Right after breakfast, they were to start out, he and Papa and Mamma, to visit General Hooker's headquarters. Fighting Joe Hooker, they called him, and it sounded like a very fighting name. He was the new general of the Army of the Potomac. They were going to stay a whole week in the camp, living in tents like the regular soldiers, eating in the barracks and watching drills. And they were going down the river by boat.

Looking out the window, Taddie was dismayed. The sky was full of swirling snow. Fat white flakes fell like cotton on the grass that had already begun to show bright green. Mamma would surely say they couldn't start out in snow. She'd say it was damp, and they'd all catch their deaths, and wipe her eyes the way she always did when she thought of Willie. She'd want the trip to be postponed. Worst of all, she might say Papa was to go on alone without them. One way or another, Taddie thought, Mamma was certain to make a fuss.

But no.

At the breakfast table there was only a little talk about the storm. Mamma, looking cheerful and nice, said it was sure not to last. Snow in April couldn't mean much, and they'd start as planned. Taddie curled his toes with happiness. Papa smiled too, though not as cheerfully as Mamma. He said they'd do just as Mamma wanted.

It was still snowing when the carriage pulled up at the front door. There had been a last wild argument with Mamma in the hall, over whether Taddie must wear his overcoat and scarf, and many warnings about racing around and getting overheated before going out in the damp air. Papa, coming down the stairs at the last minute with Mr. Hay following with three more papers to be signed, cocked an eyebrow at Taddie.

"You'd better do as Mother says, Tad, or we shan't get to go at all."

Papa hiked up one knee and signed the papers for Mr. Hay, and they were ready.

Safely started, squeezed in the seat between Papa and Mamma, Taddie squirmed around to wave at Mrs. Keckley on the steps. He'd bring her a pair of rebels' ears for a present, he shouted back. Mamma hushed him sharply, but with a face that showed she didn't really mean it, and Taddie settled back. The round, fat backs of the horses were steaming under the wet snow, and when they got to the dock the air was still thick with white flakes that fell into the gray river and disappeared.

The boat was wonderful. Full of little rooms with beds like shelves, and men who jumped around obeying orders and didn't seem to mind how many questions Taddie asked. They went slowly down the river, and when it got dark they decided to put into a cove and wait for morning. Taddie got to sleep on a shelf-bed in one of the little rooms.

Next morning the sun was warm. The snow and Taddie's overcoat were forgotten as he raced out on deck. When they reached the army camp in the afternoon all the officers were lined up smartly. General Hooker, who looked big and rather fierce, Taddie thought, made a great to-do when he met Papa, and kept talking all the time in a loud voice, as though he were afraid to stop. Every now and then the general looked at Mamma in a worried way. He would break off what he was saying to Papa about taking Richmond and say he hoped Mamma would find everything to her liking, and if not, please to say so.

Mamma, smiling, seemed pleased with the three tents that were ready for them. She said the wooden floors, which Taddie found disappointing, would keep out the damp. Taddie and Mamma would share one tent. Papa would take another. The third was where they would eat. Taddie had hoped to sleep with the soldiers, or at least with Papa, but Mamma shook her head firmly.

Once they were settled, General Hooker wanted Papa to look over the camp, and he said Tad might come along. There was a special horse ready for Taddie, and he rode beside Papa, who looked taller than ever, on a rawboned gray gelding, his long legs dangling, and his plug hat sticking up like a chimney. All the men they met seemed friendly and nice, coming out to shake hands, and once they were safely out of Mamma's hearing, General Hooker talked more and louder than ever. He said a great deal about how they would take Richmond in short order, and when he described what they would do to the Rebs, he used wonderful words that Taddie felt sure Mamma wouldn't approve of in the least. Papa talked very little, but he listened and watched everything while they rode along.

The next morning, when General Hooker asked Papa what he would like to do, Papa smiled.

"Well," he said, "Tad here has got an idea he'd like to see some rebels. If it would be possible, General, we'd appreciate it."

General Hooker looked surprised. He scratched his chin a minute and said he guessed they might manage. They rode down the river a little way. Then the general pulled in his horse and pointed across to the other side.

"There they are, son."

Taddie felt a jump of excitement, but when he looked where the general pointed, all he could see was some men in gray coats on the opposite bank. Several were standing together, leaning on their guns. Another, sitting cross-legged on the ground, was reading a newspaper. They certainly didn't look very dangerous.

Papa got off his horse and helped Taddie down, and took him by the hand. Taddie could see that Papa was watching just as curiously as he was. Just then the sitting-down soldier on the other shore jumped up and began to run down the hill toward them. Taddie's hand tightened in Papa's—but the next minute the soldier stopped. After he had stared at them a moment, he suddenly pulled off his cap and waved it. Then he kited back up the far bank and said something to the other Graycoats, and they turned and began to wave too.

Taddie couldn't understand it. Even from so far away he could see that the men were friendly and smiling. But they were Rebs, all right—he could see their silver buttons shining in the sun.

"What are they waving for?" Taddie asked.

General Hooker said he guessed the men had recognized Mr. Lincoln. "More than likely they knew you were coming down to the camp," he told the President. "When things are quiet for a few weeks, it's hard to keep the pickets from going back and forth to each other's lines. We give orders forbidding it, but they're forever swapping tobacco and newspapers. Those boys have probably heard about the President's visit."

Taddie looked up at the general, still puzzled.

"If they know who Papa is," he said, "why don't they shoot him?"

The general frowned and didn't answer, but one of the Union pickets standing near Taddie spoke up quickly.

"Why, they wouldn't do a thing like that, sonny," he said. "Those are fine fellows over there."

Papa had taken off his hat and was looking across at the men with a queer expression. He put up his hand and right away they waved again. Taddie tried it and they waved at him too. He could hear one of the men calling something. It sounded like "Hello, Abe—"

Riding back to camp, Papa kept on looking as though he were thinking about something, and Taddie noticed that he was quieter than ever when General Hooker began to tell again how they'd skin the Johnny Rebs and hang them on the apple trees when they got to Richmond.

Taddie guessed Papa must have been secretly a little disappointed, as he was, to find the Graycoats so tame.

On the third evening of the visit there was a special dinner planned for Papa and Mamma, and all day Taddie stewed and worried for fear Mamma wouldn't let him stay up for it. But when the time came, Mamma never said a word about bed. She only reminded Tad to be sure and come in a half hour early to get clean and put on his best suit. Mamma was dressed up herself, in a gray dress trimmed with shiny braid. She made him stand still while she fixed his tie and brushed his hair down flat with water. Then she hugged him and said he was a good boy, and he wasn't to forget his table manners or ask too many questions. It was funny, Taddie thought, how cheerful Mamma got when they were away from home.

When Mamma saw how they had fixed up the long tables for the dinner, she smiled at General Hooker and told him she'd hardly expected such a fine party. The general smiled too, and said he was pleased that she liked it, but Taddie noticed that his face seemed quite red, and he pulled at his collar every now and then, as though it were too tight.

There were tin cups at all the men's places, and while they ate, an orderly kept filling the cups from a brown bottle. Papa's cup seemed to be the only one that never needed filling, but he picked it up politely every time the general or one of his staff thought of another toast to someone, even though, when the men drank to "Burn Down Richmond" or "Hang Lee," Papa only touched his cup, and Taddie thought he looked sorry and not quite pleased. General Hooker seemed to enjoy these toasts most of all. He emptied his cup each time, while his face got redder and his collar tighter, and he talked to Mamma more loudly and more politely than ever.

They had oysters to eat, and steak and fried potatoes, and for dessert stewed peaches with a thick yellow cream that came out of cans and didn't taste nearly as good as it looked. Taddie was just finishing his peaches, feeling quite full, when a sudden commotion made him turn—and he saw the orderly, who had put down the brown bottle for a minute, carrying in a huge iced cake, decorated with ten fat, lighted army candles. The orderly put it in front of Tad.

Mamma stared in astonishment. How in the world, she asked General Hooker, had he found out that tomorrow was Taddie's birthday?

Well, it wasn't his doing exactly, the general said. General Sickles had reminded him of the occasion.

At the mention of General Sickles the look on Mamma's face changed slightly, but she turned to thank him, and General Sickles stood up and bowed very low, looking pleased with himself, and came around the table to Taddie.

"You must do the honors in military style, my boy," General Sickles said. He drew out his sword and handed it to Taddie, who was puzzled at first, until the general told him he must use it to cut the first slice of cake. "Make a wish now—" General Sickles's voice sounded as if he had already taken a large mouthful of the cake. "Make a wish for victory—for the finest army in the world—the Army of the Potomac!"

The cake was sliced and passed around. The tin cups had somehow, in the interval, got filled again. Now there was a toast to Master Tad, and a great many very cheerful remarks while the orderly came back, this time with a military cape, and a pair of regulation army boots with silver spurs.

"Compliments to Captain Tad—from Fighting Joe and his staff!"

Taddie thought his eyes would drop out with astonishment and delight. He must put on the cap at once—and the boots over his own shoes. He stamped them on, and jingled the spurs. General Sickles unbuckled his own sword belt and fastened it around Tad's waist.

"There you are, my boy." General Sickles drew himself up, with only a slight waver, and saluted smartly. "Captain Tad—salute your Commander in Chief." He whirled Tad around by the shoulders to face Mr. Lincoln.

"Look, Papa," Taddie said. "I'm a real soldier, Papa—*look*—"

Papa sat quiet, saying nothing, smiling at Taddie.

The next day was set for the big review. Starting early in the morning, the whole army—troops and horses and guns—was going to parade down a long field, and Papa had said Tad might wear the new cape and sword and boots and sit beside him on his own horse.

It was fun at first, watching the columns of men march past, and the big cannon trundling along the bumpy ground. But there did seem to be a great many, all looking very much alike, and even the bands all seemed to be playing the same tunes. Taddie had a hard time to keep from fidgeting. He was glad, after a while, when Papa came and helped him down from his horse and took him over to the carriage to sit with Mamma.

On the trip home, after the first hour or so, Taddie found that the time went awfully slowly. The boat wasn't half so exciting as it had been coming down. It looked so much smaller, for one thing, and no one seemed very much interested in talking to him. Mamma had gone straight to the cabin to rest, and she told Taddie he wasn't to bother people or go outside on deck where it was misting and damp.

For a time Taddie wandered around, wishing dismally they

were home again so he could play with the goats. They'd had to send Willie's pony away because every time she saw it Mamma would begin to cry, and Papa had bought the goats to make it up to Taddie. Taddie was glad, really, because he liked the goats ever so much better, but he was careful never to say so to Mamma, who surely would have cried again.

Taddie wished now he could hitch the goats to their red wagon and make them clatter down the drive. But they were still hours away from home. In the meantime he went to look for Papa, finding him in the little parlor on the top deck, his long legs stretched out in front of him, looking out the window at the slow-passing shore with the expression on his face that Willie used to say made Papa look as if his brains were racking. Mr. Brooks, a friend of Papa's, who had come along on the trip home, was there too, smoking a cigar.

Taddie climbed on the arm of Papa's chair, hoping for a story, but Papa only put one arm around him absent-mindedly and went on talking to Mr. Brooks.

"There's a good deal to be said for General Hooker, I suppose," Papa was saying. "He's kept the army in good shape during the winter—and there's something I can't help liking about him. All the same, I'd feel better if he and Sickles didn't spend so much time talking about Richmond. It makes me think of a farmer and his wife I knew in Illinois. They were set on building a new barn, and they saved up for years until they had enough money to build. But then they started arguing about what color the roof should be, and finally they fell out and got divorced, and the barn never got built."

Papa was quiet, looking out the window again, then he turned around. "Well, what did you think of the trip, Tad? Did you have fun?"

Taddie nodded, but not very enthusiastically. "Yes," he said, "only I wanted to stay longer. General Sickles said he was going to let me help shoot off a cannon. And I think," he added, "I'm beginning to have kind of a stomach-ache."

Papa smiled. "To tell you the truth, Taddie, I think I have kind of a stomach-ache myself. I don't suppose we'd better mention it to Mother, though. She'll blame it on too much excitement. Personally, I think a little excitement is worth a stomach-ache now and then, but Mother can't see it that way."

Taddie settled down in Papa's lap.

"It was good to get away awhile and rest," Papa said to Mr. Brooks after a minute. "Only it seems sometimes as though nothing ever quite touches the tired spot."

Late in the afternoon, when the boat came in sight of Washington, they all went out on deck together. Mamma stood watching by the rail. The smile that had been on her face almost all the while during the trip was gone now. She pulled her cape tighter and shivered.

"When I look at Washington," she said to Papa, "it frightens me. I feel as though the city were full of enemies—waiting for us."

Taddie looked up, expecting to see Papa laugh at such a queer remark. Papa didn't look at all like laughing. He only nodded slowly.

"I reckon our enemies are like the poor, Mother," he said. "We have them always with us."

Which was certainly, Tad thought, queerer than ever. Rebs were the enemies, and certainly *they* weren't in Washington. And when Papa had stood on the river bank and looked across at the Graycoats, he hadn't said a word about enemies, but had taken off his hat instead, and waved as though they were friends. It was all peculiar, but grownups were so often odd— and it didn't matter really because the boat was getting ready to dock and they were nearly home. Taddie gave a hop of anticipation. His stomach-ache was gone, and there would be time before supper to go out to the barn and hitch up the goats.

Forty

THAT SUMMER when the hot weather came, the President's family moved out to a cottage on the grounds of the Soldier's Home. It was near enough for Mr. Lincoln to ride the three miles down Vermont Avenue to the office every day, and far enough out of town to discourage most of the White House callers and to be a breath cooler than the simmering city. Robert would join them later for his vacation.

There was a pond for Tad to wade in, and space for goats on the sloping lawn under the tall old elms. From the porch Mary could look down the long hill toward the city that lay bordered by the curve of the Potomac.

On evenings when Mr. Lincoln was kept late in town, Mary sewed or read or played a card game with Tad and Mrs. Keckley. When Mr. Lincoln was there, they often sat on the porch long after dark. Under the bright-starred summer sky, with Taddie going first to her lap and then to Mr. Lincoln's, coaxing for one more story before bedtime, Mary knew more peace than she had for months.

There was no music, no rose-shaded candlelight for dinner, no promenade of fashionable carriages as there had been at Saratoga. But something in the brown frame cottage with its small, shabby rooms made Mary feel they had a home again.

Leaning back in a low rocker she pointed to the sky. "There's the Big Dipper, Taddie. And that bright star over the cedar tree is Venus. It's odd," she added, to Mr. Lincoln. "I don't think I've ever noticed the stars before in Washington."

"I don't think I have either," he said. "Maybe they've just come from Springfield to visit us."

Mr. Lincoln had thought Mary might find the long quiet days tedious, but for the first time since Willie's death, she began to seem like herself.

In the still country nights, she found that she could sleep. When she woke it was no longer to a sense of misery that made her want to push back the new day. The numbness that had clung so long about her heart was eased. She began to get up early in the mornings. They had brought only Mrs. Keckley and one servant to run the household. Mary went often into the kitchen—not formally, to inspect, as she did in the White House —but to consult leisurely with Jenny over the dinner. They discussed whether last night's roast might have been browned the least bit more, and whether the man who brought their supplies was giving full weight on the butter and meat.

One day, to show Jenny how Mr. Lincoln liked dumplings made, Mary put on an apron and cooked the fricassee.

Tad came in from playing and looked surprised to find his mother working in the kitchen. He asked quickly if she were going to bake a cake. "One of those big chocolate ones that Wil—" he checked himself, remembering he must never mention Willie's name, and finished lamely, "that the goats like best."

Mary hadn't noticed his slip. If there were eggs enough and chocolate, she said, she'd bake it.

Mr. Lincoln patted his stomach when he finished his second slice of cake that evening. "This tastes like Springfield cooking," he said. "Almost as good as Elizabeth's."

After that Mary put on the apron more often. She helped Mrs. Keckley make the beds and tidy the upstairs. It was strange how the things that had once seemed like fretting chores could give her such a sense of comfort.

"I never realized anyone could be homesick to make a bed," Mary said.

At first, on the evenings when Mr. Lincoln came home late, Mary tried sending Taddie to bed as usual. But he begged so touchingly to be allowed to stay up for Papa, that she began to yield more and more often. It was partly to avoid ending the day with the nerve-shattering tears of one of Taddie's stormy scenes, but more, really, because it was easier to be with Mr. Lincoln when Tad was there too. His presence seemed to hold back the queer barrier that had never quite broken down between them since the night Willie died.

Without ever speaking of it, Mary realized as the weeks went by that she and Mr. Lincoln were depending on Taddie more and more. He protected them from something, she never knew quite what it was, they dreaded when they were alone. Tad went everywhere they went. He sat between them when they drove in the evenings, through the summer dusk. He took his place, importantly, at the dinner table.

To Taddie it was a windfall. Never to be hushed or told to run out and play. Not to be left with Mrs. Keckley while Papa and Mamma drove off together. To have his conversation and questions listened to with flattering attention. Mamma hardly ever seemed to say any more that he must leave her alone because her head was aching. When he came and climbed on Papa's chair now, Papa would draw him onto his knee and hold him there, while he sat reading, or talking to Mamma over Taddie's head.

Mrs. Keckley said one morning, "I'm afraid Taddie is getting to be a very spoiled little boy, Mrs. Lincoln. He doesn't mind me as he used to. When we go back to town, it's sure to make him very difficult."

"Yes, I know," Mary sighed. "I used to think discipline was the most important thing with children. Lately I've wondered sometimes whether we oughtn't to let them just be happy while they can." She paused. "The time seems so short for any of us. . . ."

Mary was careful not to question Mr. Lincoln for news of the war. Ever since General Hooker's long-heralded attack had been defeated at Chancellorsville, there had been nothing but gloom and uncertainty.

"They're after me to change commanders again," Mr. Lincoln said, "but I won't do it. We've been enough of a laughing-stock for the South already without playing 'Going to Jerusalem' with our generals."

Often Mary watched by the front window when it was time for Mr. Lincoln to come. Seeing him ride up the long curving drive, she could judge from the droop of his shoulders whether the news had been bad again. If he looked too dejected, she would call Tad and send him running down the drive. The weariness in Mr. Lincoln's face never failed to lighten as he got down from his horse and let Tad ride the rest of the way to the porch steps where Mary waited.

It was Mr. Lincoln who did the questioning.

"Well, what's the news today, Mother? Did Tad catch a fish from the pond for our supper?"

By the first of July the wheel had turned again. Fighting Joe Hooker was down and General Meade had taken his place.

"I don't know what we can expect from Meade," Mr. Lincoln said. "I'm afraid to get my hopes up any more."

On warm afternoons the soldiers from the hospital barracks across the lane often walked on the grounds. Taddie followed them for hours, listening to their endless stories of the battles they had seen. Most of them seemed old, left over from wars Tad had never heard of. There was one, younger than the others, to whom Tad attached himself. The man had a gunshot wound in the knee. But there seemed to be something more the matter with him. When Taddie coaxed him he would come and sit on the cottage steps, his game leg stuck out stiffly, his cap pushed back on his head, while he whittled boats and guns and soldiers for Tad.

One day, when a thundershower broke in an unexpected downpour, Mary asked Taddie to invite his friend inside. The man came into the parlor, uneasily at first, leaning on his cane. But when he saw the tea and cakes Mary had set out by the fire, his face brightened.

"It's a long time since I sat down in a real house, ma'am," he said.

The shell in his knee was a souvenir of Chancellorsville, he told Mary.

"One of Jackson's own men got me," he said as though he were boasting of the honor. "They came around through the woods and got us from the side and back. I never heard anything like the yell those men let out, ma'am. Before we knew what'd hit us, half our company was down."

The man rubbed his game knee, easing it. "I don't believe the Rebs'll ever fight again the way they did for Jackson. Stonewall's men would've followed him to the devil. Lee's army will fight for him, and die if they have to. So will our army for their generals. But when Jackson was killed . . ." the soldier paused. He stirred his tea; his knee twitched. "The South lost something they can never make up."

That night Mr. Lincoln was later than usual. Tad begged to wait up, but finally Mary coaxed him to bed and crossed to her room to undress. She turned the lamp down and sat near the window where she could look down on the drive, shadowed beneath the full, high moon.

The night was breathless, as if a storm might be coming.

She remembered the night long ago when she had waited for Mr. Lincoln in their little parlor at the Globe Tavern. The night before Robert was born. She had been so frightened—and then so hurt and angry when Mr. Lincoln said he had just been playing checkers. Now it was different. She had something real to fear now. Only last week Mr. Brooks had told Mr. Lincoln he oughtn't to take the long ride out from town alone at night. Mr. Lincoln had laughed, but seeing Mary's face and Mr. Brooks's earnestness, he'd said soberly:

"There's no use being afraid. If they are going to shoot me, they will. No matter if I wear an armored vest and take a dozen men to guard me."

Mary leaned closer to the window, straining her eyes down the road. She watched for a wind to stir the leaves—anything to break the stillness that was like death . . .

Suddenly splitting the silence there was a shout from Taddie. "There's Papa!"

Mary's eyes flew wide. She had seen nothing—but in that moment there was a sound of horse's feet crunching on the gravel. There, quite surely, emerging from a patch of deep shadow, was Mr. Lincoln's tall hat.

Relief burst like a bubble. Mary's nerves, loosened from the taut suspense, jangled irritably. She crossed the hall swiftly.

"*Taddie—*"

He was out of bed and at the window, hopping up and down. "I can see Papa—Papa's come!"

"Get back into bed, Taddie. You cannot see your father tonight. I won't permit it."

Even as she spoke, it was too late. Mr. Lincoln was at the door and Tad had flown down the stairs and at him, throwing his arms around his father's neck.

"Well, well, well," Mr. Lincoln seemed astonished by Tad's noisy embrace. "What's all this rumpus about?" He carried Tad upstairs and sat down on the bed while Tad tore around the room shouting like an Indian.

Mary felt her lips tighten. "Mr. Lincoln, really, you must not encourage this child's absurd notion of waiting up for you to come home. Do you realize it's past midnight? He'll work himself into a fever going on like this."

Mary stopped.

Taddie, suddenly quiet, came over and climbed meekly into bed.

Mr. Lincoln pulled the sheet over him. "There now, Tad, will you go to sleep?"

Taddie burrowed his head contentedly. "Yes, Papa."

"No more fidgets?"

"No, Papa." Taddie's smile was angelic.

"That's a good boy, then . . . Good night."

Outside the door, Mr. Lincoln turned. "I think he'll be all right now, Mother."

"I haven't the slightest doubt of it. Now that he's had his own way and stayed awake to see you—when I had expressly forbidden it. You never see how naughty and spoiled he is. He defies me, and gets himself worked into a perfect state. The moment you come, he behaves like an angel."

Mr. Lincoln sighed. "Well, let him be good while he can, Mother. I wish we all had something that would turn us from sour to sweet as easily."

They crossed the hall, and Mr. Lincoln dropped down on the bed. Mary, turning to adjust the lamp, was startled to see how badly he looked. He sat hunched forward, his elbows on his knees, his face ashy pale.

She went to him in quick alarm. "You're not ill, husband?"

He shook his head. "We had the news today," he said. "The fighting at Gettysburg is over. It seems General Meade carried it off for our side."

Mary hesitated, confused for a moment. Mr. Lincoln seemed to be speaking of a victory and yet his words had a sound like death.

"Do you mean," she asked, still uncertain, "that we won?"

"We won," he answered, "and we lost. We lost three thousand of our men and God knows how many wounded. They tell me the South lost even more." He was silent, staring down at his hands, pulling the knuckles until they cracked. When he looked up, there was such misery in his eyes that Mary was frightened again. "How long is it going on like this?" he said. "How much more of this killing have we got to stand?"

Mary looked into his eyes, seeing the tortured doubts. She tried to speak—searching for the word that would say she understood. For the first time she saw how it must have been for him when Willie died and she had longed for comfort. How he must have been held by her grief, locked by it, as she was now by his.

Mr. Lincoln stood up. "Well," he said, "it's good news. A great victory for the Union. Stanton and the others are all set up. The newspapers have gone wild. They all say this must be the turning point against Lee. I suppose they may be right." He took off his coat, and slipped the watch from his vest pocket. He wound the watch with its small brass key, and laid it on the dresser. "I'd better see about locking up downstairs— I didn't think of it when I came in."

When he came back, Mary was in bed.

"Mr. Lincoln," she said, "I'm sorry I said the things I did— about your spoiling Taddie. I didn't mean them." She watched his face, hoping to see some sign that he knew she wanted to say more.

Instead, he bent over to blow out the lamp.

"That's all right, Mother," he said. "I know you have a lot of things to trouble you these days."

Within the week, there was more good news, this time from the West. Vicksburg had been taken. The Union now had control of the lower Mississippi. Reading the newspaper accounts of the victory, Mary was impressed.

"Mr. Lincoln," she said, "this man Grant sounds as though he knew what he was about. If I were you, I'd keep an eye on him."

Mr. Lincoln glanced up over his paper. "You needn't worry, Mother," he said. "I intend to."

Several weeks later Elizabeth wrote to tell Mary that her brothers David and Alex had been killed fighting General Grant in Tennessee. Mary crumpled the letter in her hand.

Alex, with the red hair, who had played with Robert . . .

In midsummer there was a week of unexpectedly cool weather. Refreshed by the change, Mary made several trips into town to buy new linens and china for the White House.

On the last afternoon, driving back to the cottage along the narrow shaded avenue, she was startled to have the horses rear and plunge into a reckless gallop. A sheet of paper had blown across the road and wrapped itself against one of the horses' legs. Before Tim could get control of them, they had bolted.

Thrown against the side of the carriage, Mary was pitched to the floor. She clutched at the door handle as the carriage lurched again and the door swung open with a force that pulled her with it. There was a spinning moment—she heard herself scream at Tim to stop. Then she was on the ground, struggling to get up while Tim, his coachman's tails flying, came running back along the road.

It didn't seem at first that Mary had been hurt beyond a few bruises and a general shaking up. But the next morning she woke to aching misery. Her lips were dry and feverish. When she moved a pain shot along her spine. Mr. Lincoln looked at her anxiously. He would send a doctor out from town.

The doctor looked Mary over gravely. So far as he could see, there were no bones broken. Quiet and rest, he said, would be the best cure.

She woke from a nap, late in the afternoon, to find Taddie by the bed.

"Do you hurt, Mamma?" he inquired with interest. "Maybe the doctor'll have to cut something off of you, like they do with the soldiers over at the hospital."

Taddie had brought an armful of purple and pink asters. "John said to give you these, and hoped you wouldn't mind," he said. John was the soldier with the game leg who had come to tea. "He picked them out behind the hospital, where he was sure no one would notice, only he said not to tell you that. He said to tell you if you could get some bear grease to rub on, it was very good for taking out pains. And John showed me his knee, the one that was shot. It had a regular hole in it—as big as this—where the bullet went in. He has the bullet too. He carries it around all the time in his pocket. I think John's nice, don't you, Mamma?"

"Yes," Mary said. "Very nice."

Taddie swung on the bedpost thoughtfully.

"Do you think Papa could get a real bullet for me someday, Mamma?"

"Well—I suppose so—"

"One that had shot somebody, I mean," Taddie said.

Mary was quite certain she would be up and well again before Robert arrived. But when the day came, her back was still painful. When Robert found her in bed and heard about the accident, he frowned.

"It seems to me you ought to be in town where you could have proper care," he said.

"Oh, but I'd much rather be here. I like it far better than town. Besides, it's so good for your father, dear. I wouldn't think of asking him to go back to the city."

Robert's frown deepened. "I should think Father would see for himself that a spinal injury isn't to be neglected."

Mary's smile grew strained. It was novel and rather touching to have Robert so concerned about her. All the same, she wished he had less of a knack for putting things in an unpleasant light. *Spinal injury* and *neglected* . . .

"Your father has insisted on having the best doctor from town to see me," she said. "The doctor said it was nothing more than a strained back, and nervous shock, and that all I needed was a good rest."

Robert stood up. "At least you ought to have a proper nurse then. Mrs. Keckley has too many other things to attend to, and I don't see how you can have much rest with Tad popping in and out of the room every five minutes. I mean to speak to Father."

Two days later Mary found herself in the charge of a large-bosomed nurse named Mrs. Sullivan, who had black hair and startlingly blue eyes. Mrs. Sullivan was possessed of a comforting touch and an inexhaustible supply of sickroom anecdotes, and she took an interest in other people's affairs that made conversation extremely easy. Within a few hours she and Mary were on the most congenial terms.

In the long days while Mr. Lincoln and Robert were in town and Tad was out playing, Mary found it pleasant to have Mrs. Sullivan sit by the window, rocking. Not for a long while had Mary had anyone who would listen so attentively while she talked. Gradually, as she grew more certain of Mrs. Sullivan's sympathy, Mary found herself telling things she wouldn't have dreamed of mentioning to anyone else, not even Mrs. Keckley. She spoke of the old days in Springfield, of her sisters, of little Eddie who had died.

They talked, long and companionably, about illnesses and births and deaths, and husbands and growing old. Mrs. Sullivan brought out a dog-eared pack of cards and played solitaire while Mary napped, or laid them out in mystic patterns to read fortunes. To amuse Taddie, she built a house of the cards, balancing them cautiously until a cool puff of breeze stirred through the window and collapsed the structure.

Leaning back against the pillows, Mary watched the nurse gather up the cards and slowly shuffle them again.

One dark afternoon when rain drummed on the cottage roof, she told Mrs. Sullivan about Willie. She told about his pets. Fido they had to leave behind when they came to Washington, and the black pony, and the kitten Willie had wanted on his bed when he was so ill, and the turtle that had been hanged and had come back to life. She told about the night Willie died, and the weeks afterward, and the way sometimes she could wake out of a sound sleep and fancy Willie had called her. She told it all without weeping, knowing that there was someone to listen.

The next morning Mrs. Sullivan brought Mary's breakfast tray. There was an odd look in her eyes.

"Mrs. Lincoln," she said, "he was here last night. Did you see him?"

Mary looked up. "Who was here?"

"Willie—" Mrs. Sullivan bent closer, her blue eyes burning with conviction. "He was here, the wee angel, begging to talk to you. He wanted to tell you he was happy . . . Now, Mrs. Lincoln, there's no need to go white like that. It was your own Willie. You mustn't fear him when he comes so. There's nothing to be afraid of . . ."

Mary set down her cup, feeling her wrist gone limp. "I—want to see Mr. Lincoln," she said, her voice dry. "Please get him. Bring him here."

"Now, now, you mustn't be all upset." Mrs. Sullivan eased Mary back, smoothing the pillow. "Mr. Lincoln's gone to town, an hour past. We won't talk any more of Willie if it upsets you. It's only because you're not used to it yet. But he'll come again, never fear."

1863

Three days later Mary was able to be up and dressed. It seemed unnecessary for Mrs. Sullivan to stay any longer. They had spoken no more of Willie, but before she left Mrs. Sullivan put a slip of paper in Mary's hand.

"It's the name of a medium in New York," she said. "She can get in touch with the dead. If ever you wanted to go see her, she could help you talk to Willie."

After Mrs. Sullivan had gone, Mary took the paper and stared at it a long while. Twice she made a move to tear it. The third time she actually did. But when the pieces lay in her hands, she held them a moment, and then quickly she thrust them into a corner of the desk drawer, out of sight.

✺♫♫♫✺
Forty-one
ᾺᾺᾺᾺᾺ

OCTOBER CAME. The trees began to show red and yellow. Mary found it hard to leave the cottage. Back in the White House, where there was nothing for her to do, the old lassitude closed over her like a wave.

Mr. Lincoln was busier than ever. All day now, instead of office seekers, a new tribe of callers waited outside his door. They were mothers and fathers and wives and sisters of soldiers who were reported missing, or who had deserted and had been sentenced to be shot. Mr. Lincoln's desk was piled with letters, begging for clemency, for pardons, for stays of execution.

"They come all day," he told Mary. "Telegrams and letters asking me to sign the warrant to keep some boy from being shot. I don't see how we can kill any more, when so many are dead."

Coming downstairs one morning, Mary found a man in the front hall. His eyes were filled with bewildered grief.

"I came to ask a pardon for my son," the man said, when Mary spoke to him. "Mr. Lincoln promised me he'd send word nothing was to be done until he gave orders. The boy was only fifteen when he joined up. He fought a year. After Gettysburg, he ran away and came home. I don't know what to do now . . ."

Mary touched his arm gently. "You can go home," she said. "Mr. Lincoln will never give the order to have your son killed."

After the freedom of the summer, Tad was restless and troublesome under the restrictions of town. A tutor had been engaged for him, but Taddie took unkindly to Mr. Wentworth with his pale face and thick glasses and enthusiasm for the classics.

"You must be patient with Taddie," Mary said, when Mr. Wentworth complained that his pupil was noisy and willful, and flew into tempers over having his mistakes corrected. "He's a sensitive boy, and he's had so much to upset him."

Mr. Wentworth returned to his task, paler and more resolute than ever.

One morning, while Mary was at her desk writing to Robert, Taddie burst into the room and flung himself on her. Mr. Wentworth had punished him, Taddie said. He had *whipped* him just because Tad said his father was the President.

Mary stood up. Not waiting to quiet Tad, she sent for the tutor, and demanded to be told what had happened.

Mr. Wentworth arrived, breathing rapidly. Master Tad, he said, had hidden his eyeglasses, and refused point-blank to tell where they were when it was time for lessons. Mr. Wentworth had tried every possible means of reasonable persuasion. When Taddie still refused, Mr. Wentworth had said that unless he returned the glasses, he should be whipped. Master Tad had replied that no one could whip him because his father was President of the United States, and would set the army on anyone who touched him.

"I saw nothing to do, Mrs. Lincoln," Mr. Wentworth said, "but to take his hand and strike him six blows with the ruler."

Then, it appeared, Master Tad had broken loose, howling with rage, rushed to the place where he had hidden Mr. Wentworth's glasses and thrown them on the floor, smashing them.

Looking down at Tad, Mary felt a sudden overwhelming need to make up to him for everything that had been taken away. He had no real home or playmates. Willie was gone and Robert grown up. Mr. Lincoln was lost and changed by the burdens he carried. Her own spirit was worn thin with disappointment and bitterness and pain.

"Mr. Wentworth, it's plain you don't understand this child," she said. "It was only when you frightened him that he did the first destructive, malicious thing he has ever done in his life. You may consider yourself dismissed."

The instant she spoke Mary could have bitten back her words. It was unfair to blame all her grievances against fate on this ineffectual little man.

Curiously enough, Mr. Wentworth looked anything but crushed. There was a cool gleam in his nearsighted eyes.

"Since it was Mr. Lincoln who engaged me," he said quietly, "I should prefer my dismissal to come from him." He made a slight bow and turned to the door.

For a moment Mary was speechless. Then she called, "Mr. Wentworth—" and again, more urgently, *"Mr. Wentworth—"*

He was gone. Mary found herself hurling the torrent of her outraged spirit against a closed door. The bitter words died in her throat. She couldn't think, suddenly, why she had been so angry . . . Then she remembered Taddie. Sinking into a chair, Mary put out her hand. "Taddie—"

He eyed her silently.

"Taddie, come here. Come to Mother."

Taddie did not come. Instead, he edged toward the door, a strangely wary look in his eyes as he watched his mother's face. Seeing that look, Mary was smitten with a new terror. A few times, when she had been angry, Robert had looked at her with that expression. Once, the night in Springfield when the turtle had died, she had seen the look in Willie's eyes. But never Taddie. Taddie had never watched her with that puzzled, uneasy glance. *Dear God, it mustn't be this way with Taddie. Not Taddie.* Mary forced her lips into a smile. Making her voice soft, she spoke again.

"Taddie, please come to me. I want to tell you about a surprise, Taddie. Something nice, I've been planning . . ."

Taddie wavered. A faint gleam of curiosity came through the guarded look. "What kind of surprise?"

"Oh, you must come nearer, so I can whisper. Don't you want to hear the surprise, Taddie?"

Taddie scrubbed his toe against the carpet, staring down at it. "No. I want to go out and play." The indecision was gone. An impish grin broke over his face.

Without waiting for more, he bolted for the door and slammed it behind him.

Mary heard his whoop of freedom as he clattered down the hall toward the stairs.

"Taddie, wait . . ." The words died. Her hands dropped into her lap, and she sat staring into the empty room.

Mr. Lincoln looked up as Mr. Wentworth came into his office. The young man had a peculiar look. Odd sort of fellow anyway, with his white face and thin shoulders. Without his glasses he looked queerer than ever. As if he were trying to see under water. Mr. Lincoln put down his pen.

It didn't take long to hear the story. While Mr. Wentworth spoke, Mr. Lincoln leaned back, listening without expression. When the story was finished, Mr. Lincoln looked up.

"What do you expect me to do about this, Mr. Wentworth?"

The young man drew back. "Well, I've tried to do my work satisfactorily. I felt, under the circumstances, that Mrs. Lincoln's criticism was undeserved. I assure you, sir, I've done my very best with Tad."

"Yes. Yes, I'm sure of that. But the fact seems to remain that you have failed to please Mrs. Lincoln. If she has seen fit to dismiss you, I'm sorry, there is nothing I can do about it."

"But I thought, sir, if I explained the matter to you, you might see it differently."

Mr. Lincoln shook his head. "You must realize I'm a busy man, Mr. Wentworth. I have a war to fight."

"Yes, sir, I realize that. But in a matter concerning your own son—"

"I regret this, Mr. Wentworth. There is no more I can say."

As Mr. Wentworth turned, silently, and walked out of the office, Mr. Lincoln took up his pen and bent over the desk.

An hour later, having packed his belongings, Mr. Wentworth was ready to leave his room when someone knocked at the door.

"Come in."

Mr. Wentworth glanced up, and saw Mr. Lincoln standing on the threshold.

"Mr. Wentworth," Mr. Lincoln said, "I want to apologize for speaking as I did. I'm sorry."

Mr. Wentworth smiled nervously. "I could hardly have stayed here, in any case, after what happened. I shouldn't have troubled you. Only this position meant a great deal to me. I have my mother to take care of since my brothers went into the army. I would have liked to go too, but one of us had to go on working. On account of my eyes, it seemed best for me to stay."

"I wish you had told me this before," Mr. Lincoln said. "Where are your brothers now?"

"One is in the Pennsylvania Fifth with General Sherman. The other was killed a year ago at Antietam."

There was a silence. Mr. Lincoln said slowly, "I'm sorry. Very sorry. If you need help finding a new position, I'll do anything I can."

"Thank you, sir."

"And Mr. Wentworth—"

"Yes?"

"I hope you won't think too badly of us," Mr. Lincoln paused. For a moment he seemed lost in thought. "We are a strange family these days."

❋❋❋❋
Forty-two
ʌʌʌʌʌ

In November Kate Chase married William Sprague, former governor, and now senator, from Rhode Island. The wedding was as brilliant as Washington had seen in years; the bride as beautiful with her red-gold hair and delicate, pale face. "And surely Miss Kate must be radiantly happy," Mary commented in a letter to Elizabeth, "with the prospect of a new political career to manage."

Just a week after the wedding Mr. Lincoln had to make a trip. The night before he left, he came into Mary's room and stood by the fire, his hands thrust deep in the pockets of a faded calico dressing gown. The Christmas before Mary had given him a new robe of dark red flannel ordered from Stewart's in New York. He had seemed pleased, and said it was just what he needed and very handsome. To Mary's knowledge he'd never had it on his back. He clung, instead, to the old calico he had worn in Springfield and carried in his satchel to ride the circuit, along with a venerable pair of leather slippers Mary had beaded with his initials.

"Don't make me give them up, Mother," he said when Mary

complained about his taking the slippers to Washington. "They're the only shoes I can think in."

"I wish I didn't have to go tomorrow," Mr. Lincoln said now. "I don't feel up to much, but they're dedicating the new cemetery at Gettysburg, and I promised I'd speak, so I suppose I must." He was silent, staring into the fire. "It doesn't seem as though anyone would be much interested in listening to speeches. I don't know what sort of thing they expect me to say."

"Well, don't worry," Mary leaned forward to stir the fire, "I daresay you'll think of something when the time comes, Mr. Lincoln."

Several times that night Mary went across the hall. Taddie had a feverish cold. He complained fretfully that Papa had promised to take him along on the trip. Now he was going to miss all the fun. And he might *never* get another chance to see a battlefield and look for real bullets.

In the morning Mr. Lincoln said good-bye. He stood by Taddie's bed in his long black coat, his best hat in his hand.

"Be a good boy, now, and do as Mamma tells you while I'm gone."

"Will you bring me a present if I do?"

"Well, I'll try."

Taddie's scowl lightened. "I'd like a cannon if there are any left," he said sweetly. "One that still shoots."

The evening Mr. Lincoln came home, Mary was downstairs, waiting. Taddie was much better, she told him. The fever was gone, and he had been up and dressed. She kissed Mr. Lincoln's cheek.

"How was your speech?"

"All right, I guess. It was short—but Seward seemed to think it was enough."

They went upstairs together. Mary wanted to hear about his trip, but Mr. Lincoln had little to say.

While he unpacked his small bag and put on a fresh shirt, Mary sat quietly. She looked down at her hands, needing to speak, needing to tell him how lost she had felt while he was away, needing to hear him answer.

"You know," she said finally, "while you were gone I was remembering the years in Springfield when you were on the circuit. You could be away for weeks, but there was nothing to be afraid of then. Now every messenger, every sound in the night frightens me." She hesitated. "Do you think it will ever be the same again, Mr. Lincoln?"

He turned to look at her and she saw the shadows in his face.

"I don't know, Mary." His words were slow. "Everything is changed . . ."

"But if we go back? When all this is over—" Her eyes were on him, pleading for hope.

Mr. Lincoln stood looking at her.

Before he could answer there was a tap at the door.

Mr. Hay stood outside. He was sorry to trouble Mr. Lincoln, but a number of things in the office had come up while he was away . . . Quite urgent . . .

Mr. Lincoln nodded. He'd be there in a moment. When Mr. Hay had gone, he turned back to Mary.

"I suppose I'd better see to this business, Mother. We can talk tomorrow, when there's more time." He paused, touching her arm. "I'm glad you and Taddie are all right."

The next morning Mary brought a newspaper to Mr. Lincoln's office. It said he had made a great speech at Gettysburg. "Mr. Lincoln's words were short," Mary read, "but in memory they will live long."

"You see, Mr. Lincoln," she said, "I was sure you'd think of the right thing to say."

It was January before Mary engaged a new tutor for Taddie. One thing and another delayed her. After all, she said, with the holidays so near, and Robert coming home, there would be plenty of time later for Tad to start lessons.

Mr. Lincoln, more preoccupied than usual, seemed glad enough to turn over the matter to Mary. After New Year's when Robert had gone back, she made inquiries in the city and interviewed several young men for the position. None of them suited.

"The right man isn't to be found in Washington," Mary told Mr. Lincoln. "I should do better in New York."

She planned to go, taking Taddie with her.

Taddie was entranced by the prospect of a trip. Papa promised to keep a close eye on his goats.

Once they were in New York, Taddie found everything wonderful.

"When I grow up to be President," he said, over a breakfast of cinnamon buns and hot chocolate in the hotel, "I'll change the Capital to New York. People like us more here." Everybody calls me 'sir.' "

Mary found the first days restful. It was pleasant to be bowed in and out through doors. The voices soothed her. *"Good morning, Mrs. Lincoln ... Yes, Mrs. Lincoln ..."* There were pleasant mornings of shopping and drives on Fifth Avenue in the winter afternoons.

Mr. Lincoln telegraphed each day. Mary felt safer than she had in a long time.

She interviewed tutors, hoping to find the right one.

One afternoon, coming back to the hotel in the early winter dusk, Mary found Taddie in the parlor of their suite, his hair brushed slick and his face scrubbed to a shine by the maid who had been left to mind him.

"Has he been a good boy, Mamie?"

"A *lamb*, madam. We'd a nice walk in the park whilst you was gone, and fed the pigeons. It was ever so pleasant, wasn't it, Master Tad?"

Taddie, sucking on a lemon ball, made no reply. His face was filled with a consciousness of excessive virtue as he saw Mamma's pleased look. When Mamie was gone, protesting that it hardly seemed right to take the dollar Mary slipped into her hand—"It was a pleasure, minding such a little gentleman"— Taddie went over to the sofa and sat down.

"Mamie's nice, isn't she, Mamma?"

"Very nice."

"She didn't scold me at all."

"That's because you were a good boy."

Taddie looked thoughtful. "I wasn't, though. I chased the pigeons with a slingshot and got my feet wet in the fountain when she told me not to."

"You shouldn't have done that, Taddie," Mary said. She spoke mechanically.

"Mamma—"

"Yes?"

"Why are people always nicer away from home?"

"I don't know, Taddie. Maybe they only seem nicer, because they're strangers."

Taddie reflected.

"You're nicer too, Mamma, and you're not a stranger."

When they went down for supper, there was a telegram waiting from Mr. Lincoln.

TELL TADDIE THAT FATHER AND THE GOATS ARE WELL. ESPECIALLY THE GOATS.

Mary smiled as she gave the message to Taddie. "You wouldn't want to stay away from home always, and leave Papa alone in Washington, would you?"

"Well . . ." Taddie considered. "We could send for the goats—and Papa too."

A tutor was finally found and engaged. Mary approved of him immediately. He was not in the least like the owl-eyed Mr. Wentworth. Mr. Montmorency was plainly a gentleman, and he had some notion of wit too, Mary observed. She rose from the green plush settee in the hotel sitting room and gave him her hand. "I warn you, Mr. Montmorency, Taddie can be a very spirited pupil at times."

"And I can be a very spirited teacher—at times."

"It's a fair match then."

"And may the best man win."

"Taddie and I are going back to Washington tomorrow," Mary said. "We shall expect you to follow."

That afternoon Mary took Taddie with her for a drive. It had snowed enough to make a thin coating on the street. The trees showed feathery white in the light from the gas lamps that glowed on the avenue.

Mary tucked the fur robe closer over her knees. Tomorrow evening Mr. Lincoln would be on his way to the station to meet them. She tried to picture what he would be doing now. Just coming down from the office, he might have time to walk over to the War Department for the evening bulletins before supper. If it was raining in Washington, he'd forget his rubbers and umbrella, unless Mrs. Keckley remembered to remind him . . . She thought how pleased he would be to hear about the trip—and he was bound to approve of Mr. Montmorency . . .

She turned to Taddie. "Perhaps we might go to a theater tonight. As a special treat, on our last evening."

Coming into the gilt and marble hotel lobby, Mary blinked in the sudden light. The clerk bowed pleasantly.

"*Good* evening, Mrs. Lincoln. I trust you and the young gentleman enjoyed your drive? I believe there was one message—" He selected it from the rows of pigeonholes behind the desk.

Walking between the double row of potted palms toward the elevator in its open cage of gilt scroll, Mary glanced at the envelope in her hand, hoping it would be a telegram from Mr. Lincoln. Taddie was asking something about the theater. She answered him, absently, as she opened the message. She saw the Washington dateline, and then the words. They struck like a blow, cold and deadly.

... GENERAL BEN HELM ... KILLED WHILE FIGHTING WITH THE CONFEDERATE FORCES ... TENNESSEE ...

The door of the lift clanged open. Taddie was pulling at her sleeve.

"Mamma—I said *are* we really going to the theater like you said we could?"

Slowly Mary realized what the words meant. Ben Helm was dead. She remembered the morning Ben had left the White House. She remembered his letter a few days later. [*Lee*] *cannot fight against his own people. Nor can I. . . .* She thought of her sister Emilie going home from Springfield to marry Ben Helm.

Taddie's insistent voice broke in. "Why *don't* you know, Mamma? You promised we could go to the theater."

Mary drew Taddie down on the sofa beside her. "Taddie, listen, I've had a message from Papa with very sad news. Your Uncle Ben has been killed—fighting in the war."

Taddie looked at her frowning.

"You remember Uncle Ben, don't you, Taddie?"

He shook his head.

"Oh, but you must, dear. Uncle Ben was so fond of you and Willie. Don't you remember when he came to visit, and brought the red whip for the pony cart? He was in the South when the war came and he fought very bravely . . ."

A sudden gleam of interest lighted Taddie's eye.

"You mean Uncle Ben was a rebel?"

"Well . . . yes. But that doesn't matter now, Taddie. He fought for what he believed was right."

"Who shot him, Mamma?"

"Oh, Taddie, it doesn't make any difference." Mary put her hand across her eyes. There was no use trying to explain. She went to the bedroom to take off her wraps. She might as well send Taddie to the theater, since she had promised and he'd be so disappointed. Mamie, the nice chambermaid, could take him.

Mamie was willing, and Tad went off cheerfully.

Left alone, Mary looked vaguely around the sitting room. The clock ticked loudly in the silence. There was nothing she could do. She might as well go to bed.

"Ben—wait, Ben—Ben—"

The sound of her own voice wakened Mary. She struggled up out of the heavy blackness into consciousness. What had made her call out like that?

Through the half-open door she saw the lamp burning in the parlor. Tad and Mamie hadn't come back yet. Gradually the dream began to loose its grip. She remembered now. In the dream she had been in a strange house not knowing why she had come, but only that someone had sent for her. She had looked up to see Ben on a balcony watching her. There was a way to reach it but she could not find it. She had wakened herself, screaming *"Wait, Ben—"*

Lying back, Mary tried to shake off the foolish conviction that Ben had really been there. It was only natural that she should have dreamed of him. But the feeling persisted. Long after Taddie had come in and was asleep, she stared into the dark, seeing that strange calm look on Ben's face.

Hours later Mary got out of bed. Moving quietly in the chilly darkness, she went into the parlor. There was no uncertainty now—she wanted her portfolio. She searched the pages hastily. She could remember putting the note away weeks ago, before they left the summer cottage. Her fingers touched the torn scraps of paper, pushed back into a corner.

She fitted the edges together, holding them toward the light.

There was the name, written in Mrs. Sullivan's round hand. "Mme Asta d'Estignay." An address on Washington Square. "We can reach our dear ones who have passed beyond," Mrs. Sullivan had written.

Mary straightened. There would be time, before the morning train, to drive to Washington Square.

Forty-three

BACK IN Washington Mme d'Estignay's words of hope were lost. Mary felt as though she had never been away. Loneliness came back. The old fears locked her in.

A telegram came one morning from Nashville. Mrs. Emilie Helm, claiming to be a sister-in-law of the President, was being held at Fortress Monroe on her way from Atlanta to her home in Lexington. She could not be allowed safe-conduct through the lines unless she took the oath of allegiance, and this she seemed unwilling to do. Would the President telegraph instructions?

Mr. Lincoln brought the message to Mary.

"We must help her somehow," Mary said. "Couldn't you send word to let her be passed through the lines?"

"I can do better than that," Mr. Lincoln said. He sat down at Mary's desk and wrote a single line. "Will this do, Mother?"

He showed her what he had written.

> Send her to me.
> A. Lincoln

The afternoon Emilie was to arrive, Mary waited at her sitting-room window. When the carriage finally came, she hurried down to the front hall. The door was open. Edwards was ushering in a small, tired-looking woman in mourning black. Mary felt a shock of surprise. This, surely, couldn't be Emilie. Not the Emilie she remembered the last time in Springfield, gay and laughing in her bright summer frocks . . . She would have changed, of course. But not like this. Not this worn, sad little creature with her thin face and shabby, dusty mourning crepe.

"*Oh, no—*" Mary formed the words soundlessly. "*No—*"

She saw Emilie's eyes, large and dark-ringed. With a second bitter shock, Mary realized that Emilie was staring just as she had, as though Emilie too could scarcely believe the change she saw.

"It's the war that has changed everything," Emilie said later, when they were alone upstairs. "After the things it's done, I don't think we'll ever be the same. Not any of us, Mary."

They talked guardedly at first, each careful not to say the things that might be too full of hurt.

"I've thought of you, Mary, often . . ." Emilie said. "Especially since Ben was killed. People have been kind to me—they sympathize, I know. But I kept thinking of you. It seemed to me you were the only one who would really understand what it means to lose a husband you loved."

They were strange words for Mary to hear. She looked at Emilie with a full heart.

Late one night Mary went to the room where Emilie slept. She rapped softly.

"Yes?"

Emilie had been awake. She sat up, looking small and frightened, in the big four-poster bed.

"Mary, what's the matter?"

Mary walked toward the bed, slowly. "Emilie, I have to tell

you something. I haven't spoken of this to anyone, not even Mr. Lincoln, but I must tell you." Seeing the puzzled alarm in Emilie's eyes, Mary smiled. "You mustn't be frightened. It's nothing to be afraid of . . ."

"Mary, are you ill?"

"No." Mary went closer, bending down. "It's something I've learned, Emilie. It's the only thing that brings me comfort now." She paused. "Emilie, did you hear Ben tonight?"

"*Ben?*"

Mary nodded. "He was here, Emilie. He comes sometimes. Willie comes too. And Alec and David—even little Eddie. But it was Ben who came tonight. That must have been because you were here."

"You must be ill. You've been dreaming. I'll call Mr. Lincoln."

"No," Mary stopped her. "Mr. Lincoln wouldn't understand. But you understand, don't you, Emilie? They come because they want to help us . . ."

At breakfast next morning, Mary saw how oddly Emilie looked at her.

"I hardly slept last night," Mary said. "When I did I had such a strange dream. Of course it wasn't real."

One afternoon Mary and Emilie were having tea in the south parlor when callers were announced. General Sickles and Senator Harris had come to see the President. They would like to pay their respects to the ladies while they waited.

Mary greeted the gentlemen pleasantly. She presented them to Emilie, and offered tea.

The general sat down stiffly and pointed to his missing limb. "Lost at Gettysburg, you know," he said. "Haven't got used to being a cripple yet."

They made conversation, politely enough, for a few minutes. Then the general turned to Emilie. "I understand you're from the South, ma'am."

Mary saw Emilie's expression stiffen slightly as she nodded.

General Sickles eased himself back. "Well, I expect it must seem quite a change to you, being here. We do things differently in the North. Talk differently, act differently, even fight differently."

"I suppose there are differences." Emilie spoke calmly, but Mary caught the uneasiness in her glance. "I haven't had much chance to observe, General. My sister and I have been very quiet since I've been here."

"Ah, yes, of course." The general's smile was genial. "I keep forgetting that Mrs. Lincoln is a Southerner too. No doubt you two have had a great deal to discuss. You know the old saying, 'blood is thicker than water.' " He turned abruptly to Mary, inquiring what she heard from Robert these days. "He's well, I hope."

"Yes, quite."

General Sickles nodded. "Good, good. I'd wondered if it might be poor health that kept the boy out of the army, but I'm glad to hear that's not the case. I daresay he has other reasons for not joining up."

Senator Harris shifted uneasily and murmured something about getting on upstairs. Before he could move, Mary's voice cut sharply across the room.

"Just a moment, General Sickles. If you have any doubts about the reasons for my son not being in the army, I can tell you the fault is mine. Robert wanted to enlist two years ago. He's stayed on at college because I insisted. I thought, perhaps mistakenly, that his education should be finished first."

"My dear lady," Sickles shrugged. He glanced at the senator, brows lifted. "No one said a word about any fault. I was only inquiring..."

"On the contrary," Mary said, "I think you are deliberately criticizing my son and sneering at my sister because she happens to be a Southerner whose husband was killed fighting very bravely."

"Now see here," Sickles mouth took an angry twist. "I don't

propose to let you bulldoze me, ma'am. I'm not bound to take your tonguelashings in silence as your husband is."

Senator Harris rose hastily. "I think—" he began.

"As for your sister," Sickles went on, "she's hardly to blame if the Rebs are running away from a war they can't win."

Emilie was on her feet. "Our men don't run, General." Her voice quivered but her eyes met his evenly. "You may say they are wrong but you daren't look at me and call them cowards."

The general heaved himself up, his face red. "I don't come calling on ladies, expecting traitors' talk. Good day, ma'am." He bowed stiffly to Mary and stumped out of the room, the senator hurrying after.

Mary and Emilie could hear the angry mutter of their voices and the stump, stump of General Sickles' crutch on the stairs.

"Mary. Oh, Mary," Emilie burst into tears. "I shouldn't have spoken so in your house. What will Mr. Lincoln say?"

Mary patted her sister's shoulder. "I wouldn't worry," she said. The shadow of a smile curved her lips. "Mr. Lincoln will find just the right thing to say."

That evening Mr. Lincoln told them nothing until he had had a second helping at supper. Then he leaned back in his chair.

"Sickles was in the office this afternoon," he said. "He seemed all fired up about Emilie being a rebel and a spy, and wanting us to get her out of the White House."

Mary and Emilie leaned toward him. "What did you tell him?" Mary asked.

Mr. Lincoln rubbed his chin. "Well, I told him he ought to have had more sense than to provoke a couple of Todd tempers. And I mentioned that we were in the habit of choosing our own guests, whatever house we happened to be living in."

Mr. Lincoln looked up. "Was that all right, Mother?"

The next week Emilie left for Kentucky. She had a few moments alone with Mr. Lincoln when they said good-bye.

"I wish you would come back to us, Emilie," Mr. Lincoln said. "It would mean a good deal to Mary. I'm troubled about her lately."

Emilie nodded. "I thought at first it was her grieving over Willie, but there seems to be something more. It's as if she were frightened of something—without knowing what. She talks queerly sometimes—about seeing Willie and Ben. And some strange woman writes to her from New York. The woman claims she can bring Willie back to visit."

"Yes, I know," Mr. Lincoln said. "Though she never mentions it to me."

"She doesn't want to trouble you. But if anything happened to you or Robert, I don't believe Mary could bear it."

Mr. Lincoln sighed. "Well, neither of us is bulletproof." He smiled down at Emilie. "I'm grateful to you for coming. You've helped us more than you know." He paused. "I hope you don't hold Ben's death against me, Emilie . . ."

She looked straight into his eyes. She didn't try to speak, but only reached up and put her arms around his neck.

"It's all right," he said. "It's all right, Emilie."

Forty-four

GETTING BACK to the Soldier's Home cottage seemed like coming home again to the cedar trees, and the low-ceilinged bedrooms, Mr. Lincoln's favorite rocking chair on the front porch—and the wicker swing that creaked.

Robert was to come for only three weeks, after his graduation at Harvard. Then he planned to go back to Cambridge to begin reading law.

John, the soldier with the game knee, was gone, but Taddie soon had a new friend to tag after. He was an Irishman named Joseph Greene, who stood six feet two, and said he was strong enough to pitch a bull over a fence. Mary was puzzled, seeing Joseph's apparently perfect state of health, as to why he should be in the hospital.

Joseph explained one morning, leaning on his spade. He had been digging up a garden patch for Tad to plant.

"It was the noise, ma'am," he said. "They say it made me sort of daft. Came on me gradual like, it seemed to. First I'd only notice it just after a battle was over. It'd seem like crackers were going off inside my head. Then it got so the least noise would make me go wild. One night the lad next me dropped his belt and buckle on the floor . . ." He paused, wiping his forehead, and smiled at Mary apologetically. "I don't know why it took me so, ma'am. A great husky like me. There were little measly chaps could walk into a fight where the cannons were spitting. But they say noise can do that to some. Makes them dotty, they say."

Joseph had been in the hospital since Gettysburg.

On Independence Day, Mr. Lincoln brought Taddie a package of firecrackers from town, and Taddie rushed straight out onto the lawn to try them.

Half an hour later, going to call Tad for supper, Mary almost stumbled over the big Irishman. He was crouched by the back steps, his face white and drenched with sweat. Seeing Mary, he got to his feet.

"I—didn't want the boy to see me—like this—" He spoke between chattering teeth. "It was the noise . . ."

As Tad appeared around the corner of the porch, Joseph cut and ran for the hospital. Mary looked after his lumbering figure.

"What's the matter with Joseph, Mamma?" Taddie asked.

"Nothing, dear. He doesn't feel very well, I think."

"But didn't he want to see my firecrackers? I saved the biggest one especially for him."

It was a hard summer for Mr. Lincoln.

"I'm getting used to them, though," he said to Mary. "I wouldn't know what to do with any other kind."

It had begun with General Grant's long attack on Lee's army, across the Rapidan into the Wilderness, down through Spotsylvania and Cold Harbor, and across to Petersburg. For thirty days Grant kept it up. Day by day, hearing the staggering losses the North was paying for its gains, Mr. Lincoln's face set in deeper lines. Watching her husband, reading accounts of the daily slaughter, Mary showed him a headline.

"Butcher Grant." The article began: "Grant's march is a funeral march; there is scarcely a home but mourns its dead . . ."

"In heaven's name, Mr. Lincoln, can't he be stopped? Every hospital is jammed with wounded and dying, and still they keep coming. This Grant says he means to fight it out if it takes all summer. Does he mean to take all our men as well?"

"Grant knows what he's doing, Mother."

"You've said that about every commander we've had," she shrugged impatiently.

"This time it's different," Mr. Lincoln's voice was quiet. "This is a frightful job Grant is doing, but it has got to be done, and he's the one who can do it."

Each day Mary grew more anxious about the coming election. Scanning the papers, she searched for some good word of Mr. Lincoln. There was scarcely a one. Many Republicans favored nominating a new man. "The Democrats will say the war has failed," they said. "They'll beat us unless we can get rid of Lincoln. People have got it in their heads that Lincoln is a Jonah. Right or wrong, the party has got to face it."

"It's not fair," Mary told Mrs. Keckley bitterly, "after all Mr. Lincoln has done, nearly killing himself with work, and suffering more in these four years than the men who criticize him could in a lifetime."

General McClellan was the Democratic nominee. When Mary heard that, she felt better. "If Mr. Lincoln can't win over that little stuffed Napoleon," she said, "I'll be surprised!"

McClellan's platform was designed to appeal to those who were weary and sick of the war. "Call it a failure and stop throwing good money and good men after bad," he said. "The South will be ready enough to compromise now—we can make peace while there's still something left to make it with."

"If McClellan makes it," the Republicans retorted, "it will be a peace past anyone's understanding."

The Republican convention met in Baltimore to thrash out the nomination.

Mr. Lincoln heard the news that he had been chosen while the family was at supper. He brought the telegram back to the table.

"At least it's good news for the goats," he said to Tad. "If I'm elected we won't have to find a new home for them."

The troubles weren't over. At the end of General Grant's offensive, Richmond was still untaken, and the Union had lost more than fifty thousand men. Down in Georgia, General Sherman was going for Atlanta. And the campaign grew more bitter.

Sitting on the porch in the long afternoons, Mary read long newspaper columns predicting that Mr. Lincoln would lose the election. A year ago, she might have been almost glad to think of Mr. Lincoln being free again. But she had come to realize that there was no freedom for them yet. A bargain with fate remained a bargain.

When they were together, Mr. Lincoln spoke little of the future. But in spite of the weariness that made his shoulders stoop, and the sadness that never left his eyes, Mary sensed the fatal urge that drew him along the road he had begun.

"The politicians talk about platforms and campaign promises," he said once. "There's only one platform people will vote for, and that's victory. There's no use my talking or promising. They know better than to listen to me. If we win the election, it won't be because of me. It will be because of Grant and Sherman and God . . ." He rubbed his chin. "And because the South can't fight forever with no supplies and their men outnumbered three to one."

That summer Mr. Lincoln signed the new draft bill, aimed to raise the reinforcements they needed to take the place of the soldiers who had been killed or wounded. But it still allowed for the hiring of substitutes by any drafted men who could pay the price of six or eight hundred dollars for aliens or underage boys to take their places.

"Sherman says we will get nothing much but riffraff and runaway lads," Mr. Lincoln said. "He says the North doesn't deserve to win when we are willing to sacrifice so little for our victory."

A few mornings later Mary opened the newspaper to find an article directed at the President's son. "Lincoln signs orders forcing other parents to give up their boys," it said, "while he keeps his son in luxury at a university. He writes a letter to Mrs. Bixby, speaking of the nobility of her sacrifice in laying five children on the altar of freedom. Is the rail splitter's son made of porcelain—and Mrs. Bixby's boys of common clay?"

Mary showed the article to Mr. Lincoln.

"This is my fault," she said. "Robert wanted to enlist, and you would have let him, except for me."

Mr. Lincoln put aside the paper. "Well, there's nothing we can do now, Mother. He can't enlist before the election, or people will say it's playing politics. I don't know that it matters so very much," he sighed. "Except to Bob . . ."

❊ʃ❊ʃ❊ʃ
Forty-five
VVVVVVVV

In the August twilight the sky was bright red, as though the hot sun lingered, unwilling to give up after the long day. Daddy Joe Travers, limping a little, leaning on his oak stick, walked down the path from the contraband camp toward the dusty road. His grizzled head was bent, and his brown face lost in thinking.

Daddy Joe was worried. Worried and tired, and wondering about all the folks in the camp back there. They'd come up from the slave states, just as Daddy Joe had come himself, walking most of the way from Carolina. Every day now more were coming. Daddy Joe and the others did their best to welcome the newcomers, finding them rations from the food they could scrape together, trying to keep them from learning too soon that freedom sometimes only meant you had no place to go.

They didn't try to go, most of them. Just stayed, and got what they could out of being together. The ones that went on were mostly those whose families had been broken up long ago when they'd been sold separately. Husbands would move on looking for wives, mothers for children, hoping to find them at the next camp.

Daddy Joe came to the end of the path and stood looking down the road. He always took a last look in the evening, thinking some traveler might be coming along and miss the turn-off in the fading light. He squinted down the way, but there was no sign of anyone walking. Only a carriage coming along, the dust rising in small puffs on the road where the horses stepped. Daddy Joe waited while the carriage came near. There was a man and a woman in the back, and a boy sitting between them. They passed so slowly that Daddy Joe got a good long look. He could see the man's face, and the wrinkled black coat he wore. The woman was dressed finely, all in lavender and white, with a parasol and little short gloves, like the white ladies used to wear in Carolina. Daddy Joe smiled to see those gloves.

When the carriage had gone clear by, Daddy Joe went back, but he'd hardly got to the campfire when one of the women pointed down the path, and he looked around to see the same black carriage jogging along the wagon tracks toward the camp clearing.

"Who is it, Daddy Joe?" the woman whispered. Her eyes were bright and scared in the light from the fire.

Daddy Joe didn't know who it was. He stood waiting. "There's nothing to be afeared," he said. "We don't have anyone in the camp that needs be afeared."

The carriage was almost up to Daddy Joe when it stopped, and the man in the black coat stepped out. He looked around at the circle of men and women by the fire, and they looked back, not speaking or moving until Daddy Joe came out slowly, leaning on his stick. The stranger was about the tallest man he'd ever seen. Lean as a rail, and with a plain face and nice eyes, and he just stood there giving them a chance to look him over before he spoke.

Daddy Joe came nearer. He took his time about it, straightening his shoulders so his old blue shirt hung neater. The rag-gedy trousers above his bare black feet were gray with dust.

"I hope you don't mind our coming in," the stranger said. His voice was easy. "We were driving past on the way to the Soldier's Home, and saw your fire." He put out his hand. "My name is Lincoln..."

Daddy Joe stood a minute to be sure his eyes saw right and his ears hadn't fooled him. Then the hand he put out to shake Mr. Lincoln's strong, square one was steady.

"It honors me to welcome you here, Mr. Lincoln," he said.

Around the circle by the fire, Daddy Joe's words passed round in whispers. *It's the President, Daddy Joe says. It's Mr. Lincoln stopped by to shake hands with Daddy Joe ...*

There was no excitement, no shout of welcome, only a slow gathering around the tall, bareheaded man.

"Rosaleen," one of the women bent to whisper to the child beside her, "run back and fetch the others. Tell them Mr. Lincoln's come."

"I hope you're getting along all right here," Mr. Lincoln said.

Daddy Joe nodded. "We do nicely, thank you. Nicely—" he spoke up, good and clear.

"I'm glad to hear that," Mr. Lincoln said. Daddy Joe saw how the smile lifted up his tired face. "Mrs. Lincoln and I hear you singing sometimes in the evening, when we drive past. I wonder if you could sing a little for us now, if it isn't too much trouble."

"We'd be proud to." Daddy Joe straightened his shoulders again. "Liza—"

A tall girl stepped out of the group, her handsome head bent. "Liza starts the singing," Daddy Joe said.

Liza waited a minute, not looking up, then her voice came out of the silence, low and true.

"Sometimes I feel like a motherless child ..."

The others sang with her until the last note ended in the dying light. Mr. Lincoln stood perfectly still. Then Liza's voice led out again.

"Nobody knows de trouble I see,
Nobody knows but Jesus . . ."

The lady and the little boy sat in the carriage, listening. Daddy Joe turned to see the look on Mrs. Lincoln's face. She was sitting back, half smiling, her arm around the boy's shoulders. And while they sang, Daddy Joe could see her watching Mr. Lincoln's face.

Daddy Joe frowned. He was trying to remember what people said was wrong with Mrs. Lincoln. She was queer, some said, and had a mean bad temper. She wasn't as good to Mr. Lincoln as she might be, Daddy Joe had heard. But just to look at her watching him, Daddy Joe could see what a power she thought of Mr. Lincoln.

When the singing was done, Mrs. Lincoln leaned out of the carriage to thank them all. She looked at a woman with a baby on her arm, and the woman held the baby up, shyly, for her to see.

"Is it a little boy?"

"Yes, ma'am."

Mrs. Lincoln smiled. "How old is he?"

"Just two months today. He was born the week I was free."

"He's a good baby to sleep so soundly." Mrs. Lincoln reached out to touch the round, dark head. "What's his name?"

"Abraham Lincoln Jackson."

Mrs. Lincoln turned to the boy beside her. "Do you hear that, Taddie? The baby's named for your papa."

There was a murmuring and shuffling through the group. A young girl, holding up her baby, said eagerly, "Here's another Abe too, ma'am."

"I got me a little Abe—" a voice called from the back.

"Me too—"

Mrs. Lincoln smiled again. "It must be a puzzle to keep the little Abes sorted out."

Daddy Joe explained. "We call 'em different. This one we call Fat Abe. Yonder Mother Sally's got Skinny Abe."

"I got Long Abe."

"Mine's Puny Abe—" said a mournful voice. "But just wait, he'll grow up good as the others."

"We get mixed up sometimes," Daddy Joe said, "but they'll all be proud, someday, to have the name."

Before Mr. Lincoln got back into the carriage he shook hands again with Daddy Joe. "If you need anything I hope you will come and tell me," Mr. Lincoln said. "I don't live far away."

The next day Mary told Mrs. Keckley about stopping at the camp.

Mrs. Keckley nodded. "We try to help as much as we can," she said. "But there are so many camps. So many people traveling . . ." she paused, threading her needle. "We raise all the money we can. But there is never enough."

That afternoon Mary gave Mrs. Keckley a check for two hundred dollars. "I wish you had told me sooner that you are working to help your people," she said. "I've met Mr. Frederick Douglass in New York and heard him speak to people who are raising money for the free Negroes. Next time you must come with me and meet him. He'll help you, I know."

Forty-six

THROUGH THE early weeks of Autumn the North waited to see whether General Sherman would bring his army out at salt water. When Atlanta was taken, the Republicans were wild with joy. The news had come in time for the election.

The day the returns came in, Mr. Lincoln brought a sheaf of telegraph messages into Mary's sitting room and laid them in her lap. He stretched out on the sofa and closed his eyes.

"They say we've won, Mother."

Mary looked at him in silence. She remembered the other election day, when he had come home to the parlor at Springfield to tell her the news, and patted her shoulder while she clung to him and wept. She didn't weep now. There was too much in her heart for weeping. She only sat quietly, watching him. Thinking of all who had died since the November night four years before. Ellsworth and Ben Helm, and her brothers— Alex, with the red hair, and David and Sam. Willie was dead— and Mrs. Keckley's son, whom she had never seen. The young Confederate soldier, who had looked so like Robert when she knelt beside him on the ground that afternoon in the square, and all the boys she had talked to; the ones who had come with their new regiments to march by in review and had stood in the East Room or on the lawn, drinking lemonade, shaking hands with Mr. Lincoln, telling Mary about their mothers and their sisters and their wives and children. There was no knowing how many or which ones out of the bright parade were gone.

Mary looked down at her hands. Death and suffering and war had claimed so much more than just the boys—more than Willie and Ben and Alex and Ellsworth and Stephen Douglas and all the nameless ones. There were the other deaths. Hope and courage and faith had been alive in that November in the Springfield parlor. They still lived in Mr. Lincoln's face, beyond all the weariness and sadness. But in her own heart Mary found them no more. Only the fragments, twisted and broken, were left in the emptiness.

"Well," she said, "I'm glad, Mr. Lincoln."

Now General Sherman was gone. He had disappeared with his whole army into Georgia. For thirty-three days, while Grant sat facing Lee's army at City Point, and Mr. Lincoln paced the floor of his study, and the country waited—there was no word.

Congress began to fume for news.

"I have none," Mr. Lincoln said. "I know what hole Sherman went into, but I can't tell you what hole he will come out of."

On the street one day, Mary heard Mr. Lincoln apologize to a friend for having passed him without speaking. "You must excuse me for not seeing you," he said. "I was thinking of a man down South."

Sherman's old father-in-law wagged his head. "Cump will come out all right," he said. "What's all the fuss?"

One December night the wind blew a bitter gale. Toward morning the wind died. When Mary woke she looked out the window at the unbroken whiteness of snow.

"I can get my sled out and hitch up the goats, can't I,

Mamma?" Taddie asked. "Will Papa come coasting with me, do you think, Ma?"

"I don't know, dear. You can ask him."

When Taddie asked at breakfast, Mr. Lincoln shook his head. "You'll have to make my excuses to the goats," he said. "Tell them, if they are interested, that we've heard from a man named Sherman, and things are a little busy today."

He turned to Mary. "The word came this morning that Sherman's army is in Savannah. He says the city is ours for a Christmas present."

The news was like a spring tonic after the dreary weeks. Washington came to life. Sleigh bells jingled on Pennsylvania Avenue. The ladies put on their best bonnets and furs and came out to drive. In hospital wards the soldiers brightened with new hope and asked for pens and paper to write letters home.

In the sudden excess of Christmas cheer, hampers and boxes of gifts and food began to arrive at the White House. Mary loaded the baskets straight into the carriage to take them to the hospital.

"There's more here than an army could eat," she said. "And enough wine and whisky to raise the spirits of the hosts of Egypt. They need cheering, poor boys—and they shall have it."

She stayed at the hospital, day after day, sitting by the cots, reading letters aloud and writing answers for those who were too ill to write their own. Even the prisoners had a cheerful word. One lad who had been blinded reached out and touched the sleeve of Mary's cloak.

"That's velvet, isn't it, ma'am? There was a girl I knew at home who used to wear a velvet jacket."

Everyone smiled, everyone talked about going home. The war was bound to be finished quickly. Everyone said so.

When she got back to the White House, one afternoon, Mary met Tad flying down the driveway with the goats hitched to his sled. He waved and shouted at her, pointing to the harness decorated with streamers of red, white, and blue.

"The goats have got new names, Mamma—they're Tecumseh and Ulysses."

"Sherman and Grant ought to be flattered," Mr. Lincoln said when he heard about the new names. "I doubt if even Napoleon and Caesar ever had two nanny goats named after them."

It was New Year's day, and Mary had the East Room ready for the afternoon reception. She and Mr. Lincoln stood by the door to welcome their guests to the open house. Three New Years' days before, she had seen the long room with the crimson curtains drawn and the candles lighted in the winter dusk, and watched the people filing by, strangers most of them, pausing to shake hands and say a word or two, or staring—awestruck—before they moved on to the dining room where the long tables were spread.

It was the same room. The Marine Band played "Hail! Columbia." Many of the same people passed by to shake hands and pay their respects to the President. Yet everything seemed different. Mary saw it in their faces. There was jauntiness and good will in their voices.

She spoke of it to Mr. Lincoln, in a lull toward the end of the long afternoon, and he nodded.

"They act as though the war was already done," he said. "They're right, I suppose—but I wonder how they can forget so quickly."

Late in the afternoon word was sent to Mr. Lincoln that Frederick Douglass and a group of other Negroes who had been raising money for the slave camps were arriving. "Send them in." Mr. Lincoln's face lightened. "I hope we can make them welcome."

It was past seven o'clock when the line of guests came to an end. Mary saw Mr. Lincoln's hand drop at his side.

"That's about all, I guess, Mother."

She nodded. Her hand ached. She glanced ruefully at her

white glove. The seams of three fingers were split. But she turned with a smile to take Mr. Lincoln's arm.

"Well, Mother," he said, "I expect we ought to wish each other a happy New Year."

Robert came home from Cambridge for the holidays. The morning after his arrival he told Mary that he wasn't going back to law school. If it wasn't too late already, he wanted to enlist. He looked at Mary all the while as though expecting her to burst out at him. She only nodded.

"I should have let you go sooner, Robert. I—" she stopped. There was no way to say the things she felt. No way to explain the fears—the things she had dreaded so. Robert would only go on looking at her as he was looking now. "I'm sorry, Robert," she said.

The morning Robert put on his uniform it was Mr. Lincoln who seemed more shaken than Mary. It was odd of him to take it so, she thought. Robert was going in as a captain, on General Grant's staff. There couldn't be much danger, surely, when everyone said the fighting was nearly over. She looked at Mr. Lincoln, and saw how he sipped his coffee, holding the cup in two hands to steady it. An unexpected pity stirred her heart for them.

"You look very fine, dear," Mary said to Robert. "Your father is proud of you, I know."

The fourth of March came. Robert was given two days' leave for the inauguration. He and Mary and Tad rode together, while Mr. Lincoln went alone in the open barouche, in spite of a chilly, drizzling rain.

From the gallery where she had sat four years before, Mary heard Mr. Lincoln speak. There was no large party with her this time, only Taddie beside her. Robert sat on the platform with his father. There was no Mr. Douglas to hold Mr. Lincoln's hat. None of the excitement of the first inaugural, only a job to be finished—the terrible job of war. The crowd was quiet, subdued, under a forest of black umbrellas, as Mr. Lincoln spoke.

". . . let us strive on to finish the work we are in, to bind up the nation's wounds; . . . to do all which may achieve a just and lasting peace . . ."

Mary heard the strength, sure and final, in his voice. When the speech was over, she rose. "Come, Taddie—" she held out her hand. No one stared at them as they made their way through the crowd, down the steps to the carriage.

The ball that night was in the East Room. There were the usual sightseers, noisy and pushing. Mary was used to them now. She was neither surprised nor shocked by their onslaughts on the refreshments, their gawping curiosity and shameless pocketing of souvenirs. Four years in Washington had taught her a good deal.

When the evening was over, Mary walked through the disordered rooms. Not only silverware and napkins had been carried off, but ornaments and tassels. Here and there fringe had been snipped from the upholstery by the more enterprising collectors. She said nothing until she discovered a hole a foot square in one of the draperies in the East Room, where the crimson fabric had been hacked out.

She showed it to Mr. Lincoln.

"Someone must have wanted a new red kerchief," he said.

Mary wondered what Mr. Montrose would have said. She had heard that Mr. Montrose had enlisted with a regiment of cavalry volunteers and had been wounded at Cold Harbor, in his first battle. Poor Mr. Montrose. She remembered his elegant manners and the way clashing of shades of colors could make him shudder and press his hands against his forehead. It was hard to think of him as a soldier. . . .

Mary let the drapery fall back, arranging the folds carefully so that the ragged tear was hidden.

Inauguration was over, and things settled down. Mr. Lincoln looked wearier than ever.

"I wish you could rest, Mr. Lincoln," Mary said.

"I will, Mother. Don't worry." When the war was done, they might plan a trip, he said. They could take Taddie and go out to Springfield for a visit, or to Canada or perhaps Europe. "It's been a hard pull. But we must stick it out a little longer."

Mr. Lincoln was planning to go down to City Point to see the troops and confer with Grant and with Sherman. If they could manage to join Sherman's army with Grant's the fighting would be over.

For all his weariness, Mr. Lincoln seemed hopeful of this final success, but Mary protested.

"Those men will wear you out, Mr. Lincoln. You'll be ill."

"Now, Mother, they'll take good care of me. They can't afford to lose me now."

Mary shook her head. She wouldn't have an easy moment without him. Why shouldn't she go too, and take Tad?

Mr. Lincoln was doubtful. It was no sort of place for ladies. There might be an attack any minute. If Grant decided to move his men toward Richmond . . .

"If it's no sort of place for ladies," Mary said, "why is Mrs. Grant allowed to be there? And Mrs. Ord—and goodness knows how many others? If they can stay near their husbands, why can't I?"

"Well, Mother, I'll see what can be done."

The arrangements were made. Mary and Tad and Mrs. Keckley sailed with Mr. Lincoln on the *River Queen,* on a morning when the sky was full of light clouds that scudded before a sharp breeze.

The move on Richmond was planned. Mr. Lincoln decided to stay on at City Point while General Grant took his army forward. Mary and Tad were to go back to Washington. Mary was reluctant to go. When she was home again the house seemed empty and forlorn. There was an uneasiness in the air, the old sense of waiting. She walked through the rooms, trying to plan changes here and there—fresh decorations, new curtains . . .

"I must see about some new clothes, too," she said to Mrs. Keckley. She crossed to the mirror, and was startled to see how bad she looked. She hadn't given much attention to her appearance lately, but that could all be changed. She smoothed her hair. Surely she didn't really look so old . . .

The following week word came that Richmond had been taken. The South was broken. Now it was only a question of settling the details of the peace. Mr. Lincoln had gone on to Richmond, after the army. A few days later he was back in Washington.

Mary waited eagerly to see him—to see how happy he would look and tell him the plans she had made for the house. Now they could really talk about the future. When she heard his carriage in the driveway she started downstairs. She had put on a blue silk dress for dinner, one she knew he liked.

"Mr. Lincoln," Mary's voice was eager. "Mr. Lincoln—"

He paused at the stairs and looked up. Mary caught sight of his face. The gray cheeks, the deep hollows around his eyes. She drew back, dismayed and frightened.

He came to the landing slowly, and crossed to his study. Mary followed. She stood on the threshold, watching while he dropped into a chair. He sat slumped, his arms hanging loosely, his head bent.

Mary came toward him.

He took a long breath.

"It's over, Mother." Weariness was like a leaden weight in his voice.

"Yes, I know."

When Taddie rushed into the room, Mr. Lincoln put his arm around the boy. His eyes lighted a little. "Well, Taddie—"

"Papa, did you go to Richmond? Did you walk right into the streets?"

"Yes, I did, Taddie."

"Did you see Lee, Papa? Have they killed him yet?"

"No, Lee isn't dead, and they won't kill him, Taddie. They won't have to kill anyone any more now. The war is over."

"Oh." Taddie wriggled away from his father's arm and eyed him hopefully. "Then can we go home again, Papa? Can we go back to Fido?"

"Not for a while," Mr. Lincoln smiled. "But I have a surprise that may cheer you up. General Grant gave me a rebel sword for you. One of his men picked it up in the field. I'll get it for you."

As Mr. Lincoln rose, he glanced at Mary. "You're all fixed up tonight, Mother." He sounded surprised. "This isn't any special occasion, is it?"

Mary turned away.

"No," she said, "nothing special, Mr. Lincoln."

Forty-seven

A<small>N EARLY SPRING</small> sun dissolved the Washington streets into thin, yellow mud. Stepping down from their carriages, the ladies held their skirts ankle high and trod carefully to avoid the squelching puddles. The buds on the maples were raw and tender pink. On the White House lawn the slender boughs of forsythia bloomed gold and waved softly in the April breeze.

On the Friday before Easter, Mary and Mr. Lincoln went for a drive. There was a rain in the air, and a fine mist made the dusk seem earlier than usual. They stepped into the lighted hall to find a message from Mr. Hay. General and Mrs. Grant had sent their regrets for that evening. They were sorry, but being called suddenly out of town, they would be unable after all, to join the President and Mrs. Lincoln for the theater.

"It's too bad," Mary said. "I can get someone else in their place, if you like."

Mr. Lincoln said they might as well go. If he stayed at home, he'd only work—and he'd heard the play was amusing. "Besides, people at the theater will be disappointed not to see Grant as they expected. We ought to give them something to look at, I suppose."

While Mr. Lincoln went up to his office, Mary sent off a note to a young friend, Major Rathbone, asking if he and his fiancée would join them for the evening. Then she pulled out a letter to Elizabeth she had begun that morning. There was no hurry about dressing. It would be an hour at least before Mr. Lincoln was ready for dinner. She took up her pen and went on.

. . . They were well. Mr. Lincoln said they might make a visit to Springfield in the summer, which would please them all. Taddie especially hoped to see Fido again, and claim his rightful half! . . . Robert expected his release from the army soon. He was much seen in the company of a Miss Harlan lately, but had not yet confided any *serious* plans of matrimony. . . . Mr. Lincoln seemed better these past few days than anyone would have thought possible after all he had endured. Even Mr. Seward said the President looked ten years younger since the peace was signed. . . . She must stop and dress. Some young friends were expected for an evening at the theater . . . More later . . .

It was warm in the theater. Sitting beside Mr. Lincoln in the flag-draped box, Mary fanned herself occasionally. Mr. Lincoln was in the outside chair, where he could most easily be seen from the audience. Mary noticed the frequent glances in his direction. He sat absorbed, watching the stage. Now and then, when a line from the play amused him, he laughed and turned to look at her. Young Major Rathbone and his fiancée sat in the front chairs of the box. Watching him touch her hand, Mary felt a glow of tender approval.

During the second act, her mind wandering from the play, Mary leaned toward Mr. Lincoln and took his arm. He touched her hand, not looking around.

Mary opened her fan. It was made of blue feathers, to match her dress. She moved it slowly.

The sound, at first, seemed to have no meaning at all. Only it was odd, Mary thought, not coming from the stage, but from behind her. A sharp sound—almost like a shot. She turned, but Mr. Lincoln was sitting quietly in his chair. Major Rathbone and Miss Harris had not looked around.

Queer ...

At that moment a figure, lithe and swift, leaped past them toward the railing of the box. Mary saw Major Rathbone jump up—saw him struggle a moment, in silence, with the creature. Then there was a thud. The man had jumped over the rail onto the stage—shouted some queer gibberish—and was gone.

Mary shook her head. Then suddenly she saw Major Rathbone holding out his arm. Blood was dripping from it.

"Mr. Lincoln—" Mary started up. "Major Rathbone is hurt—" She turned—and stopped. Mr. Lincoln's head hung forward in a dreadful way.

There was a confused murmur in the audience. Mary heard the words. "*He's been shot. The President has been shot.*"

Then she screamed.

"*Mr. Lincoln—*"

There was no answer.

In a moment the murmur had changed to panic. People climbed from the audience into the President's box. Others milled about.

Miss Harris called for water and brandy. Major Rathbone held up his bleeding arm. Voices rose.

"*Is there a doctor?*" Mary heard someone call. "*Isn't there a doctor?*"

A young-looking man came into the box.

"I'm an army surgeon, ma'am," he told Mary.

"Please help my husband," she said. Dark and sickening waves swept over everything. She hung onto the box rail, onto the fan, crushed and bent, in her hand.

"Please take care of my husband ..."

She saw them lift Mr. Lincoln out of the chair and stretch

him on the floor. She didn't move. The young doctor was kneeling down, opening Mr. Lincoln's coat, feeling his shoulders, his neck, his head . . .

The doctor looked up. He spoke to Mary. "The wound is mortal," he said. "It is impossible for him to recover."

Mary sat down. She spoke quietly to Major Rathbone. "Please try to keep everyone away," she said. "Please—if you can . . ."

There was a stir in the back of the box. Laura Keene, the actress from the play, swept through. She was still in costume. Her full hoop skirt seemed to fill the box.

"Please," Miss Keene said to the doctor. "Please—may I hold his head?"

The doctor nodded, scarcely noticing. He was busy taking something from his bag. Mary watched, not moving, while Miss Keene knelt down, spreading her skirts, and drew Mr. Lincoln's head into her lap.

The moments ticked by. To Mary, waiting, it seemed that a lifetime vanished, second by second, each one stretched beyond her memory.

She heard the doctor ask if there were a place to move the President.

"We can take him home," Mary said.

The doctor shook his head. They couldn't take him that far. He would die on the way.

Someone spoke. There was a house just across the street . . . a Mr. Peterson's. The doctor looked at Mary questioningly. "He could be carried—"

"Then carry him there," Mary said. "Only please take care of him."

It took a while, getting the men, lifting him, carrying him out. Mary heard their voices.

"Mind the steps here . . ."

"Be careful to keep the head level . . ."

"Take it carefully crossing the street . . ."

She followed, walking a little way behind. She felt arms around her, helping her, supporting her . . . She put them off.

"I can go alone."

Crossing Tenth Street Mary was aware of the lines of people. She saw how they were looking at Mr. Lincoln. There were moans, prayers, cries, questions . . .

Mary went in silence up the narrow twisting steps onto the stoop, into a hall flooded with yellow light, smelling of kerosene.

They carried Mr. Lincoln through a narrow passageway beyond.

"In here—there's a bed—" Mary heard someone say.

She started to follow but there were too many in the hall. She felt herself pushed into a dark little room, felt hands pulling her toward a sofa, easing her down.

"You must wait here, Mrs. Lincoln, it will be best."

She didn't know who spoke. She sat still, in the darkness, until someone carried in a lamp. She felt something in her hand, grinding between her fingers, and she looked down. It was her fan. The blue feathers stained with something dark and red that stuck to her fingers. She stared at it a moment, stupidly, then the waves of black swept over her and she fell forward. Choking, blinding, destroying—the truth tore through her . . .

When Mary looked up, someone was standing over her. A woman she had never seen was shaking her arm.

"Mrs. Lincoln—"

"Yes . . ."

"You'd better come, Mrs. Lincoln—"

The woman's arms were around her, leading out a door, down the narrow passageway filled with strangers.

"This way, Mrs. Lincoln."

"Please stand aside. It's Mrs. Lincoln."

It wasn't a room at all. Only a sort of widened hall. He was lying diagonally on the bed that was too short for him. His head lay back, his face was perfectly still.

Mary looked down. Weeping so deep that it seemed no part of her shook her. She knelt by the bed.

"Mr. Lincoln—"

There was no sound, no motion but his breathing, hoarse and slow.

"*Husband, please—*"

Arms were around Mary again, pulling her up. They led her through the hall and back to the little room again, bare and chilly in the lamplight. Mary sank down, feeling the horsehair arm of the sofa cold and slippery beneath her cheek.

They kept coming and going, leaning over her, talking about God, about the martyr, about sacrifice, country, freedom, peace, eternity. Mary heard them, but she didn't answer. She wanted to speak to her husband. Freedom and sacrifice and God were nothing to her.

It was morning, just past seven o'clock, when they came and told her he was dead.

"Come," they said, "a carriage is outside. We'll help you."

"Please give a hand here. It's Mrs. Lincoln—"

"Take her arm—"

"Who's going with her?"

"Her son is here."

Mary looked up in dull surprise to see Robert. His face was pale as wax. She put her hand on his arm as they started out.

She heard Robert say, "Please, Mother—"

She tried to answer, but the sobbing, dull and exhausted, would not stop.

Old Edwards let them into the house. He and Robert together helped Mary upstairs. She didn't know where Mr. Lincoln was. Someone hurried into her room, turning back the covers on the bed.

Mary lay down. She saw Robert waiting.

There was a voice outside in the corridor, crying.

"They've shot my Papa. They've killed my Papa."

That was Taddie. Mary heard it dimly. Still she didn't move.

"Mrs. Lincoln—"

Mary looked up. Mrs. Keckley was leaning over her. Mary stirred and put out her hand. "Why didn't you come last night?" she asked. "I needed you then."

"Indeed I tried, Mrs. Lincoln. As soon as I heard the news I came straight to find you. But the guards wouldn't let me through even though I begged."

Mary closed her eyes. "Don't leave me again," she murmured. "Please don't go away."

Days ran together like beads falling into a box, all alike, jumbled together without sequence. Lying in her room, Mary watched the morning light turn to noon, to afternoon, to night. She watched the darkness deepen, steady through the long night. She saw it pale and blanch into day again. Mrs. Keckley was there. People brought her meals, sat by her to talk. They tried, at first tearfully, then with a shade of firmness, to rouse her. She heard their voices vaguely. There was the house to be made ready and turned over to President Johnson. Plans must be made. There were trunks to pack. There was Robert, standing by so manfully. There was poor Taddie, wandering over the house disconsolate, coming into the downstairs parlor one day and finding a sightseer who had strayed in helping himself to a book that lay on the table, and flying at the visitor, kicking his shins, screaming at him to put down the book—it was his *Papa's* book.

These were the things they told Mary. She listened, not answering. She knew what they said. She heard and understood when they whispered outside her door or looked across the bed at each other, their eyebrows raised meaningly. She heard, she knew, she kept meaning to answer. When Mrs. Keckley was there she would try sometimes, sitting up a little, beginning carefully. She must tell Mrs. Keckley what it was that she had wanted to tell Mr. Lincoln.

Mary would sit up, trying to think. "You know, Lizzie. You understand, don't you?"

It was important to remember. Terribly important . . .

On the first day of June the summer air was shimmering and bright. Mary stepped into the carriage. Her black dress and long crepe veil felt wintry in the hot noon sun. Edwards was by the carriage, handing her in, piling the luggage after her, looking up to say good-bye, gruff and awkward.

Robert and Tad were beside her. Mrs. Keckley sat on the small seat facing them.

Robert gave the order to Tim, and they started down the drive. Mary looked back, and saw Edwards on the step watching, alone, his gnarled face squinting in the sunlight. She saw the house. The portico, the wide front door, the edge of the crimson draperies at the long East Room windows. The lace curtains . . .

Mary sighed. Then she remembered. She started to speak— to tell Robert. About the curtains. About having them changed. That was what she had meant to tell Mr. Lincoln . . . About changing the curtains and making everything different.

"Robert—"

He was looking straight ahead, his face set, not seeming to hear.

Mary hesitated. The carriage swung round the corner down the avenue, past Willard's, toward the station. Mary sat back, letting her hand fall into her lap.

No matter whether he had heard or not. It was too late.

PART FIVE

House of

Shadows

Forty-eight

MARY SAT at the small, rickety desk in her room on the second floor of a London boardinghouse, writing letters. The light was poor, and the damp chill made her back ache, but the letters must be finished to catch the post for the boat train next morning.

She came to the end of a page and straightened to glance out of the window. It might be any one of the windows she had looked out of in the last months, she thought. In England, France, Germany, in boardinghouses, pensions, inexpensive family hotels, the windows were so alike. They had the same curtains of coarse lace, starched as stiff as iron without ever being really clean. The rooms always had the same bed, the dresser with the scarf, the pin cushion, the round-holed container for combings. And always the desk, always rickety. Mary had found a way to steady the legs, propping one with Mr. Lincoln's old volume of Shakespeare she always carried with her.

She looked through the window at the small courtyard below. Two little boys were playing near the flower bed. Mary frowned, wanting to warn them. The manageress, in her black alpaca shirtwaist, would be sure to rap on the window with her gold and ruby ring. The manageress looked severely at all her guests, but especially at the little boys. Mary always felt sorry when the boys were scolded. A few years ago it might have been Taddie ... or Willie ...

Now Taddie was tall and lanky like his father, a student in a school near London. On a visit to the school Mary had learned that when the other boys asked Tad about his family in America, he had told them that his father was a rail splitter. At first Mary had been indignant. Then she couldn't help laughing, remembering what Mr. Lincoln might have said.

"Well, Mother, at least he didn't say a hairsplitter."

All the same, Mary explained who Tad's father was. She was always careful to make sure that people remembered what a great man Mr. Lincoln had been.

The last letter sealed and stamped, Mary went down to dinner.

Boarding house dining rooms, like windows, had a sameness. The tablecloth, fresh twice a week. Vinegar cruet and salt and pepper for the centerpiece. The same ladies, who had been guests for years. The crusty bachelors.

Each guest provided his napkin ring. Mary had her own, left from school days, but she had given Taddie one that had belonged to Mr. Lincoln, with the initials A.L. engraved in flowing script. It had lain, in the last five years, on walnut sideboards in Chicago, in New York and Florida and Paris—for a little while in Robert's house on Wabash Avenue after he and Mary Harlan were married. Mary would find herself in the midst of a meal sometimes, staring at Mr. Lincoln's napkin ring by Taddie's plate.

This evening Mary was hardly aware of the conversation around her, the complaint about the food, the small indignations. She tried to clear her mind, tried to decide sensibly what she should do.

From the beginning, after Mr. Lincoln's death, it had all been difficult. Back in Chicago, when she and Tad and Robert had been together, the troubles had begun. Troubles about money. Robert had been kind. He had made long columns of figures and sat down with Mary, trying to explain.

Mr. Lincoln had left enough money for them to live quite comfortably if they lived *carefully*. But Mr. Lincoln had left no will, which was very odd. Under the law Mary was to have one third of the estate, the other two parts going to Robert and Tad.

She had listened to Robert, trying to be patient. He said there was enough money for her to live carefully, but he didn't understand what it cost to live properly, with prices so outrageously high after the war. And Taddie to educate . . .

That was why she had come to Europe. She didn't like to trouble Robert. She could live more cheaply here, and she could write to old friends of Mr. Lincoln without Robert knowing.

A Mr. Williamson had been the first to write her about a public subscription to be raised for Mr. Lincoln's family. One dollar from every patriotic American for the cause. Mary would never have dreamed of telling Robert. He was so sensitive about money, and he had never understood how people had felt about his father.

It was too bad when Robert found out that Mr. Williamson was an agent for several department stores in New York. They only wanted to raise the money to pay Mrs. Lincoln's debts.

Debts. It was an ugly word. Surely in the days when Mary had shopped, and the clerks had been so kind, so anxious for her to have their nicest things, there had never been a word like that. But everything had changed. Everything had changed so terribly.

There had been another time when a firm of merchants on Broadway had written, suggesting that she might wish to allow some of her belongings to be sold, quite discreetly and privately of course. She had consented, though she knew Robert mustn't be told. Going to New York, with trunks and boxes and barrels, meeting Mrs. Keckley there, who had promised to help her, Mary had felt so hopeful. She had stayed at a small hotel with Mrs. Keckley, going over the old things, unpacking dresses and furs and fans and gloves she hadn't seen since the days in Washington. She remembered holding the pearl necklace and bracelets, weeping over them.

The sale had been a failure. The newspapers came out with a dreadful story about the President's widow selling her second-hand clothes.

Mary's first thought had been of Robert. But he had been very kind. When she got back to Chicago, he had said scarcely anything. Helping her into the hotel, he had touched her arm, looking a shade embarrassed. He hoped she'd stay home for awhile and not go gadding, he said. They couldn't have her running off to marry some duke or earl.

Sometimes Robert was surprisingly like his father.

There were some things Mary had never told Robert. Like the time she had met Senator Sumner on a train from Florida. He had greeted her kindly, inquired about her health and the boys. All the while, in his eyes, she had seen pity and embarrassment. When he was gone she had pressed her shabby black gloves against her eyes.

"Mr. Lincoln, oh, Mr. Lincoln, Mr. Lincoln . . ."

This evening there was no time for memories. Mary ate her dinner of boiled mutton and overcooked cabbage in silence.

Over and over, her mind went back to the letter she had posted to the men in Congress who were working for a new pension for the President's widow. Senator Sumner had introduced the bill. She had told them how grateful she was, and why certain people were opposing the pension bill. It had been painful to set down all the old grievances. More painful to discover new ones.

General Grant was the new president. "General Grant was too devoted to Mr. Lincoln and is himself too just a man to allow this public abuse of me to continue," Mary had written.

She did hope, eating her dessert—a soggy bit of cake soaked in watered rum—that she had chosen the right words.

When Mary first heard that President Grant had nothing to say in the matter of the pension, she was stunned. Then she was bitter.

But there were others, besides Grant, who had proved false. Mary knew that Billy Herndon was going about the country taking money for lectures about his personal knowledge of Mr. Lincoln and his family. Mr. Herndon told a story about someone named Ann Rutledge. He said Mr. Lincoln had been engaged to marry Ann Rutledge before she died—that he had always been in love with her—that Mary had led him a dance with her selfish tempers, all because she had been jealous of the memory of Ann Rutledge. Mary had never heard of Ann Rutledge until Billy Herndon began his lectures.

But the people who went to Billy Herndon's lectures listened.

Bitterest of all had been Mrs. Keckley's book about the White House and the Lincoln family. Mary remembered how Robert had tried to hide the book from her when it was first published. She had found it in a bookshop and stood by the counter, reading the things Mrs. Keckley had written about her—things Mary had told her in confidence. Other things Mary had never heard of. She never learned how much of the book Mrs. Keckley had written herself.

She never let Robert know that she had seen the book.

Mary had left the table and was on her way upstairs when the manageress handed her a card. There was a gentleman calling for Mrs. Lincoln. The manageress inspected the card. Her voice took on a new respect. The gentleman was waiting in the parlor.

Mary looked at the card.

General Adam Badeau
Consul General of the United States

She nodded at the manageress, smoothing her hair hastily before she went into the parlor with its gloomy hangings and faint odor of camphor and boiled cabbage.

Mr. Badeau waited. Mary saw him rise and come forward politely. His face was dimly familiar. No doubt she had met him before in Washington. Mary sat down, straightening the collar of her plain black dress. Mr. Badeau had only just learned of her presence in London, he said. He trusted she had found everything agreeable in the city? Mary nodded. If there was anything he could do to make her comfortable, she was to be assured that he was at her service. Would she remain long?

Mary shook her head. Probably not. Her plans were vague, owing to the uncertainty of waiting for word from Washington, where her pension bill was still pending before Congress. Everything in her future and Tad's education depended on that. Mary spoke quickly, warming to her subject. When she saw Mr. Badeau beginning to look uncomfortable, she stopped. She must learn to remember that people were distressed by any reference to her lack of funds. She turned the subject quickly, inquiring politely for Mr. Badeau's family. She saw the relief in his face as he rose. His family was well. He hoped that Mrs. Lincoln would do them the honor of coming to dine. One night the next week?

Mary stood up. "I appreciate your kindness, Mr. Badeau, but Taddie and I are living very quietly. I'm afraid it's impossible for me to accept any social engagements." She offered him her hand. "I'm glad you called."

Going to her room, Mary was pleased. It had been difficult receiving Mr. B. in that wretched parlor. All the same, it would show the manageress that she was someone still. It would be something to tell Taddie when he came home. And something to write Robert and Elizabeth.

Forty-nine

\/\/\/\/\/\/\/

ON A SPRING morning Mary dressed with extra care, watching the onyx clock on the mantel of her room at the Grand Pacific Hotel. She had been in Chicago several weeks. This morning Robert was calling to take her downtown. He hadn't said just where. A matter of business, he had told her. She must be ready promptly. Robert so disliked waiting.

She put on her black silk, with lace at the neck and sleeves, and laid out her ostrich boa and fresh gloves. And her newest bonnet.

Robert would surely think she looked well. It would be nice to see him pleased. He had looked so troubled lately, poor boy. She had noticed it ever since she came back from Europe. He tried to hide it from her, but she could see that he was worrying and she knew it must be about money, though he kept saying not. Only yesterday, when he had told her about this business appointment they must keep, he seemed so strange and nervous. Mary had comforted him.

"You mustn't worry, dear. I can provide for us better than you think." He'd been surprised when she told him how cleverly she had managed to keep a part of her estate out of the hands of those wily lawyers who claimed to be handling her affairs. She had bent near him, whispering. "See what I have here, Robert. No one knows, but I carry them with me every moment." She had opened her purse and showed him more than fifty thousand dollars in securities. They were hers. She'd got them all to herself, safe from the lawyers' clutches . . . Robert had jumped up, his face whiter than ever, and tried to take them —but she had put them away quickly. "You needn't worry, dear. You see, I can take care of us better than you think."

She was glad now she had come hurrying back from Florida when she had.

She had only gone to Florida because Robert insisted she needed a rest. She had been depressed and unwell ever since Taddie's sudden death of lung fever. But it had done no good. The dreams had only begun again. Taddie spoke to her often now. And Willie. And Mr. Lincoln. Always Mr. Lincoln.

She knew they were telling her to come back.

At first it had been upsetting when she arrived home. Robert hadn't seemed to understand at all that she had telegraphed Dr. Isham because she had learned in a dream that Robert was ill and must be cared for at once.

Robert kept saying when he met her that he was perfectly well. She had tried to explain to him, and to Dr. Isham, about the dream. But, though they were polite, it was plain they didn't believe she really had the dream at all. Then they had been so odd when she told them about the man on the train who had tried to poison her. They acted almost as though it weren't true, though she explained quite carefully how the man had recognized her as Mrs. Lincoln, and how he had changed her coffee cup when he thought she wasn't watching. She'd seen him do it. When she tasted the coffee and found it bitter she had known for certain he had poisoned it.

It had been a mistake, probably, to tell Robert. Robert was like Mr. Lincoln. Trusting everyone, poor thing.

No doubt this business appointment where Robert was taking her was concerned with some trouble he had got into by trusting people. She would be able to tell him who the false ones were, once she had a look at them. Hadn't she always been able to tell Mr. Lincoln? And Mr. Lincoln had relied on her judgment over any other in the world.

When Robert came to the door he wore a new black suit. His face was very set. He greeted Mary with extra kindness, but she could see he was still worrying. They drove downtown and when the carriage stopped, she looked out astonished.

"But, Robert, this is a courthouse—"

Robert said nothing, helping her out. She hardly liked to question him any more, but before they came to the door at the end of the long bare corridor he turned to her suddenly.

"I couldn't help it, Mother," he said.

She couldn't think what on earth he meant. A large woman in gray came and took Mary's arm to lead her to a seat on one of the back benches. Mary looked around, frowning, puzzled. Good heavens, she did hope Robert wasn't in any sort of trouble with the law. The jury filed in and sat down, and then the judge.

Sitting down in front near Robert, Mary saw Dr. Isham. Now, that was odd. Beside him was the other doctor who had come to see her about her headaches. That had been just after Taddie died. Why would he be mixed up now in anything Robert might have done?

They were getting on with the case. The judge said everything so fast Mary scarcely understood the words. Something about the case of Mary Lincoln, widow. It seemed an odd way to speak of her. Why did the man have to chew his words so? She leaned forward.

The witnesses were being called. First Dr. Isham. He told a story about her telegraphing from Florida that Robert was ill. He made it sound so absurd. Then Dr. Danforth testified. He told about visiting the defendant in her rooms at the Clifton Hotel, finding her a victim of hallucinations and nervous debility. Defendant had told Dr. Danforth there was an Indian pulling red hot wires through her eyes, and removing the bones of her face. On another occasion, a year later, she had said steel springs were being taken out of her head.

She'd only been trying to describe the headaches, but to hear him tell it, Mary thought, he might have supposed she was insane. The lawyer was asking something about that. Unsound mind, he called it. Yes, Dr. Danforth said, in his opinion defendant was of unsound mind.

Mary wondered who *defendant* was.

There were other witnesses. Clerks from the shops who said they remembered Mrs. Lincoln. She heard them tell about the things she had bought. Three hundred dollars for soap and perfumes. A hundred yards of moiré silk. Jewelry, fans, gloves. Six hundred dollars' worth of lace curtains . . .

"May I put a question to Mr. Lincoln, please? Has defendant any permanent home at this time?"

"No, she has none."

That wasn't Mr. Lincoln's voice. It was Robert's.

"Defendant has no reason, then, for a purchase of more than sixty pairs of lace curtains."

"No. No reason."

"Thank you."

Suddenly Mary realized that she was defendant. But it seemed a queer way to put things. Making so much of it only because she liked being in the shops, having the clerks speak politely. If they had only asked her, she could have explained. But they never asked her.

There were witnesses from the hotel. She recognized Gus, the man who ran the elevator at night, and she remembered how he had told her about his daughter's baby who was sick. Now he was saying something ridiculous about Mrs. Lincoln going down in the elevator not properly dressed, and Robert having to bring her back. That was too absurd. She had only gone out to the corridor in her dressing gown to find the maid. She could see from their faces even the jury didn't believe such a story. The man must be unsettled, poor soul, from so much trouble.

Then the chambermaid. Mary was surprised to see how pretty Stella looked out of her drab gray uniform. She was rolling her eyes at the jury box. Yes, she was employed at the Grand Pacific Hotel, had attended defendant's room for the past four weeks. Defendant was pleasant as a rule, kindly spoken, but on occasions defendant had employed peculiar language and spoken of dreams, et cetera, in which the dead appeared. Defendant appeared happy about this rather than despondent, but on other occasions was extremely depressed, spoke of imminent death, wishing same, but at the same time accusing various persons of plotting her end. Defendant was never guilty of unseemly conduct. Given to fits of weeping, tempers over small incidents, suffered from headaches, and seemed unduly concerned over money matters, insisting that the management was overcharging her, falsifying her accounts, et cetera, et cetera.

"That will be all, thank you."

Stella stepped down from the witness chair, smoothing her skirts primly. Mary reflected bitterly that she had given Stella a dollar only the day before.

"Mr. Robert Lincoln, please."

Mary watched Robert walk to the witness chair. He looked at the lawyer, his face deathly white. He was telling his name, his age, where he lived.

"You are the son of Abraham Lincoln, deceased, President of the United States?"

"Yes."

"Defendant, Mary Lincoln, is your mother?"

"Yes."

"In your opinion, Mr. Lincoln, has the testimony of these

witnesses given an accurate picture of your mother's erratic
state of mind?"

There were more questions but Mary didn't hear them. She
was looking at Robert's face, thinking of the night in the Globe
Tavern when he was born. She thought of Mr. Lincoln, sitting
by her bed in the summer twilight. Of his saying, "We must
have a regular home now, I suppose, for the little boy." She
was remembering how dreadfully Robert had cried that first
year. Especially when Elizabeth and Ninian were there. How
he took colds, and had such a delicate chest, and she had rubbed
him with camphorated oil. She felt very sorry for Robert.

The woman in gray sitting beside Mary leaned toward her
solicitously. Would she like a drink of water? Mary shook her
head. Did she feel faint? Would she care for smelling salts? "No
—no." Mary pushed her aside impatiently. "Do be quiet and
let me hear."

The judge was speaking to the foreman of the jury. He
turned to the court. "Verdict of the court—the defendant is of
unsound mind, incapable of handling her property and con-
ducting her affairs . . . Remitted to the Belleview Sanitarium at
Batavia in the State of Illinois, in accordance with arrangements
to be made by Mr. Robert Lincoln. Case dismissed . . ."

Mary stood up, quite steadily. Robert was waiting at the door.
She took his arm, starting down the corridor. There were people standing about, but they were quiet, respectful. Robert kept
his head down, hurrying her along. He'd always hated being
stared at. Mary looked back at the faces . . . It was a long while
since they had crowded around her like this, pressing close to
the carriage while Robert helped her in. Mary looked out the
window. A few were still watching. She was glad she had worn
her best black dress . . .

When Taddie had died so suddenly of pneumonia—the year
they came home from Europe—Mary felt that she had lost the
last of Mr. Lincoln. Tad had been eighteen years old, but she

always thought of him as the little boy Mr. Lincoln loved so much. And in the lonely months that followed his death, it was almost more for Mr. Lincoln that she grieved than for Taddie.

Sitting beside Robert in the carriage, as they drove back from the courthouse, Mary felt for the first time as though a corner of her loneliness had been eased. Robert had spoken so kindly about her when they questioned him in the courtroom. Robert had never been affectionate—neither shyly, like Willie, nor tempestuously, like Tad. He was always reserved, hating any show of feeling. She had been surprised to hear how troubled and sad his voice sounded.

When the judge asked whether his mother had made her home with him, Robert had said he wanted her to, but she had refused. It wasn't true, of course. It was when Mary had seen that his wife wasn't taking proper care of Robert and the babies that she had refused to stay. It was only natural—any mother would have done the same. But she was glad Robert had said in court that he wanted her to come and live with them . . .

Robert went to her room when they got back to the hotel. A woman in a blue and white uniform was waiting for them. Some sort of nurse. Mary wished she would go away, but Robert was talking to her. About packing—about taking a train next morning. The nurse must be going on a trip . . .

It wasn't until Robert was ready to leave that Mary opened her purse to look for her handkerchief—and saw that the package of securities was gone. For one frightful, chilling moment she stared into the purse. Then she emptied the contents on the floor—kneeling down, rummaging through them, searching . . . They were gone. Mary screamed. She had been robbed. She tried to tell Robert what had happened. It must have been that woman in the courtroom who had stolen them—she had sat so close—leaning over Mary.

The more she tried to explain, the less Robert listened. The nurse had Mary's arm now, trying to quiet her. They kept telling her nothing had been stolen. The money was quite safe. It would be put in a bank. But they didn't understand. The nurse was a fool—and Robert was such a child about money.

All at once Robert was holding the securities out to show her. He was going to put them in the bank for her, he said. Mary was blank for a moment with the shock of realizing what Robert had done. He was the one who had stolen them. Stolen them out of her purse behind her back. She shouldn't have let him know she had them. It had been wrong to trust him. She couldn't trust anyone—not her own child.

She flew at Robert, trying to take them back. The nurse was holding her—Robert, his face like ashes, was pushing her back. There were footsteps running in the hall outside, someone knocking at the door . . .

Mary's strength failed. She sank back onto a sofa, trembling. Robert was explaining. The nurse was explaining.

Mary put her hands over her face, shutting them out, but her fingers were like bars across her eyes and she pulled them away quickly.

Fifty

THE STATEROOM on the lowest passenger deck of the steamer was cramped and stuffy. It was a pity, Mary thought, that they couldn't have shown enough consideration to give her a more suitable cabin. She hadn't had the money, at the moment, to pay for a better room, but she had been careful to explain who she was. At the steamship office in Cherbourg, the young clerk had listened civilly while she told him she was ill, that she had had a fall, and injured her spine, and was returning to New York for medical treatment. He hadn't seemed to understand. He only said that the ship was crowded. If Mrs. Lincoln cared to wait for a smaller boat, she might find something to suit her better for the same price . . .

She had wanted to come on the *Amerique*—it was the largest and the fastest ship. After nearly four years away, she felt suddenly that she must get home. She had written Elizabeth from the south of France, explaining about the accident to her spine, and the dreadful pain she suffered. The French doctors said there was nothing to be done, but she had never trusted foreign doctors.

Elizabeth had cabled her to come at once. Robert would meet her in New York and arrange for her to see the best doctors there. When she was better she was to come to Springfield and stay with Elizabeth.

So she was coming.

But she was nervous about seeing Robert. It had been so long. He had written regularly, telling about his work, and the children, especially his little daughter who was named for Mary. The letters were kind, but there was a stiffness in them that made Mary realize he had never quite forgiven her for not staying longer at the sanitarium. She remembered how Robert had looked on the day of the second trial. Standing in the courtroom so stiffly while Ninian Edwards testified that Mary had been paroled from the sanitarium in his custody for eight months, and during that time had lived at his home in Springfield and given every sign of being mentally recovered.

The judge had turned to Robert.

"Have you any objection to this proceeding, Mr. Lincoln?"

"No, none." Robert's face had been white.

"Then it is the judgment of this court that Mary Lincoln, who was heretofore found to be insane, is restored to reason and is capable of managing and controlling her estate."

She had fought back the shadows after all.

Robert hadn't approved. If it hadn't been for Ninian and Elizabeth, who came to help her, she might have stayed in the square pleasant room of the sanitarium in Batavia.

The nurses had been kind. She wasn't in an asylum, they explained. They pointed to the curtains at the windows. The ruffles were fresh and crisp, but they never quite hid the barred windows. On nights when the moon shone the bars made crisscross patterns on the floor.

She had got her freedom back, and sometimes, in the five years, she wondered whether it had been worth the loneliness. It might have been simpler to stay where she could rest and not worry about anything—where the nurses would listen while she told about Mr. Lincoln and the boys, and how devoted they had been to her. It was hard, nowadays, to find people who cared about listening. Everyone was so busy. Still—no matter how much easier it might have been to stay on at Batavia, the thought of Mr. Lincoln had made her know she must get out, somehow.

He would have hated the bars. Besides, she never wanted to have anything about her that would disgrace his memory.

Once she was on the ship, she felt better. The pain was less, though she was still weak and ill. After the second day she felt able to go up on deck. She had hesitated at first, for fear people would stare at her too much. The stewardess said the ship was full of Americans. They would recognize her, of course. She hated to have people see her when she looked so bad. Her clothes were in wretched condition. But she had gone finally, and found a deck chair in an obscure corner. She explained to the steward that she must have a place where she wouldn't attract too much attention. He had been very kind about it.

In the dining saloon they had given her a small table, near the door. She went to meals early, so she could slip in quietly without being noticed. She spoke to her steward.

"You must be careful, please, not to let people hear you call me Mrs. Lincoln. It always attracts attention. I'm not well enough to meet strangers just now."

The last morning before they landed, Mary was in her deck chair. She had a rug over her knees. The October sun was bright on the sea, but there was sharpness in the air. People walked past, briskly, counting turns around the deck. Laughing, talking. Mary watched, keeping her face shaded. A group of children came by. Two noisy little boys tried to climb into a lifeboat and were scolded by the steward. When the steward had gone, Mary beckoned to the boys. They came over curiously, a little doubtfully. She smiled. Their cheeks were round and red and they wore blue serge suits with stiff white collars.

"I like little boys," Mary said. "What are your names?"

They mumbled their names, glancing at each other sideways.

"Are you brothers?"

They nodded.

Mary looked at them a minute.

"I had two little boys like you once," she said.

They didn't answer.

Mary beckoned them closer. "Do you know what my name is?"

"No—" They hung back.

"It's a secret, but I'll tell you. My name is Mrs. Abraham Lincoln . . ." She waited, but the boys said nothing. "You know who Abraham Lincoln was, don't you?"

The younger boy looked blank, the older one frowned a little. Finally he shook his head.

"But you must have heard of President Lincoln. Don't they tell you about him in school?"

"We don't go to school. We live in Paris and our Papa has a tutor for us. He teaches us in French."

"Oh." Mary understood then. "Do you like your teacher?"

The boys turned to stare at each other a moment, then they burst into giggles.

"No, we hate him. He has popped-eyes, and Tommy pulled a chair out when he was going to sit down once, and he went bang on the floor—like this."

Mary couldn't help laughing. The boy sounded so like Tad.

"You oughtn't to tease your tutor," she said. "When you get to America I expect you'll go to school. Then you'll learn about President Lincoln. You can tell your teacher Mrs. Lincoln talked to you—and told you Mr. Lincoln was very fond

360

of little boys—even when they were naughty. You won't forget, will you?"

The boys stared a minute longer. Suddenly the little one made a dive at his brother and turned to run—and they pounded off down the deck and around the corner, whooping.

Mary sat looking out across the sea. She was still smiling.

The boat was due to dock at noon. Mary was ready early, her bags packed, her gloves on. She had spent a long time dressing—arranging her hair carefully, so the streaks of gray wouldn't show too much—adjusting her bonnet, dusting her face with rice powder to hide the lines around her mouth and eyes. It would be a pity to have Robert find her looking old. Because, of course, sixty-three wasn't really old at all. It was only being miserable and ill that made her look so haggard.

She stood up and looked once more in the mirror. A last glance at her luggage before she went up on deck. Robert would see how well she managed alone. She must find the nice deck steward and ask him to let her go ashore quietly. It would be so awkward if word got around that she was on board and a crowd gathered.

She looked down over the rail—the ship was just being made fast. But her heart sank. There was a crowd, already. The dock was jammed with people. Milling and shouting and waving handkerchiefs as they all craned up to stare onto the deck. Mary stepped back quickly and pulled down her veil. Robert would be furious. She looked for him on the deck below, scanning the upturned faces through her veil. There he was, standing alone, toward the back of the crowd. Dear goodness, he looked almost old, with all that brown beard. But so tall and distinguished in his black suit and hat. She started to wave, and then remembered not to. She must ask the steward to help her off.

They were just lowering the gangplank. She started toward the steward, but at that moment a surge of people pushed her from behind. There was a sudden commotion. A voice called out.

"There she is—there she comes now—"

Mary looked around, startled. People were standing aside, making a clear space, and a young woman came quickly past. She was all in gray, with flaming red hair and a small pale face with enormous, beautiful eyes. She was laughing, waving her hand—calling out something in French.

"*Vive Sarah Bernhardt*—" another voice answered from the crowd.

Mary heard the name. Then she remembered. The great French actress. The stewardess had said something about Sarah Bernhardt being in first class, though she hadn't been seen during the voyage. Others were pushing onto the deck now.

It was Bernhardt's first trip to America, the stewardess had said. The actress started down the gangplank. People below were waving and cheering. A little girl came forward with an armful of red roses. Bernhardt stooped to kiss the child. Then she waved, laughing, and blew kisses to the crowd.

"The divine Sarah," a woman next to Mary said. "Have you ever seen her act? Oh, she can make you weep, that woman. She can play such tragedy as you never knew existed."

Mary moved nearer the gangplank, trying to see Robert. She had lost him in the crowd.

"Excuse me, ma'am—stand back there!" Mary heard the voice without really noticing it. She was still searching for Robert. The voice spoke again.

"You, there, step back, please. No one is allowed off yet."

Mary felt a hand on her arm. She turned, looking into the face of a police guard who had come up from the dock.

Mary was relieved. The man must have been sent to help her off the ship. "I am Mrs. Abraham Lincoln," she explained with dignity. "If you can help me find my son—"

The man pushed past her down the line.

Mary looked after him. He didn't seem to have heard her name.

By the time Mary went ashore most of the crowd had left the dock, and she found Robert easily. He came forward, his hat in his hand, and bent to kiss her cheek.

"Well, Mother . . ."

He was smiling, looking pleased to see her. She took his arm, and they turned away together. It was nice being home again. She felt stronger already. Surely the doctors here would be able to cure her. Then she would be going to stay in Springfield with Ninian and Elizabeth.

She must be very careful to say just the right things to Robert. Not to have any trouble again. She turned to look up. He would see how she had changed. He would see that everything would be better now.

Everything would be different . . .

About the Author

ANNE COLVER was born in Cleveland, Ohio, the daughter of a newspaperman. She attended Friends School in Washington, D.C., and Pine Manor Junior College, then graduated from Whitman College in Washington State. After writing five mysteries, she turned to historical fiction. The Revolutionary period and the era of Abraham Lincoln are her specialties.

She has written one other novel besides MR. LINCOLN'S WIFE, *Listen for the Voices,* and over a dozen juvenile books.

Anne Colver lives in Irvington-on-Hudson, New York, with her husband, a lawyer and writer, and their daughter, Kate.